THE PURE IN HEART

Susan Hill has been a writer for over fifty years. Her books have won awards and prizes including the Whitbread, the John Llewellyn Rhys and the Somerset Maugham; and have been shortlisted for the Booker. Her novels include *Strange Meeting*, *I'm the King of the Castle* and *A Kind Man*; and she has also published autobiographical works and collections of short stories. She is also the author of the bestselling Simon Serrailler cases. The play of her ghost story *The Woman in Black* has been running in London's West End since 1988. She is married with two adult daughters and lives in North Norfolk.

www.susan-hill.com

SUSAN HILL

The Pure in Heart

A Simon Serrailler Case

VINTAGE BOOKS
London

9 10

Vintage
20 Vauxhall Bridge Road,
London SW1V 2SA

Vintage is part of the Penguin Random House group of companies
whose addresses can be found at global.penguinrandomhouse.com.

Penguin
Random House
UK

First published by Chatto & Windus in 2005

www.vintage-books.co.uk

A CIP catalogue record for this book is
available from the British Library

ISBN 9780099534990

Printed and bound by CPI Group (UK) Ltd, Croydon, CR0 4YY

FOR
MY MOLES EVERYWHERE

Blessed are the pure in heart:
for they shall see God
The Gospel According to St Matthew

ACKNOWLEDGEMENTS

I would like to thank members of the Wiltshire Police Force – the former Chief Constable, Dame Elizabeth Neville QPM; Detective Chief Superintendent Paul Howlett, Head of CID; and Detective Chief Inspector Paul Granger – for giving me a great deal of information, help and advice, for being so generous with their time and for welcoming me to their HQ.

I must also thank the (anonymous) members of *police999.com* who have answered my many questions so quickly and cheerfully.

On medical matters, I have had conversations with any number of doctors but I would particularly like to thank Dr Ian Reekie for gallantly setting aside a career preference for saving life in order to advise me on the disposing of it.

One

At first light the mist was soft and smoky over the lagoon and it was cold enough for Simon Serrailler to be glad of his heavy donkey jacket. He stood on the empty Fondamenta, collar turned up, waiting, cocooned in the muffled silence. Dawn on a Sunday morning in March was not a time for much activity on this side of Venice, where few tourists came; the working city was at rest and even the early churchgoers were not yet about.

He always stayed here, in the same couple of rooms he rented above an empty warehouse belonging to the friend, Ernesto, who would appear any moment to take him across the water. The rooms were comfortable and plain and filled with wonderful light from the sky and the water. They were quiet at night, and from the Fondamenta Simon could walk about among the hidden backwaters, looking out for things he wanted to draw. He had been here at least once, and usually twice a year for the last decade. It was a working place and a bolt-hole from his life as a Detective Chief Inspector, as were similar hideouts in Florence and Rome. But it was in Venice that he felt most at home, to Venice he always returned.

The putter of an engine came just ahead of the craft itself, emerging close beside him out of the silvery mist.

'Ciao.'

'Ciao, Ernesto.'

The boat was small and workmanlike, without any of the romance or trimmings of traditional Venetian craft. Simon put his canvas bag under the seat and then stood up beside the boatman as they swung round and headed across the open water. The mist settled like cobwebs on their faces and hands and for a while Ernesto slowed right down until, suddenly, they seemed to cut a channel through the whiteness and emerge into a hazy buttery light beyond which Simon could see the island ahead.

He had been to San Michele several times before to wander about, looking, recording in his mind's eye – he never used a camera – and he knew that at this hour, with luck, he would find it deserted even of the elderly arthritic widows who came in their black to tend the family graves.

Ernesto did not chat. He was not a voluble Italian. He was a baker, still working out of the cavernous kitchen generations of his family had used, still delivering the fresh hot bread round the canals. But he would be the last, he said, every time Simon came; his sons were not interested, they were off at universities in Padua and Genoa, his daughter

2

was married to the manager of a hotel near San Marco; when he stopped baking the ovens would go cold.

Venice was changing, Venetian trades were in decline, the young would not stay, were not interested in the hard life of daily work by boat. Venice would die soon. Simon found it impossible to believe, hard to take the prophecies of doom seriously when the ancient, magical city was still here, floating above the lagoon after thousands of years and in spite of all predictions. Somehow, somehow, it would survive, and the real Venice, too, not merely the overloaded and expensive tourist city. The people who lived and worked in the backwaters of the Zattere and the Fondamenta and the canals behind the railway station, and would still do so in a hundred years' time, propping one another up, servicing the hotels and the tourist area.

But 'Venice she dying', Ernesto said again, waving his hand at San Michele, the island of the dead; soon this was all there would be, one great graveyard.

They swung up to the landing stage and Simon climbed out with his bag.

'Lunchtime,' Ernesto said. 'Noon.'

Simon waved his hand and walked off towards the cemetery, with its well-tended paths and florid marble memorials.

The sound of the motor boat faded away almost at once, so that all he could hear were his own footsteps, some early-morning birdsong and, otherwise, the extraordinary quietness.

He had been right. No one else was here – no bowed old women with black headscarves, no families with small boys in long shorts carrying bunches of bright flowers, no workmen hoeing the weeds out of the gravel.

It was still cool, but the mist had lifted and the sun was rising.

He had first come upon the memorial a couple of years before and made a mental note about it, but he had been spending most of his time that year at all hours of the day among the market stalls, drawing the piles of fruit and fish and vegetables, the crowds, the stall holders and had not had time or energy to take in the burial island in detail.

He reached it and stopped. On top of the stone plinth was an angel with folded wings, perhaps ten feet high and flanked by three cherubs, all with bent heads and expressions of grief, all gravely, impassively beautiful. Although they were idealised, Simon was sure they had originally been taken from life. The date on the grave was 1822, and the faces of the angels were characteristically Venetian, faces you still saw today, in elderly men on the vaporetto and young men and women promenading in their designer clothes on weekend evenings along the riva degli Schiavoni. You saw the face in the great paintings in the churches, and as cherubs and saints and virgins and prelates and humble citizens gazing upwards. Simon was fascinated by it.

He found a place to sit, on a ledge of one of the adjacent monuments, and took out his drawing pads and pencils. He had also made himself a flask of coffee and brought some fruit. The light was still hazy and it was not warm. But he would be absorbed here now for the next three hours or so, only breaking off to stretch his legs occasionally by walking up and down the paths. At twelve Ernesto would return for him. He would take his things back to the flat, then go for a Campari and lunch at the trattoria he used most of the time he was here. Later, he would sleep before going out to walk into the busier parts of the city, perhaps taking a vaporetto the length of the Grand Canal and back for the delight of riding on the water between the ancient, crumbling, gilded houses, seeing the lights come on.

His days scarcely varied. He drew, walked, ate and drank, slept, looked. He did not think much about home and his other, working life.

This time, though . . .

He knew why he was drawn to San Michele and the statue of the wildly grieving angels, just as he had haunted the dark, incense-filled little churches in odd corners of the city, wandering about inside, watching the same old widows in black kneeling with their rosary beads or lighting candles at one of the stands.

The death of Freya Graffham, who had been a DS under him at Lafferton Police Station for such a short time, had affected him far more than he might have expected and for longer. It was a year since her murder and he was still haunted by the horror of it and by the fact that his emotions had been engaged by her in a way he had not admitted to himself while she had been alive.

His sister Dr Cat Deerbon had said he was allowing himself to feel more deeply for Freya simply because she was dead and so unable to respond and therefore unthreatening.

Had he felt threatened? He understood perfectly well what his sister meant but perhaps, with Freya, it had been different.

He shifted his weight and resettled the sketch pad on his knees. He was not drawing the whole statue but the face of each angel and cherub individually; he intended to come back again to do the complete monument and then work up each drawing until he was satisfied. His next exhibition would be his first in London. Everything had to be right.

Half an hour later he got up to stretch his legs. The cemetery was still deserted and the sun was full out now, warming his face as he walked up and down the path between the black and white and grey gravestones. Several times on this particular visit to Venice Simon had wondered if he might even come to live here. He had always been passionate about his job – he had taken the opposite path to that of his entire family, doctors for three generations – but the pull of this other life, of drawing and perhaps living abroad to do so, had become increasingly strong since Freya's death.

He was thirty-five. He would make Superintendent before long. He wanted it.

He did not want it.

He turned back towards the grieving angels. But the path ahead was no longer empty. Ernesto was walking towards him, and when he saw Simon, he raised an arm.

'Ciao – something wrong?'

'I've come back for you. There was a phone call.'

'Work?'

'No, family. Your father. He needs you call him right back.'

Simon put sketchbook and pencils back into the canvas satchel and followed Ernesto quickly to the landing stage.

Ma, he thought, something's happened to her. His mother had had a slight stroke a couple of months previously, the result of elevated blood pressure and too much stress, but she had made a good recovery and it had apparently not left any after-effects. Cat had told him there was no need for him to cancel his trip. 'She's fine, it wasn't major, Si. There is no reason for her to have another. Anyway, if she isn't right, you can get back quickly enough.' Which was what he must do, he thought, standing beside Ernesto as they sped back across the now sunlit water.

The only surprise was that it had not been Cat but his father who had telephoned. Richard Serrailler disapproved of Simon's choice of career, of his commitment to art, of his unmarried state – of him, period.

'Did he sound worried?'

Ernesto shrugged.

'Did he mention my mother?'

'No. Just you call.'

The motor boat shot up to the Fondamenta, turned neatly and stopped.

Simon put his hand on Ernesto's arm. 'You're a good friend. Thanks for coming back.'

Ernesto merely nodded.

Simon ran up the dark staircase from the empty warehouse to the flat and threw his satchel and jacket on the floor. The telephone connection had improved since the new digital lines had come in and he heard the ringing tone in Hallam House at once.

'Serrailler.'

'It's Simon.'

'Yes.'

'Is Mother all right?'

'Yes. I rang to tell you about your sister.'

'Cat? What's happened?'

'Martha. She has bronchial pneumonia. They've taken her to Bevham General. If you want to see her alive you should come home.'

'Of course, I . . .'

But he was speaking to a dead line. Richard Serrailler wasted words on no one, least of all his policeman son.

There was an evening flight to London but it took Simon half an hour on the telephone and in the end the help of a contact in the Italian police to get himself a seat on it. The rest of the day was spent packing, sorting out the flat and arranging for Ernesto to take him to the airport, so it was not until he was on the crowded plane that he had leisure to think. And he had not thought, not until now. His father's telephone call had been an order in all but name and he had obeyed without question. His relationship with Richard Serrailler was so poor that Simon behaved towards him as towards one of his superiors in the force and with about as much emotional involvement.

His seat was over a wing so there was little chance to look down on to the lagoon when they took off, which was as well because he minded leaving Venice more than usual, leaving his refuge, his work, and his calm, private space. Walking about the city, over canal bridges, through the squares, down the little dark passageways between the tall old houses, sitting looking and drawing, talking to Ernesto and his friends over an evening drink, Simon Serrailler was a different man from the DCI at Lafferton, his life and concerns were different, his priorities changed entirely. Time on the journey was time in which he moved from one to the other, but tonight he was being hurtled back into his everyday life without the usual relaxed period of adjustment.

The sign to fasten seat belts went off and the drinks trolley was being manoeuvred up the aisle. He asked for a gin and tonic and a bottle of mineral water.

Simon Serrailler was one of triplets. His GP sister, Cat, was the second, their brother Ivo, a doctor in Australia, the third. Martha was ten years younger, born when Richard and Meriel Serrailler were in their mid-forties; she was severely mentally and physically handicapped and had lived in a special care home for most of her life. Martha might or might not recognise Simon. No one could tell.

The sight of his sister had always moved him profoundly. Sometimes she lay in bed, sometimes she was in a wheelchair, her body propped up and strapped in, her head supported. If it was fine he wheeled her into the garden and round the paths between shrubs and flower beds. Otherwise they sat in her room or in one of the lounges. There was nothing he could take her. He talked to her and held her hand and kissed her when he arrived and left.

Over the years he had come to worry less about whether she knew him or gained anything from his company; if his visits had no significance for her, they became important to him, in something of the way these visits to Italy were important. With Martha, he was someone else. The time he spent beside her, holding her hand, thinking, talking quietly, helping her to sip a drink through a straw or eat from a spoon, absorbed and calmed him and took him away from everything else in his life.

She was pitiful, ugly, drooling, unable to communicate, barely responsive and as a boy he had been embarrassed and upset by her. Martha had not changed. He had.

His parents mentioned her occasionally but her situation was never discussed in depth or detail and emotions were always kept out of such conversations. What did his mother feel about her or for her? His father went to visit her but never spoke of it.

If she was unwell her condition always became acute very rapidly yet she had survived for twenty-five years. Colds led to chest infections then pneumonia. *'If you want to see your sister alive . . .'* But it had all happened before. Was she going to die this time? Was he sorry? How could he be? How could anyone? Did he wish her dead then? Simon's mind veered away. But he needed to talk. When he got into Heathrow he would ring Cat.

He drank more of his gin. In the locker above his head were two sketchbooks full of new drawings from which he would select the best to work up into finished pieces for his exhibition. Perhaps he had got enough after all and the extra five days in Venice would simply have been spent mooching about.

He finished his drink, took out the small sketch block he always carried and began to draw the elaborately plaited and beaded hair of the young African woman in the seat opposite.

The plane droned on over the Alps.

Two

'It's me.'

'Hi!' Pleased, as always, to hear her brother's voice, Cat Deerbon sat down ready to talk. 'Hang on, Si, let me shift myself.'

'You OK?'

'Fine, just don't know how to get comfortable.' Cat's baby, her third child, was due in a couple of weeks.

'OK, I'm as settled as I can get . . . but listen, it costs a fortune on the mobile from Italy, let me call you back?'

'I'm at Heathrow.'

'What . . .?'

'Dad rang. He said I'd better come home if I wanted to see my sister alive again.'

'Oh, tactfully put.'

'As ever.'

'Ma and I decided we weren't going to tell you.'

'Why?'

'Because you needed your holiday and there's nothing you can do, Martha won't know you . . .'

'But I will know her.'

Cat was silenced for a second. Then she said, 'Of course you will. I'm sorry.'

'No need. Listen, I won't be back till pretty late but I'll go straight to the hospital.'

'OK. Chris is out on a call and he may well go in to see her again if he's up that way. Will you come over here tomorrow? I'm getting too big to be behind the wheel safely.'

'What about Ma?'

'I just can't tell what she's feeling, Si, you know how it is. She goes up there. She goes home. Sometimes she comes here but she doesn't talk about it.'

'What exactly happened?'

'The usual – cold then chest infection now pneumonia . . . how many times have we been there? But I don't think her body is up to fighting it now. She's barely responded to the treatment and Chris said they're now wondering how aggressive that ought to be.'

'Poor little Martha.'

Her brother's voice, concerned and tender, echoed in her ears as Cat put down the phone. Tears filled her eyes, as they did so easily in pregnancy . . . even the sight, that afternoon, of one of her daughter's soft toys, lying scrumpled on the grass after it had been left out in the rain had made Cat soften to weeping. She heaved herself awkwardly off the sofa. She had forgotten almost everything about how it felt to be expecting a baby. Sam was eight and a half now and Hannah seven. They had not planned this third child. She and Chris were the only two partners in their general practice and stretched to the limits of their time and energy. But though she meant to take the odd surgery as soon as she could, realistically Cat knew that she would be out of action for the next six months and part-time at work for the year after that. Besides, now the baby was coming and she had got used to the idea, she wanted to be at home with it and give more time to the other two, not rush back to the exhausting grind of medical practice. There would not be a fourth child. This one was precious. She was going to enjoy it.

She lay on the sofa trying to sleep but unable to stop the cycle of thought. How odd and yet how typical of their father to make the phone call to Venice and in those terms. '*If you want to see your sister alive, you'd better come home.*'

Yet how often did he ever see Martha? Cat had scarcely heard the girl's name cross his lips though he had once infuriated her by calling Martha 'the vegetable' in Sam and Hannah's hearing. Was he ashamed of having a brain-damaged child? Or angry? Did he blame himself or Meriel?

And what had been the reasoning behind his call to Simon, the other child for whom he had precious little time?

Simon, the person she loved, aside from her husband and children, above all other.

The cat Mephisto appeared from nowhere to leap softly on to the sofa beside her and settle down.

All three of them slept.

Three

The streets were dark and almost deserted though it was barely ten o'clock. But the lights of Bevham General Hospital blazed out and as Simon Serrailler turned into the slip road an ambulance overtook him, siren wailing, speeding towards A & E.

He had always liked working at night, liked it from his first days as a uniformed constable on the beat, liked it now on the few occasions when he had to take charge of a night-time operation. He was fired up by the sense of emergency, the way everything was intensified, every movement and word seemed significant, as well as the strange closeness engendered by the knowledge that they were people working on important and sometimes dangerous jobs, while the rest of the world slept.

He got out of his car in the half-empty car park and looked at the great slab of hospital building, nine storeys high and with various lower blocks at angles to it.

Venice was light years away, yet for a second he had a flash picture of the cemetery at San Michele as it had been in the cool light of that Sunday morning, of the ribbons of gravel path and the pale, still, grieving statues. There, as here at the hospital now, so much emotion was somehow held, packed into every crevice, so that you breathed and felt and smelled it.

He walked in through the glass doors. By day, the hospital foyers were more like the concourse of an airport, with a mall of small shops and a constant passage of people. Bevham General was a teaching hospital, centre of excellence for several specialties, with a huge number of staff and patients. Now, when outpatient areas and offices were dark, the real hospital atmosphere crept back into the quiet corridors. Lights behind ward doors, the screech of a trolley wheel, a low voice, the rattle of cubicle curtains . . . Simon walked slowly towards ITU, and the atmosphere, the sense of life and death together, pressed in on him, raising his pulse.

'Chief Inspector?'

He smiled. One of the few people here who knew him professionally happened to be the sister on duty.

The ward was settling for the night. Screens were drawn round one or two beds, lights on in a side ward. In the background, the faint bleep and hum of electronic monitors. Death seemed very close, as if it hovered in the shadows or behind a curtain, its hand on the door.

'She's in a side room.' Sister Blake led him down through the ward.

A doctor, shirtsleeves rolled up, stethoscope dangling, came out of a cubicle and shot off, checking his pager as he went.

'They get younger.'

Sister Blake glanced round. 'Down to about sixteen I'd say.' She stopped. 'Your sister is in here . . . it's quiet. Dr Serrailler has been with her most of the day.'

'What's the outlook?'

'People in your sister's condition are prone to develop chest infections . . . well, you know that, she's had them often enough. All the physio in the world can't make up for the lack of essential movement.'

Martha had never walked. She had the brain of a baby and virtually no motor function. She had never talked, though she made babbling and cooing noises, never gained any control over her body. She had been in bed, in chairs and wheelchairs, her head propped up on a frame for the whole of her life. When she was a small child, they had taken it in turns to carry her, but her weight had always been leaden and none of them had been able to manage her beyond her third year.

'That's the ward phone and there's no one on the desk . . . understaffed as usual. I'll be there if you want anything.'

'Thanks, Sister.'

Simon opened the door of Room C.

It was the smell that hit him first – the smell of sickness he had always loathed; but the sight of his sister in the high, narrow, uncomfortable looking bed cut to his heart. The monitors to which she was attached by various wires and leads flickered, the clear bag of fluid hanging from its stand bubbled silently now and then as it was fed, drip by drip, into the vein in her arm.

But when he went closer to the bed and looked down at her, the machinery became invisible, irrelevant. Simon saw the sister he had always seen. Martha. Brain-damaged, inert, pale, heavy, a dribble coming from the corner of her slightly open mouth. Martha. Who knew what she had ever registered about her life, the world, her surroundings, the people who cared for her, the family who loved her? No one had ever really been able to communicate with her. Her awareness and understanding were less than those of a pet.

And yet . . . there had been something of the life spark within her to which Simon had responded from the beginning, and which was deeper and greater than compassion or even a sense of simple kinship with someone of his own flesh and blood. Before she had gone to live in Ivy Lodge, he had often taken her out to the garden, or strapped her into his car and driven her for miles, sure that she enjoyed looking out of the window; he had pushed her chair around the streets to divert her. He had always talked to her. She had certainly known his voice, though she could have had no idea of the meaning of the sounds that voice made. Later, when he had gone to see her in the home, he had been aware of an intent stillness that came over her as soon as she heard him speak.

18

He loved her, with the strange, pure love which can receive no recognition or response and demands neither.

Her hair had been brushed and lay loosely round her head on the high pillow. There was no real character or definition in her face; time seemed to have passed over it leaving it quite unaffected. But Martha's hair, which had always been kept short so as to be more manageable for her carers, had recently been allowed to grow, and shone in the light of the overhead lamp, the same white-blonde colour as his own.

Simon pulled the chair out, sat down and took her hand.

'Hello, sweetheart. I'm here.'

He looked at her face, waited for that change in her breathing, the flicker of her eyelids, which would indicate that she knew, heard him, sensed him, and was comforted, reassured.

The green and white fluorescent lines of the monitor flowed on, making small regular wavelets, across the screen.

Her breaths were shallow as they passed rustily in and out of her lungs.

'I've been in Italy, drawing . . . lots of faces. People in cafés, people riding on the vaporetto. Venetian faces. They're the same faces you can see in the great paintings from five hundred years ago, it's a face that doesn't change, only the clothes are modern. I sit in cafés and drink coffee or Campari and just look at the faces. No one minds.'

19

He talked on but her expression did not change, her eyes did not open. She was somewhere further away, deeper down and more out of reach than she had ever been.

He stayed for an hour, his hand over hers, talking to her quietly as if he were soothing a frightened infant.

He heard a trolley being pushed down the ward. Someone called out. An immense tiredness came over him so that for a moment he almost put his head down on the bed beside Martha so that he could sleep.

The bump of the door brought him up.

'Si.'

His brother-in-law, Cat's husband Chris Deerbon, slipped into the room. 'I thought you might need this.' He held out a polystyrene cup of tea. 'Cat said you'd got here.'

'She doesn't look good.'

'No.'

Simon stood up to stretch his back which always ached if he sat down for long. He was six feet four.

Chris touched Martha's forehead, and glanced at the monitors.

'What do you think?'

Chris shrugged. 'Hard to know. She's had this all before but there's an awful lot against her.'

'Everything.'

'It's not much of a life.'

'Can we be sure?'

'I think so,' Chris said gently.

They stood looking down at Martha until Simon finished his tea and threw the cup across into the bin.

'That'll see me home. Thanks, Chris. I'm bushed.'

They left together. At the door Simon looked round. There had been nothing since he had arrived, no flicker, no indication, apart from the rusty breathing and the steady blip of the monitor, that the body on the bed was a living young woman. He went back, bent over Martha and kissed her face. The skin was damp and slightly downy, like the skin of a newborn baby.

Simon thought he would not see her alive again.

Four

'Gunton?'

There had to be something of course, even today, just to let him know that nothing changed, until eight o'clock the next morning.

He turned.

Hickley was holding up the garden fork. 'Call this clean?'

Andy Gunton went back into the long shed where all the tools were kept. He had cleaned the mud off the fork as carefully as he always did. If Hickley, the one screw he had never managed to get on with, had found a blob of dirt between two of the tines, then he had stuck it there himself.

'No dirty tools, you know how it works.' Hickley shoved the fork into Andy's face.

Go on, the gesture said, go on, try me, answer back, cheek me, have a go at me with the garden fork . . . do it and I'll have you in here another month, see if I don't.

Andy took the fork and went over to the bench under the window. Carefully, he wiped every prong and probed the cloth down between the blades, then he rubbed the handle over and over. Hickley watched, arms folded.

Beyond the window, the kitchen garden was empty, work over for the day. For a single, strange moment, Andy Gunton thought, I'll miss it. I've sown seeds I won't harvest, I've put in plants I won't tend as they grow.

He caught his own thought and almost laughed.

He turned and handed the recleaned fork to the screw for inspection. He didn't resent Hickley. There was always one. Hickley wasn't like the other screws here who treated them more as teachers with pupils and got the best out of them as a result. To Hickley, they were the still inmates, the enemy. Scum. Was Andy scum? The first few weeks behind bars, he had felt like it. He had been shell-shocked by everything, but most of all by the reality he could not get his head round, that he was inside because, in the middle of a botched robbery, in panic he had shoved an innocent man and the man had crashed to the concrete, fractured his skull and died. The word *killer* had rung round and round his own head like a marble in a basin, *killer*, *killer*, *killer*. What else was a killer but scum?

He waited while the man inspected the garden fork. Go on, get your microscope out why don't you, you won't find an effin speck.

'Put it away.'

Andy Gunton slid the handle slowly into the metal holder on the shed wall. 'Last time,' he said.

But Hickley wasn't going to wish him well, would have choked sooner than congratulate him on his final release. 'Don't let the bugger wind you up,' someone had advised on his first day out here eighteen months ago. He remembered it again as he walked, without a word or a backward glance at Hickley, out of the shed, through the market garden away to the east wing of Birley Open Prison.

Through one of the ventilators in the kitchen block came the smell of boiled egg; through an open window the sound of a ball to and fro across a table tennis table, pock-pock, pock-pock.

Once, overhearing him say, 'There's always a first time,' one of the screws, during his first week in Stackton Prison, had snarled back at him, 'No, Gunton, there isn't always a first time but there's sure as hellfire always a last one.'

In the raw and still shell-shocked state he had been then, almost four years ago, the words had thwacked into his memory like an arrow on to a target and stuck there.

There's always a last. He stopped at the door to his own residential block and looked round. Last working day. Last time he'd clean a garden fork. Last eyeball-to-eyeball with Hickley. Last warm boiled egg with beetroot and potato. Last game of pool. Last night on the bed. Last. Last. Last.

His stomach churned momentarily as the giddy thought of the outside world came to him again. He had been there, first on shopping trips with a screw, then on the greengrocery run, delivering, but it wasn't the same, he knew that. Open prison began to loosen your shackles bit by bit but you still had them, you still belonged inside and not out, you were still conditioned by where you ate and slept, the company you kept, your past, the reason you were there.

Your body might be allowed out, but your mind stayed behind, your mind could not, dared not, take it in.

He unlocked his door. The late-afternoon sun touched the mushroom-coloured wall making it look even dingier. The whole place needed painting. They must have tried quite hard to start with, someone had probably been proud of themselves for their efforts to make it look as little like a prison cell as possible, and the public areas more youth club or office block. Now, though, everything needed recovering, repainting, refurbishing, replacing and never seemed scheduled to get it.

Last time, last time, last time. Out of here. Out . . .

Andy opened the window. He remembered the first few days and how he couldn't get used to that little thing, being able to open his own window when he wanted to. He'd kept on doing it, opening and closing the window, opening and closing it.

He leaned out. Tomorrow, this room would belong to someone else. Another man moved from closed to open prison would do it all over again. Open the window. Close it. Open it. Close it, over and over. Tomorrow.

There was a bang on the door and Spike Jones was in the room before Andy had time to call out. Spike was OK.

'They're getting up a five-a-side.'

'Nah.'

'You what?'

'Anyway, I've handed in me boots.'

'Right. You taking Kylie Minogue?'

'She's yours.'

Spike laughed, picking up the rolled-up poster which was propped against the cupboard. He wouldn't be leaving Birley for another ten months. He'd always had his eye on that picture.

'You ent brooding?'

'Get off.'

Brooding. Andy turned back to the open window. Brooding. No. That had been at the start, in the first days and weeks at Stackton, when he hadn't known day from night and thought his mind was going. Brooding. He hadn't done that since coming here and getting out into the market garden. He wasn't about to take it up again.

The evening passed, like all the rest of them, and he was glad of that. He wouldn't have wanted anything to be different. He ate in the canteen, stood outside with a couple of the others watching the floodlit five-a-side, having a roll-up, went back in and played pool for an hour. At ten he was in his room, watching *The West Wing*.

*

He woke confused and sweating out of a night-mare. Security lights round the perimeter meant that it was never completely dark. It was just after three.

Then the shock of what was going to happen hit him again and he was terrified so that his stomach clenched and his throat felt tight. Four and a half years of prison life, of learning to conform, putting on a front, keeping his own real self so concealed that now he scarcely knew who that self was, of routine, of rules, of learning, and of every emotion there was played out, four and a half years swinging from rage to despair to acceptance to hope and back again. In five hours the four and a half years would be over. In five hours he would be out there. In five hours this room, this place would be nothing to him and, even more, he would be nothing to any of it. History. His name off the registers, his face forgotten.

Five hours.

Andy Gunton lay on his back. If it was like this after four and a half years of a sentence, how was it for the ones who came out after fifteen or more? Did they feel this sudden wash of panic at the thought of being without walls, without props, without the deadening routine which after a short time became the only thing you clung to for safety?

He remembered the first week at Stackton. He had been twenty. He'd known nothing. The stench of the place and the racket, the dead faces and suspicious eyes, the need he had had not so much to break out or run away but simply to vanish, to dissolve, the droning snores of Joey Butler, his first cellmate, that he never got used to, never slept through deeply enough, the red scaly patches on his skin which erupted in eczema after a couple of nights on the prison mattress and did not properly heal until he had come here – all of it came back to him, he lived through it all again, lying awake looking at the dull glow of the lights on the wall. They said it did one of two things to you. It took your soul away so that you never belonged to yourself again, you belonged in prisons for ever after and just went on doing whatever it took to get back there, or it scared the lights out of you, changed you, chewed you up and spat you out. Cured you.

He had been cured from the moment he had handed in his own clothes and put on the prison uniform. He could have been let out then. It had worked. He wasn't coming back.

How could he have dreamed he would feel like this, four and a half years on, terrified to go, clinging to the familiar, half longing to be told of a mistake, that he had another term to serve, that this room would be his tomorrow night after all?

He went on staring at the light on the wall until it began to change and soften to pale grey as the dawn came up.

Five

Simon Serrailler had slept deeply and woke to the sound of the cathedral clock ringing eight. The flat, the perfect space he had created with such loving care for himself, was cool and silent, filled with the bland light of a March morning. He pulled on his dressing gown and padded into the long sitting room, curtainless and tranquil with its polished elm floor, books, piano, pictures. The light was not blinking on the telephone answering machine. No one had rung to tell him his sister was dead.

He filled the grinder with coffee beans and the filter with water. In half an hour the first cars would pull into the spaces at the front and the sound of the early arrivals at work echo up the stairs. The rest of this Georgian building had long been converted into offices for various Diocesan organisations and a couple of solicitors. Simon's was the only residential flat. He had usually left for the station by eight and was not often home until after seven, so he rarely met anyone else – during the day the building had a life of its own, about which he knew little. It suited him, self-contained and private as he was, content in his orderly space. He relished his job, had enjoyed almost every day of his life in the police force, but his refuge here was essential to him.

Now, mug of coffee in hand, he went to three of his own drawings framed and hanging on the wall to the right of the tall windows. He had done them on his last visit to Venice and he saw at once that they were better than anything he had produced during the previous few days there. He had not worked so well for a long time, unsettled as he had been by the events of the previous year. The murder of Freya Graffham had hit him hard and not only because the death of a fellow officer was always a blow from which it was tough to recover. No, he said, and went briskly back to the kitchen for more coffee. Don't go there, not again. He dressed in jeans and sweatshirt and took the canvas satchel he used to hold his drawing things. The offices were opening, voices came through half-open doors, kettles boiled in cubby-holes. Strange, Simon thought. The building felt different, no longer his. Strange. Strange to be wearing jeans instead of a suit on a weekday morning, strange to be here instead of overlooking a back canal in Venice. Strange and disorientating.

He drove fast out of Lafferton.

The hospital might have been a different place too. He had difficulty finding a parking space, the foyer streamed with people on their way to outpatient appointments, porters pushing wheelchairs, gangs of medical students, flower deliverers, two women setting up a charity stall. Down here the smell of antiseptic was barely detectable.

The lift was full, the wards were noisy. Somewhere, someone dropped a bucket and swore. But in Martha's room, nothing had changed. The monitors blipped on, the fluorescent green wavelets rippled across the screens, the liquid in the plastic bag above her head drip-dripped. At first he thought that his sister looked the same but when he went closer, it seemed to Simon that the colour of her skin had darkened slightly. Her hair was damp, her eyelids tender as the soft skins of mushrooms.

He wondered, as he always did when he saw her again, how much went on in her mind, what she recognised and understood, whether she thought and if so how deeply. That she *felt* he was in no doubt. Her feelings had always moved him for she expressed them as a baby, crying and laughing as readily and absorbedly, ceasing as quickly, though he had never found it easy to make out what might have stimulated her emotion or whether the response was to something external or inside herself.

Her handicap so affected her features that it was hard to detect any family resemblance there but to Simon that only made her more completely, uniquely herself.

He pulled the chair up close to her bed.

*

He was too absorbed in his drawing to notice the door opening. He wanted to catch the spirit of his sister by freeing her, on paper, from the medical apparatus that surrounded her and as he looked at the hairs on her head, the curve of her nostril beneath the wide nose, and the eyelashes, like the hairs of a fine paintbrush on her cheek, he saw that she was beautiful, as a child is beautiful, because neither time nor experience had in any way marked her face. Drawing her eyelids with the finest pencil lines, he almost held his breath.

'Oh, darling . . .' The front of her hair glittered with raindrops. 'Cat told me you'd come back.'

They looked at the still, oddly flattened figure on the bed.

'I'm sorry.'

'You mustn't be.'

'Every time I come in through that door I feel torn in two,' Meriel Serrailler said. 'Afraid she will be dead. Hoping she will be dead. Praying but I don't know who to or for what.' She bent now and brushed her lips against Martha's forehead.

Simon pulled the chair back for her.

'You were drawing her.'

'I've been meaning to for a long time.'

'Poor little girl. Have the doctors been in yet?'

'Not this morning. I spoke to Sister Blake last night. And Chris was here .'

'It's hopeless either way. But none of them will say so.'

He put his hand on his mother's arm but she did not turn to him. She sounded, as she always did when she spoke about Martha, cool, detached, professional. The warmth in her voice, familiar to the rest of them, seemed absent. Simon was not deceived. He knew that she loved Martha as much as any of her children but with an entirely different kind of love.

His drawing lay on the bedcover. Meriel picked it up.

'Strange,' she said. 'Beauty but no character.' Then she turned to face him. 'And you?' She looked at him with disconcerting directness. Her eyes were Cat's and Ivo's eyes, very round, very dark, not his own blue ones. She waited, still and quite composed. Simon picked up the drawing and began to cover it with a sheet of protective film.

'I wish your father hadn't rung you. You needed a holiday.'

'I'll get another. I'm going for a cup of tea. Shall I bring you some?'

But his mother shook her head. At the door Simon glanced round and saw that she was stroking her daughter's hair gently back from her face.

Six

'Come over here . . . have lunch with me.'

'Maybe tomorrow.'

'Why?'

'I'm going to Hylam Peak . . . it's a good walking day. I'll get a pub lunch.'

'Brooding?'

'Not exactly.'

'I'll ring you later.'

Simon put the phone down. His sister knew him too well. Brooding? Yes. When he felt like this he was not good company, he needed to put distance between himself and home and, as Cat herself had once said, walk the brooding out of his system. It was everything – having to break off his time in Venice, Martha, and still the hangover from last year. The following Wednesday he would be back at work. He needed to brood now.

Hylam Peak was one of a chain of hills that ran thirty miles to the west of Lafferton, approached by a twisting road that climbed across open moorland. A few damp villages huddled in the shadows of the steep dips between the peaks. In summer the tracks were bright with slow-moving trains of walkers, climbers hung like spiders from ropes attached to the rocky outcrops. These peaks were Bevham's playground. People got out of the city to fly kites and microlights, hang-glide and race mountain bikes.

For the rest of the year, especially in bad weather, no one came. Simon liked it best on days like this, when he could sit at the top of Hylam Peak among the cries of the sheep and the soaring buzzards and look across three counties, draw, think, even sleep on the dry patchy grass, and speak to no one.

He wondered how people survived in families and crowded places of work, buses, trains, busy streets day in, day out, without a solitary escape to wild empty places.

He was the only one in the roughly fenced-off area that served as a car park. He took out his canvas satchel, immobilised the steering wheel and zapped down the locks. Nothing at all was left in the car apart from an old rug and neither radio nor CD player was fitted. The park might be deserted now but places like this were easy targets for thieves whatever the season.

An hour and a half later, he sat alone on the rock slab at the summit of the Peak. The March sun chased shadows like hares across the landscape below him. The air was clear and filled with the melancholy bleating of hundreds of the native long-fleeced sheep scattered over the hills.

He felt idle. He had been up here times without number and drawn the peaks and the cloudscapes over them as well as the sheep in every season, every weather until, at least for now, there was nothing left for him to put his pencil to.

Brooding, Cat had said. But now that he was up here he felt light-headed in the cool spring air and he did not brood. The sun was on his face. He rolled on to his back and crossed his hands behind his head. A single lark spiralled up into the blue sky and higher, to the whiteness beyond.

Its trail of song was sliced into and drowned by the judder of a helicopter and its shadow fell across Simon's face, blotting out the sun. He sat up, shocked. The thing was skimming the peaks in a whirl of metal blades. He saw its undercarriage, so close he might have reached up his hand to touch it and as he watched it cross the valley, going east, he could make out the outline of two of the figures inside. It was neither the air ambulance nor a police helicopter but, so far as he could tell, a private one.

As it moved across the landscape the terrified sheep fled up and down the slopes in all directions, trying to get away from the noise and the slipping shadow. The machine itself was well out of sight before the silence came down again.

The lark's song was severed.

Simon pulled himself to his feet and slung the canvas bag across his back. The intrusion of ugly sound and sight had fractured his peace and sense of ease as it had unsettled the sheep and silenced the bird.

He took the path that led steeply down the Peak, following the fingerposts to Gardale.

Seven

The bed was stripped, the mattress bare, the sheets and blankets piled by the door. There were pale shapes on the walls where his posters and calendar and photographs had been. His bag was by his feet, packed, zipped. Ready.

He was ready.

He'd been ready since six.

Only he wasn't ready, Andy realised. He was panicking. His stomach had dropped into his bowels twice and he'd had to make fast for the bog.

He thought of the days and nights spent imagining this morning, planning for it, dreaming about it, counting the hours to it. And it had come and he was shit-scared of it.

He understood why so many of them went out and chucked a brick through a shop window or grabbed a woman's handbag. Anything to get back to safety, like racing back to touch 'home' in the playground when you were a kid.

It was different when you had people waiting for you, kids to rush up to you, a wife desperate for you, you wouldn't be able to see the back of this place fast enough then.

He shook himself, got up and did thirty press-ups. He was fit; working out in the kitchen gardens and playing so much soccer and basketball had seen to that. Sweating, he lay back on the thin mattress. Right, he said, OK, you're fit, and you've got a future out there.

You hope.

He rolled over on to his side and went back to sleep.

The streets were awash and the gale was blowing so hard he could scarcely stand against it on the station platform. He went back inside the steamy buffet. The train was announced as running forty-five minutes late. Flooding on the line.

People were talking about it. He got another mug of tea and a doughnut.

An hour ago, he'd walked out of the prison gate carrying his bag, him and two of the others, but he'd got away from them fast; besides, they had people waiting for them. Families. He hadn't expected ceremony but still he was shocked how quickly it had all been over. The things they'd been holding for him were spread out on the counter, gone through and signed for; he was given his money, his train pass, waited in the passage with the others and then across the strip, and out through the gate. The jangle of keys for the last time.

Rain, driving into your face and a gale knocking you almost off your feet.

'They'd a car completely overturned in Simpson Street.'

'Eight trees down somebody said.'

'Can't have been, there ent eight trees in the bloody town!'

'Kids haven't gone to school, too dangerous.'

'St Nicholas church roof was ripped half off.'

Andy sat holding the mug between his hands. He felt unreal. People talked and got up and sat down and came in and went out through the buffet doors and no one took any notice of him. No one knew where he'd just come from.

What would happen if they did?

It wasn't being out on his own, buying a mug of tea and a doughnut, waiting for a train, none of that fazed him. It was nobody watching him, nobody taking any notice. He hadn't been invisible for four and a half years but he was invisible now.

The gale hurled itself suddenly at the doors swinging them wide open, crashing an empty chair on to the floor. A child in a red anorak screamed.

He remembered his mother. She'd only been to see him half a dozen times, scurrying into the visitors' room, head bent and eyes on the floor for shame, and after that she'd been in and out of hospital, then too ill. He didn't think of that crumpled-looking person as his mother, he thought of the one he had run to when friends of Mo Thompson's had slammed his fingers in the door

40

for fun and the one who had finally found him when they had taken him down the Wherry to one of the sheds and locked him there in the dark, but not before telling him that the scratching sounds in the roof were rats. That had been his mother, with thick arms and red hands ready to beat the lights out of his tormentors and a voice like a foghorn you could hear three streets away. She had shrunk. There had been grey stains on her coat and dirt in the folds of her neck. When she had leaned over the table between them in the visitors' room she had smelled.

The woman behind the buffet counter was trying to wedge one of the doors with newspaper but it kept coming away from her hand and now the rainwater was sloshing under it and over the brown linoleum floor.

Three men went to help her. She fetched a mop and plastic bucket and started to try to push back the tidal wave of rain water.

The child was eating a chocolate bar and screaming at the same time as the windows rattled in the gale.

Andy wanted to go back. Here it was unsafe, the ground seemed to be moving beneath his feet and the fact that nobody knew his name scared him.

Somewhere outside, part of a tin roof sheared off and crashed on to concrete.

Mam, Andy Gunton muttered under his breath, and it was the woman with the strong arms and red hands he was talking to, Mam.

A confused echo came out of the speakers, possibly announcing his train, possibly announcing the end of the world.

The lights went out then and for a second everyone froze, everyone was silent, even the child.

The weather had caught them out. Heavy rain and high winds had been forecast but not a virtual hurricane, bringing such damage and chaos at the height of a Monday morning. The electricity did not come back on in the station buffet and the trains did not run again until the middle of the afternoon.

'How the hell am I going to manage?'

The woman with the child had a baby in a pushchair and two cases. An emergency platform alteration meant that she had to cross the iron bridge. She was in tears, the children exhausted, the rain still lashing down.

'Come on, my love,' Andy heard himself say. He took the cases and after carrying them over the bridge, came back for the pushchair. The far platform was dangerously crowded. Rain was coursing along the gutterings and down in a stream.

'You hold on to your little girl, I'll get the door open and bag your seat, don't fret.'

'What'd I have done?' the woman kept saying to him. 'I don't know what I'd have done.'

'Someone else would have looked after you.'

'You can't trust everybody, though, people are funny. I can trust you.'

Andy looked at her. She meant it. Later, he thought, he would see the humour of it.

'Where are you going yourself?'

'Lafferton. Near Bevham?'

'That's the other side of the bloody country.'

'Yeah.'

'You going home?'

He didn't answer. He didn't know.

'What do you do?'

He opened his mouth. Rain was trickling down his neck inside his shirt. 'Market gardening.' But the train was drawing in. She was fretting over her children and hadn't heard him.

Andy threw himself at a door as it slid by him and as the handle locks were released he was inside the train, pushing past to a seat, throwing the woman's case across it before going back to lift the children.

'You're a saint, you know that, how'd I have managed? I'd never have done this, you deserve a bloody medal.'

It was another hour before he got on a train himself. By then, the lights were back on and the wind had quietened though the rain was still sluicing down.

There was no seat and no buffet car. He sat on his bag in the gangway, crushed next to a boy with a stereo making tinny noises.

There was no way he could let Michelle know when he might be arriving, and by now it scarcely mattered. The train stopped every now and then, for a few minutes, or half an hour. After a while, he slept sitting upright. When he woke, it was dark outside.

He wondered where the woman with the children was.

The boy nudged his elbow and passed across a can of lager.

'Cheers. Where'd this come from?'

'Had a couple or three in me bag.'

Andy took a long swig of the lukewarm gassy beer.

Four hours later, he walked up the concrete path of his sister's house. It was still raining. From one end of the street to the other there was noise, television noise, music noise, kids screaming and adults shouting noise. The orange street light shone on a plastic tractor at his feet.

'Bloody hell, you took your time.' His sister Michelle looked nearer to forty than thirty and the hallway behind her smelled of frying food. She had visited him twice in prison, right at the beginning, before she married Pete Tait after divorcing the first no-hoper and started on another lot of kids.

'What you been doing?'

Andy followed her through the house into the back kitchen where the smell of frying was strongest. Fat was spitting up from a pan of chips on to the tile-effect wallpaper. He dropped his bag.

'There was this storm. Gales and flooding, or maybe you didn't look out the window.'

'Oh ha ha, I had to bloody wade through it to get them to bloody school, didn't I? Did it stop the trains then?'

'Sort of.'

'You had your tea?'

'No.'

His sister sighed and stuck the kettle spout under the tap. From the next room the television screamed with skidding car wheels.

Andy sat down at the table. His head ached, he was hungry and thirsty, he was shattered. He didn't want to be here. He wanted to be at home. Where was home? There was no home. Michelle's was as near as it got.

'You'll have to sleep on the couch or up with Matt in his room.'

'I'm not bothered. Couch then.'

'Well, Pete'll want to watch the telly till all hours, we got Sky, he watches sport.'

'OK, Matt's room. I said I'm not bothered.'

He looked up. His sister was staring at him as she lit a cigarette. She didn't offer him one.

'You'll know me again.'

'You don't look any different,' she said in the end, through a face full of smoke. 'Older maybe.'

'I *am* older. I was nineteen. I'm nearly twenty-five.'

'Jeez.'

She put a mug of tea in front of him. 'Pete says you can stop just till you find something. Will they fix you up at the probation?'

'Look, if you want me to drink up and go, just say, Michelle.'

'Makes no difference to me. What you going to do all day?'

'Work.'

'You ent never worked.'

'I'll work.'

'What at? What can you do?'

'I've been training.'

The chip fat spurted viciously. She dragged it off the gas.

'What, sewing mailbags?'

'You don't know anything. You didn't bother to come and find out.'

'I wrote you, didn't I, I sent you stuff, I sent you pictures of the kids. It was half across the bloody country and Pete wasn't keen.'

Pete Tait. A squaddie when Michelle had married him but he'd got out when he fell off a wall on an assault course and slammed his back. Now he sat in a cubbyhole watching a shopping mall CCTV screen from two in the afternoon till midnight. Andy knew that much from the single-page notes Michelle had scrawled to him half a dozen times a year.

'They'll sort me out a place. Flat or something.'

'You want beans or tomatoes?' Michelle was opening a packet of corned beef.

'Whatever.'

Baked beans. Corned beef. Chips. Tomatoes. Prison food. He got up and poured himself another mug of tea. The woman with the luggage and the children came to his mind. Funny. You saw people. Talked to them. They went. You never saw them again. All the men in all the prisons. Never saw them again.

'The kids watching television?'

'They're in bloody bed. It's half past nine. I'm not one of those lets them stay up all hours.'

She set the plate of food in front of him.

So the television was having a car chase all to itself.

'I haven't eaten since half seven.'

'You want bread and butter as well then?'

Andy nodded through a mouthful of beans and chips.

Michelle sat opposite him.

'I don't want my kids turning out like the rest round here and I don't want them hearing stuff from you either.'

Stuff. The stuff was years ago, in another life. He hardly thought about it. He hadn't been that nineteen-year-old for nearly six years in any sense at all.

'They won't.'

'There's always jobs going on security. Pete could've put in a word, only I don't know what they'd ask.'

'They'd ask.'

'You got to do something.'

'I told you.'

'What then? You still ent said.'

The television was wailing with police sirens. 'Don't you ever turn that off?'

'What?'

'You don't even know it's on, do you?'

'I've only just bloody sat down, I've been on my feet all day. Anyway, Pete'll want it on when he gets in.'

'That's three hours.'

'Shut up, will you, who the hell do you think you are, telling me how to run my house, live my life, you've just bloody walked in after being in stir for five years, you're bloody lucky Pete didn't say no, sorry, no chance, he's not bloody coming here, but he didn't. He said you could come.'

'Very nice of him.'

'Look . . .'

'Market gardening.'

'You what?'

'I've trained. They have a big market garden, we supplied veg all round, shops, hotels, schools. Big enterprise.'

'What, digging and that, potato lifting? Sounds like hard work. You never had no practice at that.'

'Well, I have now.'

'They get you a job digging then?'

'There's a lot more to it than digging.'

'Can you cut hedges? There's one in front wants cutting and if you fancy digging up the concrete from the back I could have some flowers.'

'I don't.'

'They give you money when you came out?'

'I earned money. They keep it for you.'

'Only if you're going to eat like that . . .'

Andy reached round the back of his chair for his jacket. He took out the plastic wallet they'd given him with the money that was due to him that morning and threw it across the table.

'Take what you want,' he said, looking at

Michelle, 'I wouldn't expect my sister to give me owt for nowt.'

Above the television voices of two men arguing violently, a child began to shout in the room overhead. Andy tried to remember its name or even if it was his nephew or his niece but couldn't.

Eight

Simon was halfway down the steep track into the ravine when the sky, which had been gathering over his head, seemed to have been slashed open, releasing a deluge of rain. He cursed himself for having decided to continue in spite of the darkening weather rather than head back to the car and now he held on to the scrubby bushes at the side of the path as the water rushed down around him, taking small stones and debris hurtling with it to the ravine below. He was already saturated and his boots were full of water. The air steamed and the wind whipped up a mini tornado overhead. It would pass quickly but in the meantime he knew it was dangerous to carry on down into the ravine and almost impossible to struggle back up to the moor above him.

In the end, he crouched, holding on to the roots of the tough little bushes, and waited as the world broke around him.

Once, a couple of years before, he and two colleagues had pursued a man out here not in rain but in a snowstorm. Simon still remembered the fear he had felt as the criminal had pitched himself over the edge and begun to slither down the steep side of the ravine. He had been high on crack cocaine and armed with a butcher's knife and the car he had stolen lay upside down and on fire. Simon had been heading the pursuit; the call as to whether they went down into the ravine after the man had been his.

He shuddered, remembering. Yet police work still excited him; he still loved the chase better than anything and his only regret about his promotion to DCI had been that he would be out there in the thick of it all less than before.

He had been right. He now spent more time than he enjoyed behind a desk. But the solution wasn't easy to see. Ought he to have shunned promotion? What kind of career would he have had then, chugging along as a DC until retirement, his lack of ambition noted and derided?

The rain had soaked his canvas bag. He shifted his weight and almost lost his balance and slipped. Up had got to be better than down.

He had gone fifty yards or so, head bent against the driving rain, across the open moor, when a motorbike skidded up beside him out of the storm.

Simon could not hear what the rider was shouting to him out of his helmet visor but he understood the man's gestures and climbed up behind him, drawing up his legs against the flying swirl of mud around them.

Ten minutes later they were back in the comparative shelter of the car park. The motorcyclist lifted his visor again and shouted above the roar of the bike's engine in reply to Simon's thanks. 'You're all right.'

He had turned in a spatter of mud and stones and spun off down the track. Simon followed, driving off through the storm to the Deerbon farmhouse at Misthorpe. On very rare occasions he shied away from the silence and empty spaces of his own home.

Halfway to Cat's his mobile beeped a text message.
Ma here. Wants talk re Martha. Come 2 supper?
Simon pulled into the side of the road.

'It's me. I'm at Hassle. I was on my way over anyway.'

'You haven't been on the moor in this?'

'I have and I'm drenched. I'll need to borrow some clothes from Chris. I nearly fell down the ravine.'

'Simon, are you trying to send me into labour?'

'Sorry, sorry . . . listen, can you talk? What's this about Mother?'

'Yes, she's upstairs reading to Hannah. She came on here from the hospital. She wants to talk to us all . . . well, Chris and me, and she asked if I could raise you.'

'Dad?'

'Not sure.'

'What's happened?'

'Nothing. I think that's the problem.'

'Is she OK?'

'Who, Ma? Bit tight-lipped.'

'OK . . . anything else I should know?'

'It's roast chicken.'

'On my way.'

He loved the farmhouse. He loved everything about it, outside and in, loved the way it sat, long and low and grey-stoned in its fold of paddocks, loved the two fat ponies leaning over the hedge as he went by, loved the chicken run and the garden which was never immaculate or well weeded but always more welcoming than his mother's prize-winning designer half-acre, loved the hugger-mugger of a porch, full of wellington boots and milk bottles, loved the warmth and the tumble of his nephew and niece and the cat on the old sofa beside the Aga, loved the cheerfulness and urgent medical conversations between his sister and brother-in-law. Loved the happiness the place gave off, the smell and noise and love of family life.

He pulled in beside his mother's car. The rain had lessened. Simon stood for a moment looking at the lights of the farmhouse streaming out. From somewhere inside he heard the children shout with laughter.

Is this what's wrong? The question came back to him for the thousandth time since the death of Freya. She might have been inside a house like this one waiting for him, there might have been his children . . .

A twist of pain. Yet he could not always remember what she had looked like. They had had dinner together. She had had a drink in his flat. There had been . . .

What, precisely? Precisely nothing.

Easy to regret nothing.

He walked across the gravel and opened the porch door. The smell of roasting chicken wafted out.

'Hi.'

His sister Cat, moon-faced in pregnancy, huge-bellied, came out of the kitchen to meet him. Simon thought suddenly, this is why there was nothing. Freya was not Cat. Nobody is Cat. Nobody else can ever be Cat.

'Uncle Simon, Uncle Simon, I've got a gerbil, it's called Ron Weasley, come and look.'

He would stay the night. Now, he wore a tracksuit belonging to his brother-in-law. He sat at the kitchen table next to his mother, the remains of an apple and blackberry crumble and a second bottle of wine in front of them, Chris at the stove watching the coffee percolate.

'I wanted you all here,' Meriel Serrailler said. She sat very still, very straight. *Tight-lipped*, Cat had said. But there had been a tightness about his mother ever since Simon could remember, a smiling, alabaster, beautifully coiffed tightness.

'What about Dad?'

'I told you, he's at a Masonic.'

'He ought to be here, he has a right to say . . . whatever he wants to.'

Chris Deerbon brought the coffee to the table. 'Let's talk about it now.' He put his hand briefly on Cat's shoulder. 'I know more or less what Richard thinks anyway. I talked to him at the hospital.'

Cat turned to look up at him. 'What? You didn't tell me that.'

'I know.'

His voice alone soothed and reassured her, Simon could see it. His sister was lucky. It was a lucky marriage.

'He talked to you when he doesn't talk to me then,' Meriel Serrailler said quietly.

'Well, of course. It's easier, isn't it? You know that. I'm involved but I'm not Richard's son and I am another doctor. Don't worry about it.'

Meriel looked at him steadily. 'I don't,' she said, 'I'm past that.'

Simon could not speak. He sat across a table from a panel of doctors. They had a different point of view, no matter that the person they were discussing was their daughter, sister, sister-in-law. They had a detachment he could not find.

'She is probably going to die,' Meriel said and now her voice had changed, it was the senior consultant's voice, the clear firm tone of the sympathetic but uninvolved practitioner. 'She has been very weakened by this bout and it is not just her lungs that can't go on throwing off pneumonia, her whole immune system is exhausted and her heart tracings are poor. But we thought she would be dead forty-eight hours ago . . . more . . . and she is not. It's time to look at her treatment.'

'They seem to know what they're doing,' Simon said. But he knew what he said was not relevant, not the business they were supposed to be addressing now.

'Of course. The point is . . . how long will it take her to die? A day? A week? The longer they pour antibiotics into her, and fluids and salbutamol, the longer it will drag on.'

'You want them to withhold treatment?' Cat reached out and poured herself a glass of water from the jug in front of her. She sounded as weary as she looked. 'I haven't seen her this week so it's hard to voice an opinion. You have, Chris.'

'It's difficult.'

'No,' Meriel Serrailler said, 'it is not. It is actually rather straightforward. She has no quality of life now and none to look forward to.'

'You can't say that. How can you possibly say that, how can you know?' Simon clenched his fists, willing himself to speak calmly.

'You're not a doctor.'

'What the hell has that got to do with it?'

'Si . . .'

'You have no professional basis from which to assess her condition.'

'No, I just have a human one.'

'And doesn't that tell you she has no quality of life? It's perfectly obvious.'

'No, it is not. We don't know what's in her mind, we don't know how she feels, she thinks.'

'She thinks nothing. She has no power of conscious thought.'

'That cannot possibly be true.'

'Why?'

Cat burst into tears. 'Stop' she said, 'I can't bear this, I don't want this sort of argument in my house . . .'

Chris got up and went to her.

'It's clear no one is capable of a rational discussion about this at the moment,' Meriel Serrailler said. She got up, calmly took her coffee cup across to the dishwasher and loaded it in. 'It wasn't sensible of me to expect it. I apologise.'

'What are you going to do?'

Meriel looked at her son. 'Go home.'

'You haven't any right to make decisions about Martha, you know that.'

'I know perfectly well what my rights are, Simon.'

'For God's sake.' Cat held on to Chris's hand, tears pouring down her face.

'You should go to bed, darling,' her mother said.

'Don't speak to me like that, I'm not a small child.'

Meriel bent over and kissed Cat's head. 'No, you're pregnant. I'll talk to you tomorrow.'

The telephone rang as she picked up her bag. Chris gestured to Simon who sat nearest to it.

'Who's that?'

'Simon.'

'Yes. Is your mother there?' Richard Serrailler, curt as ever.

'She's just leaving for home. Do you want to speak to her?'

'Tell her Keats just rang from BG.'

'About Martha?' Simon felt the sudden silent tension in the room behind him.

'Yes. She's rallied. She's conscious. I'm going over there now.'

'I'll tell them.'

Simon set the receiver down and looked round. He wanted to laugh. Dance. Crow with triumph.

He saw his sister's face, tear-stained, swollen, hollow-eyed.

'Apparently Martha is rather better,' he said gently.

When he walked on to the ward again forty minutes later he was on his own. His mother had said she could not face the hospital again, Cat was exhausted.

'There's no need for you to go,' Meriel Serrailler had said. 'No need for any of us now. Your father's there.'

'I'd like to see her.'

He had assumed that his father would have left. A meeting with him at Martha's bedside was not what he wanted but when he walked into the room, Richard Serrailler was still there, sitting in the chair beside Martha's bed reading her chart.

'Your mother not coming?'

No greeting, Simon thought. I might as well be invisible.

'She's coming in tomorrow morning.'

He looked down at his sister. Her colour was better, with a faint flush of pink about her cheeks.

'What happened?'

His father handed him the chart.

'She has, as Devereux put it, the constitution of an ox. The new antibiotics kicked in, she began to surface . . . opened her eyes an hour ago. Stats are encouraging.'

'I suppose there could be a setback?'

'Could. Unlikely. Once she's over the crisis she generally hauls herself back.'

Simon wanted to touch his sister's hand, kiss her cheek, get her to open her eyes again but with his father there he could not. He simply stood, looking down.

'I'm glad,' he said.

'Why?'

'How can you ask? She's my sister. I love her. I don't want her to die.'

'Your mother thinks her quality of life is zero.'

'I don't agree.'

'We bow to your superior medical knowledge then.'

'It's an instinct.'

'The police work on instinct rather than facts?'

Simon Serrailler was a man who had never felt violent towards anyone in his life though he had never been squeamish about using an appropriate degree of force in the course of his job, but he felt an uprush of anger against his father now which made him clench his fists. At moments like this he had a clear insight into the hatred and rage that led some people to violence. The difference between him and them, he knew, was the thin but infinitely strong wire of self-control.

'When will she be well enough to go back to Ivy Lodge?' he asked calmly.

Richard Serrailler stood up. 'Couple of days. They'll need the bed.'

Simon was a foot away from him. His father was a lean, good-looking man who might have been sixty rather than seventy-one.

'What do you feel for her?' Simon asked him now, glancing towards Martha. He felt himself tense as if he might need to defend himself for having the nerve to put the question at all. But his father looked at him without anger.

'I am her father. I have loved her since the day she was born. I don't cease to love her because I have always regretted that day. What man could? You?'

'All of that,' Simon said, 'but maybe without the regret.'

'Easy for you.'

'*Easier.*'

'If you were ever to be a parent, which I presume you will not, you would know. Are you walking back to your car?'

They went together down the quiet corridors. What his father meant, what was behind his

60

extraordinary remark, how he judged him were questions Simon could not address now. He whited out all thought and merely walked, out of the hospital and into the car park. At his father's car he held open the door, waited until he was seated with his belt buckled, said goodnight, and closed the door.

Two minutes later he was on the road to Lafferton, the tail lights of his father's BMW already almost out of sight ahead.

He wanted to go back to the farmhouse; he needed to talk to Cat, but she would have gone to bed long ago, trying to rest as best she could in these last days of her pregnancy. He felt separated from her – from all of them, a feeling which would pass once her child was born, and which in any case was largely illusory and entirely on his side. It had happened before – when Cat had married Chris, and as she had borne Sam and Hannah.

He turned into the Cathedral Close. The wide avenue with the grass spaces on either side and the cathedral rising up above his head, the elegant buildings, pale in the lamplight which was a softer, more silver colour than those of the raw lights around the hospital and out along the main road, the long shadows cast by the trees . . . he had often thought that it looked artificial at night, a film set of a place, too empty, too tidy, too carefully arranged.

But it went with his mood. Tomorrow he would not hang about here. He knew when solitude became dangerous for him. He needed to get stuck into work. If it was a day or two before the official end of his leave, that was fine by him.

Nine

Andy Gunton stepped off the kerb and the car came out of nowhere, skimming his body. He lost his balance and fell into the gutter. A woman started screaming.

Traffic, Andy thought as he picked himself up, bloody cars and buses charging at you from everywhere.

The woman went on screaming and three people had come out of shops.

'I'm a first-aider, sit down.' She looked young enough to be one of Michelle's kids.

'I'm OK,' Andy said. 'Just lost me balance.'

'You could be in shock.'

'Yeah, well, I'm not.' He pointed to the woman who was staring at him and still screaming. 'You want to look at her. I reckon she is.'

He brushed at his jacket as he walked quickly off and round the corner. All the same, he was shaken. He remembered this as a quiet bit of Lafferton. How could traffic have bred like that?

There was a pub. He went in.

There were pubs enough in Lafferton and he had known a lot of them but maybe not this one. It didn't smell of beer and tobacco, it smelled of coffee. There was a mirror running along behind the bar and a barman who looked more like a waiter in a black jacket was slamming metal coffee holders into an espresso machine.

Andy Gunton ordered a pint of bitter.

'We only have bottled.' The barman rattled off a list of foreign names. Andy grabbed one as it passed.

He got a bottle. No glass. He looked round. He lifted the bottle to his mouth.

No one paid any attention to him at the bar. He went to an empty table. It was pleasant. The sun shone in on the back of his neck.

He realised that his hands were shaking, that he was breathing too fast and his ears rang as if he had just surfaced after a dive. This place panicked him, just as the traffic had. Lafferton which he had thought at first glance looked the same, was not; little things were tripping him up, it was like living in a looking-glass world, everything slightly wrong.

Jeez. What was four years? A bloody lifetime, half his youth, but then again nothing, a blink; he didn't know where he was or what he was doing, he might have landed from Mars.

The probation officer had had good legs in a very short skirt. Long slinky hair tied back. A lot of eye make-up. She talked in riddles, but he was used to that. They learned another language when they joined up, social workers, probation, briefs, whatever. Only the screws talked English.

'Your rehabilitation programme will really get under way once you start a job, Andy. Have you anything you are especially interested in doing?'

Fighter pilot. Brain surgeon. Formula One driver.

'Gardening,' he had said. 'I did eighteen months' horticulture.'

'There's a new garden centre operating at the Kingswood.'

'Garden centre?'

'I suppose most people do their own gardens, don't they? I wouldn't think there was much call for your skills in Lafferton.'

'It's market gardening. It's professional.' He had a flash picture of the raised beds of young broad beans and early peas, the beautifully arranged sandy rows of tiny carrots. He'd learned about what hotels and restaurants wanted now; earlies, picked young, not stuff that was stringy and leathery and huge in old age. Cabbages the size of a baby's fist not of a bride's bouquet.

She was sifting through the papers in the file on her desk. Was she older than him? Not much.

'You're living with your sister. How are you finding that, Andy?'

'How's she finding it more like.'

'Do you have good relations with her? The family?'

'OK.'

'Well, that seems quite positive.'

'It's only till I get somewhere. A place. They've got three kids.'

'You can put your name down for a council flat.'

'How long'd that be?'

'There aren't many for single people, I'm afraid.'

'So where are we supposed to live then? Where d'you live?'

'As I say, you're lucky to have your family, your sister is obviously very supportive, that's good. You won't feel excluded.'

'What from?'

'Your parents . . .' she began to sift the papers again.

'They're dead. Dad when I was twelve of lung cancer, Mum after I'd been six months at Stackton and don't say you're sorry because you're not, why would you be?' He felt an anger which was like foam in his mouth waiting to froth out all over this yellow-curtained office, all over Miss Long Legs.

He stood.

'Try to be positive, Andy.'

Garden centre, she'd said. He couldn't picture what it would be like and when she'd said Kingswood he couldn't place it. But it could be a start. For two years he'd been waiting for that – he didn't like the words 'new' and 'fresh' but he thought of them. He wasn't going back where he'd come from and he wasn't going down the old road that had taken him there. He'd never got much out of it in the first place, though he'd pretended to, and there'd been a few highs, a bit of speed, an escape though he wasn't sure now what from. Boredom he supposed. And he'd enjoyed being one of them. Spindo. Mart. Lee Carter. Lee Johnson. Flapper. They'd included him, and that had mattered. He'd liked the money as well. Everything had gone fine. They'd done small jobs, then bigger.

He hadn't been prepared for it all to go so wrong so quickly. The man had come after him like a mad thing, running down the street; the rest of them had been in the van, its engine running, they'd yelled at him. The man had nothing to do with anything, Andy should have left him, should have run and got into the van. He still saw it, the street, the van ahead, the man desperate and sweating, pounding along to catch him, still felt the panic. He panicked too easily. He should have kept a cool head; even if he'd been caught and the man had identified him, he would only have gone down for nine months or a year. So what had he done instead of making for the van? He'd turned on the man, waited until he was close and then gone for him in the stomach, head down like a bull and the man had crashed backwards on to the concrete, splitting his head open.

Now he got another bottle of the expensive foreign beer, went back to the table and forced himself not to think about it. His back ached. Sleeping on a blow-up bed in a corner of Matt's room wasn't comfortable and Matt didn't like him being there. Andy couldn't blame him. None of them wanted him, and he knew it, but until he had a job he couldn't get a place of his own, not even a single room in a lodging house; his allowance wouldn't run to that and so long as he did have family who would put him up he knew he wouldn't get anyone's attention in the social services. He wasn't on the streets, that was all they saw.

I ought to be happy, he thought suddenly, tipping a stream of beer down his throat. I am in a pub, I can stay or go, I can drink what I like, I can get out and walk or buy a paper. I haven't been able to do any of this or the rest for five years . . . I ought to be happy.

Three women came into the bar and dumped shopping bags at the table next to him. They were smart. One of them gave him a sideways look. Nothing else.

You've got no idea, Andy thought. Who I am. Where I've been. What I've done. How would you?

The last mouthful he took from the bottle was only foam.

He went out into the street.

On the other side parked on a double line was a silver BMW convertible. Sitting in it was a big man. As Andy came out of the pub the car slewed away from the kerb and across the road, swinging neatly in beside him as he walked.

'Get in,' Lee Carter said.

Andy kept on walking.

The car slid along, keeping pace with him. Funny, he thought, having the top down in March. There was sun but it wasn't warm.

'What's your problem?' The sound from the engine was so soft Lee hardly needed to raise his voice.

Andy had turned out of the shopping street, down a side road. He didn't know where he was walking.

'Save your legs. It's very nice. Leather seats.'

Just walk. Ignore him. Don't look at him. He's nothing to you now. Just walk.

It happened so fast he was lost. The car stopped and Lee Carter was out of it and round the front and pinning Andy against the wall.

'I said get in. I meant get in.'

'I'm getting in nothing.'

'I want to buy you a drink.'

'I just had a drink. Two drinks of poncey bottled beer. They even don't give you a glass in those places, did you know that?'

Lee Carter released him as quickly as he had taken hold. He was bellowing with laughter.

Andy stared, taking him in. He was fatter. Sort of sleek fatter. His hair was flashily cut. His shirt and jacket were nice. He looked well. Well off.

'I'll take you to my place, get you a proper drink.'

'Why did I have to crash into you?'

'You didn't. I been waiting for you. I knew you was at Michelle's.'

'Who told you? She wouldn't.'

'Course she wouldn't. I can do better than that. Now, are you getting in?'

'Not before I know why.'

'Something to ask you.'

'Right, well, I ain't interested.'

Lee walked back towards the car, but stopped before he opened the door, took out a packet of small cheroots and offered it.

'I don't.'

'Always were a goody-two-shoes, you.'

'If I had been I wouldn't have been where I have.'

Lee lit the cigar and watched the smoke drift away from him as he blew it out. 'Look, it ain't a problem, I just want to catch up.'

'Oh right, old times and that.'

'No. Old times are done. New times.'

'How do you mean?'

'I could put something in your way.'

'No thanks.'

'Legit. I'm done with all that stuff. Doesn't it look like it?'

Andy looked over the leather jacket, well-cut trousers. Cigar. Car. 'Not really,' he said.

'Come up to my new place. Meet the wife.'

'What sort of girl'd marry you?'

'Come and find out.'

Andy didn't want to get involved with any of them ever again, and Lee Carter in particular, but he was interested, he couldn't help himself, he wanted to see the place, the wife, even if he didn't want to hear the proposition.

'Oh, for Christ's sake,' Lee Carter said and slammed the driver's door.

A split second. You're not going, Andy told himself.

He got in.

The car was top of the range and had everything. The CD player blasted out, of all things, Dusty Springfield. Lee Carter drove fast and flashily out on to the Flixton Road. Andy didn't speak. He couldn't have made himself heard anyway. The wind hurt his ears. He was terrified, not having been in a vehicle faster than the prison delivery van for so long.

They sped out of Lafferton and after five miles turned into Lunn Mawby which Andy knew as half a dozen houses and a petrol station.

'Bloody hell.'

It was no longer a village but an estate of detached private houses, Tudor style, with wrought-iron gates and landscaped front lawns.

They swung round two corners and up a slope. Just three houses stood at the top. Tudor again. Twisty chimneys. Big trees at the back.

Lee drove the car at the gates and as he did so, pressed a button on the side of the steering wheel. He pressed another button and a fountain in the middle of the bright green grass spurted into life.

'Jeez.'

Lee grinned and swung the car to a stop.

'Good?' he said, and gestured to Andy to follow him as he walked cockily up to the front door.

Quarter of an hour later the guided tour was over. Everywhere they had gone, Lee had looked at him

71

for approval, admiration and envy. Andy had withheld them all, merely nodding as he took in the billiard room, the gym, the bar, the thick pile carpets, the plasma television, the wall-to-wall mirror-fronted wardrobes, the conservatory, the Olde Englishe oak-fitted kitchen.

They stood there now, Lee at the open door of a six-foot-high fridge.

'Beer?'

'No thanks.'

'Espresso. There's a machine. Lynda works it better than me.'

Lynda had not appeared.

'She'll have gone to the health spa.'

'What am I here for?'

'Tea then? Go on, let's have a brew.' Lee slammed the door of the giant fridge and picked up an electric kettle. 'Sit down.'

It seemed childish not to.

Lee turned and looked across at him with a grin.

'It's legit.'

'Right.'

'I told you. I'm not stupid. I was stupid but I ain't stupid now. But what are you going to do, And? What plans you got, now you're a free man?'

'Work.'

'At?'

His pride was up. He couldn't bring himself to say it.

'There you go then.'

The kettle began to hiss. Lee took down two mugs from a rail above his head.

'I'm looking for people. Always lookin'.'

'No chance.'

'Just listen, will you?'

'No. Where'd you get all this? House. Car. You don't tell me this is hard graft. No one gets this lot in a year or two for grafting. You was skint, you was living two rows from Michelle last I knew. You didn't even bloody go down for that job. Half the time I did, I did for you, Carter.'

'I didn't smash a man's head down into the concrete.'

'You –'

'Oh shut it, Andy. Here.' He shoved the mug of tea across the table. 'It's done with. You're out of there, aren't you?' Lee pulled out a chair with his foot and sat down.

Andy drank the hot sweet tea. Prison tea. In spite of himself he wanted to hear. Maybe it was true and something legit had bought all this. He looked out of the window behind Lee's head. The garden was mainly lawn and elaborate trellis, with a bird bath, a couple of urns, a white-painted iron pump. There was a single bed of roses which had been pruned down to their stumps. They stood out of the bark chippings at their base like rotten teeth out of a septic mouth.

He thought of the prison market garden. He didn't want to be back there but he wanted to be outside.

'Horses.' Lee said, following his eye. 'Horses bought this lot.'

Andy remembered now. Lee had always been at the bookies, or on the phone to one. He'd kept on at Andy to go to the races with him but he'd never been that interested.

'Bollocks,' he said now. If he knew anything about gambling, on horses or anything else, it was that in the long run you lost. 'Mug's game.' It had to be drugs. Had to be. He wanted the fresh air more than ever.

'Too right.'

Lee picked up the teapot and held it out. Andy shook his head.

'I woke up one morning and there it was in front of me. Big red letters. Mug's game. So that was the answer. There's always mugs.'

'You bought a betting shop then?'

Lee laughed.

'Listen. All the years I was at it, ten, twelve years – backing the gee-gees, winning some, losing some, but mainly losing, and I saw who was really making money. Yes, right, the bookies. But apart from them . . . tipsters, that's who. Not your sad little one-man, some no-hope ex-jock. Top stuff. Classy. Like an exclusive club. I paid out a fortune in my day to them tipping agencies. Promising to make you a fortune, inside information, all that crap. You got to have something different and you gotta do more than read the sports pages trying to pick nailed-on chances. The ones who can tip the real big winners, the winners nobody's picked, the 10–1 and 25–1 shots, those services can charge what they like . . . ten, fifteen grand a year, maybe more. That's nothing. I used to play in fifties, hundreds. My clients now, they deal in thousands every bet. First thing you got to do is let them believe it's hard to get in, that your service is exclusive and membership's limited. You turn people down flat. Don't give them a reason. Word soon gets round and they're crawling on their hands and knees to you. Clubs do it, it even goes on with fuckin' clothing, for Christ's sake – designer gear. Lynda has her name down for six months for some fuckin' handbag that costs two grand because there's only ever going to be fifty of them made. It's bollocks but it's a must have. So's membership of my service.'

'What's it called?'

'LER. For Limited Edition Racing.'

'So you find the outsiders that win.'

'Right.'

'How?'

'There's ways.'

'Doping.'

'No. Not these days. They test everything that moves.'

'Fixing.'

'I told you, there's ways.'

'How many members in this club?'

'Six hundred and a few.'

'Limited edition?'

Andy looked round the kitchen again. There were rows of orange-coloured iron casseroles and saucepans on top of the units. They didn't look as if anyone ever took them down to cook with.

'Is that all?'

'There's other stuff. I trade a bit.'

Andy looked at him.

'No. I never done drugs, never will.'

'So it's all clean.'

'Well, it ain't robbin' banks.'

'Yeah.'

'I'm always looking for people. You'll need a leg-up.'

Andy stood up. 'I gotta get back. There buses round here?'

'As if. Listen, you don't want to live with Michelle for ever, do you? Like your own place, wouldn't you?' Lee gestured round.

'What I get I'll work for.'

'It was work I was talking about.'

'I'll find my own.'

'What, mowing lawns? You can do that here, give you a tenner an hour. That's what gardening pays. Come on, Andy.'

'Who said anything about gardening?'

'I know what you've been doing inside. There's plenty I know. I've still got stuff on you.'

'OK, so there isn't a bus, I'll walk down to the main road, hitch a lift.'

Lee swept the car keys off the table into his hand.

'There's a lot of funny people about, Andy,' he said. 'Difficult for an ex-con to get work.'

Andy spun round. Lee raised a finger. He was grinning.

'And here was I thinking you'd changed,' he said.

Lee Carter had a baby face. Curly hair. Every mother's favourite son. Never trust a baby face. Stick Martin had told him that.

It'll never be any different, Andy thought, it'd be Carter or one of the others, or else his prison record like a weight round his neck and a brand on his forehead. You couldn't get away. Not ever. He thought of the sleek little probation officer trotting out her jargon. Whatever he did or didn't do for the rest of his life he'd never get away.

Ten

He'd made the football pitch himself out of the top of a cardboard box. He had painted it green and marked out the lines with black marker pen and the goalposts were cut out of wood from the shed. The nets had been a problem until he'd found two of the little white bags for putting washing tablets in and attached them carefully with thread. It was good. He was pleased with it. Now he was going to think about how he could construct the stands.

'David! It's twenty to.'

David Angus stood looking down at the box for as long as he dared, trying to visualise it, trying to work it out. He half closed his eyes.

'And it's Giggs, Giggs has it, Giggs has passed it across . . .'

The crowd was roaring.

'David!'

He sighed and picked up his school bag. He'd come back to it tonight.

'You've got ham and cucumber in your sandwiches, don't forget to eat those and the banana before you eat the cake.'

'Did you cut the fat off?'

'I cut the fat off. Do you need money for anything today?'

He thought. Tuesday?

'No, but I need to take the note back about the history outing.'

'On the table in front of you.'

His mother was pulling on her jacket. His sister Lucy had already gone, met by two friends to walk together down to the school bus at the corner of Dunferry Road. She now went to Abbey Grange. David was still at St Francis.

'I'm in court all day but I'll be out in time to pick you up. We need to get you some shoes.'

'Can we go for a milk shake at Tilly's after?'

'Afterwards. We'll see.'

Why did they always say we'll see first, even when they knew whether it was yes or no? We'll see, we'll see . . . they couldn't seem to help saying it.

'Come on, Doodlebug.'

David picked up his bag.

It wasn't raining, that was all he noticed. Not raining, not freezing cold. Otherwise morning was morning. His mother got into the car and held open the door. David went forward and bent in. He didn't mind kissing her here at home, especially when she was actually inside the car. He wouldn't have done it outside school.

'Have a good day, Doodlebug. See you tonight.'

'See you.'

He waited until she'd edged out of the drive into the road and driven off, then wandered to the gate. His father had gone an hour before. He was always in the hospital by half past seven. David put his bag on the ground and waited, watching for the car. It was the Forbeses' week. The Forbeses had a dark blue Citroën Zsara. It wasn't the best lift, that was when it was the di Roncos' week and the people carrier with blacked-out windows slowed up beside him. Di Ronco's father had been in one of the most famous bands of the eighties and had big rings on every finger and tattooed-in sideburns. Di Ronco's father made them laugh all the way to school and swore four-letter words.

Cars sped past him down the road. Work. School. Work. School. Work. School. Silver Mondeo. White Audi. Black Ford Focus. Silver Ford Focus. Silver Rover 75. Red Polo. Sick-green Hyundai. Blue Espace. Maroon Ford Ka.

There were more silver cars than any other colour, he'd proved it.

Black Toyota Celica. Silver BMW.

The Forbeses weren't usually late. Not like the di Roncos. They always were, once by half an hour and di Ronco's dad had just breezed into the school whistling and shouting, 'Don't start without us!'

He tried to picture Mr Forbes doing that and nearly fell over laughing.

He was still laughing a bit when the car drew up beside him, laughing too much to take in that the colour was wrong and that someone had opened the door and was pushing him roughly inside as the wheels spun hard away from the kerb.

Eleven

At the last minute, Simon Serrailler turned the car away from Lafferton and took the route along the bypass for a mile and then off into the country. Before returning to the station, he would go and see Martha who was in her care home again. Once he was back into the action he might not get another chance for days, and he knew that even if Martha did not take in his presence her carers in the home certainly did and welcomed it. Too many of the other patients had been virtually abandoned by their families, never visited or even sent cards at Christmas and birthdays. He had heard the staff talk about that often enough. He knew which ones had been left. Old Dennis Troughton whose life had begun with cerebral palsy and was ending with Parkinson's disease. Miss Falconer, huge and inert and vacant-eyed, with the brain of a baby and the body of a mountainous middle-aged woman. Stephen, who jerked and twitched all the time and had two or three life-threatening fits a week, who was seventeen and whose parents had not seen him since he was a baby. Simon had occasionally vented his anger about them to Cat, but with her medical detachment she had always agreed with him while putting forward the other point of view.

The morning traffic had eased by the time he was on the bypass and once he left it and drove towards Harnfield he saw few other cars. The fields were empty, trees still bare. He went through two villages which were deserted, dormitories now for Lafferton and Bevham. Neither had a shop or a school, only one had a pub. Few people actually worked on the land or in the villages themselves any more. Harnfield was much larger, with both a primary and a comprehensive school and some clumps of new housing. It also had a business park. People were about. Harnfield was not specially attractive but it had a community and a sense of life.

Simon turned left down the narrow lane leading to Ivy Lodge.

'I didn't know if we'd get her back.' Shirley, Martha's carer for the day, went ahead of him along the brightly painted corridor. 'She was so poorly.'

'I know. They fetched me back from Italy.'

'But she rallies every time, I suppose we ought to be used to it. She's so strong.' Shirley paused at the open door of Martha's room. 'Whatever anyone says, she must get enough out of life to want to keep going, you know.'

Simon smiled. He liked Shirley, with her slight squint and the gap between her front teeth. One or two of the other carers gave the impression that the end of the shift couldn't come soon enough and that they did the minimum merely to keep his sister clean, comfortable and fed. Shirley talked to her and spoke of her as an individual whom she knew and liked even though she could find her wearing. He knew it was rare and he was grateful.

Martha's room was bright, with buttercup-yellow walls and white-painted furniture, a room for a child; it always cheered Simon as he went in.

His sister was propped up in bed. Her hair had been freshly brushed and tied back and there was colour in her cheeks and a brightness in her eyes. She sat looking towards the light coming in through the windows and watching the breeze shift the yellow and green curtains about.

'Hello, darling. You look so much better!' He walked in and took her hand. It was soft, the skin like satin; even the bones seemed soft as the hand lay inert between his own. 'I came over when they said you were back from the hospital and I bet you're glad. All those tubes and machines meant I couldn't see you properly.'

Shirley tucked in the bedclothes at the end of Martha's bed, and closed the door of the wardrobe. 'I'll see you later, sweetheart,' she said to Martha, waved and went out.

The room was peaceful. Martha was peaceful. She would lie here like this until someone came to turn her, to clean her, change her, give her physiotherapy, move her into a chair, feed her, hold her drinking cup; she was as dependent as a baby, unable to do the smallest thing, for herself or for anyone else.

She smelled of soap and clean sheets. There was never any other smell on her, never anything sour or dirty in the air of her room. Her care couldn't be faulted.

But he had often wondered how much difference it might have made to her if she had been sitting like this at home, in the middle of the family comings and goings, the stimulus of different people talking and working and being busy around her, children coming in, Cat's children, their friends, animals on her lap. She had never known a normal life. He wished he could have given it to her.

Martha gave a little murmur, half a moan, half a sigh, half a laugh . . . it was impossible to tell. Her hand moved.

'What is it? Have you seen something?'

The little noise again. He looked at her face. It registered nothing at all yet he knew she was trying to communicate with him.

He gave her a drink from the spouted plastic cup on the table and she sipped it, but whether it had been what she had wanted he couldn't know.

'Little Martha,' he said, 'I'm so glad you're better.'

He stayed for twenty more minutes, holding her hand, telling her about the squirrel he had seen in the fir tree behind the car park, knowing that it meant nothing to her and yet sure that she liked to hear his voice.

When he left, her eyes were closing. She was like a baby, soothed into sleep by the softly blowing, bright curtains.

In the hall, he met Shirley. 'She seems fine,' he said. 'She's asleep now.'

'She'd better make the most of it then, we're going to do her bed and then she has to have her chest pummelled otherwise it'll be pneumonia again. Thanks for coming. I should think Dr Serrailler will be in later.'

The squirrel raced up the long trunk of the Scots pine tree as he approached his car but stopped halfway and peered down at him with feverish little eyes.

DCI Serrailler turned out of the drive and headed for Lafferton Police Station and work. If absence made the heart grow fonder, death did the same. He had no need to take the route through the Old Town side streets to get to the station, though it cut off a couple of sets of slow traffic lights, but as he approached he knew that he had wanted to drive down the road in which Freya Graffham had lived.

He had not been in love with her – or at least not while she was alive – though he had found her attractive, she had intrigued him and he had enjoyed her company. Her feelings for him had been fairly clear on the evening they had gone out to an impromptu dinner at his favourite Italian restaurant, not from anything she had said – she had been far too cautious for that – but from the way she had looked at him.

But things had not gone on. Freya Graffham had been murdered. Killed in her own house. The house Simon was approaching now. It was a small Victorian artisan's cottage in a row of others set among a grid of twelve similar streets known as the Apostles because they were near the cathedral. He had not been inside until after Freya's murder. He had no memories of it which were not dreadful ones. The front door had been painted. It had been maroon. Now it was smart navy blue. There were new roman blinds half down at the windows. The gate had gone. Simon stopped on the opposite side of the road. No one was about. He did not understand why he was here. But as he drove away a leaden feeling settled in his stomach and the day ahead was soured.

'Good morning, Sergeant.'

DS Nathan Coates looked over his shoulder and steadied the hand he was using to hold two paper cups of coffee piled on top of each other as the DCI went past him and on up the stairs.

'Guv? I thought you weren't back till tomorrow.'

'Change of plan.'

The door swung to behind Serrailler.

Nathan shifted the cups slightly. He was smiling. Nine times out of ten he smiled when the DCI or anyone else called him Sergeant. It was over six months since he had stopped being Acting and become an official DS but he was still not used to it, still had to check that someone wasn't winding him up. He had wanted the job and not wanted it because it had meant stepping into Freya Graffham's shoes.

And the DCI had known all the right buttons to press.

'You came from the other side of the tracks, Nathan. You might just as easily have gone the way of half your schoolmates and how many years would you have served by now, courtesy of Her Majesty's Prisons? You took the other route, and don't tell me it was easy. Do they still respect you round your way? I doubt it. They don't go for coppers much on the Dulcie estate, especially when the copper is one of their own. You now stand for everything you ought to be against, and you are exactly the sort of policeman we want. The police force ought to mirror the society it polices and it almost never does, which is why it's so important you stay in it and keep climbing the ladder. You're young, you're bright, you work your socks off and DS Graffham had a very high opinion of you. What do you think she'd say if you chicken out now?'

'That's below the belt, guv.'

'Sometimes you have to punch there. Come on, Nathan, see straight. It hit you. It hit all of us. It was a bloody awful thing to happen. I never thought we'd see a serial killer in a place like Lafferton . . . drugs, muggings, rapes, burglaries, robberies, whatever, it's all on the increase, even in a nice small respectable English cathedral town. But multiple murder? We might be able to get our heads round a shooting in the course of an operation . . . a raid . . . a panic . . . a dead policeman. We could have coped with that, but not Freya's murder. And you were the first there, you dealt with it all and you blame yourself, don't think I'm not aware of it. You've no need to but you do and you probably always will. It's none of it a reason for you giving up your career. It's a good reason for you to stay. Are you hearing me?'

Nathan was, though it had taken him another couple of weeks to admit it. He and Emma had been married quietly in the side chapel of the cathedral, with the DCI as his best man, before he had finally committed himself to remaining in the force. It had been much longer before he had agreed to go for promotion to sergeant. But he was a sergeant now and the excitement of it, the pride, the sense of achievement, woke with him every morning. Serrailler had been spot on. No one from his background had ever made it to Lafferton CID before, let alone to sergeant. He didn't intend his climb up the career ladder only to stop here.

He pushed the swing door open with his shoulder and went on towards the CID room but, as he passed, the DCI called out. The door to his room was open.

'That for me?' Serrailler held out his hand.

'Course it is.'

'Thank you.'

He took the paper cup of cappuccino which Nathan had fetched not from the vending machine at the end of the corridor but from the new corner café in the next street, run by a Cypriot couple and kept going mostly by policemen.

'DC Dell will just have to go out for his own.'

The DCI sat back in his chair. It's daft, Nathan thought, he looks younger than me, looks about the right age to be starting on the fast-track graduate scheme, not well up the ladder already. Serrailler's hair, white blond and disarranged as ever, shone in the light coming from the window behind him. 'Dishy DCI' Emma called him. Freya Graffham had thought so and they would have been just right. And then maybe . . .

Maybe nothing.

'Bring me up to speed.'

'Been a bit too quiet.'

'Don't say that.'

'Only one thing giving us grief has been this gang . . . kids, only they don't act like kids. I went up to the Eric Anderson last week, saw the head, saw a couple of teachers. They know who it is, pretty much. They're all no-hopers, they bunk off most of the time and nobody at home gives a toss. It started with small stuff only now it ain't so small. Now it's pretty well-organised shoplifting, hanging about in the evenings targeting people walking home from work and grabbing handbags, mobiles that sort of stuff . . . then there's the cars. They've started nicking top-of-the-range motors but it ain't for joyriding, they're cleverer than that, these motors are vanishing into thin. I reckon they're in with some much bigger villains.'

'How old are these kids?'

'Fourteen, fifteen . . . last couple of years at school. GCSE supposedly. Ha.'

'Names?'

'I've got some but they're fly – slippery as eels. Learned a lot of stuff from brothers and dads who've done time.'

'OK, let's target the brothers and dads. Check up on everyone who has been inside, in the last three years . . . better include those who are still there as well. There's plenty the kids can learn when they visit. We'll have a list of prisoners and then follow up children in this age group. I'll have a word with uniform about stepping up presence . . . known times. All that'll do is move them somewhere else, of course.'

'We reckon the cars are being moved at night – two, three in the morning.'

'OK, the names the head teacher gave you . . . get to some homes, talk to the mothers, see if they're aware of their kids getting up and going out at two in the morning . . . or perhaps not even coming in from the night before.'

'Guv.'

'Any other excitements?'

'The cathedral was broken into one night. Some damage done, nothing taken . . . some weird graffiti on a couple of the pillars. Seems like some religious thing.'

'Who handled it?'

'I went to talk to the Dean . . . he was very nice. Bit too nice . . .'

'Ah, forgiveness, you mean?'

Nathan aimed his paper cup at the waste-paper bin, threw and missed.

'If there's nothing else, I'll get on to this gang of kids. They want slapping down sharpish. It gets on my wick. They have everything handed to them and what do they do?'

'Everything but decent parenting.'

'Right. Thanks, guv. You have a good holiday by the way?'

'Very peaceful. I had to cut it short . . . one of my family was in hospital.'

'I'm sorry . . . everything OK?'

'Yes. It was my sister but she's fine.'

Nathan Coates went out, closing the door, and Simon sat thinking of the buttercup-yellow and white room with the curtains blowing in the breeze and Martha sitting up and making her strange little noises. He might have resented having his holiday cut short but no such feeling entered his mind.

He looked down at the files and paperwork on his desk. Petty crime. Gangs of teenagers. Small-time drug dealing. Robbery. Car theft. Some fraud and embezzlement. That was what routine CID work was about. The year in which Lafferton had had a psychopathic serial killer in its midst had been a rare one – it would be rare for any force in the country. He went on staring at the files without touching any of them. He loved his work but what was in front of him, the routine stuff which absorbed most of his time, was not stretching him. He knew that he could not stay in the relative backwater of his home city for ever unless he wanted to grow moss, but his life in Lafferton, outside work, was everything he wanted. He did not exist only for the CID. Half of him was an artist, the rest of him was brother, uncle, son – in that order.

If he went for promotion to a city force, what would he lose? And was there not just as much small crime and routine work in any big CID department? More, probably. The idea that promotion to Super in some huge city would mean non-stop excitement, difficult murder cases, story-book detective work, was nonsense and he knew it.

In Lafferton he got out a fair bit. In fact, if he spent the next two hours cracking through the files in front of him he might go with Nathan to the Sir Eric Anderson Comprehensive and then round the housing estates where the problem kids came from. Apart from anything else, he would learn a lot. These were Nathan's own places, the disadvantaged background from which he had struggled so hard to escape. If anyone knew what made the teenage gangs tick it was Sergeant Nathan Coates.

He opened the top folder and began to read.

David

What are you doing? Where's Mr Forbes? . . .
It was Mr Forbes. I don't know you. I don't
want to be in this car.

Please may you stop and let me out now,
please.

No one said it would be someone else. Are
we going to my school?

This isn't the way to my school. I go to St
Francis.

Where are we going?

I don't know you. I don't want to be in this
car.

Please may we stop now? I don't want to go
with you.

Why don't you talk? Why don't you say
anything?

Someone will have seen you in my road,
there's always someone looking out of a
window or walking there, they will know this
isn't the car I go in. They'll soon tell my
father.

You shouldn't drive like this, it's too fast. I

don't like going so fast. Please may you stop this car now? I'll walk back, it'd be OK.

Why did you pull me into your car?

When we stop at a traffic light I'll just get out.

This isn't anywhere near my school. I don't know where we are. Where are you taking me? Please may we stop? Please don't take me any further.

What do you want me to go with you for?

Why don't you say anything to me?

Why are we going this way? I'm not allowed to go here.

Please may we stop. I won't tell anyone, I can say I forgot it was Mr Forbes, or I ran away . . . yes, that's it, if you like, if I say I ran away. Then it will be me who gets into trouble. You wouldn't get into trouble. I won't say anything about you. I can't anyway, can I, I don't know your name and I wouldn't say about the car. They wouldn't know then. Why won't you do that?

Please.

Please do that. I don't want to go with you.

Please. I don't like going with you in this car.

Please.

Please.

Twelve

What was it exactly? 'Never has spring seemed so springlike, never has blossomed bloomed like this.' And who had said it?

Karin McCafferty stood in the car park of Bevham General Hospital and looked at the grey sky – a miraculous, soft, gull's wing grey – and felt the east wind cool and sweet on her face. There was a small bare tree beside her car, and a short run of stumpy hawthorn hedge. She stared in amazement at the texture of the tree's bark and at the colours of it. So many shadings of brown and charcoal, silver and mossy green. The hawthorn was like an intricate pencil scribble.

Ten minutes ago she had been sitting and waiting, dry-mouthed, in front of her pleasant, red-headed Irish oncologist, who read from the notes and reports in front of her, looked up, placed the sheets neatly together and closed the folder. And then she had smiled. 'You're fine, Karin,' she had said. 'Clean as a whistle. No new cancer cells and nothing left of the old ones.'

She could never get used to it, never take those words for granted nor fail to feel as if the whole world was ablaze with glory as she came out of the hospital buildings into the daylight and fresh air. But one thing she would also never do was gloat to her doctor, because she had disagreed with her and rejected her orthodox treatment in favour of natural therapies. They had had a short sharp fight, Karin had stood her ground, the oncologist had done some very straight talking and then agreed to continue seeing her and monitoring her progress. In return, Karin had agreed that if the cancer returned, she would look again seriously at the medical options. But so far it had not returned.

Following her own regime of alternative treatment had not been an easy option. It was time-consuming, expensive and lonely and Karin had been dealt a terrifying blow when the acupuncturist who had treated her had been revealed as a psychopathic serial murderer. But now, as she stared at a sparrow hopping about in the dust, delighting in the sheen on its wings and the brightness in its eyes, the horrors of the previous year were in another life. She was well. She had no need to return to the hospital for another half-year. She was well!

'Dennis Potter,' she said aloud. She had loved *The Singing Detective.* Dennis Potter had not been lucky. Cancer had killed him, but not before he had spoken of the beauty of what he had known was his final spring. 'Never was blossom blossomier.'

Karin dialled Cat Deerbon's number on her mobile but it was on answer. She left a quick and jubilant message, and set off for home, the CD of Eva Cassidy touching her to tears as she drove – Eva Cassidy who had fallen into the darkness of death from the cancer Karin had vanquished.

'*Somewhere, over the rainbow. . .*'

Karin slowed down at a junction to let a lorry driver turn out in front of her.

Mike's car was in the drive. But Mike was supposed to be in Ireland on business and not due home for another couple of days.

Karin sailed into the house humming. 'Mike? Where are you?'

His voice came from upstairs. 'Here.'

She ran up. She loved her house. She loved the white-painted curving banister and the turquoise-blue bowl on the ledge of the landing window. She loved the slice of light that fell through the open door of the bedroom on to the kelim runner. She loved the faint smell of citrus coming from the half-open bathroom door.

'Hi. I've got good news . . . the best.' She went on in and her humming turned into a song as she walked up to Mike to hug him. He was standing beside the wardrobe and two suitcases were open, one on the bed, the second on the floor.

'Hey . . . what's this? You look as if you're packing. Not turfing out the dirty washing.'

'Yes.'

'You're not going away again? Not straight off?'

'Yes.'

He had his back to her and was running his hand through a tie hanger, detaching one, riffling through, taking another.

'Where to this time?'

He did not reply.

'Mike? And didn't you hear me say – it was good news . . .'

There was a silence. He still did not turn round. Something in the stillness of the room and the nature of the silence made Karin's stomach clench.

'What's wrong?'

In the end, he looked round slowly, though not at her immediately, but at the suitcase, into which he laid a shirt. Then he straightened up. A big man. Greying thatch of hair. A big nose. Handsome, she thought, still handsome.

'I thought you might not be coming back till later. I thought you'd probably go over to Cat's.'

'And? I mean yes, I might have but her phone was on answer – she was probably resting. Her baby's due in a minute.'

'I'd forgotten.'

'Why did it matter what time I got home?'

He was jingling some coins in his pocket, still not looking at her.

Then he said, 'Will you make some tea?'

'OK.'

'I have to talk to you.'

Then the silence again. The awful, deafening silence.

She ran out of the bedroom.

It was after seven when she rang Cat again, after Mike had gone. Karin felt as beaten and bruised and shocked as if she had been told her cancer had returned and was advanced and inoperable, as hurt as she had ever been in her life. Not a great deal had been said considering it had taken three hours and Mike had walked out on their marriage to cross the Atlantic to a woman ten years older than she was herself. They had sat looking at one another and then not looking, drunk tea and then whisky; she had said a little, cried, stopped crying and fallen silent. Then he had gone. How could that have taken so long?

'Cat Deerbon.'

'Cat . . .'

'Karin . . . what news?'

Karin opened her mouth to speak, to tell Cat that she had neither cancer nor a husband, but no words would come from her mouth, only a strange wailing, angry noise which, as she heard it, Karin thought was being made by someone else, some woman who had nothing to do with her at all, a woman she did not know.

'Just come here,' Cat said, 'whatever it is.'

'I can't . . .'

'Yes you can, you get in the car and you drive. See you in half an hour.'

She did not know how, but she arrived at the farmhouse safely. Cat looked at her hard for a moment then went to the fridge and took out a bottle of wine.

'I'm off it but you certainly need it.'

'No, it'll make me cry.'

'Fine. Cry.' She handed over a large glass. 'The children are upstairs, Chris isn't back yet but there's a chicken pie and you're welcome to stay. You never know, I might go into labour in the night and leave you in charge, and heaven help you. Let's go into the sitting room, I lit a fire.'

Cat looked tired and uncomfortable but in every other way unchanged – capable, cheerful, firm, the perfect friend, it always seemed to Karin, as well as the perfect GP.

'So . . . you saw the doc. Was it that?'

'No. I'm clear. No sign.'

'So . . .'

'So Mike's left.'

'Left as in – left you?'

'Yes.'

'You've never said a word, I didn't know there were any problems between you two.'

'Jesus, Cat, do you think I did? I was on such a high . . . you've no idea what it feels like . . . when the scan's clear, when the blood tests are OK, when they tell you so . . . it's like . . . literally like having a reprieve in the condemned cell. The world is so good . . . then there he was packing his stuff.'

'Did you tell him?'

'The results? Oh sure.'

'And?'

'I don't know if he took it in. He said –"Good".'

'But why is he going, for God's sake?'

'A lot of reasons, a lot of things I didn't take in. The chief why lives in New York and her name is Lainey. She's fifty-four.'

'I don't believe this.'

'No.'

'What a bloody thing to come home to.'

'Yes.'

Karin moved her wine glass slowly round and round between her hands and now and then it caught the firelight and the wine glowed.

She felt warm. Warm. Comforted. Cared for. Numb.

'There is one thing you need to think about . . . you've had two major shocks . . . the murders and now this. These things can take their toll.'

'Bring the cancer back, you mean.'

'Just be aware. Step up all your therapies and be vigilant. Sorry to preach the medical line, it isn't the moment but it is important.'

'I'm not sure I care now.'

'Oh yes you do. You care all right. You don't let the buggers get you down. He'll be back.'

'Or it will.'

'No.'

'The worst thing he said was about that, actually. He said he couldn't face living with a cancer victim

102

any longer . . . that he could accept an illness that took you over and then you got better but one that changed you for good was different. He said I'd thought about nothing but cancer for the last year, paid no attention to anything else . . . that I'd . . . I'd let it define me and now I needed it and he couldn't take that.'

'Jesus.'

'I hadn't seen it, Cat. It's my –'

'Don't you dare to say this is your fault.'

'Well, isn't it?'

'And the woman in New York? I suppose that's your fault too?'

'She makes him feel alive. New York makes him feel alive. Apparently. I just had no idea there was anything wrong between us. I mean . . . there wasn't anything wrong. It never crossed my mind.'

'None of the usual? Phone calls . . . spending more money . . . being away a lot?'

'Mike's always been away a lot, he runs three international businesses, doesn't he? He spends half his time on the phone to them when he isn't travelling.'

A light flashed briefly across the drawn curtains as Chris Deerbon's car came into the drive. 'What am I going to do, Cat? What do people do?'

'They fight,' Cat said. 'Your life was worth fighting for, wasn't it?'

'I've always hated those images . . . cancer and war, cancer and battles, fighting and struggling.'

'Well, there's the alternative.'

'What?'

'Giving in. Surrendering . . . put it how you like.'

'Oh God.'

Cat got up heavily from the chair. 'You're in the blue room. I've put things out for you . . . go and have a deep bath, light a scented candle. Supper isn't for half an hour. I need to talk boring admin to Chris about the locum.'

She put out her arms and hugged her, and for a moment Karin felt the weight of the unborn baby against her. The old longing for children, usually at the back of her mind now, stung sharply again.

The expression on Chris's face as Cat went into the kitchen stopped her short.

'What's wrong?'

'You know Alan Angus?'

'Neurology. Sure . . . what?'

'His son's at St Francis . . . Year older than Sam.'

'Small for his age? A bit . . . well, an old-fashioned kind of child?'

'He's missing.'

'What do you mean?'

'They have a school lift with two other families . . . Marilyn Angus left David at their gate this morning, waiting for the lift as usual . . . it was due in a couple of minutes. It turns out that when the people arrived David wasn't at the gate . . . one of the other children went and rang the bell, but there was no answer so they just left. Thought he must have gone in with his parents after all and they'd forgotten to ring and change the arrangements. But David didn't go to school. They marked him absent and of course thought no more of it until four o'clock when his mother arrived to pick him up and he didn't come out. No one has seen or heard anything of him since ten past eight this morning.'

'Oh dear God.'

Cat's legs gave way and she sat quickly down on the sofa. Her eyes had filled with tears. 'How did you hear?'

'Local radio just now.' He sat down. 'It's not Sam,' he said quietly. 'It is terrible and all too imaginable but it is not Sam. By the way, I thought I saw Karin's car outside.'

'You did. She's in the bath. Mike's left her.'

Chris groaned.

'He can't stand living with a cancer victim so he's found consolation with someone called Lainey in New York. I suspect there's more but she hasn't said yet. Oh and her scans are clear – she had her three-monthly check today.'

They sat in silence, Chris resting his hand on Cat's stomach. Upstairs the bath water began to drain out. Cat's baby shifted its limbs, pinching a nerve in her side as it did so but she did not move. She was suddenly felled by the tumble of events one on top of the other, drained after too many uncomfortably sleepless nights. She was tired, leaning against Chris in the warm kitchen, the ginger cat purring on her other side. Then she opened her eyes.

'Chris? Go up and check on Sam . . . and Hannah.'

Chris Deerbon got up and left the kitchen without a word.

Thirteen

'Remind you of anything?' Nathan Coates stood at the window of the DCI's room, looking down at the departing press – television vans and radio cars racing off to catch the next news bulletin.

Serrailler had wanted the press on side from the start and had done the briefing and taken the usual questions. Now, he was looking at the map of Lafferton and district pinned to the wall on the far side of his office and did not reply.

'Missing persons. That's how the other started. I hate it. Rather get me teeth stuck into the Dulcie estate lot.'

Serrailler turned round. 'You're not here to do what you fancy, you're here to do the job.'

'Guv.'

'The Dulcie kids aren't going anywhere. We are.' He picked up his jacket.

Nathan followed, almost at a run to keep up going along the corridor, and two at a time down the stairs.

*

'Where first, guv?'

'Sorrel Drive. Talk to the parents. Forensics will have started on the house and you know what message that gives out.'

'Yeah, you report your nine-year-old kid missing, next minute your rooms are full of men in white suits scraping bits off the carpet.'

'Still, we know the father was doing his ward round at the hospital from before eight. Mother was the last to see the child when she left him at the gate and was at her office by eight thirty. They've nothing to worry about.'

They got into the car.

'This isn't like that missing persons case . . . OK, those women vanished apparently into thin air, and now a schoolboy does the same, but you can rule out a hell of a lot of possibilities here from the start.'

'Grown women might go off of their own accord. Nine-year-old boys don't.'

'Well, it has happened, especially where there's been bullying.'

'My gran blames the internal combustion engine.'

'Your gran has a point. Fast cars, fast roads, easy access to and away . . . People living in Leeds and doing a series of house raids in Devon, paedophiles driving commercial vans snatching a child in Kent and driving it to Dumfries . . . where do you start?'

'Are we talking to other forces?'

'We are . . . with missing children it's one of the first priorities.'

'Thought you might have wanted to bring Sally.'

Sally Cairns was one of the most experienced DCs at Lafferton, married to a traffic sergeant with the motorway force, mother of four teenagers and very happy to remain at constable rank. She was the best they had when it came to dealing with families and children.

'Sally is terrific and very sensitive . . . but she is also a mother. This case is going to be difficult and distressing. Sally can handle that, of course, but I think we need to be as detached as we can be and neither you nor I have children – OK, I have a nephew and you have younger brothers, and God forbid either of us is hard or unsympathetic, but not being parents does give us a certain distance. We're going to need it.'

If Nathan had thought before asking his next question, he might have stayed silent, but caution was not one of his strong points.

'Do you think you'll ever have kids?'

Telling Emma about it later, he said that for a split second he heard the swish of the blade.

But Serrailler only said, 'How should I know?' as they turned into the avenue and headed for the Anguses' house, cordoned off with bright, fluttering police tape. The men in white suits were everywhere.

What does it feel like, Nathan thought, going into the wide hallway of the house, with its staircase curving up ahead of them and the sort of landscape pictures he judged wishy-washy on the pale green walls. What can it be like to go out one morning and everything's hunky-dory, and at the end of the day, wham, your kid's gone, just . . . gone? Jesus.

He had only to look at the face of Marilyn Angus to see what it was like. All the pain in the world was there. She looked desperate, not so much pale as a terrible waxen colour, with brown smudges and swelling under her eyes, and a look in them Nathan was never to forget.

The uniform PC who had been sitting with her left at Serrailler's signal and the DCI went across at once. He did not offer to shake hands but put his hand for a moment on her shoulder before he sat down.

'Saying that I'm sorry is useless but I hope you know what we feel for you, and in the meantime saying that I will move heaven and earth to get your son back as quickly as possible is not useless. I mean it.'

Nathan looked at his DCI. This was what singled him out, an iron-hard determination, that honesty, the way he knew what to say when, the way he spoke the truth. That was why he himself would follow Serrailler anywhere and hoped he could be half the policeman he was.

'I'm sure I should get you something . . .'

Serrailler stopped her with a movement of his hand. 'Mrs Angus, you know how all this works, I don't need to explain. You know there are a lot of questions I have to ask which you have already been asked, and that it's going to be painful and that you're confused. But anything you tell us may be useful. I've had a briefing from the uniformed officers who first spoke to you but I need to hear some things for myself. Don't worry if you remember things you forgot or if you contradict something you said earlier, people do when they're under stress.'

'Thank you . . . this morning is like a film reel running across my mind, over and over again. What he said, what I said, what he looked like . . . whatever went on last night. His face. I just see David's face.'

'Yes. And I mean to be sure you'll see it again, just as before, and that no harm will have come to him.'

'It must have. How could harm not have come to him by now?'

Marilyn Angus got up and stood at the mantelpiece, fiddling with a tiny gold clock, turning it round and round.

'I want to ask you about David at school.'

'He loves St Francis.'

'Good. Does he have any particular friends there?'

'The boys we share the run with . . . they seem to be a little gang . . . I don't mean that as in "bad gang", just . . . they're always together. Caspar di Ronco . . . Jonathan Forbes . . . Arthur Maclean . . . Ned Clark-Hall . . .'

'Do they fall out?'

'They're always falling out . . . boys do . . . there's a bit of pushing and shoving and it's all settled. They don't bear grudges, they can't be bothered.'

'Any he doesn't get on with?'

'If you mean is there any bullying, I've thought about that but the answer's no. The school comes down hard at the first sign of it . . . they had a real problem a few years ago and they don't mean to let it happen again. I'm sure there's just nothing at all of that kind. David's a popular little boy, he's very cheerful. Is. Was . . .'

'Is,' Serrailler said firmly, looking straight at her.

'Oh God, I hope you're right.'

'Is he bright?'

'Yes, he is. That isn't a proud mother talking. I don't think my geese have to be swans. Our daughter Lucy isn't too hot academically. But David isn't bright in the obvious way . . . he thinks a lot, he's creative, makes things, works things out for himself, goes into subjects . . . the latest is Pompeii. He reads everything he can get his hands on about it . . . he likes to spend time by himself. And then of course there's football.'

'Does he support any team in particular?' Nathan spoke for the first time. She looked at him as if she had forgotten that he was there.

'Manchester United. They all pretend to be fans of one big team or other . . . Chelsea, Spurs.'

'Pretend?'

'They're just little boys . . . it's a bit of a pose, isn't it? What do they know?'

The interview went on, Serrailler leading the mother quietly through her son's behaviour at home, probing tactfully but with needle-sharp exactness into family relationships, alert to hints of any possible tensions or unhappiness. She answered without hesitation, moving about the room, touching furniture, picking things up and replacing them, running her hand occasionally through her short curly hair. They were with her for almost an hour before the DCI stood up.

'You'll have someone with you, the family liaison officer, as I'm sure you've been told and you'll be kept in touch all the time.'

'My husband had to go to the hospital . . . A patient he'd operated on developed some complications . . . no one else could deal with it.'

'Fine.'

'You mustn't think . . . read anything into that . . .'

'I wasn't going to.'

As they left, Chris Deerbon arrived.

'I'm their GP. I wanted to check them out.'

'She's OK . . . looks shattered but she seems to be holding it together. He's had to go to the hospital.'

Chris shrugged. 'He'll be needed . . . he's the best neurosurgeon in the county. Any thoughts, Si?'

'No, too early. Is Cat OK?'

'It's upset her . . . she breaks up pretty easily just now. Call her.'

'Where to?' Nathan said as Simon got into the car.

'Don't know. Let's get away from here first . . . Go out towards Starly.'

'Something up there?'

'Shouldn't think so.'

Nathan knew better than to ask any more questions but drove on out of Lafferton and into the country lanes. It was a dull day, the sky an unrelieved and dreary grey, the trees bent in the cold wind. Serrailler sat in silence until he suddenly said, 'Go right here and then take the lane to Blissington.'

Nathan did so. The roads were empty, the lane narrow with overhanging banks but at the end they came to a village, not much more than a huddle of cottages and a couple of large houses set back behind gates.

They pulled up in front of a pub set behind a raised triangle of grass with a huge oak tree. 'I never even knew there was a village here,' Nathan said.

The bar was quiet and smelled good. They ordered home-baked ham rolls and coffees.

'What do we know?' Simon Serrailler said when they were settled at a window table.

'Right – the boy and his mother came out of the house at around eight ten.'

Step by step they went through the few facts they knew, then talked their way back, to what Marilyn Angus had told them.

'Nothing,' Simon said at last. 'Normal small boy, normal family, no tensions, no problems. Nothing.'

'So?'

'Worst-case scenario? Random driver out looking for a child? When we get back, I want to know all the usual – double-check on any missing children

114

nationwide, paedophiles recently released from prison, all that. Uniform will get all the stuff on locals who always drive that way to work, neighbours, anything odd in the vicinity . . . If you were a paedophile looking for a child, what would you do?'

'What this one did . . . Pick a time of day, going to school time or coming home, lots of kids around.'

'Yes, but most of them are in gangs going to the bus or getting in and out of cars where there are plenty of people about . . . these are rush hours.'

'Done some homework first. Prospect.'

'OK, so you'd know streets where kids were more likely to be walking alone. Or waiting alone.'

'You think this was carefully planned?'

'Maybe . . .' Simon Serrailler finished his beer. 'The mother. She didn't say what you'd expect. Didn't blame herself for leaving him on his own to wait for the lift.'

'So it was her usual thing then?'

'Often enough anyway . . . she said she was in court that morning, so maybe on court days and when it wasn't her turn to do the school run, she generally left David to wait at the gate.'

'Nine years old?'

'Well . . . it was daylight, cars generally passing, the lift would be regular and reliable . . . not sure we should apportion much blame for that.'

'Someone knew just when . . . what day, what time.'

'Or maybe we're way out. I wanted to turn this over with you now because when we get back to the

115

station – unless David has been found – all hell is going to be let loose. The television and press will be going national, calls will be flooding in. Get me another of these rolls, will you? Eat while you can.'

On the way out to the car Simon stopped to look at a bench under the great oak tree. '*In memory of Archie and May Dormer. They loved to sit here.*'

'Peaceful. I'll bring Em out here next time we do a bike ride. She'd like to live in a place like this. In her dreams.'

'You never know . . . keep a lookout for a cottage . . . something like that row over there.'

'Archie and May'd have 'ad one of them. People could then. We ain't got a prayer, they'll be two hundred grand.'

'Keep looking . . . you never know. Come on, Nathan, where's your cheer?'

'Wherever the kid is,' Nathan said starting the car.

Fourteen

'The small English cathedral town of Lafferton is in shock today after the disappearance of nine-year-old schoolboy, David Angus . . . This is a blow to a place which has still not recovered from last year's murders. David Angus, son of a consultant neurosurgeon and a solicitor was last seen . . .'

'Bloody hell, kids ain't safe at their own flaming front gate now . . .'

'Heard it on the one o'clock news. They haven't found him then?'

Michelle Tait scissored open a packet of frozen pizzas and turned on the gas oven. 'Turn up in a ditch somewhere, won't he, like that little girl down in Kent.'

'He might have gone off on his own. Gone to a mate's.'

'Don't be stupid.'

'Sort of thing I did all the time.'

'Yeah, well. This kid isn't like that. Nice family, private school, posh house . . . they don't, do they?'

'Why does having all that make him less of a nine-year-old kid?'

'Use your cells. You want a pizza?'

The offer sounded grudging.

'No, I'll get something down the Ox later.'

'Afford to drink all right, can't you?'

'What, two halves?'

'You been to the jobcentre again?'

'Yes. And I'm looking in the paper.'

'Plenty of jobs . . . look, rows of jobs there . . .'

'Right.'

'You got no room to be picky, you know.'

'I'm trained. I'm not stacking supermarket shelves.'

'Trained. Right.'

'Yeah, trained, which is more than most people round here can say.'

'OOOOHH. Bloody good job you got me and Pete "round here" though, ain't it?'

'You want me out? OK. I'll get out.'

'Where?'

'Someone I know.'

'Pigs might fly.'

'You remember Lee Carter?'

Michelle sat down at the kitchen table opposite him and lit a cigarette. 'Are you serious?'

'Walked into him in the street. Drives a BMW convertible.'

'I bet he does. You went down for four and a half years for the likes of Lee Carter. Are you off your head?'

'He's straight. Making a fortune.'

'Oh sure.'

'I could work for him, no sweat.'

'Planting cabbages?'

'He's got a business . . . like this sort of executive club.'

Michelle gave him a look that could have stripped paint.

'Not what you think.' Andy heard his own voice, talking up Lee Carter, sounding defensive. His sister was right of course. What the hell was he thinking about?

Only it was something. He'd gone over it a lot since Lee had driven him out to his house, shown off, told him where it was all coming from, thought about it and asked around. He was gradually picking up some of the old threads – the right ones. He was being careful. He knew what he wanted. If he had money or if he found someone with it, he could start a proper market-gardening business, supply the best shops and hotels, good stuff, what they wanted now, organic, and not just cabbages and spuds. He had the training, he had the sense, he could do it. 'Start-up capital' it was called.

He stared down at the newsprint. 'Media Sales Executive.' 'Marketing Consultant.' 'Group analyst.' All the proper jobs seemed to have vanished. 'Youth outreach coordinator.' He folded the page over.

'You put a foot wrong, Pete'll have you out that door.'

'He wants me out of it any road.'

'Yeah, well, if I say you stay, you stay, only you want to watch it.'

The missing Lafferton boy had made Sky News. There was a picture. A mousy little kid with a small snub nose and a serious expression. School blazer. Tie. All neat.

Andy looked into the soft nine-year-old face. He remembered men inside. What they would do to a kid like that. What they had done to plenty, and if they were behind lock and key, enough others weren't.

He sat down.

Lee Carter. He saw the house. The car. The fountain starting up. The thick pile carpet. The gilded bar in the corner of the room.

Only he'd gone past that when he was a kid, wanting, wanting, doing anything to get, not bothered how. He could go and work for Lee Carter, but then what? Besides, he wasn't interested in horse racing or the people who were.

There had to be another way.

A posse of men in Stetsons galloped across the screen kicking up a dust storm. Andy got up. Westerns were just one of the things he couldn't stand.

There was still bedlam. From the kitchen came the crash of a dish into the sink.

'See you,' he shouted. No one answered.

He pulled his donkey jacket off the peg and went down the cold, ugly street towards the lights of the Ox.

It was full and they were all talking about the boy. Andy got a pint and ordered a plate of pie, peas and chips.

'Poor little sod.'

'They'll find him.'

'You reckon?'

'I didn't say they'd find him alive.'

'Right.'

'Poor bloody parents. Anyway, what's Lafferton done? After all that stuff last year it don't deserve another lot.'

'It won't be local.'

'Why not? Who says?'

On and on. The boy's face was in his head now, he couldn't get rid of it. He wanted to do something and there was nothing he could do, unless they asked for people to start searching Starly or Hylam Peak or the Hill . . . He'd be up there with them if so. What it was, he realised suddenly, he was restless. He was in prison at Michelle's almost as bad as before and in a way it was worse because he hadn't anything to do. There, he'd been outside in the market garden eight till five. He'd had a purpose to his day. He had to do something. Starting tomorrow.

His plate of food came steaming hot, mounds of it, the pie oozing thick brown gravy. A yell went up from the darts board. When he'd finished, he'd take his drink over there, have a game. Michelle wouldn't want to see him before eleven.

He cut the pie and watched the pastry sink softly down into itself.

Fifteen

'Darling?'

'Hello, Ma. Yes, I'm still here.'

'Oh, isn't it infuriating when people ask you the entire time? How do you feel?'

'You know how I feel.' Cat shifted her weight from one leg to the other and back again but the knife-blade pain in her groin did not lessen. 'The baby's lying on a nerve and it won't budge. Sorry, I didn't mean to snap.'

'Darling, I don't suppose you feel like giving me a hand on Saturday morning, do you? Only Audrey has let me down and I really don't think we have enough people . . .'

'Remind me what's happening on Saturday morning.'

'The hospice exhibition in the Blackfriars Hall . . . ten till four, and of course I wouldn't ask you, and needless to say you'll just sit in a chair and talk to people and hand out leaflets and so on, I wouldn't expect you to do coffees and teas and so forth.'

'Good of you. The problem is the baby is due on Sunday and the thought of sitting in a chair or standing about for more than five minutes is grim, to tell you the truth.'

'But what else would you be doing? It'll take your mind off it.'

'Mother, nothing will take my mind off having a baby apart from having a baby.'

'Are you doing anything else?'

Cat closed her eyes. Since retiring from the NHS, Meriel Serrailler had filled her life with a round of voluntary work, sitting on committees, acting as membership and social secretary to the St Michael's Singers at Lafferton Cathedral, and chairing the board of the local hospice. Cat remembered being told about Saturday's exhibition. The hospice needed a new day-care extension; plans had been drawn and a model made but so little money had yet been raised that the Blackfriars Hall in the centre of the town was hosting an exhibition of the plans. The Friends of the Hospice were putting on refreshments and the usual raffle and tombola and, by the end of the day, hoped to have attracted some potential donors.

'Sooner or later you are going to have to retire as Queen Bee,' Cat said wearily.

'Why? I'm good at it, I am fit and well and have plenty of free time.'

'You are also seventy-one.'

'Poof. Anyway, darling, do you think you would?'

'No,' said Cat firmly, 'but I have someone who might. Karin McCafferty's husband just left her.'

'Then she will certainly need her mind taken off things. I never really liked Michael.'

'Unfortunately Karin did.'

'I wonder why I didn't realise they weren't happy?'

Karin was the designer who had remade Meriel's garden the previous year. Cat chuckled.

'You're slipping, Ma.'

'They haven't found any trace of little David Angus, I rang Simon a minute ago. Not a trace. What do you think has happened to him?'

'I've been trying not to think about it.'

'They filmed the parents this morning . . . making an appeal. It'll be on the six o'clock news. Darling, do take care. I'll ring Karin.'

'Can't you rope Dad in on Saturday? Time he did his bit.'

'I wouldn't dream of asking him,' Meriel said and put the phone down.

Cat pulled a basket of sprouts and carrots towards her and sat up at the kitchen table to peel them. She would not watch the six o'clock news. Sam and Hannah had gone with Chris to their cousin Max's birthday party twenty miles away and would not be back until later. They would be rolled into bed, sticky and sleepy, and then she and Chris would have a late supper.

She would not watch the six o'clock news.

Would Karin mind being asked to help on Saturday? Probably not. Karin could put up a good front and besides, she was charming and beautiful and could probably sell ice to Eskimos. She was just the right kind of person to land a big donor. Her two days and nights staying at the farmhouse, pouring out everything over and over again, seemed to have emptied her of all shock, anger, resentment over being left by Mike. She was still hurt and saddened and she would undoubtedly have had him back tomorrow, but the all-clear from the hospital had strengthened her and uplifted her spirits. She had cried, she had talked, she had blamed herself, and Mike. She had dissected her marriage and gone over every incident and conversation for the previous few months, trying to understand what had gone wrong and why, whose fault it had been, whether she should have behaved differently, not said this or done that. Cat, in her present languid state, had been happy to provide an ear, and the occasional word of comfort and advice. But at the end of the two days, Karin had got up, washed and set her hair, made her face up carefully, packed her bag and gone home, head held high. 'I'm looking up,' had been her last words to Cat as she had hugged her at the door, 'up and ahead.'

Cat jumped as she nicked the skin of her forefinger with the paring knife. She had been full of admiration. She pressed a piece of clean kitchen paper on to the small cut. It was hardly bleeding.

She would not watch the six o'clock news.

Mephisto the ginger cat banged in through his flap, startling her.

125

She got slowly and heavily up from the chair and went into the den where they kept the television.

Barely ten minutes later she returned to the kitchen and to the phone.

'Everything OK?'

'I just watched television . . . the Anguses were appealing . . .'

'Oh my love, you shouldn't have watched it.'

'I know.' Cat pulled the kitchen roll to her and tore off a long strip.

'How did they seem? No, forget that, stupid question.'

In the background, Cat heard the sound of her sister-in-law's children's party. 'Where are you?'

'I came into the hall. It's bedlam.'

'They looked so awful. I hardly recognised Alan. He looked like the walking dead . . . he was seventy not forty-five. There was the most awful expression in his eyes – and hers . . . sort of wild and yet . . . I don't know . . . as if they had been beaten up and tortured beyond bearing . . . and yet they were hyper, you know? He was twitching . . . his mouth, his hands . . . God, I felt so sorry for them. I wish I could talk to Si but he'll be unreachable. I wanted to hear you.'

'I'm here and they're fine . . . and we won't be any later than we have to.'

'Don't go mad, drive carefully, Chris, I –'

'I always do.'

'I know. I'm twitchy as well.'

'Can you get anyone to be with you? Maybe Karin would come back.'

'No, it isn't that. It wouldn't make any difference. I shouldn't have watched. I can't get it out of my head . . . Chris, where is he, what's happened to him?'

'I don't know. But they've half the police force in the county out there looking . . . in the entire country, come to that.'

'There is nothing to say they'll find him.'

'Cat . . .'

'I'm sorry.'

'Have a drink. Won't hurt at this stage.'

'I'd be sick.'

'Cup of tea . . .'

'What's Sam doing?'

'Hang on, I'll have a look . . . He's sitting on the floor with a brown paper bag on his head. Don't ask.'

'OK.'

'Watch a stupid film . . . watch a DVD of *The Office*.'

'I thought maybe *Carry on Doctor*.'

'Love you.'

Cat put the phone down and wandered back into the den. It was oddly tidy. The children had not been in it since the previous evening and her daily help had decided to blitz it earlier. She wandered out again, went upstairs, closed the curtains in the bedrooms, opened a cupboard door and looked at the pile of new baby clothes. Waiting.

Waiting.

She went back to the kitchen.

The faces of Alan and Marilyn Angus were in front of her eyes and at the back of her head, they looked down at her from the ceiling and up from the floor. Cat rested her arms on her stomach.

'Dear God, help them to find him. Make him safe. Give them strength.'

If she had not been so heavily pregnant and unsafe to drive, she would have gone down to the cathedral where there was a communion service. Her faith kept her sane, gave her the commitment and strength to do her job. She did not know how Chris managed without it, or her brother, heading the team searching for the missing child. She could not have got through a day without somehow being in touch with it, however fleetingly.

After the appeal for their son by the Anguses, the screen had been filled with his face, a small, solemn, pale nine-year-old face, a face that was becoming as familiar to everyone in the country as that of their closest loved one, their own child, their neighbour, the Queen, any face they could see when they closed their eyes. David Angus. The face would be on posters in every shop window and noticeboard in Lafferton, at every railway and bus and filling station.

Cat bent her head and wept.

In the CID room, Nathan wiped his eyes, bleary from trawling through computerised data. It was seven thirty and the room was full. They had brought in extra officers from outside, another room was being equipped with more computers for the sifting through paedophile records, lists of cars, statements, descriptions, minutiae of forensic evidence from other cases involving abducted or assaulted children . . . canteen staff had stayed on duty and others had come back in, Uniform was being strengthened with assistance from outside forces . . . Nathan looked round the room. In a minute he would go and get a sandwich and a cup of tea and then see if he could be out somewhere, even doing door to door . . . anything rather than spend another hour staring at a screen.

The atmosphere in the CID room had changed, he thought. He hadn't known it like this since last year, during the hunt for Freya's killer. Tension was like an invisible electric wire strung round the room. There was none of the usual banter, no jokes, no small talk. The disappearance of a child focused everyone. They meant to find David Angus. No one talked about finding him dead, though with every hour that passed the possibility grew like an ugly fungus, taking over the corners of their minds, spreading its spores. Finding the boy and finding who had taken him – that was all that mattered. Any other business, petty burglaries, thefts of car radios, drunk and disorderlies, went to the bottom of the list.

Nathan had been present at the recorded television appeal earlier that day and had vowed to stay on duty without a break until the boy was found. The faces of the parents, the cracks in their voices, their odd jerky movements, their eyes . . . he saw them now, heard them as he went down to the canteen. On the wall, in the corridor and at the door, the posters of David Angus had gone up. Nathan looked into his young face. The face looked back, solemn, still a small boy's face, soft and round.

Nathan bought his tea, to have upstairs. The canteen was packed and he didn't want to take time out to chat. But no one had been chatting, they had been shovelling food into themselves because they had to refuel before carrying on, not spinning out a break, joshing, having a quick fag.

'Nathan . . . looking for you. My office.'

The DCI was leaning over the stairwell. Nathan ran, spilling a thin trail of tea as he went.

'We've had a report of a Jaguar XKV seen cruising a couple of times in Sorrel Drive. Once last week, and then again the day before yesterday. A woman who lives at number 10 – higher up from the Anguses – she rang us after seeing the news appeal.'

'What'd she mean, "cruising"?'

'Her word. Going slowly down the road, as if the driver was looking for a house . . . back up the other side, never stopping. Then doing it again. Same car next time, same thing.'

'Colour?'

'Silver.'

'She get a number?'

'Yes.'

'Jeez. Sort of witness you want and never get.'

'Right. The car belongs to someone called Cornhill. Leon Cornhill. Lives in Bindley. I want you over there.'

'What do you reckon, guv?'

'Nothing until you've been up there.'

'Anything else?'

'Hundreds of calls since the appeal . . . they're sifting through but no sightings. The boy's just evaporated.'

'Someone's got him.'

'We've covered every house in the grid of avenues within the area . . . people are anxious to help. Not a sniff though. The school are beside themselves . . . frightened parents, kids hearing half a tale and making up the rest.'

'What are the Angus parents doing?'

'They're at home . . . they've another child to look after . . . the FLO is with them.'

'Making tea. Drinking tea. Watching the news. Not eating. Not sleeping. Going over and over everything that morning. Heads aching with it. Poor sods.'

'We're getting plenty of help, info coming in from all over the country . . .' Serrailler fell silent, thinking. Nathan waited.

'I don't think he's hundreds of miles away. Don't know why. I think he's . . . around here.'

'They generally are.'

'I know.'

The phone rang on his desk. Simon lifted the receiver. 'Serrailler? Yes?' He held up his hand to Nathan who was at the door. 'Did he? When? OK, no one's fault. Get someone there. Get a statement . . .'

'Guv?'

'The man Cornhill reported his Jaguar XKV missing ten days ago. He'd been away on business, had a company driver to the airport so his own car was left in the garage. He got back. It was gone. Neat job apparently, careful break-in, no mess, just crowbarred the side of the garage door. No one heard or saw anything.'

'So it wasn't Cornhill doing the cruising?'

'Evidently.'

One of the desk officers trawling through data came up with a man living on the Dulcie estate who had been placed on the paedophile register during the past six months. Serrailler was looking at the printout as Nathan walked in.

'Brent Parker, forty-seven, convictions for molesting young girls, imprisoned twice, no other offences on record . . . last released from Baldney eighteen months ago . . . 15 Maud Morrison Walk, Dulcie . . . divorced, one adult daughter living away. Unemployed apart from casual jobs mainly for the council . . . underwent treatment programme at Baldney in the special unit for twelve months and again as an outpatient at BG psychiatric . . .' He handed the sheet to Nathan.

How could you say he had an evil face? How could you say, that man looks like a paedophile? If he hadn't known Brent Parker's history Nathan wondered what he would have put him down as – paedophile? GBH? Fraud? Dustman? High Court judge? He sat staring at the face, trying to empty his mind and clear his prejudices.

Brent looked older than forty-seven – ten years older at least. He had a soft, flabby face, folds of flesh under the eyes and at the jowls. Small concealed eyes, hiding their expression. Thick brows. Small chin. A self-satisfied expression, Nathan judged it – yes, Brent Parker looked pleased with himself. It was the face of a man who indulged himself, possibly in drink as well as sex.

A nasty face.

How can you say that? How can you tell? If this was the face of the man about to become the new Pope, what would you say then? What would you read into the fleshy folds and the smug mouth?

'I don't like the look of him.'

'Watch what you're saying . . . no criminologist takes the study of physiognomy seriously nowadays. I'd like to see a sample of his hand-writing though.'

Nathan blinked.

'I used to sneer at graphology so they sent me on a course. OK, get up there. If he's in, grill him, and if you're not one hundred per cent happy with every word he utters I want him brought in. If he isn't at home, find him. Take whoever's free with you.'

'Guv.'

'What?'

'I dunno . . . He ain't been in bother lately, isn't it a bit thin?'

'Of course it's thin but it's something and until we get something stronger we jump on it . . . one thing we can't do is ignore the least thing. We're under the arc lights here and they're not going to be switched off until David Angus is found. So move.'

Sixteen

Chris Deerbon had got home around nine in the evening and fifteen minutes later had gone out again on a call. The temporary locum they had appointed to the practice had left a message with the doctors' answering service to say that she was ill.

'Doctors are never ill. We can't be,' Cat said, handing him a banana and a box of juice from the packed lunch shelf. The casserole would simmer in the bottom of the Aga for as long as it had to.

'We, my love, are the last generation of GPs to have been trained to believe that.'

Chris kissed her and left. 'Go to bed,' he called back, 'you look whacked.'

'Don't know why, I've done nothing all day.'

Sam and Hannah had been barely able to stand to have their faces washed and teeth cleaned before falling into bed. Cat took her book, switched out all the lights but the lamp over the stove, put Mephisto, wailing in protest, out of the window, and went upstairs.

The children had curled themselves into their usual sleeping positions, Hannah neatly disposed with her head on her arm, Sam in a tight little ball, knees up, duvet almost over him. Cat pulled it down a little and kissed his head with the mouse-soft brown hair. It was impossible not to think of David Angus. Hannah felt cool. She would scarcely turn in her sleep all night. They were a happy little unit. Cat wondered how they would take to the baby when it was a reality, not a long-standing promise in which they had almost lost interest.

Half an hour later Chris rang. 'I've got an anaphylaxis . . . child with a peanut allergy. I'm trying to stabilise him, and now old Violet Chaundry's daughter has rung in . . . she thinks her mother has had another stroke. I'm going to be a while. Are you in bed?'

'And nearly asleep. The casserole's in the bottom oven.'

'I'll probably be past it. Got to go. Love you.'

Cat read another chapter of her Anita Brookner novel before turning out the light. Outside the wind had got up and was rattling the overhanging rose branch against the window. She found the noise strangely soothing.

She was woken by a movement at her side.

'Mummy . . .'

'Sam? You OK?'

'I needed you.'

'Oh honeybunch . . . come here.' But Sam was already wrapped round her, his feet twined about her legs, arms behind her neck.

136

'Don't squash my tummy.'

'I didn't want to go back to sleep.'

'Why? Bad dreams?'

He clung tighter. Cat shifted to try and make herself comfortable without pushing him away.

'Nat said David Angus had been murdered and thrown down a pit.'

Cat managed to lean across her son's hot little clinging body and switch on the bedside lamp. His face looked up at hers, flushed and anxious.

'Sam, Nat does not know anything . . . *anything* about David Angus. Do you hear me? What he said was not true . . .'

'He said.'

'He doesn't know. Nobody knows.'

'Why?'

'Because . . . he hasn't come home yet. The police haven't found him.'

'Why haven't they?'

'Do you want a drink?'

'If they haven't found him, they don't know he hasn't been murdered and thrown down a pit, do they? Have they looked in all the pits in the world yet?'

'Hot chocolate?'

'I don't want you to go.'

'You're OK here . . . it won't take a minute.'

'If you go downstairs I want to come with you.'

'OK . . . come on.'

How many small children in Lafferton have crept into their parents' beds? How many are having

137

nightmares about David Angus? How many other little bullying sods like Nat are frightening the lives out of the rest with stupid stories . . .?

Sam sat on the sofa, his eyes bleary as she set the pan of milk on the heat. 'Why did he go with the man?'

'What man?'

'The man who murdered him. Everybody knows not to go with a man who might murder you, everybody knows that.'

Dear God, how do I answer this child? How do I begin to reassure him and convince him that he is safe when I am terrified for his safety myself and there is no reassurance and will not be unless David is somehow found alive?

She poured the milk on to the chocolate and whisked it round.

'Can I have a biscuit?'

'If you clean your teeth again afterwards.'

'I'm too tired.'

'Then no. Come on, big boy.'

The crash from outside was so sudden it made Sam hurl himself off the sofa and on to Cat and the mug of chocolate cascade on to the floor. The wind had lifted up something loose and hurled it down again.

'Mummy, I don't like it.'

'It's OK, darling, it's fine, it's just the wind catching a bin lid or something . . . don't panic.'

'The man might be there, the one who murdered David Angus, Nat said he was a man who likes to steal boys and murder them and then he throws them into pits, there are a lot of men who do it, probably even two hundred men and . . .'

'Sam . . . come here, sit on the sofa.' She pulled him close to her. 'I want you to listen to me carefully. I am telling you that there is no man like that out there. That was the wind. There is no man wanting to take little boys. You are perfectly safe and nothing is going to happen to you. Now, I want you to tell me that you have heard me and you believe me.'

'But you don't know, how do you know?'

'I know because I know a lot of things . . . a lot more things than Nat will ever know. Do you believe him more than me?'

'I don't know.'

'If so you shouldn't. He's a silly little boy and I am your mummy.'

'And a doctor.'

'Yes.'

'Well . . .'

'Oh Sammo . . . I love you. Do you want me to make some more hot choc? And I'd better wipe that up from the floor before someone slips on it.'

Sam slithered off the sofa. 'There isn't any left to slip on,' he said, his face bright with glee. Cat looked down at Mephisto, licking up the last of the spilled hot chocolate in an efficient manner.

'Will you swear?'

'Probably.'

'What will you say?'

'It'll be secret swear. I can hear Daddy's car. If he finds us up, *he's* going to swear . . . go on, scoot.'

What do we do? Cat said fiercely to God as she waited for Chris to come in. What on earth can we do or say now?

Seventeen

He took Geoff Prince because Geoff was taciturn, so much so that he seemed to lack much interest in the job at all. But he was dogged, and good at detail. He didn't chat and never made stupid judgements.

The Dulcie estate by night was slightly more attractive than in daylight because even the sodium street lights managed to soften the concrete and blur the ugliness of the whole. In all other respects, though, it was not a place around which to walk after dark and so nobody did. The teenage thugs and junkies had it to themselves.

It was the smell as they got out of the car. Night after night Nathan had leaned out of his bedroom window smelling the smell – chips, oil, human detritus; nowhere else smelled like the Dulcie. He remembered the longing, like a sickness, to get out, to do anything to escape into a better place, a world that smelled fresher and cleaner and more prosperous – though it had never been money that had motivated him. Nathan Coates had known by the age of thirteen that if you wanted easy money you stuck around the Dulcie. It had never been that.

Maud Morrison Walk was on the other side of Long Avenue from where his family lived – the slightly more respectable side. The houses here had front gardens and gates, and not so many abandoned rusting cars and old greyhound cages in the front.

'Here we go.'

Geoff said nothing.

The curtains were cherry red and tightly drawn. There was a rim of light thin as a wire showing round the side and flickering neon blue from a television screen.

'What the hell's all this?'

Geoff flashed his torch. The front garden was decorated not with plants, nor with ancient bicycles and prams, but with hubcaps . . . several dozen hubcaps, arranged carefully against the fence and along the wall as if they were exhibits.

'Must grow 'em,' Geoff said.

The front door bell played 'Auld Lang Syne'.

'Brent Parker? I'm DS Nathan Coates, this is DC Geoff Prince.'

'You took your time.'

Brent Parker held open the door.

It was a smell again, though nothing like one he had ever smelled before and it choked him. Nathan stood in the doorway of the small, hot, frowsty sitting room and tried to locate it, to make it out. There was a three-bar electric heater full on, a television blaring, a huge neon tank of fish set against the wall.

And the smell.

'Would you mind turning that off please, sir?'

Parker ambled towards the television set.

He was a huge man, huge-bellied, huge-headed, with a black ponytail, hands like plates, fingers like bunches of bananas. Nathan looked into his face. The eyes were small, hidden behind deep lids and in folds of flesh, and the flesh was soft and pendulous beneath them.

'I almost came in. Get it over with.'

'To the station?'

Parker sat down but did not suggest that they followed suit.

'Well, you was always going to come here, wasn't you?'

'Were we?'

'Course. Kid goes missing. I take it you ent found him?'

'Why did you expect us to come here?'

'Don't mess me about, son, I been messed about enough. Kid goes missing, I've a record for kids. Stands to reason.'

'Where were you on Tuesday morning, Mr Parker, around eight o'clock?'

'In bed.'

'Alone?'

'Who'd have me?'

'Anyone else in the house?'

'Only Tyson.'

'Your dog.'

'Nope.'

'Don't mess *me* about, Mr Parker. I don't go for it.'

'I know who you are. Dinky Coates's lad . . . snotty little kid, you were.'

'Was anyone else here who can vouch for you being in bed at that time on Tuesday morning?'

'Ask Tyson.'

Nathan followed the man's sausage finger. On the other side of the room, above a shiny sideboard, stood another tank, letting off a strong glow from inside.

The smell.

Geoff Prince went over and peered in.

'You got a licence for this python?'

'Don't need no licence.'

'Think you're doing it a favour, do you, keeping it crammed into there?'

'Want me to let him out and run around?'

'Do you have a car?'

'On and off.'

'I don't suppose you drive a Jaguar XKV?'

Parker snorted with laughter and the snort sent spittle shooting out of his mouth towards Nathan. 'Yeah, right.'

'Have you ever seen this boy?'

'Don't bother, I seen the posters, I know what he looks like.'

'Have you seen him?'

'Might have. Might not. Could have passed him in the street any day. So could you.'

'Listen –'

144

'No, *you* fuckin' listen, Coates. You listen. I know what I done and I been inside for it and I done the programme for it and I'm out, finished, paid for, only you lot can't bleedin' forget it . . . I know where I am, I'm on your fuckin' register, that's where, and there I'll be till I'm frying in the Parkside Crem incinerator, but I ent seen that kid, I ent taken the kid, I ent been down that road, I don't intend goin' down that road, I don't intend gettin' near any fuckin' kid ever again. If you want to know, I've joined a marriage agency, get myself a woman, homekeeper, to look after me and Tyson, shut you up. Go on, get out. Fuck off, before I lift the lid off of his tank.'

Parker stood in the hallway with his back to the open kitchen door. Through a gap, Nathan caught sight of another illuminated tank on top of the fridge, glowing red. Parker smelled too, rank in their nostrils as they passed unavoidably close to him on their way out. For a second, he grabbed Nathan's sleeve.

'You ent checked your records careful enough, have you, you stuck-up young sod?'

Nathan pulled his arm away. 'If you've anything to tell us, Parker, you better spit it out.'

Geoff Prince was halfway to the car.

'You wouldn't have wasted your time.'

'I said –'

'I heard you. See, it's all done with now, I'm treated, en I, cured, went through a load of them psychiatrists and they sorted it, only you'd know if

145

you'd looked weren't no point in coming here talking to me. It was *girls*. Always. I never took a look at no boys. It was girls. Always. You take a look. I could have you for harassment.'

Geoff was silent as he drove back to the station.

'I feel like I need a shower and to have me clothes sent to the cleaner's,' Nathan said after a while. 'Are people allowed to keep pythons just like that?'

'Dunno. Want a check?'

'Naw, got enough on. Just hope he doesn't forget to put the top back on the tank one day.'

'It's not him. No way.'

Nathan agreed, but said nothing. The smell and aura of nastiness had hung about Brent Parker and his hot, stinking rooms, but not because he had had anything to do with the disappearance of David Angus. The DCI had wanted him brought in if there had been the slightest suspicion, but there hadn't been, not about the boy at least. 'They'll have checked on the stolen Jag time we get back.'

'You reckon anything to that?'

'Might be.'

'Bit obvious . . . crawling down the road and back in broad daylight sussing out the scene.'

'Right.'

'I reckon it was just someone looking for a house. Those bloody great detached places behind their hedges and driveways and posh gates never have anything so obvious as a number, even a name, where you can find it. I know, I did a house-to-house all round there. Never a bloody sign.'

'Right.'

'They do a nice hot pork bap out of Toni's van.'

'Go on then.'

Brent Parker's house was in Nathan's mind. He was walking round the rooms, looking at everything, trying to remember what it was that had started to niggle. Something. He had seen something, not enough to pay attention, maybe not seen it properly, but something.

He took the hot roll in its cone of greaseproof paper from Geoff's hand and the smell made him realise how hungry he was. He hadn't eaten more than a couple of chocolate biscuits for hours. He bit deep into the savoury, crumbly mass of meat and bread and hot sage stuffing, closing his eyes. But even while he was eating with such ravenous pleasure, it was there, niggling away. Something. Something.

David

I don't like this place.

I'm not frightened.

I don't like it, that's all.

Why have we got to be here? It's cold and it smells.

I'm very thirsty actually. If you gave me something to drink it might be best. We're always allowed to have a drink at school when we want, water anyway, and not anything to eat but we can have a drink when we like. It's important for people to drink, they get ill if they don't drink.

Aren't you thirsty?

If I could have a drink then I'd tell them when they come that you gave it to me, and that would be a good thing for you.

They will come.

Yes they will.

They're clever and they have tracking devices and they'll soon use those to find me and then they'll come. QED.

Don't you know what QED is?

When will we go back?

I don't like it here.

I'd like to see my mummy. It's dark, isn't it, so that means Daddy will be home and then they'll come for me together. They might bring my sister. They probably would bring my sister.

My sister is eleven and she'll soon be twelve so they would bring her. Yes, they definitely would bring her.

I don't like it here very much.

Why don't you say anything? If you said your name I'd like it better being with you. I don't really like it but I'd like it just a bit.

If you said your name.

Di Ronco's father was a famous pop star. He was in a world-famous rock band.

He's ace.

Di Ronco's dad.

He makes us laugh.

Once we wet ourselves with laughing.

I don't really like it here.

But they will be coming. I think I can hear them actually. I can hear a car coming.

Did you hear that car?

Eighteen

'I think,' Marilyn Angus said, taking off her glasses, 'I am going mad. I think if this goes on for another five minutes, I shall be mad.'

They had tried doing normal things. They should be as normal as possible, if only for Lucy's sake, though there was nothing normal about Lucy, as she sat as close as she could to one or other of her parents while trying to pretend she was not doing so, and bit the fingernails she had taken such care in growing down to the quick.

They had tried cooking supper and eating it and most of it lay congealing in the bin. They had tried answering emails, and watching television and playing Scrabble and Racing Demon.

'What are we doing this for? We never do this. We only do this at Christmas.' Lucy had got up and walked away, leaving the words frozen in mid-game on the board.

They had switched on the television and heard the terrible canned laughter like demonic cackling in their ears and turned it off.

They had poured gin and wine and tea, and the glasses stood about still full. Only the teacups were emptied, over and over again.

'I'm going to have a bath,' Marilyn Angus said. 'Call me if . . .'

Lucy slid off her chair as her mother left the room and sidled behind her up the stairs. Marilyn Angus went into the bathroom and out of the usual habit closed and locked the door. Lucy sat on the floor outside it, touching the panel with her arm.

The steam billowed up smelling of freesias. Marilyn wished she had not put essence into the water. It seemed wrong. Her bathwater ought to be plain, to smell of nothing, to be penitential. She ran cold into it so that it would not be so hot, seem so luxurious and enjoyable. She must not enjoy anything until . . .

What could be happening to David, where David might be, who was with him, what they were saying and doing to him, was there, starting out of the traps and racing round the track of the inside of her head over and over again. His face was in front of her and occasionally she saw a bit of his body, his thin, frail-looking wrist, his toes, his ear with the small cauliflower frill at the top. The thought of any part of his body not just being hurt or defiled but even being touched, even being looked at, by someone who meant him harm made her retch with a sickness that sent her to the basin but from which nothing came, though she stared down expecting black bile to be there, swirling round under the running taps, the bile her whole stomach was filled with.

Not knowing. Was it true that not knowing was the worst of this? She needed to ask someone who had been through it. The names of those people, known from newspapers and the television and radio, rang in her head. She needed to talk to one of them, anyone, to ask if not knowing was the worst, or if, when things were known, those things were the greatest horror of all and the not knowing had been nothing, a soothing, tranquil, paradisal state by comparison.

She would ask Kate, the policewoman who had been assigned to them and was now, indeed, living with them, though Marilyn would have preferred her not to be there. She neither liked nor disliked her, she simply did not want or need, or see the need for, her permanent, intrusive presence. She would ask Kate. Kate could get addresses, numbers, couldn't she, the station would have computers to talk to other computers and send the telephone numbers of those people she needed to speak to across the ether. It did not much matter which parent of what child, what had happened to that boy or girl, how long they had been missing, in what state they had been found. Anyone, anyone at all would do. Just so long as she could talk to them and ask them the questions she could ask no one else. And they might have answers. No one else had answers, but they might.

She saw David as a newborn baby writhing beside her, still attached to the cord, still covered in the white strands of mucus and caul, mouth roaring with fury at being naked under these blue-white lights.

She saw David racing down the wing with the ball at his feet and Ryan Giggs in his head and the shouting schoolboys and parents on the side cheering.

She let out the bellow of a cow that has had its calf taken away, the bellow of pain and rage and bewilderment and distress that sent Lucy backing away from the door on her hands and knees.

Alan, followed by Kate, came running up the stairs.

Lucy's bedroom door banged shut.

Marilyn sat in the cooling bathwater that smelled too strongly, sickeningly of freesia and heard the appalling noise and was puzzled, unable to tell where it was coming from or why.

The phone was ringing as she returned to the kitchen, dressed again and calmer, Kate behind her, touching her arm.

'Oh God.'

It could not be news; Kate would receive that first, on her radio, and prepare them for it, good or bad, but the sound of the telephone bell was terrifying now, any intrusion from outside could be something to do with David.

'Alan Angus . . .'

Do not answer the telephone, they had said, leave that to us. Leave us to take the enquiries and the well-wishers and the lunatics and the press, let us deal with it all. Alan would have none of that. He was permanently on call, even now, even through all of this . . . patients came first.

Marilyn sat in the chair by the fire watching as he listened and jotted down a note.

'What time did they bring her in? How long has she been unconscious? How much bleeding? OK, we need a theatre, I'm on my way.'

She could not bring herself to say anything. He had to go. He could not ignore it. Not even now.

'Woman cyclist hit by a car.' He glanced at the policewoman, coming in with yet another tray of tea.

'I'm going to the hospital. I'll be in theatre but you can page me.'

'Can't someone else do it? Can't the registrar –'

'Too difficult. I'm needed. Can't leave it to Michael.'

He got to the front door, then came back. 'Hadn't you better check on Lucy?'

Marilyn looked at the teacups. She had thought she knew Alan but she did not. She had thought they were a close couple but they were not. What had happened had separated them as if a knife had sliced their marriage in half. Alan had retreated into work, insisting on being called in for every neurological trauma, doing a full list during the day, taking every clinic. Alan did not talk about David. Alan did not talk to her. *'Hadn't you better check on Lucy?'* Alan could not face Lucy himself.

'Would you like me to go up and talk to her?' Kate asked.

She was a nice woman, Kate. Pleasant face. Neat hair. Sympathetic. Easy. If you had to have someone living in your house, at your elbow, behind you, beside you, day and night, you could not do better than nice, understanding, shrewd Kate. Marilyn thought she might kill Kate. It was not the police-woman's fault.

'No. I should.'

'Everyone has to cope in their own way as best they can. Your husband copes by being at the hospital.'

'And what do I do? I cope by not coping. I cope by having hysterics in the bath and terrifying my daughter who is already beside herself with fear. I cope. I don't cope. How can you expect us to?'

'I know.'

'No, you don't know. You have no possible idea.'

'Actually –'

'How do you? How can you imagine what it is like?'

'By . . . thinking it is my son. Peter. Or – Peter when he was nine.'

The fire which they had lit for comfort as much as for warmth shifted within itself and a little heap of coals which had burned through subsided into glowing ash.

'I'm sorry.'

'No. Never say that. You can say anything at all to me, you know that, but you absolutely do not have to apologise to me, OK?'

155

'You're very good.'

'No, I'm doing my job. I wish I didn't have to, Marilyn. I wish I wasn't here as much as you wish me away. I wish there were no reason for me to be here.'

'When they find his body there won't be any need. He is dead, you know. I'm quite sure of it.'

'I'm not.'

'Why?'

Kate shrugged.

'I'd better go up to Lucy.'

'Yes.'

'If he is dead, please God they killed him very quickly.'

She waited then. Waited for the policewoman to say that of course it was not so, that she knew, that she had evidence, that David was alive and well and being brought home now, that it was simply not possible for him to be dead. That no one had hurt a hair of his head, no one had frightened him, no one had spoken a harsh word to him. That David was as he had been the last time she had seen him, when he had leaned in through the window of her car to kiss her goodbye. That her son's body and mind were quite, quite undamaged. That time had spun backwards and nothing had happened. Nothing.

She waited. Kate got up and started to pull the fire together.

She waited.

Kate did not speak.

In the end, she went, knowing that Kate could not

speak, because there was nothing for her to say, went up the stairs as slowly as if she were an old woman carrying an impossibly heavy burden.

She waited for a moment on the landing outside Lucy's room. There were no sounds at all from inside. She gathered words up inside her head and tried to form them into sentences with meaning, to make shapes of the words which would then come out of her mouth and cross the air and be received by her daughter but the words were scattered about anyhow like spilled toys.

She turned and went on up the second flight of stairs to the small eaves bedroom. No sounds came from inside. Marilyn Angus leaned her head against the door and prayed to hear the little murmuring noise he made while he was doing his homework or the whirr of a small motor on some game. If she heard something, time would have tipped backwards and he would be there and she awake on the floor outside his room after sleepwalking here.

Silence.

She opened the door. 'Doodlebug,' she said aloud.

The room smelled of him. She switched on the light. His dressing gown behind the door swayed slightly as she went in. The model football pitch was on the table beside the window. She bent down and riffled through the books. *Harry Potter and the Philosopher's Stone. Dr Dolittle's Secret. The Chamber of Tutankhamun. The Story of Pompeii. A Guide to the Stars. Stars and Galaxies. Patrick*

Moore's Book of the Night Sky. I was there: A Boy of Pompeii.

He was here. She smelled him. She sensed him. If she reached out she would touch him. If he was here he was dead.

She lay down on her son's bed and pulled out his pyjamas from beneath the pillow. They smelled of his hair, the odd, particular boy's smell. She cradled them. He was here now. After a while, she fell asleep and David slept beside her, his small, thin body tucked into hers, as close a part of her as it had been before his birth.

In her room on the floor below, Lucy sat at the window, in the dark looking out at the dark, and thinking nothing, forcing her mind to be an empty drum and her feelings to be non-feeling.

Kate sat at the table in the kitchen, alert to the quietness in the rest of the house, a pile of routine police files in front of her. On the hour, she had telephoned in to the station where the activity was relentless and more and more manpower was being drafted in to work on the case but from which there was no news of the missing boy. Nor had they traced the silver Jaguar.

Nineteen

DCI Simon Serrailler sat in the farmhouse drawing his sister. Cat was sleeping on the sofa. One arm lay on her swollen stomach, the other was stretched out to touch the cat Mephisto. It was after midnight. He had needed to get away from the station after a seventeen-hour stretch. He had wanted the comfort of the Deerbon farmhouse, with the children sleeping upstairs, his pregnant sister close by, and the warm muddle of family life welcoming him into its centre.

He had eaten. A glass of wine was at his elbow. He changed pencils, taking a soft 4B to shade in the thick ginger halo of fur down Mephisto's back. Cat stirred slightly but did not wake.

He had spent the afternoon on the phone liaising with other forces; just after nine, a report from the Cumbria police had come in to say that a boy aged thirteen had failed to return home after a school rugby match. He had not caught the usual bus, nor been seen since he had set off to walk to the main road to wait for his father who was to pick him up. When the father arrived, the boy, Tim Fenton, had not been there so he had waited for over half an hour. His son had not turned up, nor had he been at the school, the playing fields, at home, or at the houses of any of his friends. No sightings of him had been reported in the town, or at railway or bus stations. Taxi drivers had not picked him up.

The station was in a heightened state of activity and anxiety. The CID room was alternately packed with officers, and empty as they went out to follow up reports. Uniform were trying to split themselves in two, putting all they could on to the Angus case while keeping everything else ticking over. Fortunately, a big investigation seemed to send most other areas quiet . . . reports of petty theft and vandalism, stolen vehicles and smashed shop windows were all down, pubs and clubs were peaceful. It was as though Lafferton knew the police had to put everything they had into finding the missing boy and vowed not to cause trouble otherwise.

But with every hour of the long day that had passed, Serrailler had felt more certain that the boy would not be found alive. All day, uniformed officers and members of the public had been searching the Hill, the canal banks, and every waste area, garage block and empty industrial unit, every back garden and field and paddock and strip of woodland. The reminders of the previous year's killings were everywhere.

Sometimes, turning quickly away from the window, looking up from a phone call, walking down the corridor towards the CID room, Simon saw Freya Graffham's face, or caught sight of her, swinging through the doors, pulling out a paper cup from the water cooler, smiling at him.

His pencil snapped. Cat did not stir. Mephisto was tucked deep into his own fur.

His telephone rang, waking Cat.

'Serrailler.'

'Guv . . . it just came to me. I knew there was something, it's been driving me mad all day.'

'What?'

'When we was at Parker's house . . . I just couldn't think what. Only Em had a paper and it was when I saw it on the table . . . last night the *Echo* ran a whole page with David Angus's picture . . .'

'Yes. It was a repro of the poster.'

'He had it.'

'So did a lot of people.'

'Yeah, only it was when we was leavin' and he had the kitchen door open behind him, he was wantin' rid of us . . . I glanced in there . . . he'd got another of 'is tanks, on top of the fridge, lit up. I was just wondering what the 'ell else he'd got kept in tanks in there. So busy thinking about that, I must have seen the newspaper only not properly taken it in . . . it was up on the wall. I mean, what was that for?'

'Hm.'

'Only you said if there was anything, bring him in. We didn't have nothing, to be honest, guv.'

'You said.'

'Then I remembered this.'

'It's not enough to bring him in but it's enough to pay him another visit.'

'What, now?'

'No, no, leave it till first thing. It's not enough to go hammering on doors in the middle of the night.'

'OK.' Nathan sounded disappointed.

Cat was standing by the Aga waiting for the kettle to boil.

'Sorry.'

'No, I shouldn't go to sleep like that, I get cramp. Tea?'

'No. I'll take over from you on the sofa. You go up.'

'The spare bed's made up. You won't sleep properly down here. Take a bit of your own advice.'

Simon stood up and stretched.

'What were you doing?'

'Drawing you and Mephisto.'

Cat smiled.

'How are you feeling?'

'Weary. I just want to have a baby.'

'Chris is a long time out.'

'We need that locum. He can't do this, on call most nights, and it's been hellishly busy.'

'No one yet?'

'The person he interviewed didn't want it after all. He heard about some woman today who might be interested . . . came back from two years in New Zealand and thinks she might like to be in this area but wants to test the water. Don't know any more yet. Let's pray.'

'I thought everyone wanted to be a GP.'

'Oh, they used to. Times have changed.'

'I'll go up . . . if I get called in to the station, I'll try not to make a racket.'

'You never do. Anyway, I'm used to Chris getting up, Sam coming into our bed with his nightmares. His head's full of David Angus. I can't deal with it easily, Si . . . I lie to him and he knows I'm lying. They talk about it at school, Chris says he hurls himself into the car and locks the door. He wouldn't go with the Simpkinses yesterday, Chris had to take him there to tea.'

Simon went over and put his arms round her.

'I can't stop thinking about that little boy.'

'I know.'

'How do you deal with it?'

'Cat, you have children who die of cancer, and young patients killed in stupid accidents and babies who get meningitis. Deal with this in the same way.'

'This is worse.'

'Maybe.' Simon went towards the door, rubbing his hand over his blond hair in the gesture Cat knew so well and which he had always made when he was exhausted, or over-anxious, troubled by his work or by something within himself about which he would not talk.

She put out the kitchen lights. On the sofa, the cat Mephisto stretched out a paw, kneaded the air with his claws, and burrowed back into sleep.

Twenty

The parrot Shirley Sapcote's great-aunt left her had been called Churchill but Shirley had changed its name to Elvis the day it arrived. She had tried to teach it to say 'Blue Suede Shoes' instead of 'Never surrender', but only succeeded in confusing it so much that it was now mostly silent apart from occasionally making the noise of a train going through a tunnel. It sat in its cage on the small table under the window, staring at her balefully, its sulky silence worse than its voice.

The bungalow was one of six built in a single red-brick block at the back of Ivy Lodge. Shirley had not been able to believe her luck when the job she so much enjoyed provided her with a clean, new, comfortable place to live, after years in frowsty bedsits and cheap flatlets in badly converted houses near the canal. The block had been built on a piece of land behind the nursing home where a row of condemned Airey prefabs had once stood and proved a godsend to the owners in helping them to find and keep staff. Not many stayed as long as Shirley though. She thought she would never move until she retired and even then maybe . . .

There were some trees at the back. She could lie in bed and watch squirrels run up and down the trunks and leap across from one to the other like circus acrobats and at night she could listen to the owls.

She had not wanted the parrot but as her great-aunt had also left her two thousand pounds and a Crown Derby tea service, her conscience would not have allowed her to reject him or give him away. This morning he looked cross-eyed and hunched himself into his grey feathers.

'*You ain't nothing but a hound dog,*' Shirley sang at him, '*cryin' all the time*. OK, buster, that's your lot. See you later.' She shoved a piece of apple in between the bars, half drew the curtains because it was something her mother had always done, and went out. Some people might not like living on top of the job but she found it restful to walk across a nice stretch of grass and into the building opposite without having the hassle of catching buses or starting cars, without even having to put on a coat half the year.

Shirley was forty-one. She liked her work, she liked her flat, she went line dancing twice a week and ballroom dancing every Saturday and on Sunday she sang in the gospel choir at the Redeemer Church, the only white person there. She was a happy woman.

The early-morning shift was her favourite. She liked the atmosphere of a new day. She liked to wake people up with a cheerful face. She liked the smell of the breakfasts cooking and the sound of the floor polisher whirring about the hall and the vacuum cleaner on the stairs.

She walked into the staffroom still singing 'You ain't nothing but a hound dog'.

'They haven't found him.' Nev Pacey the caretaker was sitting at the table with the morning paper in front of him.

'Oh God bless him, poor little love. What wicked people are capable of, it defies belief.'

'*Police say they are becoming increasingly concerned for David's safety as time goes on.*'

'Well, they would be. I mean, think about it, he hasn't gone off for a toddle down the road and lost his way, has he? He hasn't hopped on a bus and gone to visit his gran. Those poor parents.'

'*Mr Alan Angus, consultant neurosurgeon at Bevham General Hospital and his solicitor wife Marilyn made a highly emotional television appeal for news of their son . . . "We beg you, if you are holding David, just let him go. Ring the police. They'll come to wherever you are holding him. We want him home. We just want him home."*'

'And they say the Devil doesn't stalk the earth still. He's everywhere.'

Nev turned the paper over to the racing page.

'Right, let's get on . . . time to go and see Little Miss Sunshine and Mrs Muffet.'

Shirley had names for all the patients, something which the rest of the staff found irritating but

166

nevertheless found themselves falling in with, so that Mrs Eileen Day, who was slowly, slowly dying of motor neurone disease was for some reason Mrs Muffet, and Mr Atkinson, brain-damaged after being caught in a bomb blast, was Giantkiller. Martha Serrailler was Little Miss Sunshine.

Since she had nursed her mother through multiple sclerosis, her aunt through two years of paralysis after a stroke and her only sister Hazel through breast cancer, Shirley had found that looking after the incurably ill was a part of her life she could not conceive of being without. She was consoled by the knowledge that she was wanted and needed and that she was good at what she did, and brought something to it other than a disinterested professionalism. She brought commitment, and cheerfulness, all the benefits of lack of personal ambition, and, in the case of Martha Serrailler, love. She had loved the girl since she had first arrived here, loved her because to Shirley there was no more reason not to love her than there would be not to love a newborn baby. Martha was a newborn baby. She had no more knowledge, no more ability or personality than one; she could do no harm, could never lie or steal or cheat, never hurt or insult; she was perfectly innocent, like a white sheet of paper. Everything she did was innocent, every noise she made, every odd random gesture of her body. Her bodily functions were as innocent as a baby's too. Shirley could never understand why anyone should find them any more troublesome or unpleasant to deal with.

She went up the stairs. There was a small kitchen at the end of Martha's corridor. Shirley would get her breakfast ready, the baby cereal and the spouted drinking cup of weak lukewarm tea, the mashed banana, the plastic spoon, the bib.

After eating, Martha would be taken out of her night clothes, washed, dried, cleaned, changed; Shirley would brush her fair hair and tie it back, showing Martha the little box of ribbons and clips and rings, letting her reach out and 'choose' one. Then she would wheel her out of her room, down the corridor and along to the lift. It was a bright morning. Martha would sit in the conservatory, where the sun would warm her pale face and hands and brighten her blonde hair and the birds would come to the window feeder, which seemed to give her pleasure.

To Shirley, Martha's being like a baby extended to her lack of a sense of time which meant that she did not grow bored and restless and dissatisfied. She simply switched off and dropped into some twilight place inside herself, or she went to sleep. Only occasionally did she grunt and cry out, and in this, too, she was like a baby, if a meal was late or she was filling the nappy she wore. Once, she had screamed and flailed about, and it had taken Shirley and Rosa half an hour to find that her sandal had been buckled too tightly, pinching a fold of her skin into it.

Rosa was in the kitchenette now, waiting for the kettle to boil.

'Morning, Shirley.'

'Good morning, darlin', how's things?'

Rosa sighed. Rosa so often sighed as a prelude to any response or remark that Shirley took no notice, though she had once said that Rosa was like the boy who cried wolf and when she had something to sigh about no one would ask her what was wrong.

'Can't wake up this morning and Arthur's wet his bed again.'

'So what's new?' Shirley bent to the fridge to get out the fresh milk.

'They heard anything about that little boy yet?'

'Not when I listened at half past five they hadn't.'

'If they catch him . . .'

'Or her . . .'

'No woman would take a little boy from his parents like that, no way.'

'Myra Hindley?'

'That was years ago.'

'Human nature don't change.'

'I'd like them hung at a public hanging like they had in history. I'd pay to go, I would.'

Shirley spooned Ready Brek into a plastic non-tip bowl.

'They said her brother was in charge.'

'Yeah, well, he's the top man at Lafferton, he would be.'

'Do you think he's handsome?'

'Mr Serrailler? Never thought about it.'

'Course you have.'

'All right then, I have . . . yeah, only his hair's too fair for a man. Looks lovely on Martha though.'

'Sad that.'

'Why?'

'If she was normal, it'd be really attractive.'

'Rosa, you haven't got to say that sort of thing, not in here and not anywhere.'

'True though.'

'Move over, let me get at the fridge. They didn't mean this kitchen for two.'

'Don't get me wrong, I do feel sorry for her, poor girl.'

'You needn't. I think she's happy.'

'How can you know that? Don't be daft.'

'I just know. Like a baby's happy. Well, she doesn't know any different . . . like a baby. If she'd been . . . like us . . .'

'Normal.'

'If she'd had an accident or what, like Arthur, then she might remember . . . but what you don't have . . .'

'. . . you don't miss. Really, what would have been kindest would have been for her to have died of that last go of pneumonia.'

'That's a terrible thing to say.'

'No, it isn't, it's the truth and you know it. She'd have just drifted off and never known and that would have been that. She can't get better, she'll grow old like this.'

'So?'

170

'So where's the point? You believe in God and heaven and that, so wouldn't you say that'd be better for her? Certainly be better for her poor family anyway.'

'They're OK . . . they can afford for her to be looked after properly here. They come and see her . . . Dr Serrailler was here again last night wasn't he, I saw in the book, and Simon, until all this little boy business . . . and Dr Deerbon'll come only she's having a baby any minute, maybe had it . . . they don't ignore her, they haven't just dumped her.'

'That's true. Like Arthur's wife.'

'And son and daughter.'

'Right. If I had my way –'

'You'd have a public hanging. OK, let's go. Bloodthirsty little thing you are, Rosa Murphy.'

Rosa chuckled.

'Morning, my darling. How's my Little Miss Sunshine this morning?'

Shirley often wondered if Martha moved at all in the night. Every morning, she was lying on her right side, looking towards the door, her eyes open. She lay like it now and made her little murmur, of recognition and, Shirley always thought, pleasure. Shirley bent over and kissed her forehead and pushed her hair back from where it had fallen over her face.

Martha smelled of warmth and dirty nappy.

Shirley looked down into her eyes. The eyes looked back, but what was *there*, she wondered, thinking of what Rosa had said, what was really behind them? It worried her that any day anything could happen to Martha, and she would have no say in it at all. They could take her from here, have her at home, send her somewhere else, give her to strangers, and she would lie as she lay now, she would eat and drink messily, fill her nappies, make her noises, flail her arms. Look up into the face of anyone, with that unfathomable blue-eyed stare.

'Poor Little Miss Sunshine,' Shirley said softly. Maybe Rosa was right. If she'd simply gone to sleep quietly in the hospital, overcome by the infection, if her lungs had given out, wouldn't that have been the best for her? It would happen one day. She'd been at death's door two or three times. What was the point of her getting better?

She stood upright quickly, shocked at herself, shaken by her own thoughts.

'Lord Jesus Saviour, forgive me my sin and bless this girl. Lord Jesus Saviour, touch me with your love.'

Martha lifted her arm and twisted her hand about, and her eyes followed the movement and she smiled.

'All right then, my darling, you're off to see the birds.'

Shirley lifted the brake on Martha's chair and went out of the room and down the corridor, singing 'Jesus Saves'.

Twenty-one

'You want to make yourself useful you could wash up.'

'You only have to ask.'

'I'm asking.'

Michelle swept crumbs and bits of sugar flakes from the kitchen table into her hand and threw them in the direction of the bin. Andy went to the sink. The dishes were piled up from the previous night's fish and chip and ketchup supper.

'I'm buyin' you a present next time I go out, new washing-up brush. Look at this.' The bristles were completely flattened and there were tea leaves stuck down between them. He turned on the taps.

'Guess who I saw just now anyway.'

'Go on then.'

'That Nathan Coates.'

'Right.'

'Wasn't you in his class?'

'No. Dean's.'

'Oh yeah, Dean. That Nathan's up himself. I waved at him, but oh no.'

'He's a copper.'

'Didn't look like one to me.'

'CID.'

'Gawd. What's he doing up here then?'

'Probably spends half his time this way.'

'He went down Maud Morrison. What do you reckon?'

'Bloody hell, how should I know . . . could be a dozen things, couldn't it . . . you know more about what goes on round here than me. I been away, remember, ha ha.'

'Yeah, well, it isn't like that up this end.'

'Oh no.'

'Oh no, there's people buy their own houses this end, it's got a lot more respectable.'

'Right.'

'I shall find out, mind.'

'I bet you bloody will.'

'Don't use up half a bottle of that, it costs.'

'Needs half a bottle to get this fat off, you want to wash them up straight away.'

'You watch yourself, you're only here . . .'

'OK, OK . . . I've got to see the probation officer today, maybe she'll have something . . . flat or summat.'

'Probation won't get you a flat.'

'Anyway.'

'Or a job. You gotta do that for yourself.'

'I might have already.'

'You what?'

'Got a job.'

'What, street cleaner?'

Michelle lit a cigarette, put on her leather jacket and went out without waiting for a reply.

It took her all of ten minutes to find out why the CID were up this end of the Dulcie and two minutes more to join the other women at the end of the close. There were half a dozen of them but others were on their way, some pushing buggies and pulling toddlers, others returning from taking older children to school.

'They kept it dark,' Michelle said to the woman beside her.

'Don't they always? Try and get past us!'

A few laughed. Then, after the laughter, came the first shout.

'Paedophile out.'

It was taken up. 'Paed out. Paed out. Paedophile, paedophile, out, out, OUT.'

After a moment a curtain in the upstairs window shifted slightly.

'Get out here, Brent Parker, we know who you are.'

'Yeah, and what.'

'Child molester.'

'Rapist.'

'Paed out, paed out, paedophile, paedophile, out, out, OUT.'

Placards came, home-made from sheets of old wallpaper tacked to board. 'No Paedophiles.' 'Paedophiles OUT OUT OUT.' 'Protect our children.'

The curtain did not move again.

Andy Gunton went to the upstairs front-room window, from where he could just see the gathering crowd in the close. He did not need to open the window to hear them.

Nonces. They'd been hated inside, never safe, never off their guard, always looked out for by the screws. Beat up a nonce, trip him in the shower so he cracked his head open, knee him in the balls during a game, it was the quickest way to becoming a hero. There hadn't been many of them but you could tell a mile off, even if they didn't wear NONCE across their foreheads. They had a smell about them, they were shifty-eyed, there was just something. You never cured them, a screw had said. Treatment programmes, shrinks, rehab . . . might work on junkies, often did, surprisingly often really. But on nonces, never. Once a nonce, always a nonce . . . they were clever though, they knew the game and all the tricks, they could pull the wool. But they didn't change.

He didn't fancy the chances of one against Michelle multiplied by fifty . . . even against Michelle on her own come to that. What were they doing, putting him on a family housing estate anyway? Nonces wanted segregating off, putting in blocks of flats for singles, so the police knew where they were and what they were up to.

It was his only prejudice. He prided himself on not caring about blacks and browns and yellows.

Live and let live. Even gays. But not nonces. No way.

In the end, uniform had to go round to the back of Brent Parker's house and break in, while back-up tried to clear the crowd outside. By the time Nathan Coates arrived, Parker was in the kitchen, shaking, standing beside his snake tank.

'I want protecting.'

'We'll get rid of them. I was coming up to have another word with you anyway.'

'You won't leave alone, will you? I served my time, I done with all that, but you'll never leave alone. I told you last night, we don't need to start again. And I ain't stopping here without protection. You drive off, what do you think they'll do? You think I'll be safe, do you?'

'You could try letting one of your reptiles out for a walk. I doubt they'd come close after that.'

'Reptiles need heat.'

'Plenty of it out there. OK, they'll be gone in a half a minute. Forget about them. Sit down.'

'I'm all right standing.'

'Suit yourself. You said last night you didn't know anything about the missing boy.'

'I don't.'

'You weren't involved, weren't even interested.'

'I'm not . . . no more than most people.'

'What do you mean?'

'Stands to reason.'

'Tell me.'

177

'Kid goes missing, it's a terrible thing. You don't want that happening. Kids aren't safe.'

'No.' Nathan looked at the man. He was unshaven, he smelled, his hair was filthy, and he had his hands on the snake tank as if it were a protective talisman. He had shifty eyes. Only that was the sort of thing you were told not to think . . . eyes were eyes, call them anything else other than blue or brown, you got told it was inadmissible. But Nathan knew shifty eyes when he saw them – they shifted.

'So you're not interested in David Angus?'

'Not specially. I said.'

'Then why do –' Nathan stopped.

'What? Why do I what?'

The newspaper poster of the missing boy had gone. Last night Nathan had seen it through the half-open door, clear as day, stuck to the wall above the snake tank. He got up.

'Move.'

'What you doing? You leave me be.'

'Just move.'

Parker hesitated, then edged round, his hands still touching the snake tank. Heat came off it and it smelled rank. Nathan preferred not to look closely at the inside.

'What's been up here?'

He touched the slightly sticky patches on the wall.

'Nothing.'

'Nothing been stuck up here? Not a notice . . . or a poster maybe? Sheet out of a newspaper?'

'Yeah . . . no. There was a note.'

'What sort of note?'

'About the snake. Feeding times.'

'You need a reminder?'

'No. It was for . . . someone else. Someone else was feeding it while I was out.'

'Who?'

'A mate.'

'You got mates? What's his name?'

'I don't have to tell you.'

'Yes, you do. If you don't tell me so I can check it out with him, I might think you was making that up. I might think you'd had a sheet out of the newspaper stuck up there . . . with the picture of David Angus on it.'

'Well, you'd be wrong.'

Nathan turned quickly and took two strides to a pedal bin with its lid hanging half off. The pedal didn't work. He didn't fancy touching it with his hands but it fell open easily enough when he poked the lid with his shoe.

'Empty that out, will you? Don't look too clean in there.'

'Empty it yourself. What you want? You need a search warrant.'

'To get to the bottom of your manky rubbish bin? I don't think so.'

'You want to look in my rubbish, you look. I ain't moving.'

'I suppose asking for a pair of rubber gloves would be a waste of time?'

179

'Right.'

'Newspaper?'

'Under the sink.'

It took Nathan Coates three minutes to spread the only newspaper he could find, an ancient copy of the greyhound section of the *Racing Post*, on the floor and tip the contents of the bin out on to it. The congealed mess of egg remains, hair, tea bags, and dirty wood shavings which had probably come from the snake tank made a soggy clump. But there was no newspaper, not even shredded up. No poster of David Angus.

'OK,' Nathan said. 'For now.'

'Where you going?'

'Get some fresh air.'

'You ain't leaving that lot.'

Nathan grinned, turned his back and got out of the house fast. The air of the Dulcie estate had never smelled sweeter.

Only a couple of the women were left, a few yards away from the house, talking closely together. The patrol car was still parked at the kerb. Nathan bent down to the window.

'They'll be back, minute you've gone.'

The PC shrugged.

'He'll ring again.'

'We'll take that as it comes then. You got anything on him?'

It was Nathan's turn to shrug. As he went towards his own car, one of the women turned round. 'It's that jumped-up little prick Nathan

Coates. Surprised you show your face round here these days, thought we was all beneath you.'

Leave it, Nathan said to himself. Let it go. 'Morning, Michelle,' he said, before slamming the car door and accelerating away from the Dulcie estate as fast as he knew how.

David

I'm hungry. Do you have anything for me to eat? You ought to give me something to eat.

I'm a bit thirsty as well.

I don't like this place. It's very cold here.

Are you still there?

I want to see Mummy now.

Can we go back home now please? I won't say anything to anyone, if you just leave me I can walk back to my house. I'm very good at walking.

I'm quite a good walker. Everyone says that. I'm good at games.

Where have you gone?

Can you hear me?

I don't want to stay here. It's cold here. It's horrible here.

I'm thirsty now. And hungry. I haven't had anything to eat. Why haven't you given me anything?

Are you going to kill me?

I didn't say anything wrong. If I did I'm sorry I did.

I didn't do anything. I haven't done anything.

I don't really know why you brought me here.

I don't really understand this.

I just want my mummy now.

I wish someone was here.

I wouldn't even mind it if you were here. I don't like you but I don't like being here by myself.

I wouldn't even mind if there was a dog here.

Or a rat.

It's very cold.

I don't mind the dark. It is dark but I don't mind that. I'm not frightened of the dark. Not very frightened.

I want to go home please.

I'm not crying or shouting, am I?

I won't cry or shout. If you take me home. Or just let me out. Open the door. Or lift the lid thing. I can walk home. I don't know how far it is but I'm a good walker.

I don't want to be here.

Please.

I don't want to be here.

Twenty-two

'I want uniform up there on a rota, two at a time, round the clock. Parker is going to scream for protection the minute our backs are turned, so let's not turn them.'

The DCI put his feet up on his desk and his hands behind his head.

'I wanted a word about things up at the Dulcie, guv.'

'Screaming harridans.'

'It's my patch, it's my territory. I knew half of them women shouting the odds outside Parker's house this morning. I went to school with 'em.'

'What's your point?'

'Mebbe I ought to keep out of the way of there.'

'The fact that it's your patch makes you more valuable there than anyone else. You've got the smell of it, you know them, know what goes on in their houses, who's who . . .'

'They don't like it.'

'Someone been winding you up? You can take that. I'm not putting the Dulcie out of bounds to you, Nathan.'

'They'll clam up on me. I'm a traitor, see.'

'Tough.'

'I got a sniff of something else though.'

'It'll keep. Meanwhile, we're up against a brick wall and the press is on my back. They got hold of the Parker story of course and they're smelling blood. Are we doing enough? Why haven't we made progress? Well, why haven't we? It's gone cold. Correction, it was cold from the start.'

'Nothing come in from anywhere else?'

'Not a peep. They found that boy in Cumbria. Tim Fenton.'

Simon leaned back perilously in his chair, tipping himself against the window ledge. Nathan waited. When the DCI went quiet, something always came next.

'OK, we should have done it before. Reconstruction.' He stood up. 'Day after tomorrow. I want a boy David's age, size, height . . . wearing the clothes. I want all the parents who take kids to school that way doing what they did the morning he vanished. Talk to the school . . . I want everything set up with the neighbours . . . the whole road. Everyone doing exactly as they did it that morning.'

'Guv.'

'I'll go and tell the Anguses.'

Twenty-three

The garage was cold and lit by a fluorescent light. The back wall was covered with grey metal racks stacked from concrete floor to ceiling. In the corner beside the door leading to the house, a chest freezer stood open. Marilyn Angus stood beside it. She wore an old sheepskin jacket belonging to her husband and some black gloves that she had found on one of the shelves and which smelled of oil.

She had switched off the freezer and emptied it completely. A lot of the food she had bagged in black sacks, to be thrown out; the rest she had put into carriers, to be returned to the freezer when it had defrosted.

Now, she was going to start on the racks. God knew what was in most of the boxes. Old toys. Old tools. Old files. Old clothes. Old. Old. Old. Why had they kept all this stuff? Because there was space to keep it in. She was going to take down every box and open it, go through the contents, sort them, and throw away, ruthlessly. It was the only thing she could do, a job which occupied her, tired her, needed doing and could be done while most of her self was elsewhere.

With David.

Where?

A small rail ran round inside her head like a toy train, carrying boxes and bundles and bags and every so often an item would fall off and down a chute, to land in front of her, demanding her attention. She had to pick it up. She could do no other. She had to open it. She had to examine the contents.

This time the box contained a picture of David as he had first emerged from her body, slippery, flushing pink as she looked, eyes tight shut against the light, arms flailing. Hair. A shock of dark, Struwwelpeter hair. For a split second he was upside down. His genitals had looked huge, like strange growths against the tiny damp limbs.

She stood in the cold garage staring, staring at the contents of the box under the forensic light. She was conscious of the smell of oil on the old gloves but not of the cold at all.

For a moment, she wondered what she was doing here and why. For another moment she could not remember her own name.

'Marilyn?'

The door into the house had opened. There was a woman. Who was she? She looked slightly familiar. Friendly. Marilyn felt she ought to be polite but did not know quite in what way.

'The Chief Inspector is here.'

The woman came forward quickly. The woman laid her hand on her arm.

'There isn't any news. He just needs to see you.'

The woman standing beside her was the FLO. Kate? Yes, Kate something.

'Thank you.'

'You're freezing. You've been out here too long.'

'Have I?'

She could not remember how long or what she had been doing. There seemed to be a lot of bags and boxes at her feet and the freezer lid was up.

'Come on, I'll finish this after I've made some tea . . . come into the warm.'

She let the girl lead her into the kitchen, and help her off with what seemed to be Alan's old sheepskin jacket. Her hands smelled of oil.

'Do you want a minute? He'll wait . . .'

He?

It was warm in the kitchen. Thawing was like coming out of a dream.

'The DCI.'

There was a sudden pain through her heart as she remembered.

'Yes,' she said, 'of course.'

Simon Serrailler. She still could not think of him as a policeman. Serraillers were doctors.

She walked into the sitting room.

'Sit down please . . . there'll be some tea.' She smiled. 'I dread to think what our tea bill is going to be.'

Then she put her arm up and leaned it on the mantelpiece before bursting into sobs so desperate and raw that Simon was startled by them.

He got up and handed her the box of tissues from the coffee table. It happened often enough and he understood it, this terrible, heart-rending crying. He waited awkwardly. In the end she shook her head, wiped her face and sat down.

She looks a hundred years old, Simon thought, or no age, no human age looks like this.

'I want to be dead.'

'Mrs Angus, we're —'

'No, please do not tell me you are doing everything in your power to find him. You think you are, but it isn't enough . . . nothing is enough, nothing short of every single human being in this country dropping what they are doing and looking for him.'

'Yes,' Simon said quietly.

The FLO handed him a cup of tea.

'But I'm here to talk to you about what we plan . . . With your agreement, I'd like to do a reconstruction of David's last-known movements.'

Marilyn stared at him. She lifted her teacup but set it down again, her hand shaking.

'How can you do that? David isn't here.'

'We'll have a boy the same age, same height and colouring, same school uniform . . . as much like David as possible . . . he would . . .'

'Pretend to be David.'

'That's the way it works, yes.'

189

'And I would . . . be myself?'

'Yes . . . we'd try to get neighbours and people who were driving down the avenue that morning . . . people walking . . . everything . . . as near as possible to replicate it. It's a hard thing to have to do but it really could give us the key. Someone doing the same thing in the same way as they were doing it that day may have a flash of recollection . . . something they saw, a car, a pedestrian . . . something they heard. I know you want to do anything possible.'

'Will Alan have to do this?'

'He will have to do as he did that morning. He left for the hospital forty minutes before you and David came out of the house?'

'Yes. The only way Alan can deal with this is by working.'

Simon stood up. 'Everyone has their own way of trying to cope. We'll give Kate details of the arrangements for the day after tomorrow. I know how distressing it will be but it could be vitally important.'

'But what boy can you get . . .? You don't know the boys.'

'Leave it to us.'

'I was clearing out some shelves. It was so cold out there. Do you think David is cold? Whoever . . . if they are looking after him . . . he only had his blazer, you see.'

Leaving the house, Serrailler felt angry with Alan Angus, so anxiously defended by his wife, so wrapped up in work that he left her alone all day with a policewoman. It might be his way of coping but Simon questioned the humanity of it, let alone whether a neurosurgeon required to perform intricate life-saving brain operations and whose nine-year-old son had been missing for several days was able do his job properly.

Before returning to the station, Serrailler drove into Lafferton and stopped at the florist. She liked something bright . . . a big bunch of red and orange and yellow. He added a red balloon. The whole looked garish and festive and slightly ridiculous sitting in the boot of Simon's car. It pleased him.

Twenty-four

'Lee?'

'Who's this?'

'Andy Gunton.'

For several seconds there was nothing but loud and derisive laughter. Andy almost put the phone back.

'Dear oh dear, let me wipe my eyes . . . tell you what, I knew you'd be on to me before long. But it's making me laugh all the same. You coming to cut my lawn or what?'

Andy clenched his fingers into his palm to stop himself from swearing. Calm and reasonable, he'd decided.

'You said there might be a job – in your club.'

'You said you wanted to work in God's fresh, couldn't stand being cooped up in an office, you said.'

'OK, is there a job or isn't there?'

'Depends. Not in the club there isn't, I've got a couple of smartly dressed young chaps right here . . . besides you ain't interested in racing.'

Andy waited.

'I might have something else.'

'Legit. It'd have to be.'

'For who?'

'Legit.'

'I don't do criminal. I'm grown up, And.'

'Right.'

'Know the Crown on the Starly Road?

'I'll find it.'

'Half six.'

The phone went dead.

Andy Gunton stepped out of the kiosk. If he hadn't made the call he'd be stacking shelves in the supermarket overnight – either that or homeless.

'You don't get yourself a job by this time next week, Pete says, you're out of here; there's jobs, And, you ain't dossing in Matt's room any longer.'

He had given up on anything he was trained for, at least until later on in the spring. He had to get some money behind him somehow, then a place of his own, then find a way of starting up his market garden. He needed a backer, or a partner at any rate, and working for Lee Carter might lead him to someone.

The pub was a mile out of the town centre, on a nondescript corner, not the sort of pub anyone would find their way to unless it was their local. Andy wondered how it kept going. It smelled stale.

The mirrors behind the bar wanted cleaning. There was a poster on the wall for a circus that had left town three weeks ago. Next to it was the poster about the missing boy. Andy looked at his face and looked away again. He saw him everywhere.

Lee Carter's car turned into the pub drive at exactly six thirty. He walked into the bar and straight up to the counter, ordered a double tomato juice, came over to Andy and took off his leather jacket with a flourish.

'Like it?'

The jacket was like the car.

'Very nice.'

'You work for me, all this could be yours, my son. You got all you want to drink there?' Andy nodded.

'Cheers. Now then, And . . . cars.'

'What about cars?'

'Know anything?'

Andy shrugged. 'I'm no mechanic.'

'Wouldn't need to be. See, what I do is, I dabble in import-export and sometimes it's cars. Export mainly. I buy this, sell that, ship the other . . . good money.'

'What'd I be doing?'

'Driving, picking up from here, dropping off there, bit of smartening up . . . whatever.'

'What kind of cars?'

Lee Carter smiled a fat, smug smile. 'Top of the range. No money in heaps of rusty tin. Mercs, Beamers, Jags, Rangers.'

'Bloody hell. Where'd you get 'em?'

Lee's smile iced over. 'First thing you know when you work for me is how to keep this shut.' He gestured.

'When do I work, nine till five sort of thing?'

Lee laughed, picked up Andy's glass without asking or answering, and went to the bar.

Andy wiped the back of his hand across his mouth to make it feel cleaner. He had buzzing in his ears. Buzzing along his veins. Buzzing through his head. Warning buzzing. Get up, he told himself, get up now and walk away. Remember where you've just come from? Remember what it felt like?

Lee set the pint glass in front of him. The head frothed up over the rim.

'Here's to it.'

Andy drank without speaking.

'When you work,' Lee said, straddling the chair, 'is when you're told. I ring you, or someone else does. You'll be told where to go, what to do. When.'

Andy shook his head. 'I don't think so. This don't sound legit to me, this don't sound like straight car dealing.'

'You reckon? Like I said, this is export. Not your garage forecourt with your Aftershave Nigel trying to flog you a tin coffin. I told you, this is different.'

'Yeah, illegal different.'

'Nothing illegal about exporting cars, And. Happens every day. Why not? You come to the office, you see the yards of fucking paperwork I have to fill in, customs this and excise bloody that . . . I ain't doing that if exporting isn't legal, right?'

Andy looked at him. He had that straight, blue-eyed gaze which held yours. There were lunatics and murderers and paedophiles who couldn't look you in the eye and then there were the conmen, who always did.

Only he needed a job.

'When do I start?'

'You got a mobile?'

Andy laughed.

'Right, I'll sort it. Meet me Thursday, Dino's in Queen Street. Eleven o'clock.'

'Bloody hell, Dino's . . .'

'He's still there . . . only it's Alfredo taken over now, and he's got a missus. Dad sent him off to Italy, they'd got it all fixed before he went, came back with Lina. Smashing girl.'

For a second, Andy Gunton forgot who he was talking to – forgot Lee Carter had been one of the reasons he'd done five years in prison, forgot you couldn't trust him, not ever, and that he'd be daft if he went to work for him. Forgot he ought not to be in this pub drinking with him now. All he remembered was when they'd been in school together and Fredo Jaconelli had been with them and they'd all piled into Dino's after school and on Saturday afternoons and drunk Cokes and eaten Knickerbocker Glories in tall glasses with long spoons. If Fredo's dad was feeling generous, they'd had one each; if not, one between them and however many spoons it took. Dino's.

'Machine still makes the same noise. They still got cherries on the wallpaper and plastic pineapples full of sugar.'

'Bloody hell.'

'They weren't though.' Lee Carter stood up.

'What?'

'The days. Just in case you said they was. Crap, those days were. These are the days, Andy, and don't you bloody forget it.'

Lee Carter shrugged on his leather jacket and walked out of the pub without a backward glance.

By the time Andy followed him it was raining, hard, straight, steady rain which had him dodging in and out of doorways and hanging about under shop awnings which then tipped water down the neck of his jacket. He had no raincoat – no coat at all. He stood, looking into the window of an electrical shop at convector heaters and steam irons. He knew what he wanted. He wanted his own house, his own front room, sofa, television, radiator, carpets. His own door, his own key. Freedom as freedom was no longer enough. The thrill of being able to go out and walk about as he pleased, enter a pub or a shop or a café when he liked, all of it had worn off. He was a stage further on. He had started to be discontented, even irritable. To want more. A lot more.

He dodged between doorways and stood waiting for a bus to the Dulcie estate.

Michelle was out. Pete was in the kitchen.

'Been wanting to have a word with you,' Pete said, standing in the doorway with his hands on either side, his stomach falling out over his belt. He had a line of moustache and a line of beard drawn round his chin and stubble between. Underneath, his skin was pink as pork. Andy imagined him in prison as one of the screws who bullied and had favourites and played nasty little tricks. He'd never understood his sister having anything to do with Pete.

'I hope Michelle's not standing outside that paed's house in this lot,' he said, pulling off his jacket.

'Up to her. We don't want them perverts here. This is respectable.'

'Since when?'

'Since until you got out.'

'Can I put this by the stove to dry out.'

Pete stood solid as a chopping block, unmoving in the doorway.

'OK, suit yourself.'

'How long was you thinking of stopping? Been here a bit now. Feels like years. I was going to tell you it was time you got a job, only funnily enough, I got one for you. Warehouse down Culvert Street. They want a loader. I put in a word. Foreman's a mate of mine.'

'I got a job.'

Andy walked away from his brother-in-law and into the living room where the television blethered away to itself. Andy stood looking at it. A man was standing in a garden waving his arms about.

'I don't believe you. You just made that up.'

'Nope.'

'Doing what? What sort of job?'

'Cars.'

'What do you mean, cars? You ain't no mechanic.'

'Export.'

'Talk English.'

'Top-of-the-range motors, sorting them for export.'

The man stopped waving his hands and started to walk slowly down the grassy garden avenue between mixed flower borders fifteen feet wide. Roses and clematis climbed up old brick walls.

Pete stood, fumbling about for words. Andy ignored him.

'Where'd you get this job then? You don't get jobs like that down the jobcentre and who'd give you one, with your record?'

'Thought you said you'd got me one – with my record.'

'Never mentioned it.'

'Right.'

'What they paying you?'

'Enough. Can I get a cup of tea?'

The man was leaning on a lead statue of a naked woman. A bee was zizzing about his head.

'You got a job then, you'll be looking for somewhere to live?'

Andy turned and faced Pete.

'Too right.'

The back door opened and slammed shut behind Michelle.

'Bloody soaked I am. Pete, ain't you got the kettle on?'

Pete turned from the doorway. 'He's got a bloody job,' he said. 'Exporting bloody cars. What's he know about cars? Who'd give him that sort of a job?'

Michelle came out of the kitchen.

He couldn't tell her who, Andy knew that. He could never mention Lee Carter's name in this house, he'd be flat on his back on the path and the door locked behind him.

Michelle went on looking.

'That right?'

Andy headed for the stairs. 'That's right.'

He pulled off his wet shirt and trousers and changed into dry. There was hardly room for him to turn round in the room he had to share with his nephew.

He ought not to have rung Carter, he ought not to have listened to him. Carter was trouble. He'd ruined his life once. Why give him a second chance?

This was why. Andy looked round the frowsty, overcrowded room, with Matt's soccer poster and heavy metal stars all over the walls and his wardrobe spilling out with clothes and gear, the top of it unsteady with piles of old toys. Under his bed were half a dozen pairs of manky trainers and the trainers smelled. This was why, this and his piggy-faced brother-in-law.

Besides, who was to say the car business wasn't perfectly kosher? Probably was. He'd do it for a year, maybe eighteen months, until he'd saved the money he needed. It'd be OK.

He went back down, carrying his wet clothes. At the doorway of the sitting room he glanced through to see if the man was still wandering about the garden but the screen was manic with a cartoon.

In the kitchen, Michelle was pouring water on to tea bags in two mugs.

'We seen the bugger off,' she said as Andy came in. 'Police took him away half an hour ago.'

'Where to?'

She shrugged. 'Don't care so long as it's a long way from here. We don't want him.'

'Trouble is, he's got to live somewhere.' Andy put his trousers over the oven rail.

'I don't see why. Have my way they'd hang the lot of them.'

'Nah, you're going too far there, darling, castration'd do the trick.'

Michelle laughed.

Andy sat down at the kitchen table and put his hands round the tea mug.

'You see Nathan Coates again?'

'Yeah, he was up twice. Snooty little bugger he is now, just cos he's a copper. Don't know what he's got to be like that for, his brother's never up to any good.'

'They found that kid yet, did he say?'

'Never asked. They won't have though. Poor little bugger'll be dead in a ditch somewhere and it'll be down to a paed. Like that Brent Parker. What else?'

She lit a cigarette from the gas sparker. 'It don't stop things happening,' she said.

'What do you mean?'

'People like them, you know . . . posh family, live on Sorrel Drive . . . all of that don't make any difference. It don't save you from anything. You're just as well off being like us when push comes to shove. Now get your backsides out of here, the both of you, I got things to do.'

The two men wandered into the living room, where the television had gone black and white and calm with an old romantic comedy.

Andy went to the window. The Dulcie estate looked down at heel and deserted in the rain. Grass sprouted up between the paving stones and in the corners of the guttering. Runnels of water ran down from the drainpipes on the block of flats opposite, making dark stains. It wasn't that he'd be as well off in prison. He wouldn't. He hadn't been. But if he'd come out to nothing better than this for the rest of his life he would be suicidal. All the same, Michelle had a point. He knew that. They had what he wanted, those people – big house in a nice area, smart cars, good jobs, everything you'd envy if you were living here on the Dulcie estate, everything you'd want. He wanted.

But when it came to losing their kid one Tuesday morning, to God knew who or what, none of it had made the slightest bloody difference at all.

Twenty-five

'Aw look, darling, look . . . so pretty!'

Shirley propped Martha over her arm expertly, plumped up the backrest and pillows with the other, and set her comfortably in place again. It was like moving a giant doll, Simon thought.

His scarlet, orange and yellow flowers were a slash across the pastel room.

'Your brother's lovely to you. I wish I'd got a handsome man bringing me bouquets. I'll pop them in a vase, Mr Serrailler, all right?'

'Thanks, Shirley. Has anyone else been to see her?'

'Oh, we've had a proper little party in here this afternoon. We had been going to have her down in the lounge only she had a bit of a runny nose this morning and you know how she is if she gets a cold . . . and there's some nasty ones about. So she stayed up here and we had the party, tea and a cake and candles and some ice cream and we sang. Look, Rosa brought her that sparkly balloon . . . she loves it. You should've seen her face when she saw it, she waved her hands and her eyes were that bright . . . and she loved the ice cream and we opened her cards.'

His sister's room was festive with the balloons and flowers and some red ribbons they had tied to her bed and dressing table. They do love her, he thought, they care for her and look after her, which they're paid to do, but they love her too.

Martha was dressed in a yellow knitted shawl over her nightdress and her hair had been freshly washed and tied back in an orange ribbon. Colour registered with her, so did music. Simon had brought her a new CD of brass-band music. He had often watched her face when music started up and seen the flicker of life and recognition which surely must be pleasure.

'She seems well, Shirley.'

The nurse had come back with the flowers in a huge fan-shaped vase which had a pearlised sheen to its surface.

'Yes, maybe it wasn't anything, only we just always have to be careful with our little Martha, you know?'

'She's twenty-six today.'

'She's little to me . . . well, all of us. You know how it is.'

'I know.'

Simon took Martha's hand between his own. She moved her head slightly.

'Happy birthday, sweetheart.'

'Dr Chris came in this morning, brought her this . . . look.' Shirley picked up a bright pink stuffed octopus with huge eyes that rolled about. 'We put it on her lap all afternoon. She kept reaching out for it.'

Soft toys. Balloons. Bright objects. Colours. Baby things.

He remembered when she had been born and he had peered into the cot. She had seemed like a lump of putty to him, dough-coloured and inert. Only her hair was beautiful. 'Many Happy Returns' one of the cards said in glitter, a vast heart in pink and purple. Is that what they ought to wish her? More of this? Year after year of next to nothing. He stroked the soft, silken skin of her hand as it lay floppy and motionless in his.

'I hope you find that little boy, Mr Serrailler, I can't sleep for thinking about him, you know? I wondered if you'd get in today with all of that.'

'I shall have to go in a minute. I wasn't going to miss her birthday but I don't have long.'

'Any news?'

'Not really.'

'I suppose you can't say . . .'

'I keep telling people, Shirley, if I had anything to say I would. It's a cold trail at the moment.'

'I saw you were going to do one of them reconstruction plays . . . maybe someone will remember seeing him.'

'Maybe. It works occasionally.'

'Poor little kid. The Lord Jesus bless and keep him. Praise be to the Lord.' Shirley had closed her eyes and put her hands together and her voice was fervent. 'And may those that have taken him know that the Lord will avenge His little ones and the flames of hell await the wicked and the ungodly. Amen.'

Simon went quickly out of the room, startled by the passion in the otherwise gentle nurse's voice. He glanced back at his sister, lying among the brightness and the balloons and the sight cheered him through the rest of the day.

As he walked into the station ten minutes later his heart stopped for a split second. On the bench in the front office sat a boy, aged about nine and wearing the uniform of St Francis school. He had David Angus's hair, pale slightly freckled face, protruding ears, serious expression. At his feet was a school bag identical to the one they knew he had been carrying when he left his mother.

The boy was not David Angus.

'Hugo Pears, guv . . . couldn't believe our luck. Kid's an identikit.'

'Is he OK with it all?'

'Great – wants to be an actor. Wants to star in films about the Roman Army.'

'Dear God – I suppose he thinks this will be good training?'

'Mother's a bit wary. Only she says your brother-in-law's been so good to her she couldn't refuse your family anything.'

'Oh right, one of Chris's patients? Yes, they'll do anything for him. Even this.'

'Everything is set up for seven forty-five tomorrow morning.'

'Good work, Nathan. What about Brent Parker?'

'He's in a hostel at Bevham. We've nothing on him, guv. It wasn't him. He doesn't even have a car.'

'Who said he had to have a car?'

'You mean the boy just walked off holding the hand of someone he didn't know?'

'Don't make assumptions. No one has reported seeing him getting into a car and we have no idea whether he went alone, with someone, with someone he knew, or did not know. Keep an open mind – wide open.'

'Guv.'

'Any reports from outside?'

'Not a whisper.'

'Bugger.'

'Well, no other reports has to be good news, don't it?'

'I don't mean I want to hear a report about another child who's disappeared on the way to school. But this silence is getting on my nerves.'

'He's clever then.'

'No, just lucky.' Simon banged the desk hard. 'What about the number-crunchers in there?'

'Nothing yet.'

'Get me a coffee from the Cypriot, will you? Double espresso and one of their toasted sandwiches . . . I haven't eaten since seven. I've just been to see my sister.'

'Dr Deerbon had her baby then, guv?'

'Not that sister. Martha. It's her birthday.'

Nathan looked embarrassed. He felt embarrassed. He never knew how to react on the few occasions the DCI mentioned his handicapped sister so he changed the subject instead. As they always do, Simon thought.

'Couple of cars nicked last night . . . same story, top of the range, one Jag, one Range Rover . . . one from a garage, one outside a house in the drive. No one heard or saw anything . . . clean as a whistle.'

'Cars don't even make it on to my list right now. Let uniform deal. I want some more digging; any cases in the last three years of children reporting someone hanging about, strangers speaking to them in the street . . . anything. And we'll have another check round the rest of the country. I'm looking for unsolved cases . . . child abduction, or maybe children missing for a short time and found safe but no convictions. Remember the Black case? He travelled the country by van, the children he murdered were taken long distances, he picked them up at random, wherever he happened to be. Is someone else doing the same?'

'There's a lot of that sort of checking already going on, guv.'

'Then I want a whole lot more, right? What about that poster up on Parker's wall, by the way?'

'Do you believe this? He suddenly remembered he'd stuck it up there – it reminded him, he said. What can happen. Said he needed a bit of reminding.'

'You believe him?'

Nathan paused. Then said, as if to challenge Serrailler, 'Yes, guv. Funny that. But I do.'

'OK. Then so do I. Now get out of here.'

Nathan went. The DCI almost never raised his voice. When he did it was more a sign of frustration with himself than rage at anyone else but it was still best to keep out of his way. Serrailler had always struck the DS as a man who, for the most part relaxed and easygoing, had a simmering cauldron deep inside him which might one day boil over spectacularly.

'Sex,' Emma had said when he had mentioned it one time.

'I don't think he's got any.'

'Bollocks.'

'You going to tell me he needs the love of a good woman?'

'Something like that.'

Twenty-six

'I painted her fingernails, did you see? That pink polish with all glittery bits in . . . they looked ever so pretty.'

Shirley handed Rosa the umbrella while she put her keys into the lock. The wind drove rain at their backs.

'I don't know why you bother, she doesn't know. She doesn't notice anything.'

'She noticed your balloon.'

They got inside as the gale took the door and slammed it behind them.

'Get your things off and bring them into the kitchen. I'm soaked just from across there, the water's gone right over the sides of my shoes.'

In ten minutes the curtains were drawn, lights and heating on and they were huddled in the kitchen. Sometimes, at the end of the long day shift, Rosa came to have supper and sleep on Shirley's sofa bed to save the trek on the bus across town. She could have slept in one of the staffrooms in the home but it wasn't as cosy and, besides, at the end of work you wanted to get out of the building. It was odd, the bungalow was just across the grass – you could see the home from the windows – yet it felt a different world.

It was a world Rosa liked after the stuffiness and mess of her family house, full of her brother's computer kit and music decks, her grandmother's bazaar knitting, her mother's black sacks of stuff from her market stall. Shirley had been to tea once or twice and said she liked being part of a family again, but there was nowhere to talk, nowhere without the noise of a television or sound system. Here was better.

'Funny old day.'

They had a routine. Always when they came off this shift they had a breakfast, at eight thirty at night. Shirley took eggs and bacon and tomatoes out of the fridge, Rosa put on the kettle and sliced the bread. The wind shook the badly fitting metal window frames now and again and the rain lashed.

'I don't know how you can stand it here on your own with those trees moaning. I'd be scared out of my wits.'

'The Good Lord and His angels look over me. Praise be. I don't know what's to be scared of in a bit of wind.'

'Do you really think she liked the balloon?'

'Didn't you see her face? She laughed at it.'

'Poor little thing.'

'I think she had a really nice day . . . all those things, those lovely bright flowers the Chief

Inspector brought and just about all her family come to see her.'

'Poor Mrs Fox. No one came to see her for four years and now she's gone.'

'It was best, Rosa, she's with the Lord and she'd no life. There was nothing in there, just a shell. I mean, Martha's got more.'

'What do you think God made them like this for then? You always say there's a reason for everything, only look at Martha Serrailler, look at Arthur . . . what reason's God got for that?' Rosa found Shirley's robust religion by turns fascinating and repellent. She had once been to the Gospel Chapel with her and the singing and dancing and clapping had been great, really uplifting. People came from miles. Only then there was the funny stuff.

'It's not up to us to question. The Lord knows.'

'You can't say it's a punishment, can you? Not for Martha, at any rate. She's never done anything. She's never been able to.'

'Oh no. Martha's one of God's innocents. One of His chosen angels.'

'I don't get it.'

'You will one day. I pray for you every night, Rosa.'

'I don't need any praying for, thanks.'

'Of course you do. We all of us do. Praise the Lord.'

Shirley slipped eggs and bacon neatly on to their two plates as Rosa buttered the toast. The wind almost broke the pane in one roaring gust. The lights flickered.

'That's all we'd need, a power cut in this.'

'I am the Light of the World,' Shirley said, and began to pour out the tea.

Across the wet grass, past the wildly flailing trees, the lights shone from the back of Ivy Lodge. In the end there was no power cut.

Hester Beesley took the drinks trolley round and filled spouted plastic beakers with lukewarm Ovaltine. Those patients who had medication were seen to last by the nursing staff.

Absent-mindedly, Hester pushed open the door of Room 6 and for a moment was puzzled that it was in darkness and felt cold. She clicked the light on. The bed had been stripped. The radiator was turned off. The wardrobe door was hanging open. It didn't take long, she thought, backing out again. Mrs Fox had only been dead half a day and her room had lost all trace of her. She might never have existed.

Mr Pilgrim existed, though, sitting motionless and silent apart from the trembling of his hands and the line of dribble that went from his chin down on to his bib. When she had seen to him, she went in to Martha, whose room was bright with flowers and cards, a new soft toy and the balloon still tied to the corner of her bed.

'Don't settle her down yet,' Sister Aileen said, putting her head round the door. 'Someone else is coming in to see her – there was a message on the pad from the doctor.'

'I'll freshen her up then. Oh look, someone's painted your fingernails, lovey, I bet that was Shirley. Do you like it? You're a pretty girl.'

Aileen Whetton made a face at the baby talk but it was Hester's way and how was Martha to know the difference?

Animals left the runt of their litter out in the cold to die. People used to do the same. Now there was everything to bring them back every time they were ready to go through the door. No one would let them just slip away.

But at least Martha's family did more than write cheques.

Aileen unlocked the drugs trolley and counted out Lady Fison's sleeping tablets into the plastic cup. To get her to take them could be a fifteen-minute job. She opened the door. The old, bald woman sat up in bed, staring into space, while her radio played Irish dance music. Lady Fison's radio played some music or other from morning till night. If it went off, she cried; if it stayed off, she screamed.

'Here we are,' Aileen said, rattling the capsules in the little transparent cup.

Down the corridor, Hester was sponging Martha Serrailler's face and retying her ribbon.

'Make you look lovely for the ball, Your Royal Highness.'

214

On a whim, she took one of the bright red flowers out of the bouquet on the table and pinned it in the girl's soft, blonde hair.

'You're my beauty,' she said. 'Who's my beauty?'

Martha did not move.

In the bungalow, the parrot Elvis made his train noise quite suddenly, making Rosa start in her chair. They were playing Racing Demon.

'Bugger off.'

'Elvis, I'll put your cloth on. I won't have swearing.'

'God save the Queen.'

'Yes, that's better. We love Her Majesty, don't we?'

'Did you see that picture of Prince William in the *Mail*? Image of his mother, the way he looks down all shy, you know.'

'I like William.'

'Well, I like Charles. He does such a lot of good things you never hear about . . . all that stuff with young people, and trying to stop them putting up too many of those skyscrapers.'

'Sod me, sod me, sod me.'

'Right, that's it, I warned you.'

Shirley picked up the red velour cover and dropped it on to the parrot cage.

'Never surrender,' Elvis said before descending into silence and the dark.

They stayed up until eleven, watching television, talking about royalty, playing cards. At ten, Shirley had brought out the bottle of Harvey's Bristol Cream for their usual glass.

'I always thought chapel people were teetotal,' Rosa said.

'That's Methodist chapel . . . English . . . that's nothing to do with us.'

'Oh.'

'Wine that gladdens the heart of man.' Shirley held her glass up.

'Cheers.'

'Oh good, it's Huw Edwards,' Rosa said as the news came on.

The wind blew more strongly, lashing the trees. One or two cars came up the drive, rain streaming sideways in the headlights. One or two of the residents had visitors. There were no rules, people could come and go as they wished. It made the place more like a home than a 'home', Matron Scudder said.

The corridors were quiet. Some slept. The drinks were finished, the drugs given out. Lamps were still on beside beds here and there but the lounge and the conservatory were empty, the chairs set back against the walls ready for the morning cleaners.

In the hall, the bright fish swam soothingly in their neon tank among the little trees of vivid weed.

Shirley and Rosa were in bed by ten past eleven, asleep not much later. They were on early shift, which was how the rota worked. Both would finish at two the following afternoon and then have thirty-six hours off.

The last visitor's car drove away. The lights began to go out.

The storm worsened.

Twenty-seven

Tuesday morning and an overcast sky. Rain threatening. In Sorrel Drive a police van and two cars arrived at seven, a few yards from the house of Alan and Marilyn Angus. In a blue Ford Focus behind them, Hugo Pears, ashen-faced and anxious, sitting between his parents.

'I hate 'em, reconstructions,' DS Nathan Coates said through a mouthful of crisps. 'They spook everyone. Poor kid.' He nodded towards the Pearses' car.

'Yeah, well, but if it turns up something –'

'Won't.'

'How can you know? What's up with you?'

Nathan scrunched the crisp packet. 'It's got to me, this one . . . he's in my head, know what I mean? All day he's there . . . it feels bad.'

He had told Emma as much the previous night. 'He's dead.'

'You don't know that.'

'I do though. So do you. Don't you?'

Emma had not replied.

'In my head,' he said again, and got out of the car into the dark avenue as the DCI pulled up just ahead of them.

'Guv.'

'Morning, Nathan.' They stood together for a moment, looking towards the Anguses' house, set behind its hedge. The lights were on upstairs.

'Poor sods.'

Serrailler shook his head. 'There's got to be something,' he said, half to himself, 'there has to be. Something . . . or someone . . . It's going on too long.'

'Anything come in overnight?'

Serrailler barely shook his head, turned his collar up against the drizzle which had begun, and walked away towards the house.

It's got to him too, Nathan thought. It's in his head.

A car slowed down on seeing them and slid slowly past, the driver staring, but as Nathan made a move, picked up speed and shot away.

Nathan got back in beside DC Martin. 'You get his number?'

David Martin gestured to his notebook.

'Bloody voyeurs.'

The drizzle greased the car windows. It was still dark.

In the bungalow, Shirley Sapcote scalded her mouth with tea. Rosa was repinning her hair which was slippery and all over the place. The parrot Elvis was silent, the cloth still over its cage.

'Like the middle of the flaming night,' Shirley put a dribble of cold water in her tea mug.

'Roll on summer.'

'You want toast?'

'No thanks.' Rosa came into the kitchen. She went to the window and twitched the corner of the curtain.

'Black as pitch. Raining. Days like this you feel like pulling the blanket over your head.'

Shirley pulled the cloth off Elvis's cage.

'Bugger me,' the parrot said, bouncing on and off its perch. 'Bugger me. Bugger me.'

They crossed the grass, arm in arm, through the dark drizzle towards Ivy Lodge.

'Things can only get better,' Rosa said.

Shirley put her foot into a puddle of muddy water by the back step, which sent them first into giggles and then into gasping laughter so that they had to stand just inside the door struggling for breath.

Outside, the drizzle turned to heavy rain.

It was not yet light when Shirley carried the tray into Martha Serrailler's room, so she did not draw the curtains back, but switched on the bedside lamp and set down the tray.

'You're in the best place there, my darling, it's horrible outside and I stepped up to my ankles in a puddle and you should have heard that parrot swear fit to make you blush . . . you've never heard words like it in your life . . . well, you haven't, have you, sweetheart? Wake up.'

'I knew,' she said afterwards, 'straight away. It wasn't that she looked different, she looked just the same, only there was that . . . that silence in the room, that stillness, you know? Everything's changed. I looked at her and her face was the same . . . only it wasn't. It just wasn't. God bless her. God love her spotless soul.'

But she had cried then, sitting in the staff kitchen with Rosa holding her hand, the tears had run down her arms to her elbows. In a house where death was so often at hand, and dealing with death merely part of a working day, that of Martha Serrailler distressed them all.

'It wasn't raining,' Marilyn Angus said over and over again. 'It wasn't raining. How can they do this if everything is so different? I would never have left David outside in the rain.' She was right, Serrailler knew. She did not want the reconstruction to go ahead because she couldn't face it and that was a normal reaction . . . but rain made things look different, made people who would have walked that other morning take their cars and those who still went on foot hurry, looking down. And David Angus would not have been on his own in the rain at the gate.

'You have to call it off, don't you?'

He could hardly bear to look into her haggard face. Her hair was unwashed and roughly combed back and she wore no make-up. Marilyn Angus had aged twenty years.

'No,' he said gently. 'We'll do it. Everything's in place and the rain is easing . . . and I don't know if Hugo could manage it twice.'

The boy Hugo Pears stood with his parents near one of the police vans. If he had fantasies of acting in films about the Roman Army, his real-life role in such a police reconstruction had made him so anxious they had been uncertain if he would take part after all. In the end a lot of encouragement and a pep talk about how much good he would do had got him as far as the doorway of the Anguses' house, where he was now, huddled against his mother, stricken-faced.

Marilyn had on the jacket and pashmina she had been wearing the morning of David's disappearance, carried the same bag and briefcase. But she would have looked smart, the DCI knew, made up, hair freshly washed.

There was no way he could tell her. He opened the front door. They were running.

Somehow they got through it. Somehow, Marilyn dredged up the courage to lead the small boy, who looked so extraordinarily like her son, out of the house and towards her car which was parked in the drive. The rain began to teem down. Simon Serrailler cursed, watching from the opposite side of the road as cars sloshed past, and a couple of neighbours valiantly followed their own routines exactly as they had then.

Somehow.

His phone rang as Marilyn's car turned out on to Sorrel Drive. Hugo Pears was walking slowly towards the gate.

He spoke into the phone. 'Serrailler.'

For a second or two he could not take in what his brother-in-law was saying. His eyes were on the small white-faced boy with a school bag and cap, now standing by the gatepost of the house opposite. A man rode past on a bicycle, head down against the rain. Had he been there? Had he ridden by in that way at precisely that moment? Simon turned round to look at him as he pedalled away.

Chris's voice sounded odd coming out of his mobile.

'Si?'

'Yes.'

'Can you hear me?'

'I'm in Sorrel Drive – we're in the middle of the David Angus last-known movements mock-up.'

'Jesus.'

'Is it Cat?'

'No,' Chris said gently. 'Not Cat . . .'

Simon Serrailler listened and when his brother-in-law had finished, said, 'Right. Thanks,' and then disconnected.

He stared at the mobile in his hand. Hugo Pears was still waiting. Just waiting. Soaked to the skin.

Nathan Coates waved from the police car a few yards away.

The DCI looked at his phone again. Then pressed his sergeant's number.

'OK, let's call it,' he said calmly to Nathan. 'Tell the parents to come down to the boy. And get Mrs Angus back home.' The rain was running off his hair into his eyes and his jacket was sodden.

Nathan Coates came running down the road towards him, slipped and almost fell on some wet leaves. He was calling out something, talking about how it had gone, what they had noticed, but as he got closer to Serrailler his words petered off.

'Guv?'

Simon stared at him.

'You OK?'

'Yes.' He stared down at his mobile again, as if it would ring and he would listen to Chris Deerbon telling him there had been a mistake. 'My sister's dead.'

Twenty-eight

Dr Derek Wix, GP to Ivy House, sat in the staff-room drinking tea and eating the bacon sandwich they had brought to him. He had revised the dosage of Mr Parmiter's tablets, given an antibiotic for Miss Lemmen's ear infection, and signed the death certificate for Martha Serrailler.

'You checking up on me?' he mumbled through a mouthful of bread as Chris Deerbon walked in.

'Don't be ridiculous.'

Derek Wix was a good doctor and a morose and curt man. His patients seemed to like him. Chris and Cat had often wondered why.

'Your sister-in-law . . . it wasn't the chest infection as such.'

'Heart?'

Wix nodded, slurping tea. 'You want to see her?'

'I'll go in of course. But you're the GP – whatever you say, Derek.'

Derek Wix stood. 'Staff seem cut up.'

'They loved her. They looked after her so well.'

'Best thing though.'

'Of course . . . just don't say that in front of anyone else.'

'Richard will agree. Always told me she shouldn't be here.'

Chris had no doubt that his father-in-law would have said just that many times. 'Still . . . point is, if someone loves them, they're –'

'Point is, to get them before they start barking. Give them nothing, no affection, no attention . . . what are you left with? Sarah's working in an orphanage in Thailand, did I tell you? No one loves those poor little sods. Never have. They turn into animals.'

He stalked out.

Chris had to remind himself that Derek Wix had a charming wife and three daughters, including Sarah, who had qualified as a doctor the previous summer and gone straight out to work in the Far East.

Shirley Sapcote came down the corridor as Chris went towards Martha's room. Her eyes were red.

'God rest her beautiful soul, she's an angel with the angels. She never did a wrong thing or said a bad word in her life, Dr Deerbon, and how many can you say that about? Newborn babies, that's all, and that's what she was. Innocent as that.'

'You're right. I know how fond you were of her and how well you've looked after her. We all do.'

Shirley followed him into the room. 'As soon as I looked at her I knew. I didn't have to touch her. You know how it is, Doctor.'

'I do.'

'She seemed OK yesterday, happy, you know . . .
I knew when she was happy. Everybody saw her,
except Dr Cat of course . . . How is she, Dr
Deerbon?'

'Tired of waiting . . . and now upset about this of
course.'

'Yes . . . but I tell you what, it'll be the Inspector
who takes it hardest. It was ever so touching, seeing
him with her, hearing him talk to her. He'll be the
one.'

Chris stood beside Martha's bed. Death, as ever,
flattered to deceive. Apart from the deep stillness
she might have been sleeping. But death had no
work to do here in smoothing out the lines of age
and trouble, for Martha had had none. Her skin
was a baby's, her hair fine-spun, her expression
bland and smooth and, as Shirley had said, entirely
innocent – innocent of experience, of knowledge, of
wrongdoing, of emotion – of life.

Cat Deerbon had seen Sam and Hannah into Philippa
Granger's car – the Grangers were their nearest
neighbours and Philippa had cheerfully taken on the
school run for the last few weeks. She had cleared the
breakfast things from the table, wiped it, loaded the
dishwasher and got out a tin of food for Mephisto.
As she bent down to put his dish on the floor, water
flooded down her legs and made a pool on the tiles.
Cat gave a sigh of relief and pulled the telephone
towards her across the work surface.

'Hi, babe.'

'Chris, you need to ring Carol Standish.'

Carol was the locum who had replaced Cat for her maternity leave. She was new to Lafferton, seemed efficient, pleasant but slightly cold. They were lucky to get her, locums were becoming hard to find.

'She's not in this morning.'

'She will be now. I'm in labour.'

David

Where are we going?

I don't want to go in that car again. I just want to go home now please.

Is this a game? Or a dare?

That's OK but can it finish now and say you won it?

Don't pull my arm, it hurts where you pulled it before, it really, really hurts . . . don't pull it.

I don't want to go in that car but I will, I will go in it, please don't pull my arm.

It's dark.

It's always dark.

I haven't seen the daylight for a long time. Not since . . .

Why do we go everywhere in the dark?

I'm very tired of going to different places.

Why are we always going somewhere else?

I think it's a long way from home now.

I don't like that.

I wish you would stop.

Please stop.

Twenty-nine

The DCI looked round the room. He could see it in their faces. Exhaustion. Disappointment. Flickers of stubborn determination. But no hope. They expected the worst now. It was only a question of when.

'OK, the reconstruction this morning wasn't worth much . . . the rain altered the scenario of course but it wasn't only that . . . no one came forward saying they'd seen anything because no one did see anything . . . simple. We put the boy and Mrs Angus through it for nothing.'

'Guv, a minute ago there was a call in from a cyclist . . . said he went past this morning without knowing about the recon, but he just heard about it at work.'

Serrailler remembered him, flashing past on a mountain bike, head down against the rain. 'Is he coming in?'

'In about an hour . . . he can't get off work sooner. He remembers seeing the boy at the gate that morning.'

A couple of people in the room punched the air.

'Anything else?'

'Not so far.'

'Thanks, everyone. I know how frustrating this is but we can't let up.'

'Guv? What do we really think here?'

'I'm not concerned with the thinking, it's doing. We redouble our efforts to find him, Jenny. We have no other option.'

Serrailler walked out of the room, leaving the usual subdued buzz as the relief broke up.

'He knows he's dead,' Jenny Humble said, 'why the hell doesn't he just come out with it?'

Nathan Coates turned on her. 'If he is, ain't we still got to find him? Think of them parents. The worst is not knowing and never finding, you ask anyone out there who's had someone go missing, they'll tell you.'

'My dad spent a week doing nothing but look for our dog. He's never given up really, still thinks it'll come back.'

'Right. The worst is not knowing.'

The room emptied and the door banged shut.

Simon Serrailler stood at his office window looking down on to the car park. It was gone noon and still only half light. He felt as if he had lived through a century since getting up that morning.

His telephone rang.

'Chief Constable for you, sir.'

Here we go, he thought wearily . . . Why no progress? . . . What exactly are you . . .

231

'Simon?'

'Good morning, ma'am.'

Paula Devenish was one of few women chief constables, in her late forties and a police officer since she was twenty, with a QPM and a medal for bravery. She had arrived eighteen months ago and turned the county police around, the crime stats around, morale around. She was efficient, energetic, frighteningly knowledgeable about all aspects of policing, and hands-on. She was also approachable and sympathetic. Simon respected her a great deal.

'How is everybody bearing up? I know what these cases are like when days go by and there's nothing . . . everyone feels frustrated.'

'That's just what they are . . . determined and frustrated. We're as much in the dark as we were.'

'I'm planning to come into the station on Friday, but will you put the word about that I'm on side? I don't want them feeling got at when they're already under so much pressure.'

'Thank you, ma'am, I will. They'll appreciate it. The team needs a boost.'

'Finding the boy will do that, but I'll try my best. Now, what about you? Are you taking the day off?'

'Ma'am?'

'I've just heard about your sister.'

It was one of the things that gave the CC such a formidable edge – knowing everything almost before it happened, including personal matters like this.

'Take a couple of days' leave . . . you'll be at the end of the phone if you're needed.'

The rain had cleared for the moment but the sky was heavy with iron grey, scudding clouds. Car lights were on. A woman towing a child took a chance and darted across the road in front of him. Simon cursed and banged the flat of his hand on the hooter, startling her and making the child cry.

He eased his foot off the accelerator.

Martha was in his head. He knew that what had happened, the quiet death in her sleep, was the right end to her hopeless life . . . for it had been hopeless, he would not lie to himself. He was not sorry for her, he was sorry for himself. The closeness he had felt to her had been severed abruptly, his feelings left in limbo. There was no one now towards whom they could be directed. Her death left an uneasy, unhappy hollow within him.

His mother was in the kitchen, standing in front of the range waiting for the kettle to boil and to his surprise she was in her maroon dressing gown, her hair down as she never let anyone see it.

She turned as Simon went in, and he put his arms round her. Without make-up and smart clothes she looked older – gentler too. The polished surface she always presented to the world often seemed to him as hard as varnish, but this was the real woman, holding tightly to him for a moment and then stepping back as the kettle began to sing.

233

'I went to see her. Then I'm afraid I came home and went back to bed. I needed to blot things out for a while.'

He had never known her do such a thing in her life before. He wondered how his father was dealing with Martha's death, which he had so long and loudly anticipated.

'I'm not crying,' Meriel Serrailler said, 'I cried all the tears I had for her years ago. Do you understand that?'

'Yes. It's a shock though. She was fine yesterday – or seemed fine.'

'Well, but that was always the way. She couldn't tell you how she was.'

His mother filled a cafetière and set it in front of him.

'I'll go into Ivy Lodge,' Simon reached for the milk jug. 'I'm taking the rest of the day off.'

'I'm surprised they can spare you.'

'The Angus case? We've nothing.'

'Oh darling, what a host of black clouds gathered overhead. I can't see my way through them to the light.'

'Not like you.'

'I don't feel like me. I feel as if I've lost what I thought was a burden, only to find that it wasn't one after all . . . well, whenever you carry your own child, in whatever sense, it isn't a burden, is it? But I didn't understand that until this morning . . . about her. About the rest of you, yes, but it was always . . . so complicated with Martha.'

She stared down into her cup. Her skin was meshed with the finest wrinkles. But she was still beautiful, Simon thought, her high, prominent cheekbones, and elegant straight nose – beautiful, austere, slightly forbidding. And now, having to come to terms not only with the death of her youngest child, but with an uprush of strange and unanticipated emotion, for the first time vulnerable.

'Where's Father?'

'Undertaker . . . all of that.'

'Inquest?'

'No . . . why would there be?'

'I suppose not.'

'Richard doesn't want any fuss . . . just the crematorium service. The ashes will be buried in the cloister garden later and there'll just be a small stone.'

'And what do you want?'

'Oh darling, I'll leave it to him, he needs to deal with it – it's what he's best at.'

'Why can't she have a proper service? Isn't that what you'd do for the rest of us? Why is Martha any different? We could have a small family funeral in the cathedral – one of the side chapels.'

'Simon, I can't cope with a battle. Leave it.'

'I'll organise it. Let me argue with Father.'

'Please. Don't. Besides, what difference would it make?'

Simon emptied the cafetière into his mug. 'It would make a lot of difference to me.'

His mother sat very straight and upright in her chair, not looking at him. It had always been like this with her, he thought, always leaving things, letting things go, not stirring anything up, placating his father, humouring his father, keeping things quiet. It was the way she had survived a long and unhappy marriage to a bully – that and by separating herself from him in her work and, after retirement, in all her committees and trusts.

He did not want Martha to have a bleak cremation, over in ten minutes, the whole thing shoved out of the way as if they were ashamed, and he knew that Cat, the only firm believer and regular churchgoer in the family, would side with him. But Cat was in no state at the moment to join him in a fight with their father and Simon wondered if he had the heart and strength to go it alone if it was going to upset his mother so much.

'Her room looked so bright,' Meriel said now, 'the red balloon and your flowers.'

'Shirley had painted her fingernails pink and tied that ribbon in her hair. She loved her.'

His mother looked across at him, her eyes distant. 'How strange,' she said slowly. 'How strange that was.'

She looked up sharply as Richard Serrailler's car stopped outside.

'It's OK,' Simon said, putting his hand out and covering hers across the table.

His father came briskly into the kitchen. 'That's done.'

Meriel got up to make fresh coffee.

The morning's post was in a pile on the table and Richard Serrailler picked off the top letter, read for a few seconds, then looked up at Simon.

'Why aren't you out catching criminals?' he said with a small smile.

Thirty

'If the phone hadn't rung at that moment, and it hadn't been Chris with the news, I honestly think I might have punched him in the face.'

'How very suitable for a DCI,' Cat said, speaking to Simon, but looking down at her infant son.

The light from the bedside lamp shone in a soft circle on the two of them as they lay together in the high hospital bed.

It was just after six in the evening. Simon sat beside her looking at the charmed circle. 'Damn, I wish I'd brought my sketch pad. It's perfect.'

Cat smiled. 'Plenty of other times . . . we're not going anywhere.'

'Sam and Hannah been in?'

'Of course. Sam made his aeroplane take-off noise the whole time and Hannah was pink with pleasure.'

'So am I.'

When Chris had phoned, seconds after Richard Serrailler's cynical remark about catching criminals, Simon had felt a lift of the heart which made him realise how low he had been.

'What did Mother say?'

'The inevitable . . . the one about heaviness lasting a night . . .'

'. . . but joy cometh in the morning . . . Well, someone had to.'

'Odd how it's so often true though . . . a death and then a new life.'

'Every day,' Cat rubbed her son's back gently, before putting him to the other breast, 'every, every day.'

'Has he a name?'

'He has two. Felix Daniel.'

Simon watched his new nephew snuggle into the breast, his mouth working, eyes tightly closed and a wave of emotion came roaring up through him. There was no one else in the world before whom he could have wept openly as he did now.

Cat reached out her hand to him. She thought when he had gone that tears might overcome her too, but Simon had pent-up emotion which had been simmering since Freya's murder. Martha's death and now this new birth had released it and she was glad. But she said nothing, merely kept her hand on his. Now was not the time for a doctor's pious words.

After a few moments, he got up and went into her bathroom. She heard the taps running. Felix nuzzled more deeply into her breast and his fingers curled in bliss.

The door opened on Chris as Simon emerged, his fair hair wet, his face slightly flushed.

239

'OK, I'm off . . . I think I'm going to sleep the clock round.'

Simon bent and kissed his sister and cupped his hand round Felix's damp, warm head. 'Good,' he said, and left, touching Chris briefly on the arm as he went out.

In the corridor, he stood to blow his nose, and wipe his arm over his eyes again. His hand was shaking.

Thirty-one

'Remember, you're a policewoman not a friend. You're on our side not theirs. You don't go native on us.'

The reminder from the DCI had been necessary at times like this, when Kate had to keep out of the way and be tactful and unobtrusive, yet to see and hear and pass on everything she heard of the row between the Anguses. An FLO was just that – a liaison between the family and the police, not a counsellor nor a shoulder to cry on, not a family friend. It was a thin tightrope on which to balance and Kate had already caught herself siding with Marilyn.

They had been in the kitchen making a cottage pie, Kate peeling potatoes, Marilyn browning the mince, when the front door had slammed. It was not much after six and Alan Angus had not been home earlier than eight since Kate had been here.

Marilyn had looked at her in alarm and gone quickly through to the hall, leaving Kate to pull the meat off the gas ring.

'What's happened?' she heard Marilyn say urgently. 'What's wrong?'

'What do you mean? Nothing's wrong.'

'Have they rung you? Have you heard something?'

'No. You're the one with the police here, you'll be the one to hear anything.'

'Then why are you early? You're never this early.'

'Just a cancelled operation . . . it does happen.'

'It never happens.'

'Death happens and this patient died. All right?'

'Alan, I have to talk to you . . . it's very hard to do that.'

'Why ever should it be?'

'You're never here.'

'I'm here now.'

'You've cut yourself off from me . . . and from Lucy. She notices.'

'What good would it do for me to stay in the house all day? Would it help find him? Would it help you or Lucy? Not to mention my patients?'

'Oh yes, your patients.'

'If you can convince me I'd be better hanging about here with you all day instead of doing my job I'll happily stay.'

The voices retreated as Alan Angus headed for the stairs and his wife followed.

Kate finished peeling the potatoes, cut them up and put them in a pan of water, then looked around for a carrot. As she did so her phone rang.

'DC Marshall.'

'Hi Kate, it's Nathan.'

'Something happened?'

'Not much . . . only something came up as a result of the recon. Bloke phoned this morning. He's just been in. He's a cyclist. Says at first nothing clicked, only when he got to work he remembered.'

'What?'

'Remembered that he saw David Angus standing at the gate . . . his school bag was on the ground . . . he was looking up the road . . . round about ten past eight.'

'And?'

'And that's it.'

'Oh.'

'So eyewitness . . . he was definitely there.'

'Well, we knew that already . . .'

'Mightn't have . . . might have been a wind-up.'

'How?'

'Dad might have come back. Said he was taking him after all.'

'Oh come on. Anyway, forensics have been all over the dad's car – always do. You know as well as I do – suspect the parents first, so try and pin it on them first. Well, they couldn't. Did the cyclist see anything else?'

'Nope. Sorry.'

'OK. Thanks, Nathan.'

Kate found a sharp knife and an onion and began to slice it, with the cold tap running the way her mother had always done, and which wasn't a damn bit of use for stopping your eyes watering.

So now she had to tell the Anguses that there was news, but no news . . . nothing they didn't already have. If only the man on the bike had been a minute or two later, he might . . . But you couldn't think like that. Deal in facts, she'd learned over and over again, never speculation. Never dash hopes but never build them up either. Stick to what you know, don't indulge in fantasies, don't get involved in theirs . . .

From upstairs she heard their voices, raised and angry. The slam of a wardrobe door. One single shout of anguish.

She went out of the kitchen as Marilyn was coming down, hands to her head, her face contorted with tears and rage.

'Don't say it's all right, because it's not . . . it's never going to be all right again. What's happened? You've heard something . . .'

Kate led her into the kitchen.

All over Lafferton David Angus's face looked out from posters, in shop windows, and the windows of houses, on noticeboards, in pubs and clubs, the library, the sports centre, the swimming pool. But not only over Lafferton; now, the poster had been taken up countrywide. David Angus, the nine-year-old schoolboy with an earnest face and protruding ears, saw, if he could have seen, mothers pull their own children closer to them and schoolteachers watch anxiously at school gates and in playgrounds; heard, if he could have heard, what everyone said about 'that poor child', 'those poor parents'; and worse, heard the words 'dead' and 'murdered' and, most frequently of all, the word 'hopeless'.

As Simon Serrailler walked down the blue carpet towards the exit doors of the maternity wing at Bevham General, David Angus's eyes followed him from the noticeboards. He realised that the extreme tiredness he felt was partly the result of hunger. There was precious little in his larder and the last thing he felt like was eating out, even in a pub, but the sight of the Sprat and Mackerel Fish Shop on the corner of March Street was cheering.

He bought freshly cooked haddock and extra chips, had them double-wrapped and sped down the road towards home.

The sound of the silence as he opened the front door had never been more welcome. He closed the wooden shutters against the wet night, switched on the lamps, and put his supper in the warming oven, before pouring himself a large glass of Laphroaig. He was not a big drinker, especially when at home alone, so that what he had now would be plenty to relax him and take the edge off his tiredness and the chill in his bones which he knew was more emotional than physical.

He would eat and drink, make coffee and read – not the new biography of Stalin which he had bought the previous day; glass in hand, he browsed along his bookshelves. *The Diary of a Nobody*. *Three Men in a Boat* . . . but he knew he did not want to laugh and in the end took down a

Hornblower novel he had not reread for some years.

Before eating, he rang in to the station.

'Is Nathan still there?'

'Just gone, sir.'

'Anything happened?'

'Afraid not . . . most people have called it a day . . . they're all a bit dispirited.'

'I know. Everyone needs a good night's sleep.'

Except the people who most need it, he thought, putting down the phone, the Anguses. The FLO had told him Marilyn Angus only slept when she took one of the tablets Chris had prescribed for her but that she hated doing so, in case there was news and she needed to be alert.

And David? Was he sleeping? Or dead?

Some lines danced through Simon's head.

From the kitchen came the smell of warming paper. He opened the oven door and was about to take out the plate and the package of fish and chips when his doorbell rang. He remembered Chris saying that he might call round on his way home, and went to the intercom.

'Hi, Chris, come on up.'

He went to meet his brother-in-law at the flat door.

'Hi . . .'

But it was not Chris Deerbon who came up the last flight of stairs towards him.

'Hello, Simon. I took advantage . . . I realise it wasn't me you were expecting.'

The last person, Simon thought, the last person in the world.

'Diana.'

He stood in the doorway looking at her and she was a total stranger, this tall, red-headed, slim woman, smart, scented, well-made-up. He did not know her. Had he ever known her? Yes, in another life, when he had been another person.

'What are you doing here?'

He did not want to let her in. The flat, his sacred space, was forbidden to her. She had never been inside it. They had never met in Lafferton at all.

'You're hard to track down.'

He did not reply.

'Do I take it you would rather I turned round?'

'I'm sorry . . . of course not.' He held the door open.

'If it isn't convenient . . .'

Sod it, no, it is not 'convenient' – your coming here will never be 'convenient'.

'Can I get you a drink?'

'That depends.'

'Sorry?'

'I do have the car. So it depends on how long I stay as to whether I have a drink – or not.'

'I was about to put some coffee on. Sit down. Just give me a moment.'

Simon went into his immaculate galley kitchen, closed the door and leaned back against it. Damn. Damn and blast.

He filled the coffee percolator with water and pulled the overhead cupboard open too hard. The packet of fish and chips was on the plate in front of him, cooling. He ripped it open and stuffed a handful of chips and a lump of fish and batter into his mouth. He was starving. Anger that Diana should have come here made a knot in the middle of his chest. He had met her abroad, and for a few years they had had a loose relationship uncomplicated, for him at least, by much emotion. They went to a play or a film, and often out to dinner. Afterwards, they usually went to bed, at Simon's hotel or Diana's mews house. She had always asked him to stay there with her. He never would. He enjoyed her company . . . she was attractive, intelligent, informed; ten years older than him and a widow; hands-on owner of a highly successful chain of brasseries.

And that was it. Or rather, that was that.

Diana had telephoned him a couple of times the previous year, once shortly after Freya Graffham's murder, once a few weeks later but had had to leave messages on his answerphone. He had not returned them. He had assumed she would have understood what his silence meant, and until now she had barely entered his mind.

There was no uncertainty about what he was going to do when she had finished her coffee. He took up the tray and opened the door.

She was wearing a cream knitted suit and emerald earrings, expensive shoes and she had her back to him as she studied one of his drawings on the wall.

'I'm sorry, I don't have any biscuits . . . empty larder.'

She turned and looked at him coolly. 'That's fine, Simon. Just coffee will see me on my way.'

He did not respond, only bent to the cups.

'Are you involved with this missing schoolboy case?'

'I'm heading it up.'

'Oh God. Any news of him?'

'No. Do you take sugar?'

'Don't you remember?'

No, actually, and if I did, I would not own to it, those are the personal details I do not want in my head.

'I'm sorry.'

'No, I don't. I like that drawing.'

She nodded towards the portrait of his mother which he had done earlier in the year and put up to see if he thought well enough of it to have in his next exhibition.

'Thank you.'

'Your mother?'

That is nothing to do with you. My family is not your concern, that is a part of my life in which you will never belong.

He remembered how quickly Freya had become friends with both his mother and with Cat. Diana held her coffee cup and looked at him. Simon had taken a chair some distance from hers.

249

'All right, Simon, might I be told what happened between us? I called you a couple of times – you weren't here, but you didn't respond. Either time.'

He couldn't answer.

'I don't think we parted on bad terms, did we? I've tried to remember . . .'

'No, of course we didn't.'

'So . . .'

He hesitated, about to make excuses, to blame work . . . then recovered himself. That was unfair. Diana deserved the truth, or a version of it. And once he had told it and things were clear, then she would go, and there would be no possibility of a misunderstanding.

'I had a fairly traumatic year . . . someone I was becoming close to died. I'm not sure what would have happened between us. And then of course nothing could. But it wouldn't have been fair to you for me to come to London and . . . seeing you isn't something I feel I want to do now.'

'By "now" do you mean "yet"?'

He saw a look on her face, in spite of her effort to remain aloof, a look of hunger or need which he recognised and which made him want to open the shutters and the window and throw himself out to get away from it.

'No,' he said.

'Ah. You mean "at all".'

He was silent. Diana stirred her coffee and sipped it. He saw that her hand trembled.

250

'I have hated this year,' she said, 'I've missed you. Your visits. Going out with you. Going to bed with you. I've been busy as hell. I hardly seem to have been off the road between the restaurants.'

'Are they doing well?'

'Oh yes, they're doing well and making me rich. It doesn't mean much. It stops me from thinking, that's all.'

'Rubbish. You love your empire.'

'I'd give it up tomorrow . . .'

Simon got up. 'I have to ring in to the station,' he said.

'Please have the decency not to lie to me, Simon. If you were needed, you would be called. Wouldn't you? If you are waiting for me to leave, say so.'

'No . . . finish your coffee, of course you must.'

Diana stood up and looked slowly round his room.

'I longed to come here,' she said quietly. 'I longed to see where you live. I imagined it. I longed to be in this room – this flat – with you. It's perfect.'

He stood in silence.

Go. Go, please, go now. This is my room. I hate people coming here, I don't want this. I don't want to know anything of your feelings, your hurt, you.

Please.

'I don't want to leave. There now, I've no pride left, have I? Don't make me go.'

The silence in the room was like the seconds before some terrible explosion or act of violence, electric as a high-voltage wire.

But it was a silence and it was not broken by any blast.

Diana took up her coat and put it on quickly before he could move to make the polite gesture of helping with it, picked up her bag, and walked out of the room. She did not speak to him either there or at the door, but went down the stairs without looking back. After a moment he heard a car start, turn on the gravel far below, and roar away.

The room settled back, as if dust had been disturbed and was falling quietly again, to lie invisibly over the chairs in which they had sat, the tray of coffee things, the picture she had looked at.

Simon closed his eyes. He could smell her scent though he had no idea what it was. He had never bought her anything so personal, just taken flowers or a bottle of wine.

Relief warmed him. He went across to the cupboard and poured himself a second whisky. His supper would be inedible and he had nothing else to eat in the flat. But in any case, his appetite was gone.

Thirty-two

'Who the hell's sending you a parcel?' Michelle threw the brown box at him as he came into the room.

Andy took it and turned it over twice. His name was on a printed label, with the correct address. 'CIM-communications.com' was the name of the sender.

'I 'ope it ent a bleedin' bomb.'

'Don't be stupid.'

'Well, what is it then?'

'How do I know?'

'You expectin' anything?'

He wasn't. Michelle watched him closely. 'Open it, why don't you?'

'I'm going out.'

In the front room *Coronation Street* was just ending.

'I hate that bloody tune . . . waaw waaw waaw . . .' Michelle bounced out of the kitchen. Three seconds later, the tune changed to gunfire.

Andy grabbed the brown box and went out before she could come after him, demanding to know more.

The only place he could take it was the Ox, and that was packed for a darts final, but he found a seat by the door to the lavatories, got a half-pint and looked at the parcel and the people around him. But those who were not round the darts board were in front of the television watching Chelsea go one up on Arsenal.

He ripped the box open with the edge of his front door key. A new mobile phone nestled among the wrappings. He took it carefully out and weighed it in his hand. It was very small and very light. Silver. 'Cool,' his nephew would have said.

Andy knew where it had come from and it felt like a ticking bomb in his hand.

He drank slowly from his glass. The box contained a charger, instruction booklet, guarantee. Nothing more.

A roar of approval went up from the darts watchers.

He didn't dare start to fiddle with the keypad or try to find out how it worked. He didn't want it near him. Having it meant a commitment to Lee Carter and his job and for days Andy had been having second and third thoughts about that.

He thought back to prison. He had a glimmer of understanding why people sent themselves back there. Not that he would, not ever. But the world was difficult. Freedom was difficult. Nothing was as he'd expected it to be, everything, once the novelty of being out had worn off, was either a shock or a disappointment. He felt aimless and frustrated. He wanted to get on with something . . . life, he supposed. Was this life? Hanging about the Dulcie, spending hours making half a pint of cheap beer last in places like this, sleeping crammed in with his nephew whose trainers smelled?

He rewrapped the mobile phone, finished his beer and looked across to the darts board. Boring. Andy had played them all in prison. Darts, ping-pong, pool . . . and darts took the prize for being the most deadly boring of them all.

The arrows flew, and hit the right segments of cork, thwack, thwack, thwack. Another cheer.

Andy went out into the drizzle, the package tucked away inside his jacket.

Nothing happened for two days. When he had an hour alone in the house he read the instruction booklet through and set the phone on to charge, hiding it under his camp bed. No one would look there. Michelle never seemed to tidy in here, just made the beds every so often, and opened the window for a bit.

A lot had happened in his time away and mobile phones were one of them. Then they had been mainly fixed inside cars, now they were everywhere. Ten-year-old children rollerbladed along the street talking into them. The world had lurched forward and not taken him with it.

At quarter to nine that morning his nephew came downstairs carrying the mobile and threw it at him. 'You got a text,' he said, and carried on out of the back door.

He went upstairs, consulted the instruction booklet, and opened the first text message of his life.

Apprentice Rd. 2.30am. Slvr jagXK8. cntct Dnny.

He reread it a number of times. He did not know Danny. He only knew that picking up a Jaguar XK8 in the early hours of the morning from a smart residential road on the outskirts of Lafferton was unlikely to be legit.

So, he wouldn't go then. Simple. Lee Carter couldn't make him. He wasn't going to come banging on Michelle's door asking for him at that time in the morning, was he? He just wouldn't go. Bloody stupid to expect a kosher job from Lee, even for five minutes, and even though he said it was all different now. Of course it wasn't different. Did it look different? Had the house and the lawn and the in-corner bar and the fridge stocked with booze looked legit?

He put the mobile in his trouser pocket and went out. The streets were empty. Kids were in school, most people who worked at work, those who didn't watching telly or in the pub or hanging about town. Like him. He caught a bus and went to hang about town.

The bus took him to Dino's corner. The steamed-up windows and the name in curly neon, the same as ten and more years ago, came from another world, the old world, one he felt at home in. Below the neon sign, the face of the missing schoolkid looked out at him from the poster.

Andy pushed open the café door. Fredo was at the espresso machine.

'Andy . . . you come in for a Knickerbocker Glory?'

Those were the days. Andy laughed.

'Espresso, cappuccino, mocha, latte?'

'Tea.'

'OK, I give in. How are you, Andy? Gotta job?'

No. Yes. He wasn't sure.

'Looking for a job. You know anyone wants to set up a market garden?'

'No. Maybe I know someone who wants a hedge cutting. Me.'

'Yeah, right. Thanks, Fredo.'

He took the mug of tea, hesitated, then added a doughnut from under the glass dome on the counter.

As he set them down on one of the marble-topped tables by the window the mobile phone made a buzzing noise. He looked round. No one had taken any notice. Well, they wouldn't, would they?

Andy took it out of his pocket. 'Gunton,' he said. Silence. He hesitated then pressed the green rubber button and tried again. 'Gunton.' Bloody stupid object. He bit into the doughnut and jam squirted sideways on to his cheek.

Fifteen minutes later, as he was finishing his second mug of tea, the phone buzzed again and, this time, as he lifted it to his ear he caught sight of the square display. *Message.*

It took him five minutes. He didn't have the booklet with him. Alfredo was polishing spoons by the handful and watching him. The schoolkid on the poster was watching him. A woman stared in through the misted-up window at him. Shit.

In the end he got there.

Reply.

Jesus.

'You OK, Andy?'

'OK.'

'You keep cheerful, right?'

'Right.'

'Know what you want?'

'What do I want, Fredo?'

Fredo bent under the counter, took out a small leather photograph wallet and handed it across. Inside were two pictures, one of a dark-haired, dark-eyed girl with gold hoop earrings, one of the same girl dressed as a meringue with Alfredo on their wedding day.

'Great,' Andy said, handing back the wallet. 'Terrific, Alfredo. Good for you. How much?'

'One pound.'

'Nah, come on.'

'I can't make it free, Andy, but only a pound.'

For a split second, Andy felt a surge of anger roaring up through him, so that he almost slammed Alfredo's hand full of spoons down on the counter hard and told him he didn't want favours. He looked into his old school friend's face. Alfredo looked back, still smiling.

'Thanks, Fredo,' Andy said, 'only next time, I have to pay the whack or I can't keep coming in and I want to keep coming in.'

'Deal,' Fredo said, putting the pound coin in the till. 'I want you to keep coming in.'

As Andy reached the door, Fredo shouted after him. 'Any time you wanna cut a hedge, Andy?'

He found a bench in the new pedestrianised shopping square. Two old men were sunning themselves. One looked asleep. How could they stand it, day in, day out, nothing to do, sitting on benches?

So, what was he doing? He took out the mobile phone. The message had gone from the screen. He wondered what would happen if he just didn't reply. He could pretend he hadn't received the phone at all, that he'd never worked one so he had no idea there had been any message, that . . .

Yeah, right.

He'd have to go, that was all. He had to pick up a car at two thirty in the morning. If he didn't, Lee would come to him and then what? He knew what.

Michelle and another woman were eating sand-wiches and drinking out of cans of cider when he got back.

'What you been messing at?' She didn't offer him a sandwich.

The other girl had a stud in her nose and black-painted fingernails.

'Just out.'

'Not out where you should have been. Bleedin' probation officer rung up, didn't she?' Michelle wiped her mouth and reached across the table for her cigarettes.

Shit. He'd forgotten, because the appointments were a waste of time like Long Legs was a waste of space. Where had the chats got him? A job? Somewhere to live?

'What she say?'

Michelle shrugged. 'Ring her and find out.'

'Great.'

'Then if you don't mind, we was having a girl talk.'

Black fingernails giggled.

The bedroom smelled stale. Andy opened the window wide, stuck two pairs of Matt's trainers on the ledge to air, and then sat on the edge of his camp bed reading the mobile phone booklet until he had the instructions for sending text messages by heart.

The Dulcie estate was quiet and would be until half past three when the schools turned out and then bedlam until one in the morning. It wasn't like prison, it was worse. His sister was no nicer to him than any of the screws and at least there he'd had a room to himself. Under his nephew's bed he could see rolls of grey fluff and a pile of porn magazines.

So what was the answer? There was one. He took out the phone, found the message in the inbox, and carefully pressed out a reply.

Undrstd.

He pressed Send.

*

260

He guessed it would take him forty minutes to walk from the Dulcie, cutting across the railway waste ground to Apprentice Road. He had no alarm and even if he had he dared not risk waking Matt, so in the end he went to bed at midnight and just lay awake on his camp bed, hands folded behind his head. He was in no danger of sleeping, he was so pent-up. Beside him, his nephew slept noisily, snuffling, grunting, talking to himself, heaving over and back again.

It was bright moonlight. It shone in on Andy through the window and silvered the heavy metal and Harley-Davidson posters on the wall opposite. He'd never liked the moon much. Spooky and cold, he thought it, but it would be handy tonight.

He had the mobile in his pocket.

At one, he got up and put his shoes on quietly. Matt stirred and mumbled, but nothing more. The house was still. His brother-in-law was at work. Michelle had been watching television with a couple of cans of cider until after Andy had gone up. He went quietly down the stairs, making barely a sound, unhooked his jacket and slipped out. The Yale lock dropped with a clunk. He froze. But he reckoned he could have slammed the door and no one would have heard.

He set off to walk through the empty moonlit streets, and after a while he realised that what he felt was not fear and foreboding, it was excitement. It was something to do with being out alone at this time, with not having had any excitement

261

whatsoever for so long . . . and more. Whatever it was he was set up to do was not legit, though how far it was not he couldn't guess. But it was the fact that he was out on a job again, in the night and pitted with the others against the sleeping world which was giving him a buzz. He had difficulty admitting it to himself.

Here and there a light shone in a bedroom window. A minicab went past him and instinctively he flattened himself into the bushes. On the waste ground beside the railway line he saw a fox race across ahead of him, brush down, eyes glinting. He liked the smell of the night.

Apprentice Road was further away than he remembered. It was twenty to three when he reached it. He started to walk more slowly, keeping to the hedge. No one. No lights. No cars.

It was a longish road, with Edwardian houses mostly turned into flats, and one or two 1960s semis crammed into the plots between. Then he saw it, almost at the end. A Jaguar parked away from the street lamps. Just the car. No person.

Andy approached it cautiously. Paused. Waited. Rubbed his finger over the phone in his pocket.

He stood for perhaps four minutes, barely breathing. Nothing. No one. He went up to the Jaguar. It was empty but on the driver's seat was a route map. He reached out cautiously and touched the door handle, ready to leap away if an alarm went off but none did. The door was unlocked.

He bent in and moved the map. The keys were underneath it. As he touched them the buzzer went on his mobile, terrifying him, loud as a siren in the sleeping street. He pulled it out. The display screen was backlit in weird luminous green.

Airfld. 4 mls, edg Dunstn by hangar 5.

Andy looked behind him. Not a light, not a sound, but someone was out there, someone had known the instant he had let himself into the Jaguar. He felt sweat round his collar.

He waited. Nothing. There were no more messages.

He knew the airfield. They used to muck about up there as kids. He thought it would have been all built on by now.

He got into the car and adjusted the seat. It smelled wonderful, of cold leather. When he put the key in the ignition the dashboard lit up in a deep soothing blue. The gear was leather-covered and stubby, fitting perfectly into the palm of his hand. He started the engine. He had not driven a car for five years but it felt like five minutes and the sound of the engine purring up excited him. A Jag was something else. The interior was immaculate. It had only done 3,000 miles. He let off the handbrake and went slowly and quietly, without putting on the lights, to the end of the road. Beautiful.

The main road was deserted. Andy put the beams on to dipped and fastened himself into the belt. Three miles then on to the bypass, second left and out on the winding country lane towards the airfield. His heart thumped. He accelerated and the Jaguar powered forward.

There were some lorries on the main road, but the bypass was deserted and after he turned off that he saw nothing but an owl and a little further on a rabbit picked up in the car headlights. He swung off the lane across the potholed track that led towards the airfield. Nothing much seemed to have changed. He slowed. Nothing. No vehicles, no lights, nobody.

At the far end the old barrel-roofed Nissen huts were still in place. Andy drove slowly past them then turned and headed back across the open ground; as he did so, the mobile phone buzzed. Bloody thing, like a disembodied watcher.

He stopped, and picked it up.

Lve car kys undr map.

He slid up beside the second hangar, number 5, doused the lights, switched off the engine and sat waiting. He waited for quarter of an hour. No one came. The place was dark and silent. He got out and stood holding open the Jaguar door. So, he was to leave the car here. Then what? Walk back?

Yeah, walk back.

Fucking hell.

He pushed the keys under the road map, then slammed the door and set off through the darkness. He wasn't bloody doing this again for Lee Carter or anyone else. He'd walk holes in his shoes.

A mile down the lane he heard a car coming towards him. For a second he was blinded in the headlights.

'Get in.'

It was an old Land-Rover. He didn't know the voice, didn't recognise the man. He hauled himself up into the seat which was covered in sacking and smelled of manure.

'Dropping you off at the corner of Barton Road.'

'Who are you?'

'Ian.'

'Ian what?'

'Ian.'

It was like riding in a tank after the Jaguar. Andy felt every stone in the road jar through him. He glanced at the driver. He wore a fishing hat. Perhaps he was thirty, thirty-five.

'You work for Lee regular?' he asked.

'Barton Road.'

'OK, Barton Road, Mr Mysterious.'

Ian grunted. 'Want a toffee? One in front of you.'

'No thanks.'

'Suit yourself.'

'Where'd you come from?'

'Not far.'

'Pardon me for asking.'

They rode in silence for the rest of the way, though the silence didn't seem hostile. As he got out, Andy took one of the toffees and chomped it.

'Thanks. Thought I was going to have to leg it all the way.'

Ian laughed. The sound of the diesel engine seemed to echo round the entire estate. Andy watched the Land-Rover's tail lights disappear down the road before heading into the Dulcie. It was five to four. The moon had gone in behind a cloud but the streets here were bright orange from the lamps.

He felt drained and oddly let down. Not enough had happened. He'd driven one car and been driven back in another. Legal or not, the only decent thing about it had been the Jaguar. There'd been no mention of money at any point.

Tomorrow, he'd ring up Lee Carter, say he couldn't do any more.

Thirty-three

Chief Constable Paula Devenish sat on the other side of his desk.

'Nice to see you again, Simon. Just give me a quick briefing and then I'll go along and talk to everyone.'

'Would you like the team in the meeting room in half an hour, ma'am?'

'No, no. They'll think I've come to get at them. I'll just say a few words and then talk to people as I go round the room.'

'They'll appreciate it.'

'How's morale?'

'Bit low. They need an energy recharge . . . that's why it's good you're here.'

'The only thing that will really give them a boost is some sort of breakthrough and there hasn't been one. They don't have anything to get their teeth into.'

'Let me send out for some coffee. I don't know if you've sampled the delights from our Cypriot deli on the next corner?'

'Sounds good. I don't want to offend the canteen though.'

'They're used to it. Cappuccino?'

Simon picked up the phone. 'Nathan? Could someone go out to the Cypriot and get a cappuccino for the Chief and a double espresso for me? Yes, I thought you might. Thanks.'

'Nathan Coates?'

'Nathan Coates.'

'How is he doing?'

'I'm delighted with him. He's keen as a terrier, he knows Lafferton so well, especially the estates, he's got good judgement . . . he's working round the clock on the Angus case. I've had to send him home for some sleep a couple of times.'

'No worries there then.'

'He can be a bit volatile . . . very high when something's going well, bouncing about like a puppy, but he goes crash down easily. He's angry about this case.'

'He's young. How did the reconstruction go?'

Simon groaned and told her. Paula Devenish listened sympathetically and with her usual full attention. It was one of the things he admired about her. You never felt her mind was elsewhere, never felt she was trying to rush you. She asked, she listened, she thought, she decided. He remembered Chris Deerbon once saying that the best surgeons were those who made a decision about what they were going to do, did it and never looked back.

'How are the parents?'

'Kate Marshall is the FLO. She says the father is hardly there – burying himself in work. His wife is close to cracking up.'

'Have forensics finished in the house?'

'Yes. Nothing. And now we know for sure that the boy was waiting outside the house at eight ten. We have a definite sighting.'

'So, where are we, Simon?'

'Searches have drawn a blank. Every known paedophile within ten miles of Lafferton has had his file reopened and gone through. Nothing so far . . . Come in.'

'Coffee . . . ma'am . . . guv.'

Paula Devenish stood up. 'Good morning, Nathan. That was good of you, to go for it yourself.'

'Never miss a chance, ma'am. The wife's barred me from the pastry counter though.' Nathan put the plastic beakers down on the DCI's desk, having carefully placed paper napkins beneath each one first. He winked at Simon and disappeared.

'What happened about the paedophile who was being harassed?'

'We had to move him to a safe house. Things got quite nasty up there. Television got wind of it and of course that attracted even more crowds.'

'This will leave scars that will never heal properly, you know, Simon. Just like Freya Graffham's murder.'

'I do know.'

'Meanwhile, what about you?' Paula Devenish looked at him carefully.

'I'm fine. I take everyone's advice about getting enough sleep and eating properly.'

'Good. But that wasn't all I meant. Have you thought about your next move?'

'Ma'am?'

'There are some tempting jobs coming up . . . special incidents, fast-response units, paedophile squad to be based over at Calverton but operating over the eastern region –'

'Absolutely not.'

'Drugs ops coordinator?'

Simon laughed. 'Have you got it in for me?'

'OK, but I don't want to lose someone of your ambition and talent to another force.'

The incident room was packed. Heads were down at computers, telephones glued to ears. There was a hum, as if a great deal was happening, and in a sense it was, but the DCI knew that the air of purposeful industry was largely an illusion. People were working on long shots, following up thin leads and hopeless hunches. There was a lot of number crunching, and file sifting . . . and a strangely dead atmosphere in spite of the noise.

It went quiet as the Chief walked in. Phones were set down and hands froze on keyboards. A tension ran through the incident room. Paula sensed it at once. 'I'll have a word,' she said quietly to Simon, and walked to the far end of the room, where the whole wall was given over to the Angus case. In the centre of it, the poster, blown up to twice life-size. David Angus's face looked out at them.

Paula Devenish was not tall or physically prepossessing. She had neat brown bobbed hair and mild features and although fit and active was more plump than lean. But there was a presence about her which gave her authority. She had a quiet, ordinary voice but everyone listened to it, a quiet manner which commanded immediate respect. Now, she stood in front of the white board, slightly to one side of the poster and the room fell silent.

'Good morning, everyone . . . I want to say that I understand absolutely what a sense of frustration you must be feeling at the moment, how demoralised . . . I don't blame you for a moment. It's entirely natural. You must have thought, as we've all hoped, that within twenty-four hours, with such a high-profile case and a high-powered team and so much extra put into this inquiry, David would have been found safe and well. You now know that this is very unlikely and you all feel you are plunging about in the dark. That's understandable too. But what I don't want a single one of you to feel is that you are not supported completely, by me, by everyone at HQ, and indeed by the whole force. This is a case that has a very high media profile. That puts extra pressure on you, I know, but you have to try and set those things aside and stay focused. Please know that everyone is behind you. And when you have a long dull day trawling through stats at a computer or old files looking for

271

distant details, remember: it may well be some snippet of information gleaned from just such a day that provides the lead we need. It must seem as if the people out there dredging the river and the canal and going through every ditch and hedgerow have a more interesting time, but they don't. It's dreary back-breaking work. It's got to be done, that's all, just as all the detailed searches have to be done here. I'm here to encourage you and to say that if anyone feels the need of a break, a day's leave, whatever, then speak to the DCI and take that day. Get out, do something different, and you'll come back in here recharged. It's easy to get stale and you'll be called in quickly if there's a development. Don't sit looking at a screen for hours on end, go and take a walk and you won't only feel better, you may suddenly see this case from a different viewpoint – and that again might yield the break we need. OK, thank you all . . . what you are doing is very, very much appreciated. Now I'll just wander round and have a closer look if I may – you can brief me about what you're doing as I go.'

She stepped aside and turned to Simon. 'No need for you to stay, it'll be better if I just blend in for a bit. I'll see you before I go.'

He left. The Chief was already talking to Nathan, going over the marker notes for the day on the white board. The room was settling back to work, and he noticed that there was a more focused air about everyone; people were sitting straight not slumped in their seats, someone had opened a window, the phones were ringing and being answered crisply. The Chief had revived their spirits and their enthusiasm in a few words. It was the shot in the arm that had been needed.

He went back to his room feeling a fresh charge of energy himself. He took out a sheet of paper, asked for all but urgent calls to be turned away, and began to look at the case again from the beginning, making a flow chart from the time the boy had gone to bed the night before his disappearance, and adding side lists of notes as they occurred to him. He worked fast, his imagination alert, seeing the boy in his mind's eye, following him, and then looking at the case from someone else's point of view . . . that of an abductor.

It was forty minutes before Paula Devenish came back. By then, he had filled three sheets with careful notes.

'Simon, I have to get back, but I'm up to speed with what everyone is doing. I'm impressed. It's an efficient and well coordinated inquiry.'

'Thank you.'

'They were a bit down but that's always the way. They're a good team. And don't forget what I said about your career. I could use you to head up something I want to develop over the next year or so. Don't get too comfortable, Simon.'

He escorted her to her car and watched it sweep off.

Was he too comfortable? He had never thought so but if he was then why not? It suited him here.

He wondered how ambitious he still was. But two women had ruffled him within a few days. He did not object to the Chief's questioning him about his future – she had his best interests at heart and he also knew that she thought highly of him and he was not about to underestimate the value of that. Diana was different. He did not want to think about her at all.

He stood in the chill breeze for a few moments before returning, taking the stairs at a run and ringing for Nathan Coates as soon as he got back to his room. They had to move. If David Angus was dead then his abductor and murderer would now be working himself up to taking another child.

Thirty-four

'I can't see,' Meriel said, 'I need you to tell me. You'll choose the right thing and set it in the perfect spot . . . you're so good at it.'

Karin stood beside her. In the two years since she had redesigned and planted Meriel's garden, everything had begun to mature, so that it looked less raw and new. Shrubs were filling out, bulbs had spread so that the small beds at the side of the steps leading up to the terrace were thick with iris reticulata and miniature narcissi. By June the wide borders at the far end would be coming into their own, the climbing roses fuller.

Meriel had asked Karin to lunch. It was the day after Martha's sad little funeral at the crematorium in the cold and grey. Now, the sun was shining. Meriel wanted to plant a tree in Martha's memory but she seemed not to know what kind or where it should go. She simply stared vaguely out at the garden.

She looks drawn, Karin had thought, suddenly old. Frail even. There was something about her eyes, too, an anxious look which Karin had never noticed before.

'You do think it's the right thing to do?' She turned now, needing confirmation and reassurance.

'Of course I do, it's perfect. I was wondering about a winter flowering cherry; they have those delicate pink blossoms on bare branches when there's almost nothing else and you often get a flowering twice, in November and again in late January. They're easy, they look wonderful in snow, they give a pretty dappled shade during the summer.'

'I knew you'd think of the right thing and you have. But where?'

'You want to see it . . . to have it stand out from everything else . . .'

'There?' Meriel pointed vaguely. 'Oh, but you choose, you decide.'

'It's your garden,' Karin said gently, 'she was your daughter. I don't want to take over on this one.'

'I'll only get it wrong.'

'Of course you won't.' Karin stepped down off the terrace on to the grass and stood looking all around her. There was no warmth in the sun. She needed the scarf she had tied twice round her neck. Meriel stood above her watching, tall and straight-backed, her legs long in black jeans. How many women of her age could wear black jeans to such effect? Karin wondered.

'What about there . . . in the middle of the side lawn against the dark background? You'd see it from the kitchen, from the drawing room and from your bedroom. It wouldn't grow too big for that space.'

'Yes. Thank you.' She seemed anxious to get the decision out of the way, to have the tree chosen, bought, planted and then to move on.

Karin was puzzled. She had no idea what Meriel's feelings had been about Martha's life or now her death. Yesterday at the crematorium she had been dry-eyed, moved a little stiffly, once touched Simon's arm before moving quickly away to the waiting cars. She had been grave. Nothing more.

It had been Richard Serrailler who had wept, discreetly but for some time, he who had read a poem over his daughter's coffin and barely been able to finish. Afterwards he had not joined the others or looked at the flowers laid on the grass but walked quickly away into the memorial garden at the side of the chapel. Chris Deerbon had made to go after him but Simon had shaken his head.

There had been so few there – three people from Ivy Lodge, Karin, Chris on his own as Cat was only just home with the baby. Karin had looked at Meriel again and again. Something had happened to her. She had been a woman still in middle age and now she had moved forward into the first stage of being old.

'Do come inside, the wind is too cold to stand about here. I want to talk to you about the hospice exhibition.'

Karin followed her. From the study at the end of the corridor she heard the faint patter of a keyboard.

Richard Serrailler still wrote medical papers and co-edited an online journal in ophthalmology.

Meriel put a fresh filter paper in the coffee percolator and a bag of peppermint tea into a mug for Karin, who was still strictly following the anti-cancer diet. Karin sat at the kitchen table looking at the plans for the hospice extension.

'Do you feel it,' Meriel asked abruptly, setting down the cups, 'not having children?'

Karin was taken aback. Since Mike had left her, she had been on an emotional seesaw; half of her was grateful that, after years of struggling to conceive, they had not managed to have children after all – children who would now be torn apart by his actions. But some of the time she believed that children might have meant Mike would never have met the woman in New York, not have left home . . .

'Yes and no . . . probably more no than yes, just now. But when I go to see Cat and little Felix I daresay it will be a very strong yes.'

'It is the hardest. Losing your child, having your child die before you die. It's the wrong way round and you feel guilty. You've failed, you see. You should protect them from death and you have failed. I had no idea that I would feel like this about Martha . . . Perhaps I feel it more than I would have done with one of the others . . . she was so vulnerable. She was innocent and helpless and vulnerable.'

She sipped her coffee. Karin noticed the pale smudges under her eyes, as if someone had scored thumbprints there.

'Medical advances mean we are so much less accepting of death. And we have to accept it. All of us.'

'I don't think I accept it, or I wouldn't have spent the last year fighting so hard against the prospect of it.'

'No. But you would have been dying before your time. Did Martha? When was *her* time to die? At birth probably. Before birth. People bewail miscarriages but they are almost always right. Almost always.' She stared across the kitchen, not out of the window but simply into space.

Karin reached out to pull the plans towards her. 'What time would you like me to come to the hall on Saturday?' She wanted to break the atmosphere, to have the usual Meriel back, full of energy, organising, arranging and in charge, not this sad and rather defeated woman. Karin felt like a child whose seemingly invincible parent has suddenly demonstrated a weakness.

'Yes,' Meriel looked vaguely at the papers in front of her. 'Well, we open at ten. There's the model to set up and the display boards . . . we can't have the hall the night before unfortunately, it's in use.'

'Half past eight?'

'Could you bear it?'

'Oh yes, I get up pretty early. Are there people lined up to do refreshments or do you want me to help with those too?'

A door opened and closed and they heard footsteps along the passage.

'Oh no, goodness, there are plenty of cake bakers and coffee servers . . . no, I need you with me. We must talk to everyone who comes in, persuade them how badly this day-care unit is needed. I aim to have promises and interest enough by the end of Saturday to feel confident that we can go ahead. God knows there's plenty of money in Lafferton, we just have to dig for it. Have you seen the model? I never think plans and drawings give a proper impression of any building, but the model makes it come alive.' She leaned over the table. 'Karin, it is so important . . . we have got to make this happen!'

This was the old Meriel Serrailler back, enthusiastic and determined, her face alight. Karin relaxed. The right order of things was restored after all.

The door opened and Richard Serrailler stalked across the kitchen.

'Coffee hot?'

'I made it five minutes ago.'

'Good.' He opened the cupboard and took out a cup and saucer. Then, as he was about to pour his coffee, turned to Karin. 'It was good of you to come yesterday. Please know how much it was appreciated.'

Karin stammered a reply. Richard Serrailler had barely spoken to her before, and never without appearing curt. How strange death was that it should not only shatter people and change things for ever, but bring different people out of the ones you thought you knew. Even this death of a child-woman whom no one had ever really known had changed things, hurt Meriel enough to age her and reveal her vulnerability and softened her husband to the point where he acknowledged Karin's presence at the funeral with real gratitude, for all the formal way he had expressed it.

'I was glad I could be there,' she said. He nodded, and went out without further comment.

'The model has to be placed so that it's the first thing people see and then they'll be drawn straight to it,' Meriel said.

Her husband might never have been in the room.

Thirty-five

Sam Deerbon was in the porch of the farmhouse, his small figure lit by the overhead lantern, as Simon drove up. As he opened the car door, his nephew ran up and stood in the way.

'Have you found David Angus yet?'

Simon looked at the little boy's earnest face with its strangely upward-sprouting hair and his mother's eyes.

'You haven't found him, have you? Are you looking hard enough? A lot of people at school say you aren't looking properly. A lot of boys at school say he's dead but I don't think he is, I think a gang has got him somewhere, in a loft or in a cave and they'll ask for money to let him go. It's called a ransom demand.'

'It is, yes. But what makes you think that might have happened to David?'

'Well, I should think his dad's quite rich. Well, a bit rich anyway. He could pay a ransom, couldn't he?'

'That would depend.'

'Why?'

282

'On all sorts of things.'

'Like on how much money the gang wanted?'

'Sort of.'

'Not millions and billions, I don't mean, but he could pay quite a lot I should think, wouldn't you?'

'I don't know. Sam, can we go inside please.'

Sam hesitated then slowly opened the door wider. 'Don't forget to lock it. People steal cars from places in broad daylight, you know.'

'Thanks for reminding me.' Simon zapped the remote button and the doors clunked shut.

'Good,' Sam said. 'Rivers's mother's car got stolen from their garage and it was even locked with a warning alarm set but they got in and stole it.'

'Where does Rivers live?'

'Yoxley Crescent. I should think they would have kidnapped Rivers, his father has a mega big factory, they'd pay loads and loads.'

'I don't think anyone should be kidnapping anyone at all, do you?'

'Not really, but if people needed money to buy food for their children they might.'

'I think that's what's called a false argument. Robin Hood, you know?'

Sam looked puzzled.

'Never mind.'

Simon stepped into the kitchen and wanted to freeze the moment. He was tired and irritable and cold. The kitchen was warm and smelled of baked potatoes and a bottle of red wine stood on the worktop. Beside it sat the huge ginger cat Mephisto, his tail curled round his body, green eyes blinking at Simon. In a corner of the sofa, Cat was curled up in old tracksuit bottoms and a T-shirt, which was lifted for her to give the breast to Felix, who was pressed close to her, one hand curled to touch Cat's pale skin with its blue veins running towards the nipple.

'What a picture.'

'Fat woman with infant.'

'Maternal, not fat.'

'Thanks, bro, just what I need.'

Sam had wormed his way into the crook of her arm and was trying to get as close to her as the baby was. Simon raised an eyebrow but Cat shook her head.

'You could open that bottle now. God knows when Chris will be back, the locum's called in sick again. I don't know how much longer he can cope with this.'

'No good?'

'OK . . . when she's there. Patients don't like her much, she's too sharp – tells everyone to stop smoking, lose a couple of stone and go to the gym before they've got in through the door and hasn't been known to prescribe an antibiotic in her entire career. Tough cookie. But then always ringing in that *she's* not well.'

'Can I have a gin before the wine?'

'You staying the night then?'

'Yup. OK?' Simon threw his car keys on to the table.

'Sure. You know where the bottles are.'

When he returned with his drink, Cat had shifted Felix on to the other breast and Sam had vanished back to the playroom.

Simon went to sit beside his sister. 'He was waiting for me . . . he's worrying about David Angus, isn't he?'

'Of course he is. '

'Told me he thought David was being held to ransom.'

'And is he?'

Simon avoided his sister's eye. 'I doubt it.'

'He's dead.'

'You don't want to have this conversation.'

'Not really. How do you think your new nephew is looking?'

'Bigger. Sort of – smoother.'

'So he was small and wizened and you didn't even mention it.'

'What's to eat?'

'Mary put a lamb thing in a casserole. She's here every day all day for the next two weeks.'

'Has Ma talked to you today?'

'Yes. Didn't sound good.'

'Karin was at the funeral.'

'I know, Ma said.'

'It was pretty meaningless. I wish it hadn't been up at Farnley Wood. I hate that place. I hate crematoriums, period.'

'How do you feel now?'

Simon shrugged. 'Don't say it's for the best, that's all . . . I'll miss going to see her. I always felt so peaceful with her, you know.'

'Ma says you did a drawing of her.'

'When she was in BG, yes.'

Simon drank, then got up and went to the cupboard in search of crisps. Mephisto gave him a glare. 'Hello, evil one.' Simon stroked his ears but the cat twitched away and jumped down.

'Diana came to the flat,' Simon said, his back to Cat. He heard the baby making small snuffling sounds.

Cat said nothing.

'It was very late.'

Still nothing.

He turned. Felix was over her shoulder having his back rubbed. His head was bright pink and had a small bald patch in the middle of the fluff of dark hair. Cat looked at Simon.

'I was bloody furious.'

'Why?'

'I don't like people turning up unannounced, uninvited.'

'You only like people on your terms.'

'That isn't true.'

'Not us. People as in "women".'

'Is that so terrible?'

'Have you asked yourself what she felt?'

'She was taking things for granted.'

'That isn't what I said. What did you do anyway? Let me bet you didn't open your arms wide to embrace her.'

Simon flushed.

'No, I thought not. Maybe it took a lot for her to beard you in your den . . . maybe she felt desperate. How long is it since you were in touch?'

'I don't have to be in touch.'

'Did you ever tell her you weren't going to be? She probably left your flat feeling humiliated and crushed and very, very hurt.'

'It's her own fault. She shouldn't have come at all. We had a perfectly good understanding, I didn't owe her anything . . . nor she me.'

'Right.'

'Bloody hell.'

'Get me a glass of water, would you – big glass?'

'I thought you'd be sympathetic,' Simon said, taking out the spring water.

'I'm a woman.'

'So? I'm your brother.'

'I love you, Si, but I have to say so far as women are concerned, you are bad news. Harsh, I know.'

'Indeed.'

'So let's talk about something else.'

'Just not work.'

'The economic state of the nation? The Booker Prize? '

'Do you think I'm too comfortable?'

'As in . . .?'

'The flat . . . the job . . . just in general.'

'I don't know that I've thought about it. What's wrong with comfort?'

'Quite.'

'Dad been getting at you?'

'No, the Chief Constable.'

'Does she want to move you?'

'She muttered something. New units, new challenges. It'd be in the county . . . and promotion.'

'Don't move far,' Cat said, and her eyes filled with tears. Easy, easy to cry, she knew, just now after the birth of Felix, too easy, but she could not have borne her brother to go away. 'I didn't mean what I said just now.'

'I know.'

'I did feel a pang for Diana though.'

'Save it. Diana's a tough cookie.'

'Hm.'

'Uncle Simon, what would be the most money a kidnapper would ever get? What would a nine-year-old boy be worth, would he be worth hundreds of pounds to be kidnapped or thousands of pounds?'

Cat and her brother exchanged appalled looks and Simon stood at once, picked Sam up, threw him over his shoulder and whirled him round. Sam began to laugh.

'Tell you what, Samuel Christopher Deerbon . . .'

'What? What?'

'I'm going to throw you in the bath . . .'

'And me, and me, and me.' Hannah came racing in and threw herself at Simon's legs. Cat sat holding the sleeping baby as the three of them ran for the stairs.

He had handled it as Chris usually did, by diverting Sam and causing an uproar, but she knew that the disappearance of David Angus was inside her son's head night and day and could never now not be there. The boy's disappearance had changed everything. Every child, every parent. Everyone.

At half past eight the children were asleep; they decided to eat.

'Lay the table, Si – the casserole will keep warm in the bottom oven. I've fed Felix twice since I ate last and I'm beginning to feel faint.'

'Are you worried?'

'About Chris? No . . . he doesn't always call in . . . there'll be some emergency he's in the thick of.'

'Exhausting.'

Simon fetched wine glasses and took the bottle to the table.

'None for me, I'll have water. How did you think the folks were yesterday?'

'Hard to say. Buttoning a lot up . . . maybe grief, more likely relief. Dad was more upset than I'd expected.'

'He often went to see her. Sat for hours. So the Ivy Lodge girls said.'

Simon poured out a large glass of red wine and took a swig. 'She was no threat of course. Couldn't disappoint him any more than she had at the start, unlike me.'

'Oh, get over it, Si.'

Simon shrugged.

They were eating when Chris walked in ten minutes later, grey-faced. He went straight to the table, poured a glass of wine and drank half of it before he said, 'I've put calls on to the agency for the rest of the night, I'm bushed.' He turned to Simon. 'Have you heard?'

'What?'

'Alan Angus tried to commit suicide.'

'Jesus.'

'By some miracle his registrar went to his office to pick up a file and found him just as he'd slashed both wrists. He knew which way to do it too, of course, he wouldn't have had long. But they think he'll be OK.'

Cat pushed her plate away but Chris filled up his glass and went across to get food.

'I'd better call in.' Simon was going to the house phone when his own mobile rang.

'Nathan? . . . I've just this minute heard.'

'Mike Batty's there, guv . . . he and I had been in to see Angus earlier. Went through everything again. I told him he wasn't suspected, I said we was just taking it from the beginning again, no way could he have thought we was questioning his story. I never went for him, guv, no way.'

'No one's going to think you're to blame.'

'He was soddin' lucky, I tell you, someone was lookin' after him, no one's around them offices at that hour, not normally.'

'I know. Where are you?'

'Wherever you want me to be, guv.'

'Right, go check out Marilyn Angus.'

'Nah, she's at the hospital, I'm outside there now. Want me to talk to her?'

'No, in that case leave her for tonight. She's had enough. You go home.'

'Guv, just before I got called about Angus I was looking back over everything. I come up with that silver Jag again. Thought it'd be worth checking out.'

'Hasn't it been done?'

'We just did Lafferton and Bevham . . . maybe we could go nationwide?'

'Too many. You can't start on that tonight.'

'Guv.'

'I'll go into the hospital first thing, then see Mrs Angus. Knock off now, Nathan.'

'OK. Guv, that was really appreciated, the Chief coming in, everyone was saying full marks to her.'

Simon smiled. 'I'll pass it on. Goodnight, Nathan.'

'Cheers, guv.'

They finished the lamb casserole and opened a second bottle of wine, but they scarcely talked. Deaths and near-deaths hung over them.

Cat went up to bed before ten carrying the sleeping baby.

Chris held up the bottle.

'No thanks.'

'No. God, what a week. I've never felt more like packing up and joining Ivo in Australia. We talked about it, you know, Cat and I.'

Simon looked at his brother-in-law, trying to assess whether he was even halfway serious. Simon would never be able to bear it. How could he remain here, with their parents growing older and his father more morose and bad-tempered with age, and everyone he loved either dead or thousands of miles off? Yet he had once been to visit Ivo in Melbourne and hated the place – the only person, his brother had said with amusement, who ever had. Following the others there would never be an option for him. His life, designed so carefully and exactly as he loved it, suddenly seemed in danger of caving in on him.

David

This is the worst place.
   I'm really, really hungry.
   I'm really thirsty as well.
   My arm hurts.
   Why was it me?
   It's cold.
   I'm all shivery now.
   I just want . . .
   Don't . . .
   Please . . .
   Not . . .
   Pl . . .
   Mu . . .

Thirty-six

'I can't do this,' Marilyn Angus said. 'Waiting for the worst news, waiting and there is no news. I cannot do it, but I *do* it. What is wrong with you?'

Her voice was a whisper. She sat beside Alan's bed, among the blipping machines, and hated him. What had happened to David had torn them apart when everyone assumed it would have brought them much closer together; she would have assumed so beforehand. But it had revealed to her a husband she did not know or want to know – one who in her eyes was a coward. Running away to work before seven every morning and staying there until late at night, taking on other people's caseloads, putting himself on permanent call – she saw it all not merely as unsupportive of her but as cowardice. This was cowardice too. His wrists were bandaged, there was a drip into his arm, every monitor was switched on to every function of his body and she despised him. It was the most terrifying feeling of her life. She did not know this man, her husband, Lucy's father. David's father.

His head was turned away from her. He had not spoken to her since she had arrived with the police officer. Kate cares more than you, she thought, staring at his bandaged wrist.

'I don't know what to say to you,' Marilyn said. 'I don't know what's going on in your mind any more. I don't understand why you did this.'

'No,' he said, so softly that she could hardly hear him.

'If David had been brought home tonight, if –'

'David is dead.'

The words came out of his mouth and rested on the air, heavy and full of black bile. They frightened her. If she had reached out, she could have touched the words and they would have entered her body, her bloodstream and her belief. She opened her mouth but no words came out of that, neither poisonous nor hallowed.

'I was operating. I looked at the monitor and saw my probe hovering inside a patient's brain and I simply knew. Don't ask me why then. I don't know why then. I looked and saw that David was dead and then there was no way of living myself.'

'Is that all?'

He moved his head. She saw his face, drained of colour, grey as the face of something dead, his eyes flat and sunken into his head, lifeless.

'Is there nothing else in your life?'

'What?'

'Not Lucy? Not me?'

'Of course.'

'Not worth going on living for?'

'I don't know.'

'I said, if David were to be brought home, alive and well . . . wouldn't he need you?'

'Of course.'

'You didn't think of that?'

'David is dead.'

Marilyn put her head down on the hospital bed and screamed into the covers, stuffing the sheet into her mouth so that nothing could be heard. She felt a desperate need to hurt someone and the only way she knew to stop herself was by hurting herself, trying to choke on the cotton bedding.

The bell rang. A nurse and Kate Marshall were in the room and behind her, talking to her gently, their hands on her shoulders, lifting her back.

'Marilyn, it's all right,' Kate had her arms round her now. 'Don't worry –'

Marilyn swung round and stabbed her elbow hard into the policewoman's face. Kate gave a cry of pain. The room seemed to explode with people and voices.

They led her out to a waiting room with blue chairs. Someone brought her a glass of water. Someone else came with a cup of tea. Marilyn sat with her arms clutched tightly round her own body, rocking, rocking, trying to keep every sound out, every word, every clumsy attempt at reassurance or comfort. Alan's words had gone home. There had been a place she had kept secure, a place in which there had been a small bright patch of warmth and hope into which she had been able to retreat. No one else knew that it was there but she had relied on it because in there was the truth, that David was alive and well and would come home. Alan had sent a blade slicing through the wall and all the light and brightness and hope had leaked out and turned black, a pool of darkening blood on a floor. The place was empty now, the air foul and contaminating. He had killed the last resource she had. Now there was no hope or comfort. David was dead. Everyone else had known it but she had not. Now, she did.

She unclenched her cramped body slowly. The muscles around her ribcage and in her back ached, and there was a dull pain beneath her heart.

A nurse was beside her, holding a glass of water patiently. Marilyn tried to take it but her hand shook so violently she could not, so the girl held it to her lips and tipped it, letting her drink as a child first learning from the cup. She tried to thank her but her throat was constricted. The nurse stroked her arm.

'Kate . . .' the word came out eventually, an odd croak.

'She'll be here in just a minute. Don't worry.'

The girl now lifted a cup of warm sweet tea and held that to Marilyn's lips. People walked by in the corridor. A door closed with a strange sucking noise. There was a chink of metal on metal. This room was very warm, very calm. There was a picture of a wave curling over on to a beach, another of a garden in the snow. '*Donated by the Friends of Bevham General Hospital. 1996.*'

Marilyn tried to find a handkerchief in her coat pocket. Her face was scored with tears. The nurse handed her some tissues. She shrank from the thought of the violence that had welled up inside her, of how she had turned so angrily on the policewoman; she had never struck out at anyone in her life, never hurt a spider or trod on a snail. Neither of her children had ever been given the lightest smack. Yet she had felt rage enough to want to kill.

The door of the room with the blue chairs and the quiet pictures opened. A young doctor in a white coat came in.

'How are you feeling, Mrs Angus?'

Why were they being so kind to her, speaking so reassuringly, looking so sympathetic? They should be locking her away, straitjacketing her, leaving her alone with her own anger – not this.

He took her pulse, then held on to her hand. 'That's fine. When you feel ready the police have sent a car – someone will drive you home and stay with you. I've prescribed a sedative, you can collect it at the nursing station as you go out . . . you need to sleep. Is there anything else I can do?'

She looked into his face. He had a tiny mole beside his eye, and a scar on his upper lip. He might have been fifteen years old. How could he be speaking to her with such calm confidence? How was it that she was ready to do whatever he asked?

She shook her head, then again managed to say Kate's name.

'She's fine but she's going off duty for tonight.'

'What did I do?'

'Gave her a bloody nose actually. No lasting damage.' He smiled. 'You packed a punch.'

She didn't mind that he was trying to lighten her up, make her relax. She didn't mind. She smiled back at him. Then she said, 'My son David is dead,' and knew that it was the simple truth.

The young doctor did not insult her by contradicting her or trying to jolly her out of what she had said, he merely took her hand and held it firmly in silence, and stayed with her until a different police officer came and took her down to the waiting car and home.

Thirty-seven

The room smelled of damp coats. Outside
Blackfriars Hall the square was like a sluice and
the guttering poured water on to everyone
stepping inside. A great many people had come,
mainly, Karin McCafferty thought, to escape the
wet rather than to support the exhibition of the
proposed new day-care centre. The helpers in
charge of refreshments had been serving coffee
and cakes non-stop, and the raffle and tombola
tables had attracted a queue since the opening.
But people wandered vaguely round the model of
the centre without asking any questions or, save
for a few, writing their names in the book left out
for those who wanted to be contacted with
further information. It was a very nice model. The
day-care centre would be at the side of Imogen
House and have facilities for patients to meet
together, to paint and sew, make models, play
games. There would be consultation and treatment
rooms and a conservatory opening out on to the
garden. Not everyone needed to be an inpatient at
the hospice, and not all inpatients simply went

into Imogen House to die; many went for respite care and pain relief and returned home for weeks or months of better quality life. If they had a day unit to attend, their care package would be complete. Karin and Meriel Serrailler had been ready with the answers to every conceivable question, ready with explanations and leaflets, ready, as Meriel put it, with a better sales pitch than any used-car dealer. But they had scarcely been asked a question and no one had wanted to stay long enough to have the idea of the day-care centre sold to them.

Now, the room was thinning out as people finished their coffees and got ready to plunge back into the rain. Meriel had gone to help with washing-up. Karin sat beside the model, finishing her second cup of tea and feeling dispirited.

A second later, she looked up at a young woman who had just come in. She wore a cream belted raincoat and a pale pink cashmere stole, and her hair gleamed with raindrops but was neither tangled into damp rats' tails not plastered round her face. She was beautiful. Karin stared at her. She was probably the most beautiful woman she had ever seen. She was slim with a perfect skin and very large, dark eyes, as dark as the sheet of hair.

Karin stood up. It was, she felt, what you did in the presence of such beauty.

The girl made her way slowly across the room towards the model.

'Good morning.'

'Hi there.' American then. The accent was gentle, educated, soft. The girl held out her hand. 'You are?'

'Karin McCafferty.'

'Lucia Philips. Now please tell me what is going on here – what this model represents. I guess we came in out of the rain and to see the old building, and here is something going on we should maybe know about?'

Five minutes later she knew everything that Karin could tell her and she listened with intelligent attention. They walked round the model. Karin pointed out this and that feature, the girl looked carefully. At the back of the room, Karin was aware of Meriel and a couple of the other volunteers peering out, wondering.

The girl, Lucia Philips, turned at the sound of a footstep behind her. 'Cax, come and see this.'

He was in his fifties and good-looking. He wore the American equivalent of Savile Row and had an accent to match. But the downpour had been less kind to him. His mackintosh was soaked at the neck and sleeves, and the rain ran down the sides of his face into his neck.

'Please, let me get you some coffee . . . and I'm sure I can find a clean towel for you to get a little drier.'

He held out his hand. 'Well, thank you. George Caxton Philips. I see you already met my wife Lucia.'

Karin looked again. The girl could not be more than twenty-two or -three and Karin had taken the man for her father. But whatever he was, she sensed that they ought to be given the best attention. She went off to the kitchen in search of fresh coffee and a towel. Meriel backed her in beside the sink. 'Who?'

'American. Charming. Can you make them a fresh pot of coffee?' She rummaged in one of the drawers and came up with a couple of faded but clean tea towels with pictures of St Michael's Cathedral.

'I'll bring it out,' Meriel stage-whispered. 'You go back there.'

The couple were examining the model together and, as she approached, Karin sensed a frisson of intimacy and sexual electricity between them which startled her, though they stood inches apart and were intent on speaking about the display.

'I'm sorry this is all we have for you to mop up with but they're quite clean.'

'Thank you so much.' He turned a smile on Karin which explained in a second his attraction for any woman, even a stunning beauty at least young enough to be his daughter. He rubbed his hair vigorously with one tea towel and wiped his face and neck with the second, while making a rueful face. His wife glanced at him and rocked back on her heels with laughter; as she did so, Karin noted the expression on his face in response – adoration, she thought. Not merely love but totally bewitched adoration.

'Now, let me take these somewhere to be laundered.'

'Good heavens, no, please.' Karin held out her hand as Meriel came up with a tray. From somewhere she had made not cups of instant but a cafetière of real coffee materialise. Karin moved away and started to gather up litter from the tables. A few more people came in and headed for the tombola. A couple asked for tea.

Meriel had taken over, as Karin had been perfectly sure that she would, but not before she had heard the American say, 'We're so interested in everything. We've bought Seaton Vaux, maybe you know it, just a few miles out of town?'

Karin shot into the kitchen where three of the others were huddled. 'Seaton Vaux,' she said, indicating with her head.

'I'd heard there was somebody . . .'

'My God, that is serious.'

The tiny kitchen buzzed.

Seaton Vaux, a few miles west of Lafferton, was a Grade I Elizabethan manor house with several hundred acres and an estate village and had been owned by the Cuff family until the death of the last member ten years before. Since then, it had fallen from disrepair into semi-ruin. It had been on the market for a long time, and the usual rumours of pop stars, film stars, royalty and exotic foreigners had done the rounds. Lately, there had been silence. Until now, and this good-looking Ivy League American with the young wife who could put any film star or princess into the deepest shade.

Karin looked out of the kitchen. The lull was over. More people had come in. She went over to take sandwich orders, passing Meriel who was now sitting with the Caxton Philipses. Meriel ignored her.

Meriel saw them out of the hall. Karin hesitated, then climbed on to a chair to look from the high window. A dark blue Bentley glided to the kerb as the George Caxton Philipses appeared in the doorway.

Royalty, Karin thought. Money and royalty. What else?

They closed the doors at four. Mary Payne sat at a card table for twenty minutes surrounded by piles of money and cash bags while the rest of them cleared the hall of everything except the architectural model and displays which would be taken separately.

'One thousand, one hundred and eleven pounds and fifty-eight pence, two Irish pennies and an Israeli shekel.' Mary sat back and rubbed her knuckles into her eyes.

A small cheer went up. Everyone was exhausted. Outside it was still raining. No one asked anyone else if the Americans had made a donation.

Two days later Karin was in the garden early, repotting and feeding half a dozen camellias which stood on the sheltered terrace at the side of the house. She heard the postman's van and walked round to meet him. She still waited, knowing that there would be nothing, uncertain even if she wanted to hear from Mike. She was not happy but she had begun to adjust, focusing on her work and her own garden, and spending as much time as ever on keeping to her organic diet and therapies which had held her cancer at bay for almost eighteen months. The postman leaned out and handed her a pile of mail banded together. She did not want to see a New York postmark. She did want to.

She fanned the letters out on the bench. Nothing from New York. Did she mind? No. Yes. They were all bills and circulars except for one letter in a thick cream envelope, addressed in black.

Dear Karin,
It was such a great pleasure to meet you on Saturday and we do thank you for your kindness to us and your attentiveness in showing us the very interesting exhibition of the proposed hospice day-care centre.

I look forward to welcoming you to Seaton Vaux and not only after we have come to live there. As my husband told you, our main attention has been to the house but I am so anxious to make a real English garden and especially to recreate something of the great glory that we know was there in former years and which we have seen from photographs. Dr Serrailler enthused to us about your garden design and planning genius and I would so love it if you were able to come and look at ours as it is now, share any ideas you may have, with a view to your being involved in the new work.

We are in London next week and can be reached at Claridge's Hotel, after which we fly back to New York for a time. I have enclosed a card.

We look forward to renewing your acquaintance.

With all good wishes

Lucia Caxton Philips

The phone rang inside the house.

'Hallo . . . Meriel, I was just thinking of you. I'm reading a letter from the beautiful American girl. She wants to restore the gardens at Seaton Vaux.'

'I know. I sang your praises. Now listen, never mind the gardens, *I* have had a letter from the handsome Mr Caxton Philips. He's offered to pay for the day centre.'

'What? All of it?'

'All of it. He's giving us a million pounds.'

'Bloody hell.'

'Quite. It means we go ahead without having to cut any corners or send out any more begging letters.'

'And all because they walked in out of the rain to look at the Blackfriars Hall.'

'Now I must ring John Quatermaine. He won't believe it.'

Meriel put the phone down, as ever without saying goodbye. She would enjoy telling the consultant to the hospice about George Caxton

Philips. Within half an hour one American couple had changed the world around. Money, Karin thought. Never despise it.

She re-read Lucia Philips's letter, written in the slightly unformed hand which gave away her age.

For the first time since Mike left, Karin found herself looking forward. To work on the redesign and planning of the gardens at Seaton Vaux would be a dream job. It was also a daunting prospect. She would need all her skills, her health and strength.

'Life,' she said out loud into the kitchen. 'Life!'

Thirty-eight

My Darling

I am sitting over a glass of Sancerre, chilled just as you like it. It is half past two in the morning and I can't sleep. I have scarcely slept since I drove fast back to London like something scuttling back to its hole, after you threw me out of your flat. Harsh? Yes . . . I'll revise it. 'Made me so unwelcome at your flat.'

I felt ashamed of myself. I felt a fool. I felt with the deepest certainty of my life that I am, and have long been, in love with you. I think it all began as a friendly game, didn't it, on my side as well as on yours? I think we both wanted a companion for a pleasant evening out, a social partner isn't it called? And some light-hearted sex. It worked like that for a time but I now realise that for me it was a very short time indeed.

I fell in love with you. I did not want to do so, and I barely admitted it to myself for a long time. Certainly I never admitted it to you. It spoiled things. It has spoiled things. But there we are. I came to see you out of desperation, after having left the messages you never returned. I wanted to know what I felt when I saw you again. Perhaps I had been wrong, and perhaps I would no longer love you and want you so much. It would have been a relief. But I did. The moment you opened the door, I knew nothing within me had changed, but only grown and strengthened.

We were so good together but we could be so much better. I think we should be. I think you are a lonely man who has no idea of the strength of his emotions. But if you admit them, you will find that you are a free person after all, free to be in love, free to be with me.

You mentioned in our brief meeting that there had been someone else. That stabbed into me like a blade until I realised, as I drove home, that it was not true. There was never anyone else, was there? I know you enough to know that you have never had a lover. You wanted to get rid of me, you were in a mild panic, and you invented the 'someone'. It doesn't matter. So long as you know how much I love you and will see me again, nothing matters. Please, Simon, phone me, come to me, anything. But don't ignore me. I can't bear the silence and the distance from you.

Ever, ever with love,
Diana

Simon Serrailler held the paper as if it were alight. When he had finished reading he banged open the kitchen pedal bin with his foot and dropped it inside. The lid clanged shut again. He went to the sink and drank a glass of water, then took out the Laphroaig bottle. It was nine thirty and he had been with first Marilyn and then Alan Angus for several gruelling hours. He had eaten a plate of canteen fried food and come home fit for nothing but a drink, and some time sorting carefully through his portrait drawings to find three to enter for a prize.

He had not recognised Diana's writing. If he had he would have dropped the letter into the bin before, rather than after, opening it.

It felt like an invasion of his territory, his private space, another attempt to get under his skin, like her visit. He was angry with her for disturbing him, angrier that she hadn't believed him when he had mentioned Freya. Angry.

He hesitated, took another shot of malt, and shoved the bottle back in the cupboard. It solved nothing and he had less time for drunkards than for most criminals.

He pulled out one of the flat portfolios from the drawer, began to undo the black ribbon ties, but then stopped. He couldn't look at his work now. He would have no judgement. She had spoiled that for him too.

'Fucking woman.'

He would not reply and at least now he knew her writing he could tear up any future letters unopened. 'If you don't know what to do, do nothing' had been one of the few lessons he had learned from his father. So, no reply to the letter, no returning any telephone messages. He would do nothing and if he did nothing for long enough, she would leave him alone. He wished her no harm, he just wished her out of his life.

The cathedral clock struck ten, the grave, measured notes sounding through the room, cleansing it from the stain left by his angry swearing. It calmed him. He lay on his back on the long sofa.

Freya Graffham was in his mind, her neat cap of hair, her fine features. So that had been love and he had been too stupid to recognise it, too slow to act upon it, too . . . He imagined her in this room, not as a visitor but as a familiar part of it, her books on the shelves, the scores of whatever piece of choral music she had been learning for the St Michael's Singers opened on the table. In his mind, it was no longer his room but theirs. 'Have you asked yourself what she felt?' Cat had asked him when he had told her about Diana's visit. Now Diana had told him and it had not made him ashamed of himself or sympathetic towards her, it had simply annoyed him.

He got up. There was a team review of the Angus case at nine the next morning, a press conference at ten. The news of Alan Angus's suicide attempt had not yet become public knowledge and Simon was anxious to brief the media and control their reaction to it. He needed to be fresh. He locked up, put the lamps out, and stood for a few moments looking out of the window at the floodlit cathedral. The sky was clear, the night immensely still. Gradually,

Simon felt the calm seep into him. He went to bed to read another chapter of *Hornblower* before sleep.

But he did not sleep. At two he was still turning about in bed, his peace frayed. He read more, then got up and ate a couple of biscuits. He went back to bed and still did not sleep.

Half an hour later, he left the flat and ran down the hollow-sounding staircases past the darkened offices and out to his car. If he could not sleep and did not want to lie thinking about Diana's letter, and least of all about Freya, then he might as well be working. The Audi slipped out of the close into the night streets.

Thirty-nine

Three days after he had left the Jaguar at the airfield, Andy Gunton had received another package in the post, a white Jiffy bag taped with FRAGILE and sent special delivery. Michelle had stood in the kitchen doorway as he came down the stairs.

'There's tea in the pot and there's bread. I'm round to school, ten minutes tops, and when I get back you and me is going to sit down and 'ave breakfast and talk, OK?'

She had yanked Otis's scarf tighter round his neck and yelled up the stairs for Ashley, lit a cigarette and gone out leaving Andy to close the door. Pete was in bed. In the sitting room the television advertised leather sofas on interest-free credit.

The packet was on the table. She'd signed for it and no doubt turned it over and over and upside down. There was no way he could pick it up and pretend it had never come. After the mobile phone, something else arriving for him by special delivery was going to be up for discussion.

He put the kettle back on the hob, took down a mug, got out a tea bag, found the sugar and a teaspoon, opened the fridge and took out the milk, and between each move he either looked at the packet on the table, touched it or weighed it in his hand. He dreaded opening it. Nothing had happened since he had been dropped at the end of the road in the middle of the night. No one had contacted him, there had been no phone messages. It might never have happened. Andy half believed it had not.

He sat down at the kitchen table with his mug of tea and picked up the packet again. It was the size and thickness of a small paperback book. He ripped it open.

Inside the packet was a brown envelope. Inside the envelope were fifty ten-pound notes. There was no message. Just the money.

He broke out in a sweat. He was going to have to either explain five hundred pounds in cash, or lie about what had been in the packet. If he was going to lie, he needed a convincing explanation to occur to him within the next few minutes. On the other hand, if he simply handed Michelle a couple of hundred pounds and said nothing, answered no questions, went straight out . . . then what?

He got up and stuck four slices of bread in the toaster. What was he frightened of Michelle for?

He knew what for.

He scooped up the packet and the money and ran upstairs to stuff it into his nylon holdall and put that back under the bed next to the box that had contained the mobile phone.

The back door slammed.

Andy opened the bedroom window to let out the thick stench of his nephew's trainers, and went downstairs, his heart in his mouth as if it were his mother come home and he had been nine years old and up to something.

'What's going on?'

Michelle stood facing him, her back to the sink. For a split second he did indeed think she was their mother. She was starting to look like her, broom-handle thin, flat-chested and sour-faced. Only Michelle had yellow hair and a bad skin. Their mother's skin had always been peachy, her hair mouse-turning-grey. But the way she stood was the same, and the set of her head, up and back, chin stuck forward.

He picked up his mug of tea which had cooled and tried to get past his sister to reach the microwave but she moved forward suddenly and he sat down hard, the tea slopping down his sweatshirt and on to the floor.

Michelle swung round, picked a cloth off the draining board and threw it at him.

'Did you hear me?'

'I heard.'

'And are you going to tell me? Don't you bloody wind me up, Andy Gunton, don't you bloody start lyin'. I wanna know. What was in that envelope for starters?'

'Mind your own fuckin' business.'

'It is my business if you're up to your old tricks. You get out of my house if you're into anything dodgy, anything, I don't care what it is. Out.'

Andy finished wiping his shirt, then bent to the floor and swirled the cloth vaguely round the spilled tea at his feet. Then he got up, threw the cloth in the direction of the sink, and went upstairs two at a time, not bothered if he woke Pete or not. He could hear snoring like a road drill from the front bedroom.

He got the packet of money out from under his bed, removed a hundred pounds and slipped it into his back pocket, then went back down to the kitchen. Michelle had not moved. She was waiting for him.

Andy put the money on the kitchen table.

'Can I have my tea now?'

'Where'd you get that?'

'You wanted to know what came in the post. That came in the post.'

He stood in front of her until she moved slightly to let him get by. Andy put the kettle back on and more bread in the toaster. He started to whistle.

'I knew it.'

'You don't know nothing.'

'You find that lying in the gutter then?'

'It's wages. You wanted me to pay my way, I'm paying my way. There's four hundred.'

'You nicked it.'

'I did not. I told you, it's wages. I did a job. I got paid.'

'Job. Oh yeah, right. What sort of job? Picking peas?'

He almost said it. 'Driving a car.' The kettle boiling and the toast burning together saved him.

'You're a liar, you done a job – and I don't mean job as in honest day's work and you bloody know I don't.'

There was a crash upstairs as the bedroom door was flung back against the wall. Pete Tait came heavily downstairs and appeared in the kitchen doorway, wearing a vest and tracksuit bottoms.

'What the fuckin' hell is going on? Am I going to be allowed any sleep or what? You both yelling. I'll have some of that tea. What you think you're on at, Michelle? Worse than the kids, you two.'

Andy wondered if he might break the spindly kitchen chair as he crashed down into it. The money was in front of him on the table. Pete reached out a finger gingerly and flicked at it.

'You can leave that where it is, that's dirty money, ask him.'

Pete ignored her. He pulled the notes towards him and shuffled them about a bit. Andy put a mug of tea in front of his brother-in-law and sat down opposite him with his own. He spread margarine and jam on his toast and began to munch it, paying Pete no attention. Michelle watched.

But Andy didn't need to look. He knew Pete and money. There was the sound of tea being slurped down Pete's throat. Under his eyelids, Andy saw the fingers slide back towards the cash again.

'I told him, he can bloody get out if he's started his tricks again. We don't want him here. I got kids. I ent having them mixed with criminals.'

Pete slurped his tea again. 'Where'd you get three hundred quid?'

'Four,' Andy said through his toast. 'Four hundred.'

'Four hundred?' He almost laughed at the oily tone of his brother-in-law's voice.

'Don't matter if it's four grand, it's not stopping here, it's dirty money. Next thing we'll have the police at the door, that stuck-up Nathan Coates.'

'Now hang on, just hang on.'

'What?'

'Give him a chance to tell us where he got it.'

'Working, he said. Wages. Job. Ha bloody ha.'

'Now hang on . . .'

Andy lifted his head and stared straight at Pete for the first time. 'I said it was a job and it was a job. I said it was legit and it was. I just never said what and I don't have to say what. Do I?'

'Well . . . no, no, I don't think you have to, And. No.'

'I offered it to Michelle. Rent and that. She wouldn't touch it.'

'Now hang on.'

'So you have it, Pete. Go on, stuff it in your vest.'

Andy stood up. He scooped up the money, rolled it together and leaned over. Pete grabbed his wrist and stopped the money from going down between his underwear and his skin. He was laughing. Andy leaned away from his breath.

'You want me to have it? Four hundred?'

'Four hundred. I told you. Rent.' He slapped Pete on his spotty shoulder. 'Good on you, Pete,' he said, and walked out grinning, leaving them to it.

Upstairs he put on his shoes and jacket, folded his own hundred pounds up, still grinning. He'd be staying here until he chose to leave now, not until his sister chose to sling him out. It had been worth it.
In the kitchen they were arguing. In the sitting room the television was playing host to Richard and Judy.

As he reached the gate, the mobile phone beeped receipt of a text message from Andy Gunton's pocket.

Forty

Diana was stalking him and he was beginning to know why unrequited love made people violent. He shot too fast round a corner and headed for the Old Town. He needed to look at Freya's house.

The street was quiet. It was two thirty. Not a single light shone from any of the terraced houses. He slowed. But as he did so, he thought, And I am stalking the dead. Is that possible? What in God's name was he doing? If he had discovered that one of his team was behaving in this way he would have signed him off and recommended he see the FME.

At the top of the road, he noticed that the petrol gauge was below red. There was one all-night garage, on the bypass going towards Bevham. He filled the car and got a coffee from the machine. The man at the till wore a strange red woollen hat that made him look like a gnome and was half asleep. The coffee tasted foul but it acted like an intravenous shot of adrenalin, so that as Simon pulled out of the forecourt and saw the silver Jaguar XKV ahead of him, he was alert. He clicked on the hands-free and called in to the station.

He kept the Jaguar a hundred yards ahead. There was nothing else on the bypass. Then the Jaguar took a right turn and another, and was heading out into the country. The roads narrowed quite soon. Simon called up again, gave his location and requested a patrol car.

The Jag was being driven carefully and not fast. The driver took the sharp bends well into the centre of the road and with caution, as if anxious not to risk any damage to the car body from overhanging branches or the verge. One careful owner, Simon thought, making his sedate way home. If it had not been getting on for three o'clock in the morning he would probably not have followed. The station had already confirmed that the number was different from the car that had cruised Sorrel Drive.

They were heading towards Dunston. Simon doused his main beam and drove on sidelights, not wanting to draw the attention of the driver ahead. There was no sign of a patrol car behind him. If the Jaguar turned in to one of the driveways in Dunston, he would make a note of the house and call uniform off.

A moment later he remembered the disused airfield, its concrete runways broken and sprouting weeds, the sides littered with old hangars. Whoever owned it did not want it, but was not prepared to clean it up or let it go. It had long been a blot on the landscape about which neither the council nor anyone else seemed to be able to do anything.

The Jaguar continued for another mile. Simon had to drop to just over thirty to keep well behind. He switched his radio on and told the patrol to move. If the car was going to a deserted area full of old hangars, he might need back-up urgently.

The Jaguar was slowing right down, and turning left on to the track leading to the airfield.

Simon doused his sidelights, waited until it was well ahead, and then followed again, weaving in and out of potholes and crunching on shards of broken concrete. His heart was thumping and he was conscious that he was alone. He called in again, gave his new location again. The voice from the station was steady, professional. Reassuring.

'I need urgent back-up, repeat, urgent back-up.'

'Understood. Back-up on way.'

The Jaguar was moving towards the far side of the airfield. There were no other cars, no signs of movement or activity of any kind, so far as Simon could see. He pulled up beside the gateway, hoping it would shelter him from sight, unless the Jaguar drove back close to him with headlights on. He watched as the car slipped along the broken-down rear fence, reached the end, and then swung right, and back towards the hangars. Was he looking for someone else? Checking that the coast was clear? It was difficult to see what was happening so far off and in the dark.

The Jag edged towards the hangar furthest away from view, and went out of sight. Simon got out but did not close his car door. In wide open spaces at night the tiniest sound carried. He heard nothing. There were no lights anywhere. He waited.

The moment the patrol car turned into the gateway and headed up the track, Simon saw the moving figure at the other side of the field. He jumped from his hiding place, shouting. The patrol slowed.

'Put your main beam on, there – see him? He's running. Move.' Simon leapt into the back as the police car shot forward.

The man stood no chance. He zigzagged, turned and tried to hide behind the hangars, but it took them a few seconds to reach him. The uniform first in line had the man on the ground.

'OK, OK, no need to smash my head in.'

'Take it easy,' Serrailler said. The PC was shining his torch as he let go and the man scrambled to his feet.

Simon reached for his ID. 'I'm DCI Serrailler. I've been following you since we left the bypass. I'd like a word please.'

'What am I supposed to have bloody done?'

'If you'll walk back to the patrol car.'

'You taking me in?'

'Do I have any reason to?'

'No, you fuckin' do not.'

'Fine.'

They stood beside the car and the driver switched on the beam.

'What's your name?'

'I'll tell you that when you tell me what you've been following me for when I ent done nothing.'

'Any reason you don't want to give me your name?'

The man sighed. He was young, early twenties. Simon didn't recognise him.

'Gunton. Andrew Gunton.'

'Where do you live?'

He gave an address on the Dulcie estate.

'Thanks. You were driving a silver Jaguar XKV out of Lafferton. Is that your car?'

'Yes.'

'So why have you parked it behind that hangar?'

'Why shouldn't I?'

'Valuable car like that? Aren't you afraid it'll be nicked or vandalised? Top-of-the-range motor I should guess. New, is it?'

'Yes.'

'So why park it out here and walk off?'

'I was leaving it for a mate.'

'I see. What mate?'

'Just a mate.'

'What, he was going to pick it up from here?'

'That's it.'

'How was he going to get hold of the keys?'

'Left them in the car, didn't I?'

'Really? A bit careless. Car like that.'

'He'll be here any minute.'

'And how are you going to get home?'

'He'll give me a lift, OK?'

'Have you been here before, Mr Gunton?'

'What if I have?'

'How many times?'

The man scraped his toe in the concrete. 'Used to muck around here when I was a kid.'

'I meant more recently than that. Have you been here recently?'

No reply.

'Why did you park over by that hangar?'

'Out the way.'

'I see. You didn't go in?'

'What would I want to do that for? I told you I was just leaving me car.'

'Have you ever been inside that hangar?'

'Dunno. Might have. I told you, when I –'

'No, not when you were a kid. In the last week?'

'No.'

'Sure?'

'Course I'm bloody sure, I don't sleepwalk, I haven't lost the use of me memory. I haven't been in there.'

'In any of the hangars?'

'No, not in any of them. Look, what is this?'

'Do you know anything about a nine-year-old boy called David Angus who went missing from outside his house?'

There was a stunned silence. Andrew Gunton stared blankly at Serrailler in the harsh glare of the car headlights.

'Fuckin' hell,' he said softly after a moment, 'is that what this is about?'

'Answer the question please, Mr Gunton.'

'Yes I know about him. You couldn't live in Lafferton and not know about him, could you, he's everywhere, isn't he, on every window on that poster. Poor little sod.'

'Why do you say that?'

'Well, of course I say that? Don't you?'

'Do you know anything about where he might be?'

Andy Gunton took a step forward. He spoke between clenched teeth and his face was angry. 'No, I bloody do not. I wish I did. I wish I could tell you I knew he was tucked up somewhere safe and warm and take you there but he ain't, you and I know that.'

'Do we? Do you?'

'Listen, I might have done a lot of things –'

'Such as?'

'But so help me God and on my mother's grave, I have never and would never so much as touch or harm a hair of any kid. I'll bloody swear on any Bible right now, you listenin'?' He was speaking the truth. There was a pure and almost righteous anger in his tone and his words. Serrailler felt the truth blaze out of him.

'You were driving a silver Jaguar XKV. You say it's your car.'

'Right.'

'A silver Jaguar XKV of that model was seen in Sorrel Drive, near the Anguses' house, the day before David Angus disappeared.'

'Shit,' Andrew Gunton said softly.

'I'm going to ask you to come in to the station and make a statement.'

'Yes.'

'I'm not arresting you, you understand?'

'I don't fuckin' care if you do. I'll make a statement. I'll do anything you like, if it helps you find that kid.'

'Thank you, Mr Gunton. If you'd get in the back of the patrol car please, I'll meet you at the station.'

Simon sent them on their way, and got into his own car. The moon had come out and the hangars cast great shadows over the old runways. They were rusty, their curved roofs blackened and broken open. Instead of following the patrol car across the airfield and out of the gateway, he drove towards the hangars and parked up beside the Jaguar.

It was silent. There was no wind, not the slightest movement of air.

He did not care to follow instincts and hunches, but he had a strong sense of emptiness about this place and no sense of either evil or danger. Nothing had happened here of any relevance to David's disappearance, no child was hidden here, alive or dead. Simon was certain of it as he stood in the mild night, hearing nothing but the occasional hoot of an owl far away.

He went towards the first hangar. The door hung off but on this one the roof was more or less intact. He went in. There was grass beneath his feet. The air smelled faintly metallic. Nothing. He coughed. No one was there.

He came out and walked across to the next hangar a few yards away. As he did so, he heard the sound of a vehicle coming down the lane and turning on to the track. He froze against the hangar wall. Headlights sliced across the grass and then the hangar itself, before swerving away. Simon edged his way out, keeping to the sides of the building. There were no voices. He heard a car door click shut and the scuffle of a footstep. He moved around the side of the hangar, ducked, and ran quickly to the shadow of the next. As he did so, car lights came on and an engine started up. Simon dodged out and into the open, holding up his arm. There were two vehicles, the silver Jaguar with its engine running, and what looked like a small pickup truck.

'Police!'

He banked on their not sussing that he was alone, and stood in the path of the Jaguar.

Seconds later, he was on his side, rolling over and over across the concrete towards the edge of the hangar, having missed being run over by inches as the driver had accelerated the pickup truck straight at him. He lay, an agonising pain thrusting through his right arm and shoulder. The Jaguar and the pickup were away, out of the airfield and along the road, tyres screaming. Serrailler cursed himself for a bloody fool and felt with his good arm for his mobile. It had fallen out of his jacket and must have landed somewhere on the ground. It took him some minutes to crawl and feel about, wincing with pain. The palm of his hand was painful too and wet with blood.

He swore on, sweeping about blindly. It was only when his phone rang that he located it, to the right of where he had been searching. It stopped as he managed to pull it to him but it was easy enough to press redial.

Ten minutes later, two police cars and an ambulance came on to the airfield. His arm hurt badly, his hand was full of gravel. But he realised that he was on a high in spite of his injuries, adrenalin pumping through him; he was no longer brooding. He had the buzz that had always come from being in the action, as he rarely seemed to be these days, the buzz which he had gone into the police force to find, and which kept him there. Little over an hour ago he had been lying in bed, tossing and failing to sleep. It might have been in another life.

Forty-one

'You can tell by those densely packed isobars . . .'

Meriel Serrailler knew that she could not but leaned forward all the same to stare at the whorls and swirls across the television map. Impossible to see where Lafferton could be in the midst of it all, but the general picture seemed to be wet and very windy.

She pressed the red button on the remote control and the picture shrank to a pinprick.

'Any news?' Richard Serrailler came in.

'Wars and pestilence.'

'Weather?'

'Rain and wind. But not until tomorrow or the day after.'

He made an impatient noise and retreated. Meriel got up and followed him into the kitchen where he had begun to set out the tray for their late-night tea.

'I'm rather keen on rain at the moment. If it hadn't been raining on Saturday, the hospice would be a million pounds worse off.'

Her husband glanced up. 'You don't seriously believe this nonsense, do you? It's quite ridiculous.'

'Why is it ridiculous?'

'You cannot tell me some unknown American walks into Blackfriars Hall out of the rain and genuinely offers a million pounds to build a day centre. Why on earth would he do that?'

'Because he's a generous man. And very rich.'

'It's a nonsense. Some scheme.'

'Now *you* are being ridiculous. What sort of "scheme"?'

'No idea. But you won't see your million pounds.'

'Why must you be so dismissive? You should trust people, Richard.'

'I trust some.'

'Who?'

'You.'

She looked at him in surprise and something in her stomach tightened.

'Well, of course I do.' Richard Serrailler poured the water into the pot and replaced the lid. 'I know you. Not some Yank. People like that get their kicks from shows of power. There'll be no money.'

He picked up the tray. He wanted her to argue, to come back at him. It was what he most enjoyed. Usually she would have done so, partly to keep him happy, partly because she believed in George Caxton Philips and his million.

'You didn't meet him,' she said quietly.

'Didn't need to.'

She let it go. She was trembling.

They went back into the small sitting room.

At that moment, walking behind him, she knew what she would do.

She had thought she could carry it locked within her until the end of her life and if he had not said that he trusted her, she believed she would have done so. Why not? She felt no guilt. She did feel regret, but regret she could live with. Regret was part of the fabric of her life. But sitting here now in the quiet room, watching her husband lift the china cup with the blue-and-gold band to his mouth, looking at the way his hand curved round it, seeing him close his eyes as he swallowed, no, she could not carry it.

The clock had a white china face and slender gold hands. It had been a wedding present from a friend of her mother's, forty-three years ago. As Meriel watched it now, it seemed to grow and become distorted, its face to shine, then to glare out at her in anger, the gold hands blazing as if they were on fire. The pale green wallpaper behind it wavered.

She took a couple of sudden deep breaths.

'You all right?'

If she could get up and go back to the kitchen and be alone there for a few moments, then she would be calm and no longer afraid of what she was about to do. Or else she would not do it. She would carry on. Nothing would be said. When she came back everything would be normal again, the white-faced clock quite familiar, the green wallpaper still. She could not get up. She could not even lift her cup. If she did she would spill the tea everywhere, her hands would shake so violently.

'Ron Oldham's dead by the way. Announced it at the lodge tonight. Another.' He reached forward to refill his cup. 'All dropping off their perches. Time of year.' He looked at her sharply again. 'Hadn't you better go to bed?'

She felt frozen, her limbs locked together, the muscles of her mouth, her neck, her face, paralysed. This is what it must be like to have a stroke, she thought, to think and know what you want to say, should say, but unable to speak or move. To have to wait for someone to help you. Lift you. Speak for you. Feed you. Undress you. As she had done.

The clock struck the quarter-hour. It had a pretty chime, she thought. Delicate. The room seemed to be humming faintly, as if invisible wires were being plucked. It was a beautiful sound.

There was a sour taste in her mouth. Her throat had a lump of congealed greasy matter embedded in the centre which she could neither swallow nor expel.

Richard Serrailler sipped his tea. His collar was disarranged at the back. He had been to his Masonic lodge where they played their silly dressing-up games and no one ever laughed, or that was what she had always believed, for if they could laugh they would see themselves and laugh until they were sick. He had tried to persuade Simon and Chris to have their names put forward. They had laughed, both of them, laughed until they shook. She wondered if Freemasonry would survive for many more years.

Quite suddenly, the humming in the room ceased and the lump in her throat dissolved. She felt perfectly calm.

'I have to tell you something,' Meriel said.

He did not reply but his eyes remained steady on her face.

'What do you think about Martha now?'

He set down his cup. 'Think about her?'

'Do you think about her?'

'Do you?'

'Oh yes.'

'And what do you think?'

She had not meant to allow him to become the inquisitor but he twisted things around and now she was on trial. She was unsurprised.

'I think . . . that twenty-six years was a long time for things to be as they were.'

'For us?'

'For us. All of us. But for her most of all.'

'How could you know that?'

'I couldn't. No one could. But the burden of existence . . . even of consciousness . . . must have been almost insupportable for her.'

'We will not know.'

'No.'

'When you asked me what I thought . . .'

'Perhaps I meant . . . feel. What do you feel now?'

He was sitting staring down at the cup and saucer in front of him on the low table, his head bowed, hands joined between his knees. She tried to remember what he had looked like when he was

Simon's age . . . and younger than Simon, but they were physically so different, apart from a dismissive gesture they shared, as well as the way each had of shutting himself off, that it was difficult. They had both been handsome – Simon still was.

Richard? Was he handsome now? His face had for so long worn the mask of sarcasm and disapproval that it had changed him for good. Had he ever been a gentle man? With Martha. Yes, and with Cat as a small child too. Never with the boys, and especially never with Simon.

'I feel anguish,' Richard Serrailler said. 'I feel bitter regret and a bitter bitter helplessness. What do we do?' He raised his head and she saw that his eyes were bright with tears. 'What do we do now, in medicine, with our relentless desire to maintain and prolong life at any cost? Why do we insist that any life at all, any sign of breath and consciousness, has to be the best and to be striven for? Why can we no longer let old people go when they should? What did we call pneumonia when we trained? The old man's friend. Not now. There is no such thing now. Pneumonia should have been her friend years ago.'

Stop, she said to herself, stop now. Turn the conversation round, or away, get up, leave the room, go to bed. There is no need for this. Stop now. You have to go on bearing it alone. You cannot do this.

'There is something I must tell you,' she said.

The silence in the room was so great she wondered if they had both stopped breathing. Richard waited. A hundred years went by.

'Derek Wix believed that the last chest infection and pneumonia had exacerbated the congenital heart weakness,' she said at last. 'He gave heart failure as the cause of death.' She waited. Nothing. He did not react. 'Which of course it was. I caused her heart to stop. I killed her.'

She wanted him to help her but knew that he would not, that she was alone in having to get to the end of this and that she must tell him everything, there must be no detail which he did not know. Her throat was dry but she could not move to pour herself a drink, not until it was over.

'She was asleep. I went to see her late that night – after ten. I went to choir practice and then I drove to Ivy Lodge. The room was very peaceful. She was peaceful. She had no idea I was there. I gave her an injection of potassium. Her heart stopped at once of course but it was as if she just went on sleeping. I kissed her and sat with her for a moment, and I said goodbye to her. Then I drove home.'

She felt all the breath go out of her body, leaving her weak, but with all tension and anxiety gone too. She was shaking, every part of her was shaking.

'There is nothing more to tell you, Richard,' she said.

Afterwards she could not have said how long the silence went on for. She rested her head back on the chair and closed her eyes. Behind them, she saw Martha, peacefully sleeping.

Some time later, Richard got up, went to the cabinet and poured whisky into two glasses. He handed one to her without speaking. Fearfully then she looked up at his face. It was set and slightly flushed. He did not meet her eye.

In the end, when he did speak, his voice was strange, as if he had half choked and was recovering, or as if he were forcing back tears. 'I find it hard to believe you have done this.'

'I have done it.'

'You bore her and gave birth to her.'

'I think that was why. Finally. I loved her.'

'Did you?'

They looked at one another for a second then.

'Of course I loved her. How could you have ever doubted it? I loved her as you did.'

'Oh yes.' He sipped his whisky.

'You know, barely a day went past when I didn't think of it.'

'Of killing her?'

She flinched, but said, 'Please do not tell me it never occurred to you too. Every time she had another chest infection, another bout of pneumonia, you said she should die now.'

'Yes.'

'Is this so very different?'

'If you mean, is the end result the same . . .'

'I mean . . . you wished that she would die. I wished it. But she didn't die and so I took her life. And she knew nothing at all, and she is – free. Whatever that means, yes, she is free. I freed her.

She was locked in a terrible prison and I released her. That's the only way I can see it.'

'You feel no guilt? Have you simply put it to the back of your mind?'

'It has been at the front of my mind every minute since. But I feel no guilt. No, none.'

'I could never . . .'

'I don't believe you.'

'My God, do you think I could commit murder?'

Murder. The word sounded peculiar in the room, like a word in a foreign tongue which did not belong with the rest. It did not frighten her or alarm her. She simply did not understand it and then, after a moment, rejected it as irrelevant.

'It is not murder . . . whatever you call it, it is not that.'

'Killing.'

'Yes.'

'Why mince words?'

'They're important.'

'Our daughter was important.'

He had finished his whisky. She had not touched hers. He was slipping the empty glass about and about through his fingers. Then he got up. He came over to her, put his hand on her shoulder.

'I know. And now one of us must tell Simon.'

'Absolutely not.'

'Because he is Simon or because he is the police?'

'Both. He felt closer to her than any of us. That strange way he had of talking to her, singing to her, when he was a boy, do you remember? The times he went to sit with her . . . it would devastate him.'

'Nevertheless, he is the police.'

'You think I have to tell them? Bring all that down on our heads?'

'Your head.'

'I don't mean bring shame and disgrace, and besides, no one would react in that way, no one. I mean a prosecution and a trial, the newspapers, and for what? "Another doctor in mercy killing" . . . It happens all the time, you and I know that. Every doctor knows it.'

'We used to be trusted. Not any more. Doctors are suspected . . . since Shipman and the cases in Holland.'

'All the more reason. But I didn't do what I did as a doctor. I sent her to her peaceful end because I was her mother. If being a doctor gave me the knowledge of the right way – that's incidental.'

'You won't rest easily until you tell someone.'

'I have told you.'

'I wish you hadn't,' Richard Serrailler shouted out, and as he shouted, tears of anguish and rage exploded from him in a torrent. 'I wish to God I didn't know.'

She slept at once and dreamlessly but woke in fear, her heart hammering through her eardrums, sweat running down between her breasts. In his own bed Richard was turned away from her, on his side.

After a moment, she got up quietly, went to the bathroom and took a warm shower. She hesitated on the landing but in the end went back to the bedroom. Richard had not stirred. She drew the curtain slightly. It was calm with a bright three-quarter moon, catching the first blossom on the pear trees, making it ghostly. She pulled the basket chair from her dressing table and sat, looking out on to the garden. She never saw any of this, Meriel thought, not any of it, neither the house nor the garden, nor the country around. It should have been her home but it never was.

She remembered Martha's birth. Through her pregnancy she had known that something was wrong and once tried to tell her husband, who had dismissed her imaginings, pointing out that she was perfectly fit and well and had had her first children more easily than any woman carrying triplets had a right to do. She had heard him, and still known. When, years afterwards, she told Cat, her daughter had been unsurprised. 'Of course, it happens. You knew. You were right.'

But the sight of the child had still been shocking. She had lain, flabby and inert, her head too large, her skin pale and clammy. They had worked to make her breathe and they should not have done so, any more than all the doctors over the years should have worked to save her from mumps and German measles, chest infections and otitis media and every other attempt by God or nature to end her life.

It had been left to her instead.

She had not simply 'withheld treatment'. If the elderly had DNR posted above their beds, why not the ones like Martha?

She had taken life. Was it murder? She did not know. But there was no ambiguity about the word 'kill'.

Her head was clear, her mind calm. She felt rested. The sight of the moonlit garden came to her as a balm. What she had done she would do again. She knew that. She could accept herself now.

She started to remake her bed and smooth the pillows. A sliver of moonlight was falling on the pale blue carpet through the chink she had left in the curtains.

Abruptly, surfacing as if from deep beneath the sea, Richard woke, sat up, said her name.

'It's all right. Go back to sleep.'

He stared at her. 'Do you remember what you told me?'

'Darling, you're not awake . . . it's three o'clock.'

'You told me you had murdered Martha.'

'I didn't use that word.'

He lay back on the pillows and turned his head slightly so that he could not see her.

'Richard . . .'

'You must go to the police.'

'No,' she said.

'Someone must.'

'Will you?'

He did not reply. The moon went behind a cloud. Meriel waited, lying on her back as he was on his.

Like effigies on one of the tombs in the cathedral. She saw them so – cold, grey and silent in death.

In the end, still waiting for him to answer her, she slept like that, hands at her sides, and the moon slipped out and silvered the room again and the space between the two beds was the width of the world.

Forty-two

It was the smell of the place. Andy Gunton sat on the bench in a cell at Lafferton Police Station and smelled it. Police stations. Courts. And after that prisons. They smelled. They each smelled different but you knew them with your eyes shut and as he sat down he had felt anger and shame and recollection and self-loathing crash over him, wave after wave. It was four o'clock. They had put a plastic beaker of tea down in front of him and left him and even the way the constable set the drink down told him something about how he was seen.

He put his head down on his arms. You blew it, he said. You blew it. You stupid fuckin' idiot. What did you expect, working for Lee Carter, where did you think you were going to finish up except here? He hated and despised himself to the extent that if he could have seen a way he would have killed himself. He'd spent five years inside and learned nothing then?

He saw how it happened, over and over again, and there was nobody he was going to blame. He'd had no time for the ones that kept coming back until the only thing they knew was prison but he'd turned into one of them without seeing it coming.

He wanted to cry. He did cry for a moment which only made him loathe himself more. Michelle would throw him out. He could see how you ended up homeless as well. How people got to sleeping in shop doorways. Better inside. Three meals and a halfway decent bed. Better that.

He wondered when they'd come. He watched the clock for half an hour then forty minutes. Then he rolled over and faced the wall and went uneasily to sleep.

They had X-rayed Simon Serrailler's arm, strapped it up, cleaned out his hand and told him to go home to bed. But he knew that if he did, he would take the painkillers they had given him and in the morning be half doped and too stiff and bruised to want to move. He told the taxi to take him into the station.

'You sure you're all right to be here, guv?' The desk sergeant gave him a hard look.

'Fine. I'll interview Gunton as soon as Nathan comes in, then go home. Any tea?'

'Guv.'

Simon took the stairs slowly. The station at night was an odd place, quiet for the most part, especially up here, but with the occasional racket below when the D and Ds were brought in and started banging on the cell doors.

He switched on his desk lamp and drew up the slatted blind. In the yard, the amber lights shone in pools on to the asphalt.

His arm hurt.

He had a strong feeling that the Jaguar XKV had been stolen and also that following it out to the airfield was the first stage in uncovering part of a large operation that involved a lot of people; it would turn out to have tentacles spreading out far beyond Lafferton. But he was also pretty sure that neither the car nor the driver had anything to do with David Angus.

He went to look at the map on the wall. Lafferton and district. The cathedral. The old town. The Hill. Sorrel Drive. He made his eye follow routes outwards from where the boy had been, standing outside his house. Any car heading out of town would have turned right at the bottom of Sorrel Drive and within three minutes would be on the Bevham Road, from where it would either continue on or hit the roundabout and take the bypass, to east or west. Within twenty to thirty minutes, it would be on the motorway.

He looked at the grids drawn from Sorrel Drive, again, spreading out and out, taking in the Hill, the canal, the river, the parks, the old railway tunnel and so on, out into the country. By now, every obvious dumping and hiding place for a body had been combed. A corpse had been found in woodland near Starly – that of an elderly man who had been missing from home for ten days. His body

346

had been just out of sight of the traffic passing on the main road but his death had been from natural causes.

Of David Angus there was no trace.

Simon went back to his desk and sat trying to forget about the pain which had now spread up into his shoulder, as the doctor had predicted. 'That's where the impact was as you rolled over. Bloody lucky you didn't fracture it.' It felt as if he had.

Somewhere, someone had the boy's body or else had disposed of it. When an abductor took a child then the child became a liability the longer it remained alive. A nine-year-old boy, articulate, bright and observant, would be a liability of the most frightening kind to an abductor, one able to describe and identify and remember. Whoever had taken David Angus might not have known him and might well never have been to Lafferton before. He had seen, grabbed and sped off. Then . . .

Simon stared at the sheet of paper on his desk. It was blank. No clue, no lead, no evidence, no trace, no results. Blank.

He dreaded that it would remain blank for ever.

Forty-three

They woke him with a mug of tea and a soggy bacon roll. He felt cramped and stiff. The sky through the high window of the cell was grey and dead-looking. They'd asked him if he wanted to phone anyone but he'd said no. He wondered what had happened at the airfield. What Lee Carter was doing. What Lee Carter would do. Safer to be in here.

Jesus. In here. He looked around in disbelief. What had he said? What was the one thing he was never going to do? Still, they couldn't send him down just for picking up a car in one street and driving it to an airfield and leaving it there. If he said nothing, they'd have to let him go. They opened the door again to let him out to the toilets. He washed his hands and sluiced his face, combed his hair. He looked like the sky, grey and dead.

'OK, interview room. Hope you know it was the DCI tailing you last night.'

Bloody hell.

He waited, sitting at the table. There was the same rectangle of blank sky. They brought him another cup of tea he didn't want. Then the two of them came in.

'Andrew Philip Gunton.'

'Yeah.'

'I'm DCI Simon Serrailler, this is DS Nathan Coates.'

Bloody Coates. What would Michelle say? 'Jumped-up little prick.'

Andy said nothing. The DCI looked terrible and his hand was bandaged. He was holding his arm awkwardly.

'Interview commenced 8.13 a.m. OK, Gunton, what were you doing driving a stolen Jaguar XKV, registration number 188 KVM, at around 2.30 a.m. on Tuesday March 14th?'

'I didn't know it was stolen.'

'Really? Dreamed you won the lottery?'

Bloody cocky little Coates.

'No.'

'What were you doing with it?'

'Taking it to the airfield.'

'Why?'

'I was told to.'

'Who by?'

'No comment.'

'Where did you take it from?'

'I picked it up.'

'Where from?'

'Grasmere Avenue.'

'What was it doing there?'

'How should I know? I just went to collect it.'

'So someone told you it would be there.'

'No one told me.'

'How did you know?'

He did not answer. He'd said enough.

'Had you driven this car before, Gunton?'

'Never seen it.'

'What's the scam then? You just the runner or is there more?'

'Don't know what you're on about.'

The DCI shifted in his chair and winced faintly. Leaned forward. 'Who was it tried to run me over last night?'

'What?'

'On the airfield.'

'Not while I was there.'

'No, just after you'd gone. Someone drove in there and picked me up in the headlights. When they did that, they thought they'd better flatten me. Who was it?'

Andy shrugged. But he was thinking hard and he didn't like what he'd heard. Driving a car from A to B was one thing. Getting involved in anything like he had before . . .

'You heard of David Angus?'

Andy looked up. The DCI was boring holes into him.

'Be hard not to. I told you before.'

'Did you ever see him?'

'No. Not that I know of, any road.'

'You didn't pick him up in the Jaguar on the morning of –'

Andy stood up, almost knocking the chair over. 'No I fuckin' did not.'

'Sit down. Did you drive the same Jaguar down Sorrel Drive on –'

'No, I did not,' he shouted.

'Listen, Andy . . .' So it was Andy suddenly. 'It don't look too brilliant for you. Two thirty in the morning. Driving a stolen car. A car of the kind known to have been in the street from which the boy disappeared.'

'That's got sod all to do with me. I wouldn't touch a kid and you know it.'

'Do I? How do I?'

'Gunton,' the DCI said wearily, 'listen. Just tell us who told you to pick up the car and take it to the airfield. Tell us anything you know about why and how many times you've done it before.'

'And?'

'Just tell us.'

Andy didn't believe Lee Carter had anything to do with the little boy. Money was his thing, not taking kids.

'Come on, come on.'

'OK . . . and this is all. And when I've told you, I wanna go and I don't want no more questions about the missing kid because I swear to God I would never, never have –'

'Just talk,' Serrailler said.

He believed him, Andy Gunton could tell.

He leaned on the table and started. There wasn't a lot to confess when it came to it. Meeting Lee

351

Carter. Saying he'd do some driving for him. Getting the text messages. Picking up the cars, twice, and leaving them. That was it.

'How do you get paid, Gunton?' Coates again. 'Cos you ain't doing it for kisses.'

'Cash. Through the post.'

'How much?'

'Hundred pounds,' he said quickly.

'And the rest.'

'Hundred pounds.'

'Who else is involved?'

'I never saw anyone else.'

'Just Carter.'

'Yeah.'

The DCI stood up. 'Interview terminated . . . 8.28 a.m.' Coates switched off the tape.

'You charging me?'

'Taking and driving away. The duty sergeant will bail you. And don't go anywhere. We might want to talk to you again.'

They left him at the duty desk, waiting.

He counted himself lucky.

Forty-four

'How about Karin?'

Silence. The clock struck half past ten with its sweet chime.

'Chris?'

He was in the armchair opposite the horrors of a suicide bombing on the television news and he was asleep. Cat got up and switched off the set. In his crib beside her Felix stirred and sucked his lips but Chris slept on. She was making lists of possible godparents and so far there had been no obvious candidate for Felix's godmother.

She went into the kitchen. Mephisto was rubbing his great ginger body against the window and she opened it to let him in. Cold air on the north-east wind came like flying knives into the room.

An hour ago she had meant to ring Simon to find out how his arm was. It was five days since he had injured it and he had still complained to Cat of pain when he had called in for a quick sandwich the previous afternoon. He had seemed low-spirited, frustrated and pessimistic about the David Angus case.

'Don't know where else to turn.'

The case was now entered on HOLMES, the central database for major police inquiries, which meant that every force in the country was linked into it and able to access and cross-reference the information. If there were any other cases with similarities to the abduction of David they would quickly come to light.

Chris came blundering into the kitchen rubbing his hands through his hair. 'I think I fell asleep.'

'This can't go on, Chris. Look at you, you're absolutely exhausted.'

The new locum was ill again. Chris had tried the agency who could not, for the moment, give him any more night cover.

'I'll come back to work sooner than I said. I'll get help with Felix. Sally Warrender can't wait to have more of him, she said so today.'

'No, you won't come back any sooner. You are taking a year out. End of story. I'm fine.'

The phone rang.

'Sure, sure, you go to sleep straight after supper and you sleep like the dead through the night, you walk about like a zombie, the children wonder if you actually live here. It's like your first year as a houseman, only you're not twenty-four years old.'

But he waved at her to be quiet as he took the call.

'Yes, I'll come straight away. Just give me directions again. I know roughly where you are.' He wrote. 'Fine . . . will you wait at the main road and lead me up? Thanks, Sergeant.'

'Police call?'

'Man found dead in a car in the woods near Starly.'

'Not a hosepipe job?'

'Seems like it. Never too much fun.'

'Have a cup of coffee first. If it's a certification and the police are there you've got time.'

'Thanks.'

He went out to fetch his bag and jacket. Cat poured water into the cafetière. Five miles there. Certify death. Five miles back. He'd be home before midnight and with luck maybe the phone wouldn't ring again. With luck.

'You've got to get a more reliable locum.'

'I don't know what's happening to general practice.'

'I do. Bloody paperwork and red tape is happening, just as it's happening in the whole of medicine, plus attitudes have changed.'

He winced as he sipped the scalding coffee and stuck his cup under the cold tap. 'Right, babe, I'm off to the woods. Don't wait up.'

'I'll be feeding. Another nice chapter of my William Trevor to enjoy while his lordship tucks in. He's such a slowcoach.'

'I like a man who makes the most of his pint.'

Chris kissed her cheek and went out.

Cat remembered that he had been asleep when she had suggested Karin McCafferty as Felix's godmother, and made a mental note to mention her name again if she was still awake when Chris got in.

She wiped the draining board, switched the dishwasher on and the lights off and went out. On the sofa, Mephisto curled himself tighter and spread his claws luxuriantly.

The police car was waiting on the lane. He flashed his lights as he drew up.

'OK, Doc . . . get in. We need a four-wheel drive. It's pretty steep.'

Chris and the constable got into the police Land-Rover and headed up the track that climbed steeply between the trees. At the weekend this area was full of off-road bike riders. Deeper in the woodland, teams of people came to do paintballing. But tonight the headlights of the police car picked up only the lichened rows of tree trunks and the leaf mould and mud of the track. They wound through the woodland for almost a mile before the police car pulled into a rough clearing beside the tapes which had been run across between a couple of trees. Chris got out.

'You'll do best to walk from here. He forged his way through the undergrowth but he wasn't worrying about the damage to his car at that point, I suppose.'

'Do we know who it is?'

'He's making it difficult – took both number plates off. We haven't found them yet, only we haven't looked too far – it's not easy in these conditions.'

They both switched on torches and struck off into the trees. Brambles and scrub had been broken down to form a rough path.

'Who found him?'

'Gamekeeper. This is right on the edge of the Pennythorn Estate. He was cutting across with his dog, heard a car engine . . . at first he thought it was rutters.'

Chris smiled. Rutters. The local word for couples in cars late at night.

'Here you go. After you now, Doc.'

'Evening, Doc.' The second PC was standing just behind the car.

'All yours.'

'Thanks a lot.'

It had begun to rain and the path was slippery with mashed down leaves. It was cold. The car was silver and not familiar to Chris. He went up to the open driver's door and bent over. It was a job he particularly hated, tramping up a lane in the night and the dark with the police champing for you to get on with it, having to certify death from carbon monoxide poisoning which caused the body to flush pink so that you had to be even more sure than normal that it was dead. There was rarely any doubt, but he was always afraid of making a mistake, so that the job took twice as long as it should, and his back took the punishment of leaning halfway through a car door for several minutes.

He shone his torch. The man was slumped over the steering wheel and Chris had a struggle to raise and turn him. When he did so he looked into the flushed face of Alan Angus.

He made sure, checking and double-checking, pulses, heart, eyes.

Then he backed out.

'He's dead. Carbon monoxide poisoning. I can tell you who it is as well, only you're not going to like it . . . Alan Angus.'

'The boy's father?'

'Yes. He had a previous go – slit his wrists in his room at the hospital . . . only someone happened to come by.'

'Not this time.'

'No, this time he knew where to go and he was doing his best not to be found.'

'Poor bloody wife.'

'And the other child. There's a daughter.'

'Makes you think . . . he couldn't take it, could he, but she has to – twice over.'

'It's a bugger.'

Chris slithered down the track and almost fell on the last section of the slope beside his car. The station would ring Simon. The body would go to the mortuary and after that Alan Angus would belong to the pathologist and the coroner. Chris's own job was done. He had seen his fair share of suicides, certified plenty of such bodies, but it always upset him at a deeper level than almost anything in medical practice. It was the last desperate, hopeless act of someone who at that moment was the loneliest in the world. As a doctor, he felt he had failed when the body was that of one of his own patients. As a human being, any suicide distressed him.

He knew that the first reaction of many people close to the dead husband or wife, daughter or son was very often anger. Grief was complicated and muddied by it. He felt angry himself at Alan Angus, for leaving his wife to cope alone with yet more agonising uncertainty and loss. But he knew the despair the neurosurgeon must have felt, the desperation at the disappearance of his son and the complete silence and blankness since.

*

simon.serrailler@lafferton.pnn.police.uk

Darling, I can't stop thinking about you. I just wanted to tell you how much I love you. I read in the paper this morning about the suicide of the missing boy's father. It must be dreadful. I know how you feel your responsibilities. Try and take a break when you can. Someone came out of the blue to make an offer for the restaurant chain – such an offer I had to sit down. I may accept. Tired of being a single career girl.

Love to talk when you can. Ever, your Diana.

Forty-five

He was shaving when the phone rang. It was barely seven o'clock but he was sleeping badly at the moment and going into the station early was no hardship.

'Guv.'

'Morning, Nathan.'

'They've found a body.'

'What sort?'

'Child's.'

'Oh Christ. OK, where?'

'Gardale Ravine – in a shallow grave on the steep bank beside the river, just before it disappears underground.'

'They were supposed to have searched Gardale.'

'Yeah, right. Only it's rained quite a bit since then, lot of stuff been brought down – probably uncovered it.'

'Who found it?'

'Caller wouldn't give his name. Said he'd been walking his dogs along there.'

'OK, on my way. Tell forensics.'

'I just did.'

It was raining now, a soft, steady rain that misted the windscreen. Lafferton was just getting on the move but the traffic was still light.

Simon put his foot down as he headed out of town. He had already been called about Alan Angus. Now this. It might not be the boy. But if it did turn out to be David's body in the ravine, Marilyn Angus had the worst day of her life ahead.

Gardale was a steep ravine. There was a narrow, vertiginous road down to it in one direction and another out of it at the other end. In summer it was a fisherman's paradise; trout swam in the unpolluted clear water of the river which appeared here and vanished again, only to reappear mysteriously further down, the stuff of local legend for generations. On sunlit summer afternoons Gardale held no fears, no sadness or mystery. It was dappled and peaceful. People picnicked beside the water and children shouted up and down the ravine to hear the peculiar echoes.

Now, on a grey March morning of cold wind and rain, the ravine was difficult to get down to, shadowy and menacing. The sheer sides with their overhanging rocks and shallow caves closed in and the air was fetid. The space beside the track was littered with cars – the usual police clutter plus forensics. Simon got out of his own vehicle. Two men were clambering into ghostly white suits. Another was pulling out a bag.

'Morning, Simon.'

'Jonathan.'

The duty pathologist, Jonathan Nimmo, was an unattractive, wire-thin man of six feet five or six, with a mouth full of small, pointed rat-like teeth.

'I suppose this might be your boy.'

'Hope not, afraid so.'

Nimmo finished pulling his boots on. 'OK, let's go.'

'Hang on, I'll change my own footgear. It'll be treacherous as hell down that slope. You ever tried it?'

'Nope.'

'Then I suggest I go first.'

'I don't need a nanny.'

'Just a guide.'

Simon bent to lace his walking boots. They had a grip that would keep him upright on the face of a mountain.

The descent was slow and they took it with caution. Below, Simon saw the small area already taped off, and the figures of a couple of uniform.

'All right?'

The pathologist grunted, trying to keep his balance and hang on to his bag.

The rain was falling softly and steadily, making the ground a mulch of leaves and mud on the tarmac surface. Simon did not look up, only at his feet, placing them carefully. But he had the picture of the whole ravine in his mind. If the grave was that of David Angus, how had he been brought down here, by whom, and how long ago? He tried not to imagine what the journey would have been like, if the child had been alive. If dead, how had he been killed and how long before he was brought here?

By the time they reached the bottom, others were coming down behind, more forensics, the photographer and Nathan Coates.

They crossed the river, which was swollen and moving fast, by the place where it disappeared underground, and climbed the short slope to the taped-off area. Serrailler's hair was soaked, his anorak running with water.

'Guv.'

'Morning.'

'Over here.'

They ducked under the tape. A small area had been disturbed. Brush and stones had been pushed aside by the coursing rain.

'Whoever phoned in more or less said where it was. Very accurate. We hardly had to search around. This had been partly uncovered anyway.'

Simon stepped forward. Looked down. A trench about three feet deep had been scraped out of the earth and undergrowth.

'There was still quite a bit of greenery and mulch covering it over. But it was loose. Easy to see.'

The ground had been cleared just enough to reveal the grave.

There was a body in an advanced stage of decomposition, bones revealed. It looked as if it had been naked.

'Looks as if it may have been here too long to be David Angus.'

'What we thought, guv.'

'All yours, Jonathan.'

The pathologist had his bag open, his white suit half on. There was a look of eagerness on his face, but the DCI had seen that plenty of times before. Pathologists were either world-weary and apparently bored out of their minds, or they licked their lips with anticipation and the nastier the corpse the better they liked it.

Nathan Coates came up.

'Guv? What we got?' His squashed-in face was apprehensive.

'I doubt if it's him. Too far gone. Still, I also know what effect weather can have – he'll tell us more in a minute.'

They both stood looking up. The ravine rose sheer on either side.

'I 'ate this place, you know. Me dad brought us here once when we was kids, frightened us to death. He said there was robbers and that hiding in them caves, great big giants with red hairy beards and sweaty armpits and wooden clubs. I never stopped believing him really, had bad dreams about it for years.' He looked up at the scooped-out caves.

'How old were you, for God's sake?'

'Four, five? Bloody terrifyin'. That was what he did, me dad . . . he thought it was a laff.' Occasionally, Nathan's cheerful front gave way to let slip just this sort of titbit about his childhood.

'Simon.'

'Coming.'

Please God, don't let it be. Let this be . . . Well, what? Some other child's body, hastily buried in the ravine?

'What've we got?'

'Child. Between eight and ten years old. Cause of death probably fracture to the skull. There's quite a split at the back.'

God.

'How long has it been here?'

'Hard to say. The body had been partially exposed, we've had a few frosts and then heavy rain . . . I'll know when I've got it back to the mortuary.'

'Could it be three weeks, maybe less?'

'Unlikely.'

The pathologist looked up like an owl from out of the white hood with the strings drawn under his chin. He was standing in the shallow grave beside the body.

'Anyway, however long, it isn't the body of your missing schoolboy.'

'How do you know?'

'Because this is female. You got any of those unaccounted for?'

Forty-six

The conference room was packed already with radio, television and press. The DCI walked in briskly, his stance telling them he was on the attack not on the defensive. He looked in control and confident, Nathan thought, taking his own seat, and he knew he was not.

'Thanks, everyone. OK . . . we need your help. This morning the body of a child was found in Gardale Ravine. It was in a grave, covered in undergrowth and leaves. The body is of a female child aged approximately eight to ten years. Cause of death was a fractured skull, possible other injuries. We can't release any other information because we don't have any. Dental records, if any, are being checked of course . . . the body was naked, no trace of clothes so far. The whole ravine has been cordoned off and we are searching. At this stage there is nothing to link the finding of this body with the disappearance of the nine-year-old schoolboy David Angus but nor is there any evidence to the contrary. We have no leads yet as to the where-abouts of David.

'We want public involvement here. Not many people go down into Gardale Ravine at this time of year as you know, so anyone seen parking a car in the area . . . any vehicle . . . people walk on the moor at all times of year, so any sighting by walkers in the area above the ravine of someone with a child of this age, will be of significance. We have no reports of any missing child of this age in this area. We're liaising with other forces but there's nothing yet.

'OK, any questions?'

The room erupted, as Simon had known that it would. Why hadn't David Angus been found? One more missing child – when would there be another? What efforts were . . .? Would anyone from outside the force . . .? What about a review . . .? Would the DCI comment on the suicide of . . .?

He answered quickly and without ducking or trying to conceal his own frustration at the lack of progress in finding David Angus or the distress in finding the body of another child this morning. The press liked Serrailler, Nathan Coates thought. They knew bull when it was given to them, they were experts at probing out the weak spot, and hostility was always bubbling below the surface in a case like this. The media could turn on the force very quickly, especially if it sensed the public would be behind such a move, but they were still on side. They trusted what they were told, they appreciated being called in early and spoken to honestly.

The questions dried up and the room emptied.

The story was local headlines within half an hour, the national radio bulletins half an hour after that.

While the phone calls began to come in – 'Nutters and publicity seekers first', as Nathan had it – and they were sifted by the telephone teams, Simon went out to Bevham and the mortuary. He wanted to know whatever more there was to know about the child's body and he wanted to get out of the station. When he had got in from Gardale there had been another two emails on his screen from Diana. Last night there had been a message on his answerphone. He was angry. He also hated kicking about the station. After he had been to Bevham he wanted to go back to the ravine, and he also knew he had to go to Marilyn Angus.

Jonathan Nimmo was already at work. The child's body lay on the slab, pathetically small and little but skin and bone.

'Morning, Simon. You caught the killer?'

'She was killed?'

'Well, she didn't die in her bed. No, she died from a blow to the back of the head . . . see?'

Simon bent down.

Nimmo pointed. 'See . . . there? And here . . .'

'What hit her?'

'Actually, I'm inclined to think nothing in the sense you mean, I think she fell backwards, possibly from a height, though not a great height, and cracked her skull on a hard surface.'

'Oh.'

'Oh indeed.'

'So we might or might not be looking for a killer.'

'She could have been pushed, she could have slipped and fallen . . . impossible to say.'

'Anything else?'

'Fractured arm . . . and elbow . . . she probably fell awkwardly. I would say it was behind her, beneath her. Otherwise, no. Normal.'

'Was she sexually molested?'

'Hard to tell. Not with any violence. I'd need to have had her earlier. We've taken swabs but there won't be anything.'

'If she died accidentally . . .'

'What was she doing in an earth grave in Gardale Ravine. Quite.'

Nimmo was lifting the bones of the child's fingers one by one very gently, examining each, and setting it down again. His expression was intent and concentrated.

'Well, we have no reports of a girl of this age missing in our area.'

'Been brought in from outside then.'

'Maybe. It would be someone who knew where he was. Gardale is on the maps but otherwise it isn't a well-known spot to people out of the district.'

'Oh, I don't know – in summer plenty of people go down there.'

'And in winter almost none, so somebody knew he wouldn't be disturbed and the child might never be found.'

'Thinking aloud, Simon?'

Serrailler looked down at the body, so exposed under the glaring light. He felt near to tears. He thought of his niece Hannah, a child of similar age, sweet-fleshed and overflowing with zest and energy – with life.

'Let me know if you come up with anything else,' he said, and turned away from the slab.

'I won't. I'm pretty well done now. I'm happy with a fractured skull from a fall on to the back of the head.'

'Doesn't make it easier.'

'Sorry, not my problem,' Nimmo said cheerfully.

Simon went up to the fourth floor of the hospital and one of the League of Friends snack bars. He was hungry. The mortuary had never interfered with his appetite. Perhaps it was one tiny gene inherited from that long line of doctors. He bought coffee and a cheese roll. 'Over to you,' the pathologist had said but, for the moment, it was not of the small body he had just seen, or even of David Angus and some possible link between the two that he thought. It was of Martha. The last time he had been in Bevham General it had been to see her, after his return from Venice. He thought back to it. She had lain still and pale, attached to so many tubes and machines. He had drawn her. He had looked at the sketches only last night and to him they were death masks, even though she had not been dead. His feelings about her now were a confusion of simple grief, a measure of relief, sadness that he would not sit with and talk to her ever again – and something else. Deep under all of this something niggled at him, some vague doubt or uncertainty or anxiety. He could not define it, could not place it, but it was there, like a faint echo or a question, a strand of unfinished business.

Someone dropped a piece of china and it shattered, someone else had a coughing fit at another table and was given a hasty glass of water. A wheelchair squeaked on the floor. A bell rang. Life.

He drained his cup and walked quickly out to the next job. Sorrel Drive. Marilyn Angus. Somewhere in the depths of this building her husband's body lay in a mortuary drawer. Somewhere, David Angus's body lay.

His phone rang as he went across the car park.

'Guv?'

'What's happening?'

Nathan sounded odd – apologetic? Embarrassed?

'Sorry . . . only . . . you'd better come in.'

'I was on my way to see Mrs Angus.'

'Yeah, I know . . . only, maybe you'd better come back in here first, OK?'

'This is Simon Serrailler. I'm not here. Please leave me a message. Thanks.'

'You never are there, are you? Not for me. Or maybe you are and you are listening and not picking up . . . Simon? If you're there please just pick up the phone, darling . . . OK, well, whether you're there or not, I need to talk to you sometime. I miss you so much. I can't bear this. I don't understand it. What went wrong with us? Darling Simon, please, please call me. All my love.'

'We got a call,' Nathan said. He had an expression which Simon could not fathom. He had closed the door of Simon's room and stood with his back to it. 'Member of the public. Came in about half an hour ago.'

'And?'

'Bloke says he saw a car up near Gardale about the time we want . . . says he was up near Hylam Peak, in the car park. He reckons –'

'Jesus Christ.'

'Guv . . .'

'It was mine. He saw my car parked up there.'

'Yeah . . . it does check out with your number, only I said –'

'Bloody hell, I'd forgotten.'

But he remembered now. Lying in the turf with the sun chasing across the Peak and the sheep bleating. And then the helicopter shadowing the sun and the sheep fleeing madly up the hill. He knew now that the helicopter belonged to the American millionaire who had bought Seaton Vaux.

'There was a motorcyclist. He gave me a lift back to my car.'

'Right.'

Simon sat down at his desk. 'Can you get us some coffee? We need this sorted.'

'Guv.'

'Don't bother to go across the road, canteen stuff will do. And get the details of that call.'

He sat quite still after Nathan had gone out, eyes closed, hands behind his head, piecing the afternoon together, remembering every detail of his walk. Martha. He had gone after seeing her in the hospital and fearing that it would be the last time. He had wanted to walk things out of his system and needed to be on his own.

Nathan came back and set down the plastic beaker of canteen coffee. Simon had already opened a file on his laptop.

'I'm writing this down as a formal report. I've got the date and the time. I parked in the public car park and walked across the Peak towards Gardale. I was going down into the ravine but there was a downpour – it would have been too risky. I was making my way back when a motorbike appeared out of the deluge and he picked me up and dropped me back at my car. I saw no one else . . . there wasn't another car in the park, no other walkers that I came upon.'

'It ain't a problem, guv, you know that, just I thought you ought to know right away.'

'Thanks. You were right.' Simon took a swig of the powdery coffee. 'I don't know whether not getting down into the ravine was a good thing or not now. I might have seen something. Pity.'

'No way of telling, is there?'

'Nope. Anything else come in?'

'Half the bloody county calling in since that local radio appeal . . . all a load of nothing.'

'And no missing girl?'

'No. They're searching HOLMES but there ain't nothing yet. It's like it was someone's cat. People don't bother to report them missing.'

'Oh I don't know. When I was in my first uniform job we had a woman who used to report her cat missing every other week . . . then it turned up and she reported it found . . . then it went AWOL again . . .'

'Gawd. What was wrong with her?'

'Lonely,' Simon said.

'Nah, she fancied you, guv.'

'That too.'

'You seen Mrs Angus?'

'I was on my way there.'

'Sorry. Only . . .'

'Oh get out, get out, Nathan, stop apologising.'

'Guv.'

Simon turned to the laptop screen and began to type what he had called a report but which felt like a statement.

Forty minutes later he had finished and dropped a copy on to Nathan's desk. He also emailed it, with a note of explanation, to Paula Devenish. As he was doing so he checked his messages.

'*Darling. I can't stop thinking about you . . .*'

Delete. He banged the key, closed the machine and headed out.

Forty-seven

'Do I have to let you in?'

Marilyn Angus held the front door only slightly ajar and stared out at Simon. He had expected her to be carelessly dressed, unmade-up, distracted, as she had been the last time he had come to the house but today she wore lipstick and a silver necklace over a cashmere jumper; nothing might have happened were she not peering out at him with such a hostile and unwelcoming expression from a crack in the door.

'I would like to have a word if I may.'

She hesitated. Two days before she had asked the FLO to leave, refusing to discuss the subject, simply telling Kate that she must go.

Abruptly, she opened the door and walked away. Simon followed her into the kitchen. She stood with her back to him. She was indeed smartly dressed but there was something that troubled him about her, an air of unreality, as though she were not fully in touch with what had happened.

He hesitated, then sat down. Marilyn stared at him as if he were from a species she simply did not recognise, but then picked up the kettle from beside the sink and began to fill it. Her hands shook.

'I am concerned that you felt unable to have the family liaison officer with you any longer. If there was a problem I do need to know.'

'Kate? No. I liked Kate.'

'You're under no obligation to have an FLO with you, as you know, but if you're here alone . . .'

'I'm not. Lucy is here.'

'Lucy is twelve.'

'We are perfectly all right. The full inquest into Alan's death will be held at a later date, by the way. The first was opened and adjourned.' She spoke as if she were discussing one of her clients or a case she had read about in the paper.

'Yes. I'm sorry – it's distressing when these things are dragged out.'

'What do you think about what my husband did? What's your view of it?'

'I was extremely sorry – it . . .'

'It was cowardly. Wasn't it? Easy to do.'

'I doubt that, you know.'

'A few minutes of unpleasantness maybe . . . but then escape. He's out of it, isn't he? And what do I do? My husband is dead and my son is missing. I have to look after Lucy. But that is difficult in itself. She doesn't speak. She locks the door of her room. She goes off alone, she doesn't talk to anyone at school. When it was just David it was bad enough but now her father has killed himself she's lost to me completely. I have no idea what to do.'

'I think you should see someone . . . talk to someone. With Lucy. She needs you and you have to find a way of reaching her.'

'Some counsellor?'

'You could talk to your GP first . . . it's Chris Deerbon, isn't it? I saw him here. He would be able to advise about the best person for you to see.'

'I'm sure he would.'

The electric kettle was pouring steam. Marilyn seemed not to know that it was there so Simon got up. He switched it off, and began to open cupboards, found mugs and a jar of coffee, got milk out of the fridge. She stood watching.

'Where is Lucy now, at school?'

'I expect so.'

'You don't know?'

'I thought David was at school for the whole of that day, didn't I?'

'Do you take your daughter to her school?'

'She goes on the bus. A gang of her friends call for her.'

'And they came this morning as usual?'

'I expect so.'

Simon set the coffee things out on the table.

'I don't know how you like to drink it.'

Marilyn stared but made no move.

'I'm worried about you being here alone in the day and with just Lucy at night. Is there anyone who could come to be with you? I understand you prefer not to have an FLO but is there a friend or a relative who could come?'

377

'No.'

'No one?'

'I don't want anyone. Why would they want to be with me?'

'It's your need I'm worried about.'

'Oh, as to that . . . I need my husband. I need my son. I need my life to be as it was before the days when one disappeared and the other killed himself. I need what no one can give to me. How would having someone else sleeping in the spare room help those needs?'

He had no answer for her.

'I don't suppose you have any information for me, have you?'

'I'm sorry . . .'

'Well, there you are then.'

She pulled out a chair and sat down heavily. Simon moved the mug of coffee towards her. She had been told about the discovery of the girl's body in the grave at Gardale by Kate Marshall, who had called at the house specially. Kate had reported that Marilyn had seemed undisturbed by the news, as if it could have nothing to do with her. 'She asked why I was telling her this. It wasn't David's body, so it meant nothing to her. The thing is, guv, I had a feeling her reaction would have been the same if I'd told her it was David. She's like someone in a trance.'

Simon stayed to finish his coffee. He could think of nothing to say and felt that even if he had Marilyn would not take it in. The house oppressed him. She seemed scarcely aware that he was leaving, but sat on at the kitchen table, the coffee untouched in front of her.

In the car the DCI rang in to the station. Kate Marshall was out but Sally Cairns was the inspector on duty. She was the right person.

'I'm worried about Mrs Angus.'

'She won't have an FLO back, she was adamant. We can't make her, as you know.'

'I know. But I'm unhappy about her being on her own with just the daughter. She's not in a fit state to look after her.'

'I could get someone from CSU to go round. Social services would be a bit heavy, don't you think?'

'Yes. I don't want to frighten her or to put her back up. She's in shock, not irresponsible and Lucy is twelve, not a toddler. But Sorrel Drive isn't very neighbourly. Too damned posh – lawyers and so on.'

'Trouble is we're pretty stretched. There's been a serious pile-up on the bypass – two coaches have crashed, seven dead so far. The driver of one was drunk and managed to get out and run for it and he hasn't been caught yet. Plus there's been a knife fight in the underpass leading from the Eric Anderson . . . drug dealing down there again and some PE teacher went to try and sort things out himself.'

Simon groaned. He knew what it was like for the relief when everything came in at once. 'Is that all?'

'No, a young man has been found in a ditch. Badly beaten up. Someone you had in here the other day for questioning.'

Andy Gunton. 'Who's dealing?'

'Nathan's gone to BG.'

'Fine. Thanks anyway, Sally.'

'If I had another body you could have it – though come to that I could do with one myself.'

Simon smiled. Inspector Sally Cairns was the wrong side of thirteen stone. Her dressings-down, which could reduce the toughest cops to jelly, were the stuff of legend.

Simon turned the car round and headed out to Cat's village by the roundabout route, but even so got caught in the traffic blocks caused by the pile-up and a slow tail heading back towards Bevham.

It was after three when he reached the farmhouse. He let himself in by the back door. The kitchen was empty and quiet. Mephisto was sitting in the lozenge of sunlight falling on to the wide window sill.

Serrailler helped himself to the ingredients for a sandwich, made a mug of tea and slumped on to the sofa. At once, the events of the morning fell away and the peace and warmth of the kitchen, the atmosphere of the whole house, soothed him into a state of deep relaxation. For half an hour he would forget the Angus case, forget the body of the child in the ravine, forget . . .

He remembered Diana but immediately pushed her to the back of his mind. He would not let her in here or allow her to enrage him. She did not belong in his life and he would keep her out of it, whether she stalked him with phone messages and emails or even unannounced visits to his flat.

He had better things to think about. That morning he had been contacted by a Mayfair gallery suggesting a co-exhibition of his drawings. His fellow artist would be a man whose work Simon admired. The call had come as a total surprise and made him feel as he had felt very few times in his life; for five minutes everything else had receded into the distance. Nothing had ever seemed so important. If he could change his life . . . if he could afford to . . . would he?

A strange cloudy band seemed to spread across him, blotting out two-thirds not only of what he did but what he was. No colleagues. No challenges. No satisfaction when a case was concluded. But there was everything else. His flat. His drawing. Travel, anywhere, everywhere, for half the year. He could be a nomad with a canvas satchel.

The door opened.

'Hi, bro. Saw your car from the bathroom window. Here, have this a minute . . .' Cat held the baby under one arm like a rolled-up newspaper, which she dumped into Simon's lap.

'Hi, Felix.'

'Prop him up or he'll sick on you.'

'Thanks.'

'He's been sicky all day. Here . . .' She threw a clean kitchen towel across. 'Be prepared. I was asleep.'

'Thought so . . . nap while you can. What a life.'

'I'm loving it, Si. If it weren't for the fact that Chris is on his knees with exhaustion I'd seriously think of giving up being a GP for good . . . just do the odd clinic and locums. But how can I? I might have to go back to take over some surgeries soon anyway, I can't let Chris go on like this.'

Simon leaned his head back and tucked Felix into the crook of his arm. The baby's head dropped sideways on to him. He listened to his sister chatting as she unloaded the dishwasher and put things away, poured herself a glass of water, let Mephisto out of the window.

Suddenly, he wanted a kitchen full of warmth and tea and a cat and a baby, full of happiness and a contented everyday domestic sound. Full of love. The memory of Freya lanced through him.

'You OK?'

'Yes. No.'

'Hang on till I dump these things in the washing machine . . .' Cat picked up the laundry basket and went out to the scullery. Felix opened his eyes and was sick at the same moment. Simon reached for the towel and wiped them both up.

'Oh God. I don't think he's ill. I ate a curry and it's disagreed with him. You forget. Amazing but you forget.'

She took Felix to the sink, wiped his face gently with a damp piece of tissue, and returned him to Simon. 'Do you want wiping as well?' Cat sat down on the sofa.

He had thought that he had come to talk to her about Marilyn Angus and to hear her advice, and when that was done, to tell her about the gallery. He had thought they were the things that most concerned him, were at the front of his mind. He had not expected to hear himself say, 'I want to ask you something about Martha.'

'Martha?' Cat raised her eyebrows.

'It's been niggling.'

'What?'

He sighed and shifted Felix gingerly but the sickness seemed to have spent itself.

'When she was in BG and I came back from Venice, she was pretty ill. When Dad rang me there he said if I didn't come home I wouldn't see her again, or words to that effect.'

'Yes. She was very ill.'

'But she didn't die.'

'No. They gave her an antibiotic she hadn't had before, something pretty new, and she responded. It happens. They didn't expect it to but it did.'

'Yes. But then she died without any warning, in her sleep . . . when she was better. It's bothered me.'

'OK, let me explain. You know that anyone as badly handicapped as that from birth is likely to have all sorts of weaknesses and defects . . . can be anything – kidneys, lungs, but most often it's the heart. In her case it was known about and checked regularly. It wasn't serious enough to kill her as a baby, but every time she had an infection, whether it was in her lungs, her bladder – she got a lot of kidney infections – whatever, and she was given very powerful drugs, the heart weakness was exacerbated. The last bout was very serious . . . if she hadn't responded to the new antibiotic she would have died, no question. But obviously her heart was affected more seriously than anyone recognised, or else it was just one last straw that broke the camel's back, we can't be sure. Either way, her chest infection was cured, but her heart wasn't, so it just gave up. It isn't uncommon. Not a bad way to die either.'

'I suppose so.'

Cat looked at him for a long time. 'What is it?'

Everything seemed to bubble up from somewhere deep below the surface of his consciousness.

'Is there any possibility that someone took her life? I'm choosing my words carefully here . . .'

'Who? And even more, why?'

'I don't know . . . well, yes, the why is easy enough.'

'Is it?'

'It was generally thought that she had no quality of life. I never thought so, but you all did, and everyone at Ivy Lodge, except that sweet girl Shirley. No one thought her life was worth living.'

'Sweeping.'

'But true.'

'Yes, I suppose so. Yes, especially in the last couple of years when she was succumbing to infections so easily. But if people thought that – it's a big step to doing something about it. I mean to murdering her. That's the word you have to use, Si. You should know.'

'Yes.'

'Derek Wix saw her first and he was confident it was heart failure. Chris went in to see her. He didn't examine her, true, but he saw her and he didn't question Derek's opinion. Nobody at Ivy Lodge questioned the cause of death. You bloody detectives see crime everywhere you turn.'

Simon's mobile rang, waking Felix, who wailed in fright.

'Nathan, where are you?'

'Standing outside BG, guv. I been in seein' Andy Gunton only he's still in a bad way, they wasn't letting anyone in.'

'Have his family been told?'

'Sister's there now. I know that Michelle Tait. She had a mouthful for me when she saw me down the corridor, but then she's always had a mouthful for anyone.'

'Do we know what happened?'

'Naw. Man with the 'edge trimmer was going along there, looked down and saw him in the ditch. Called the ambulance straight off. He'd been beaten up and dropped out of a vehicle, seems like.'

'Nasty.'

'He's mixed up with some nasty people . . . I'm off up to see Lee Carter.'

'You know him?'

'Oh yeah, I know Lee Carter all right.'

'Well, be careful, take someone tough with you.'

'You mean I ain't tough?'

'You know what I mean.'

'You see that Mrs Angus, guv?'

'I did. She's in a bad way.'

'Well, she was always going to be, wasn't she?'

'Yes,' Serrailler said. 'Yes, I suppose she was.' He liked the way his DS went straight at things.

Simon turned back into the kitchen. 'Cat, Marilyn Angus is your patient, isn't she?'

'Chris's.'

'But you know her?'

'Not very well. Why?'

He pulled out a chair and sat on it back to front, facing Cat as she sat with Felix at her breast.

'She worried me a lot.'

He told her about his visit to the Angus house. Cat listened carefully, stroking the baby's small head. His feet curled and uncurled with the extreme pleasure of suckling.

'She's obviously in shock, but that's not surprising.'

'She didn't seem to connect with me. It was as though I was there but not there. She seemed in a trance.'

'Detached?'

'Yes . . . more . . .'

'Zombie-like?'

'That describes it well enough, yes. It's the daughter I feel most concerned about. She was at school but it sounds as if she isn't talking to her mother at all – she locks herself in her room the minute she comes home. Marilyn Angus won't have anyone else in the house, said they were fine.'

'Could she be suicidal?'

'No. She didn't seem to have enough focus, enough energy or sense of purpose for that.'

'Would she be a danger to Lucy?'

'Only in the sense that she'd neglect her, be unaware of her or what she was doing, not bother with her.'

'Not good. Do you want me to ask Chris to call in?'

'Someone should.'

'He's got so much on his plate. But he'll go. I think the locum actually did a surgery this morning.' She lifted Felix and began to rub his back.

'OK, I'd better hit the road.'

'Oh no. You sit there until you tell me what you were driving at before your phone rang.'

He had known she would bring him back to it. He had never been able to evade her, even when they were children.

'You asked if I thought someone could have killed Martha.'

'Not in so many words.'

'Oh, don't be jesuitical, it's what you meant.'

'All right. Do you?'

'But who?'

'That isn't part of the question. I just meant, is it possible?'

'Well, anything might be. Is it likely? No, of course not. Why would anyone do that? Because they wanted to be rid of her?'

'Because they felt sorry for her?'

'Who felt sorry for her?'

'God, Cat, stop challenging me.'

'You've challenged me by starting this. Bloody policemen. There is such a thing as natural death, you know.'

'Let's drop it. I've got to go. Nathan has gone to see a potentially dangerous man. I ought to be there.'

'Suit yourself. I just wish you hadn't walked in here and sown all sorts of doubts and left them to sprout up between the cracks in the floor tiles.'

Simon turned from pulling on his jacket. His sister was crying, holding the baby close to her face.

'Oh Christ, I'm so sorry. I didn't think, I shouldn't have said anything.'

'You meant it, you should say it. It's OK, I'm still full of hormones, take no notice.'

Simon squatted down, handed Cat a clean handkerchief, and took Felix from her while she wiped her eyes. The baby smelled of warm flesh and milk.

'I'm sorry.'

'I honestly don't think there's a one-in-a-million chance of it, Si. I really don't. Put it out of your mind. Go and find David Angus, please.' She looked into his face. He said nothing. There was nothing to say. 'And now there's another thing, this child's body in Gardale,' Cat said. 'They've got to be connected, haven't they?'

'Not necessarily. We don't know anything at this stage. I'm not ruling it in or out.'

Cat's eyes filled with tears again. 'Put him in his crib, will you? He's had enough and I'll only sob all over him.'

Simon settled his nephew down, then went to sit beside Cat. He put his arms round her.

'I am a shit.'

'No more than usual.'

'Forget it all.'

'Not sure I can. Now, hop it, I'm going to read a nice comforting book for half an hour before they come piling in wanting tea and homework. I'll ring Chris. He's in an antenatal clinic, he can call in on Marilyn Angus on his way home.'

'Thanks, sis.'

'What do they pay you for, DCI Serrailler?'

Forty-eight

Andy Gunton could scarcely move. His neck was in a collar, his right arm in plaster. He was on a mattress which was supposed to ease the pain of his leg and his bruised back but he wondered how much difference it made.

He couldn't do anything much. Only think.

Michelle had been in twice and harangued him in such a shrill voice they had asked her to go. No one else, apart from the police. He hadn't been fit to talk to them, but they'd be back. He wasn't complaining though, he knew he was lucky to be alive. Had Lee Carter meant him to be alive? The van had run at him, blinding him with its headlights at the same time as it headed fast out of nowhere towards him. One minute he'd been walking home from the airfield, the next rolling in agony in the deep ditch beside the black lane. He remembered little else . . . just a blur of noise and lights and pain, and the desperate need to stop anyone moving him. Then he had woken up in A & E.

The message had come as usual via a text. *Brrtts Lane 2am.*

He wasn't going. How could he? He'd been caught, he'd talked to the police. He was in a sweat already. But Pete had made it plain that if more money in envelopes through the post was not forthcoming he was out on the street. He meant it. The police would be watching him round the clock. They'd want him to lead them to bigger fish, they'd be watching and waiting, laying a trap.

No, he wasn't going to do another Carter job. Not till he woke up at one o'clock and lay there wondering what would happen if he didn't. When it occurred to him that they might come here, he shot out of bed and began pulling on his jeans and sweater. It was a cold night. Matt was lying on his stomach, one foot sticking out from under the duvet. Andy lifted it and shoved it back. The foot was freezing. He hesitated but his nephew merely groaned slightly.

Barrett's Lane was not far away. He didn't mind the walking at night. It was keeping him fit, but it was so cold that a half-mile was pleasanter than two or three. The lane was a snicket between the backs of some old, dilapidated houses and he saw the car waiting as soon as he turned into it. It was a black Ford Focus and he didn't know the driver who started the engine as soon as Andy came towards him and accelerated away before he'd properly climbed in and got the door closed.

'Watch it, I nearly fell out.'

Silence. Andy looked sideways. He was a handsome lad with a shaved head and four rings in one ear. He drove fast, screaming the wheels on every corner and said nothing at all the whole way to the airfield. Once there he had driven to the hangar. 'Out.' Andy got out. The Focus screeched off. The airfield was silent, deserted, so far as he could make out, freezing cold and pitch black. He huddled into the lee of the hangar but the wind found him out. He edged round the other side, turning up his collar. His hands were stiff with cold. On this side it was worse, the wind coming straight towards him. He waited. Waited for maybe almost an hour. He was so cold he couldn't think and he felt sick. In the end, he walked across the airfield and back, jogged a bit on the spot and then made for the gateway. Nobody was coming. Lee Carter had been taking the piss. Probably he could see him from some satellite, could track him the five and a half miles home through the freezing night and laugh about it.

He had turned out into the lane and was jogging along it. Then there had been the headlights and the van heading for him and the crack of pain and terror as it hit.

Whenever he closed his eyes he had a rerun of it.

The doctors had seen him again that morning. His arm would heal fine, though they told him his bruising would get more painful before it got less. They had been watching for concussion but decided he had none. Tomorrow morning someone would take him down to X-ray and if his neck was OK he'd only need to be in another couple of days.

He wanted it to be a week or a month. He felt safe, warm and quiet and away from both his sister and Lee Carter. He wondered if he would be allowed back to Michelle's and if not where else he could go.

A woman in a green tunic came into the cubicle with a trolley of magazines and sweets. He wanted a bar of chocolate but he had no money. He'd gone out without any that night and he couldn't ask Michelle.

'Thanks,' he said, 'nothing.' And gave the green woman his sweetest smile.

'Afternoon.'

Nathan jumped-up bloody Coates and a sidekick with one of those weird, pencil-line beards. Must be like doing dot-to-dot trying to shave round that.

Sidekick looked fed up and didn't say anything. Nathan Coates pulled up the visitor's chair.

'Feelin' better?'

'Yeah, great.'

Nathan grinned. 'You was lucky, mate.'

'I'm not your mate, Coates.'

'Don't suppose you feel lucky either.'

'Can you lend me a quid?'

'What for?'

'I fancied a bar of chocolate from the trolley only I got no money.'

'Go on then . . .' Nathan took some change out of his pocket. 'Get a couple of Mars bars, Bevin.' Sidekick caught the money and wandered off.

'I owe you.'

'You bloody do. OK, Andy, you was in no fit state to answer questions before. Let's have another go. What happened?'

'I was run over.'

'Who by?'

'Couldn't see.'

'Just like that – you was walking along a country lane near an airfield at three o'clock in the morning by yourself, out for a stroll, and blow me, car comes and runs you over. Come on, don't mess me about.'

'He shone his headlights into my face. How could I see who it was?'

'Could have been a she then.'

'Yeah, right.'

'What sort of car?'

'Van.'

'What sort of van?'

'Couldn't see.'

'But you saw it was a van?'

'It was big . . . bigger than a car.'

'What were you doing?'

'How do you mean?'

Nathan sighed. Sidekick came back with the Mars bars and handed them over. Nathan scooped both into his pocket.

'Here –'

'You give me some straight answers, I'll give you the Mars. Right. You're already in a mess, aren't you? Let's see what you can do to get yourself out of it. Who sent you down to the airfield this time? What kind of car was you picking up?'

'I wasn't. I got a text telling me to go down to Barrett's Lane, two o'clock. I'd be met.'

'And were you?'

'Yeah and I don't know who he was, I never seen him before. Black Ford Focus.'

'And?'

'Drove to the airfield. He dropped me by the hangars. Told me to wait, then he drove off. I waited . . . waited till me balls was frozen off just about. No one was there, no one came. I started to walk home. I was walking up the lane when this van come out of nowhere straight at me. Had me in the ditch. I don't remember any more till I woke up in A & E. Don't even remember much of that. Can I have me chocolate?'

Nathan hesitated, then threw it on to the bed. It was out of Andy Gunton's reach. But he did not protest. It was as if the stuffing suddenly went out of him. He sank back looking exhausted and tried to turn his face to look out of the slab of sky.

Nathan reached over, opened up the Mars bar and handed it to him.

'Thanks,' Andy said dully.

'OK, you sure that's it?'

'Yes.'

'Nothing else at all?'

'No.'

'Do you think it was Lee Carter drove at you?'

'No.'

'Why not?'

'Because he wouldn't do it himself, would he? Be tucked up in bed. He don't get his hands dirty these days, pays other people to do that.'

'Right – people like you. You're a bleedin' idiot, Andy. You had your chance. What got into you?'

'You got no idea, have you? None of you. I was trained, I was getting a good job in market gardening, I was straight, I was clean, I had it all sorted. Only there ain't no good jobs . . . it ain't like you plan or like you want.'

'And then you bump into Lee Carter.'

'Right.'

'And everything goes out of your stupid head.'

Andy looked at him. If he had not ached everywhere, if his arm wasn't hurting, if he hadn't felt so crap, he'd have yelled into smug Coates's mushed-up face. But he hadn't the energy and where would it get him?

'Everything,' he said.

Nathan Coates stood up. 'That'll do. When you out of here?'

'Couple of days.'

'Back to your Michelle's?'

'She's thinking about it.'

'Where else is there?'

'Shop doorway.'

'Your probation officer can sort something, that's what he's for.'

'She. Nothing doin'.'

'They won't let you sleep on the street.'

'Don't hold your breath.'

'Come on,' Nathan said to sidekick. 'Here.' He threw the second Mars bar on to Andy Gunton's bed. 'On the house.'

Andy watched them go out of the cubicle. Sidekick's shoes squeaked.

It occurred to him that something Nathan Coates had said, or maybe behind what he had said, had been a hint. He was hinting at a chance – and it would be a last one too, Andy knew that. Not that Nathan had power to give him anything but he could speak to people who had and what he had to do now was decide. He'd decided before, in prison, and it had all gone wrong though he couldn't quite work out how, it had happened too quickly, almost while his back was turned. Now he might have a chance to decide again and see it through. Somehow he had to avoid Lee Carter and anyone to do with him. Somehow he had to get away from Michelle's. Somehow he had to get a job, preferably one he was trained for but to start with, any job. Somehow . . . You had to feel strong to see that sort of thing through and he wasn't feeling strong. When Carter found out that he hadn't been killed by the van he could be in danger again too.

A nurse came in. The plain one with the weird hair like his mother used to have, in flat waves. Her front teeth rested on her bottom lip, like rabbits' teeth.

'Now Andy, let's have a look at this dressing, see if we can't get it off you for good.'

Forty-nine

'I want to talk to someone.'

'What is it concerning, sir?'

'I'm not talking to anybody, only the Boss.'

'That doesn't give me much to go on, sir, if you –'

'The kid.'

'Which kid would that be, sir?'

'I'm not talking to you, I want the Boss. You found a kid's body . . .'

There was a long silence. The operator waited.

'Are you there, caller?'

'Gardale Ravine.' It was like a soft snarl.

'Just hold on a moment. I'll put you through. Don't hang up please.' The operator went through to the DCI.

Three minutes later Serrailler banged open the door of the CID room and shouted for Nathan.

'Where we off to then?'

They were heading out of Lafferton, Serrailler driving.

'Not sure . . . get the map out, will you? I know round here pretty well but I can't place this one exactly . . . other side of Hylam Peak . . . Fly'ole, he called it. Out to Hylam, he said, but take the track before the climb up there, beside a metal oil drum, four miles on, pull in behind a Dutch barn.'

'Sounds iffy.'

'He knows something. This isn't a wind-up.'

Nathan did not argue.

'While we've got five minutes, guv, I wanted to run something past you about Andy Gunton.'

'Go ahead.'

Nathan sketched out his visit to the hospital, how he had found Andy Gunton, what he thought.

'Look, what gets me is this. He's not bad, Andy Gunton . . . his family was a step-up from ours, I can tell you; his dad was a layabout but his mum was salt of the earth, she kept them together. That Michelle's a nasty piece, give you a face full of abuse soon as look at you and she's got no time for me at all, only she's bringing them kids up OK . . . But Andy . . . He done well inside. It's since he come out it's gone pear-shaped. What'd he have to bang into bloody Carter for?'

'Lafferton's a small place. He needn't have got tied up with him again though.'

'That's easy said, guv.'

'I know.'

'He ain't had a proper chance.'

'What are you asking for, Nathan, me to give him a job?'

'If he hadn't got to live with that sister, if he had a job he liked. I think someone ought to give him a go, that's all.'

'Fine. Who?'

'Have a word with housing? His probation officer?'

'On what grounds? I had him in last week and charged him with TADA.'

'Yeah, right.' Nathan slumped miserably down in his seat.

'Your heart's in the right place, DS Coates. OK, we're looking for an oil drum.'

It was fifty yards further on. They turned on to the cinder track. The grass had virtually grown over the dirt. Above and ahead of them, Hylam Peak loomed up green-grey in the poor light. A pair of buzzards circled and soared and a few sheep looked as if they were about to tip over the steep ledge but continued to graze unconcerned.

The car bumped over the rough ground. There was no sign of a house or even of the Dutch barn.

'Something about this place,' Nathan said.

'Good or bad?'

'Not good.'

'Get it on a bright sunlit afternoon it's very different.'

'Still looms over you though, don't it?'

They turned and followed a scraggy line of hedge. Sharp stones and bits of brick jutted out of the ground.

'A fiver says I get a flat tyre.' Simon cursed as he swerved.

'This is a wind-up, guv.'

But as he spoke, a pair of dogs raced towards the car, mangy, ribby and snarling. The track dipped suddenly, and to their right they saw first the rusty tin roof of an ancient Dutch barn, and beside it, a caravan. Another two dogs were tied up to a post beside it. The DCI pulled the car up and hooted and the dogs started to hurl themselves at the tyres, until the door of the caravan opened and a man appeared. He yelled and the dogs scurried back to the van, running low to the ground.

'Seems safe.' Simon got out of the car.

'DCI Serrailler, Lafferton Police, this is DS Coates. Mr . . .?'

'I never said.'

'So you didn't.'

The man watched them walk towards him. 'Who's the Boss? I said I was talking to the Boss, that's all. I don't trust policemen.'

'I'm the Boss and I'm a policeman.'

'Talk to you then. Go on, scrubber, 'op it.'

The DCI nodded at Nathan, who began to walk round to the other side of the caravan. The dogs growled.

'Other way.' The man pointed. Nathan went slowly in the direction of the car, but stopped after a few yards and stood with his arms folded, watching.

'Right, I'm the Boss, talk to me. But not until you tell me your name.'

'Murdo.'

'Mr Murdo.'

'Come in here then.'

Serrailler followed him into the caravan, glancing back at Nathan, who moved nearer again. He had expected filth, stench and disarray, judging by the look of the man and the dogs, as well as the mess scattered about outside. But the interior of the van was clean and orderly, though stuffed with furniture and bric-à-brac that would have been more in keeping in the front room of a terraced house.

'Sit down or you'll crack your head open.'

Simon was already stooped. Murdo indicated a wooden wheelback chair.

'Right, you said you had some information, Mr Murdo. Can you tell me exactly what it's about?'

'Cup of tea?'

'No thanks.'

'Suit yourself.'

Murdo sat down on the bench beneath the caravan window. He was a huge man, brawny with red hairs thick on his chest and grey hair sprouting from his ears and nostrils. He picked up a tin from the ledge and began to pull out strands of tobacco and roll up a cigarette.

Serrailler waited, looking at him closely. He wished he could draw Murdo, just as he was, vest, hair, roll-ups and the inside of the caravan too . . .

'I live here because it's what I choose. I don't bother no one, no one bothers me. Straight on that, are we?'

'I've no problem with it.'

'I don't go far. No desire. But I get about round here and I see this and hear that. Last autumn they was here – travellers. Not gyppos, you get me, travellers.'

'I know the difference.'

'Right. Slovenly lot. Litter, vans, filth, fires where they ought to know better. They camped for maybe three weeks, half a mile further along towards Gardale. Glad to see the back of them. Set the dogs off every night, kids came round here giving cheek, peering in these windows. They'd have nicked the shirt off me back only they was too frit. Week before they left, there was an accident. Kids mucking about; one of 'em fell off the roof of a camper van.'

'How did you find out about this?'

'I told you. I see and hear this and that.'

'Did the child go to hospital?'

'Child was dead, Boss. Girl. Fell on her head on a heap of stone slabs. That's what I know.'

'What else do you know, Murdo?'

Murdo took a long slow drag of his roll-up, looking at Serrailler all the time through half-closed eyes, as if summing him up again. Then he said, 'I know they buried her.'

'Who did?'

'Family. You know they buried her as well. You know where.'

'You tell me.'

'I go along with the dogs. I get rabbits and that, along the ravine. They buried her up a bit of sloping bank. They was digging one afternoon. Next day they buried her and next after that they was gone.'

'Why didn't you come and tell us about this before now?'

Murdo shrugged. 'Not my business. Not yours, not then.'

'It was ours. By law every accidental death has to be reported to us and an inquest has to be held.'

'What good is that supposed to do?'

'It's a safeguard, apart from anything else. Think about it. And you can't bury human bodies where you please without permission.'

'She was theirs.'

'Oh come on, Murdo, you know very well . . . and why have you waited to come to us till now?'

'Heard it on the radio. Asking about it.'

'You needn't have come forward, any more than you didn't at first. Something's made you.'

'Well, it's that other kid. When they said it might have to do with the other kid . . . the boy . . . shook me up.'

'Why? You just told me the girl fell off a van and hit her head. Why would that have anything to do with the disappearance of the schoolboy in Lafferton weeks later?'

'It didn't have. That's what I mean. I know what happened to the girl, I know when and who she was and how. Nothing to do with the boy. Got no idea about the boy. I heard all about him and I never thought anything till you lot started to put two and two together and make five. I got no friends with the travellers. They're nothing to me. But they ent child snatchers, Boss. They need someone to stand up for 'em; it might as well be me.'

'Do you know where they went after they left here?'

'Cornwall way.'

'Any more than that?'

Murdo stood up. He pinched the end of his roll-up out with his thick fingers and dropped it into a tin ashtray.

'You heard the lot. You can go, Boss. I told you, I don't like police. Fewer police I see the better. You do what you have to and I never said anything to you about it and there's no witness, is there?'

He held open the caravan door and waited. Serrailler passed close to Murdo as he left. He smelled Old Holborn tobacco and sweat.

'Thanks. We may be in touch again. You'll be here?'

'What for? I got nothing else to say and I said nothing anyway, did I?'

As Serrailler walked back to Nathan, the dogs started up again behind the van.

'I wasn't keen on that, guv,' Nathan said as they moved off. 'I come right up under the window when you was in there.'

'Thanks. Hear anything?'

'Naw.'

'Pity.'

They bumped along the track.

'Anything then?'

'Yes and no. It'll need looking into but I don't think he's guilty of anything except maybe withholding information . . . which he has now given it to us voluntarily.'

'Any help on David Angus?'

'No,' Serrailler said grimly, 'absolutely bloody none.'

Fifty

'Guv?'

'Hold on . . .'

Simon switched off the heat under a saucepan in which he was about to cook pasta and went back to the living room. Reception on his mobile was best beside the tall windows overlooking Cathedral Close, now empty and silver under the lamps.

'OK.'

'Sorry – only did you know Mrs Angus was doing an interview on telly in half an hour? Late night, after the news. They're doing a special on the case.'

'*What?* No one's been through me. Have you spoken to Ken?'

Ken Mather was the force area press officer.

'Yeah, he don't know about it either. All done on the quiet.'

'Bloody hell. How'd you find out?'

'Em saw a trailer. Half past ten.'

He wondered whether to ring the Chief but he decided against it. The television broadcast had been sewn up behind their backs, it was not the fault or the responsibility of anyone in the force and Simon had nothing to apologise for. He was angry with Marilyn Angus and he did not understand her. If she felt another public appeal about David was necessary she should have come to them but now she had refused to have a family liaison officer with her it was difficult to keep abreast of everything she was thinking and doing. He cooked his pasta and opened a jar of tomato sauce, grated parmesan on to the lot and poured a glass of wine. As he sat down at the kitchen table the house phone rang. He hesitated, then decided to let the machine pick up for him.

At ten thirty, he turned on the television.

The presenter was a smart young woman with long blonde hair wearing a pinstripe trouser suit and the familiar media expression of grave sympathy.

'Three weeks ago, Marilyn Angus kissed her nine-year-old son David goodbye in the drive of their spacious house in the leafy cathedral city of Lafferton.

'Nothing has been seen of David since that morning. There have been no reported sightings, no one has come forward with any information. Police have searched the whole of Lafferton and the surrounding area. The river and the canal have been dredged and nearby peaks and moorland scoured. But nothing has been found of David. It is as though he vanished into thin air. Last week there was a possible development. A body was found in a grave in a deep and lonely ravine. The remains were those of a girl, aged between eight and ten.

'Earlier today Marilyn Angus came into the news studio and talked to our special reporter Lorna Macintyre. She did so because she is desperate for news of her son and desperate that not enough is being done to find out what has happened to him – where he went that Tuesday morning – with whom – and why. Here is that interview.'

In the studio background, the photograph of David Angus was blown up to huge proportions. Marilyn had been placed so that he was slightly to her right, his face constantly in view when hers was. She wore a black skirt and blouse and a single strand of pearls. Her face had the hollow look, her eyes were sunken, but they were wild, too, as wild as Simon had seen them the last time he had faced her. Her hands were clasped together in front of her and she moved her fingers constantly, rubbing them together, linking and unlinking them.

The young woman interviewer spoke the usual sympathetic platitudes. It was unfair to dismiss them as false, and yet they sounded so.

'Mrs Angus, can I ask you, first of all, how you are managing to cope? Obviously it's impossible for anyone to imagine what your feelings are, what you are going through, but perhaps you can tell us how you try and get through each day?'

There was a terrible, long moment of silence. It seemed as if Marilyn Angus might not be able to continue at all, but then she said in a low voice, 'By determination. I am determined to find out what has happened to David. Determined he will be found and that whoever has taken him and is holding him will be brought to justice. That's the only thing that keeps me going really.'

'It's a very brave statement . . . and obviously you are determined. Are you finding a lot of support in this?'

'I support myself. You have to. Neighbours, work colleagues . . . people ring, come to see me. They've been splendid. But in the end, I'm on my own.'

'With your other child, of course . . . your daughter Lucy.'

'Yes, but I can't put any of this on to her shoulders.'

'How old is she?'

'She's only twelve.'

'Now as I just mentioned, your husband, Alan, apparently committed suicide. This has obviously been another devastating blow –'

Marilyn interrupted. 'It was his way of coping. He got out. He couldn't take any more.'

'I see.' Lorna Macintyre looked down at her notes. She seemed faintly embarrassed. 'I imagine you are being helped in other ways, too . . . by the tide of public sympathy, by your own community in Lafferton and by everyone's assistance, by the police –'

'The police do their job, but that's about all.'

'I'm sorry . . .'

410

'They haven't found him, have they?' Marilyn's voice became shrill. 'They have found no trace of David, they have no idea what happened and the whole trail seems to have been allowed to go cold.'

'Is that how you feel? That not enough is being done by the police to find your son?'

'I think plenty was being done – they were very active at the beginning, we had teams of officers going over my house with a fine-tooth comb an hour after I reported him missing. I don't see so much sign of urgent activity now, though. Perhaps I'm judging too harshly.'

'Now I gather you had a police officer, a family liaison officer, or FLO, living with you but that you asked her to leave, is that right?'

'I wouldn't like anyone to think I had anything at all against her personally – DC Marshall – she was a nice person. But having a police officer living in your house is an intrusion when you're trying to cope with something like this. We're – I'm – very private. I didn't like it. Also . . . well, she was working for the force, and answerable to them first and foremost. I don't know if people realise that . . . perhaps they think a family liaison officer is there to help the family and be on their side but it isn't the case. You don't really feel an FLO is on your side, you know. Essentially, you are under suspicion and they are spies. I'm sorry if that sounds harsh.'

'I know this is a difficult question for you, but have you any idea, any at all, about what might have happened to David, where he might be?'

'I wish to God I had. But no, of course not. I have none. What possible reason would someone have for taking a small boy from outside his own house in broad daylight?'

'And have you anything to say, any appeal you'd like to make?'

'Yes.'

Marilyn Angus looked at the camera directly. Her eyes were wild again, her hands working. 'If you know where David is . . . if you are holding David . . . please, please think hard about what you are doing. Imagine what it's like for me . . . for his family. This has killed his father already. Can you live with that? Can you? Let David go. Bring him home. Call the police and bring an end to this. I beg you. And if anyone can think and think again about some little thing they might have heard or seen . . . that might have something to do with David's disappearance . . . no matter where you live, who you are . . . please come forward. Please. I've lost the most precious thing in the world and this ordeal is –' She fell suddenly silent and turned her head abruptly away from the camera.

At once, the screen was filled with the picture of David, bright, alert, intelligent David, the picture everyone in the country now knew so well.

Simon switched off the set and went to the phone. He was uncertain whether to call the press officer, or the Chief, and as he hesitated it rang.

'Simon? Paula Devenish.'

'Ma'am. I take it you saw the interview?'

412

'Yes and I'm very annoyed about it – not with you, with her, with the irresponsible media. Let me repeat what I said when I was at the station – you know that I'm on your side and even more so now. I'm absolutely certain you are still doing your utmost . . . all of you. Let's get that straight.'

'Thank you, ma'am. But . . .'

'Exactly. But what I know and what the public will now believe, let alone what Marilyn Angus feels, are different things. I think we need an outside review.'

'I'm glad you suggested it and I agree. It's very important, particularly after tonight.'

'I'll see to it first thing. Don't let this get you down. It's unfortunate – bad publicity always is – but Mrs Angus is in a state of shock and they should be ashamed of themselves for exploiting her in the way we just saw. I gather they acted completely behind our backs.'

'Totally. I knew nothing, nor did Ken.'

'Right. I have every confidence in you. Understood?'

'Understood. And thanks.'

'Get some sleep. We'll speak tomorrow.'

When he replaced the receiver, Simon noticed the red message light blinking and pressed it, to hear his mother's voice.

'Darling, I would like to talk to you. Can you come over tomorrow, I suppose it's too late now? Will you call me back?'

He replayed the message. She sounded worried, almost panicky. It was ten to eleven and his parents were early to bed. The message had come in before nine.

He dialled the farmhouse. 'Dr Deerbon.' His voice was soft.

'Hi, Chris. You on call?'

'As ever.'

'Has either of you spoken to Ma tonight?'

'Don't think so. Cat's in the bathroom, I'll ask her when she comes out but I'm pretty sure she hasn't. What's up?'

'Not sure. I just picked up a message from her. She said she wanted to talk me, sounded a bit . . . I don't know . . . not her usual cool self.'

'Hang on, Cat's just come in. It's Si.'

'Hi, bro. OK?'

'I had an odd-sounding message from Ma.'

'Oh. She hasn't rung here. What sort of odd?'

'Don't know exactly – nothing she actually said – just wants to talk, would I go round if it wasn't too late – but she sounded strung-up.'

'Can't think why. But then I haven't spoken to her for a couple of days.'

They chatted for a few more minutes. Felix had been colicky, Cat was tired, Chris was still on call too often, Hannah had had a tooth out and been frightened by the experience and was waking every night, Sam was still full of stories about kidnapped boys.

They had enough on their plate. Simon hung up with reassurances about their mother and without mentioning the television interview which they clearly had not seen.

414

He was getting ready for bed when the phone rang again.

'Serrailler.'

'Simon? Darling, don't hang up, please . . .'

'Diana, I can't talk to you, I'm in the middle of calls to the station.'

'The David Angus business, yes.'

He did not reply.

'I saw the interview with the mother. How dare she accuse you of negligence? It made me so angry.'

'She is a very distressed woman. I can't discuss this any more and I'm afraid I need to keep the phone line clear.'

'Don't you have your mobile?'

He did not answer.

'Simon, I need to see you so much. We need to talk.'

'Do we? Why is that?'

'Please don't be like this, please don't do this to me. This hurts so much. I want to see you, I want to be with you. I miss you, I . . .' She spoke more and more quickly, trying to hold him on the line.

Simon thought of this or that reply . . . that he was busy, that he would rather she did not go on making contact with him . . . but he said none of it. He simply put the receiver down.

Outside, the rain had begun to fall softly, blurring the lamps and making the cobblestones shine.

Fifty-one

When she had first come down the wide flight of steps out of the house she had seemed cautious and restrained, the perfect hostess welcoming a guest. Within seconds, she had burst out of the veneer of maturity she had put on and started to laugh. Now, Lucia Philips almost danced along beside Karin as they walked around the gardens, like a child let out to play, full of excitement and enthusiasm for this new toy, the Seaton Vaux estate. It had been neglected, neither money nor love had been spent on it for years and it had a weedy and disconsolate air. But it was magnificent. The Elizabethan house of rose-red brick and barley-sugar chimneys, the garden with its sunken Italianate terrace, walled orchard and acres of wild grass. Beyond a ha-ha lay the deer park, its trees overgrown and wild-looking; beyond that over another wall lay the small estate village through which Karin had driven.

Lucia Philips wore a pair of perfectly cut jeans, an understated tweed jacket, a pale pink shirt, together with ludicrously high, strappy shoes in matching pink. Her hair had been tied back but as she and Karin had come outside she had pulled the band out and let it shake loose, curling on to her shoulders.

Over coffee earlier, she had shown Karin her wedding photographs. 'We married in Switzerland . . . in a beautiful village . . . we took it over. The church had those sweet little bells, you know? We came out married, and walked down to the lake . . . it was late afternoon, the sun was setting. It was golden. We had seven hundred guests, everyone flew in, but it was so simple really.'

Karin glanced at her but there was no hint of irony in her tone of voice. Simple was what she had said and how it had seemed to her.

'Your dress is so beautiful . . . all those tiny crystals. Where did it come from?'

'Oh, Valentino.'

'Ah yes.'

'We went through Switzerland down to Venice, then on to southern Italy, before we flew back to New York and had a post-wedding reception there too. The flowers – oh, you should have seen, you would have so appreciated the flowers – all round the room, simple flowers, you know? Nothing showy, not awful stiff designer flowers.'

'It sounds wonderful.'

'It was. My God, I want to have it all again. To marry Cax all over again.'

They had talked garden restoration, garden history, garden plans . . . trees, flowers, walls, arches, statuaries, water, and Lucia had proved to have knowledge as well as desires, serious interest as well as money.

'I just love what you're telling me, how you see it all. I would so like you to take this place on, Karin.'

They sat down in the last of the sun, on a low wall.

'Listen, I am not a major garden designer, Lucia. I qualified fairly recently and I have never undertaken anything like this. I think you ought to perhaps take advice on more important names.'

Lucia took her hand and looked at her earnestly. She is, Karin thought, too beautiful to live.

'Karin, I don't want "important names" . . . phooey. I want someone I can like and trust and who can come to love and nurture this beautiful place. And that is you. I knew it straight away.'

'There's no doubt that I could love it. Who wouldn't?'

'Well then . . . it's done?'

'What about your husband?'

'Oh, Cax will have what I want.'

Yes, Karin thought, that much was clear.

'I have good taste, you know, Karin . . . he trusts my taste. He knows how I feel about it here. You will take it on?'

'I'll think about it. I'll make some preliminary designs . . . do some costings . . . work out a time scheme.'

'Of course, whatever you like.'

'Not with the design and planning – that would be down to me – but I want hands-on help pretty early . . . I wasn't well a year ago and I take a bit of care.'

'Oh, I'm so sorry . . . what happened to you?'

Karin hesitated. One of the things Mike had said he hated was living no longer with a wife but with a cancer victim. Her entire being had been focused on her illness, her time and energy and drive had been given up to it, for too long. It had come to define her. That had to stop. She shrugged and jumped off the wall.

'It's not important,' she said lightly, 'it's over and dealt with. I just want to keep it that way.'

Lucia had the best brand of American good manners. She smiled and the subject was dropped.

'Let's go round to the west of the house,' she said, 'there is the most perfect walled kitchen garden . . . well, the wall is half there, but it's just wild. I so want to grow all our own fresh stuff – vegetables, salads, fruit, herbs. I'd even like to start a business of this, you know, an organic garden store? I care so much about preserving the land, growing with respect. I think we have the land on trust, don't you? And because I'm just a newcomer, jumped in on your territory, I really so want to nurture and respect it.'

Coming from anyone else it would have sounded phoney.

'This is where you and I do shake hands,' Karin said. 'Organic fresh produce is my own passion. I'd love to take on a project like this.'

Lucia turned to her, kissed her on both cheeks, and then danced off again.

They went on happily towards where a broken gate led into the old kitchen garden. Karin felt a burst of energy and renewal. The place and the girl were filling her with enthusiasm and a bubbling up of excitement. She realised she had barely thought about either Mike's absence or her illness since arriving here. Instead, she had started to plan and dream and urge herself forward.

Lucia caught her shoe in a tuft of weeds, wobbled and fell over. She lay there for a split second looking startled and then began to laugh, and as she laughed, lifted her legs and pulled off her shoes and threw them in the air. She turned to Karin.

'Well, doesn't that just serve me damn well right?'

They laughed, there in the warmth of the sun that came off the old brick walls, until they were crying with it.

Fifty-two

'Darling, how nice! Are you staying for tea?'

Whatever had happened in her world or the world in general, Simon thought, his mother would never present anything other than this calm, cool charming face to it. She looked as elegant as ever in a pale blue cashmere sweater and navy jeans. Her hair was swept up, her brooch and necklace were in place.

He put his arms round her. 'I think you'll look like this at the Second Coming, Ma. "Darling, how nice! Are you staying for tea?"'

'Well, I hope I shall be polite, and don't call me Ma.'

'No, Ma. Any cake?'

'Probably. Tell me about Marilyn Angus. I thought that broadcast was perfectly shocking. Whoever set her up to do it?'

'She's in a very bad state – unsurprisingly.'

'No need to slate the police in that way – of course you are doing everything. And I do so dislike these public parades of grief. Well, are you any nearer to finding the little boy?'

'Nope.'

'It is simply unimaginable. Who has done this, Simon?'

'A pervert . . . a psychopath . . . a random murderer. I came for some tea and cake, Ma.'

'Darling, I know, I'm sorry, I am thoughtless.'

'And to ask why you rang me in such a state the other night.'

He looked at Meriel closely. She opened her eyes wider.

'I was in no such thing.'

'Your message was a bit odd . . . panicky?'

'Why on earth should you think that?'

'You tell me.'

'I simply wanted . . . well, now, I have fixed a date for a short service, but I did want to check it with you. The stone which will cover Martha's ashes is ready. It will be in the walled burial ground behind the cathedral of course . . . and the stone is very plain. It's made of Welsh slate.'

'What does it say?'

'Martha Felicity Serrailler, her dates and then "Blessed are the pure in heart".'

'I like that.'

She had put her spectacles on and was flicking through the diary. He watched her. He knew her too well. Something had made her agitated.

'Here we are . . . Sunday May 12th. At two. We'll gather in the Lady Chapel – only the family and one or two others, nothing formal. Is that all right with you?'

422

'Fine. Is Dad in?'

'He's playing golf. Now . . . cake. Yes.'

'Are you sure something wasn't worrying you when you rang me?'

But his mother had gone towards the larder. Simon filled the kettle and began to take down cups and saucers. Something had been wrong but there was no point in pushing at it. She had blocked it out and she would not now refer to it again.

As she came back carrying a couple of cake tins there was a ring at the front doorbell.

'Darling, that will be Karin McCafferty – she did say she might come – will you let her in?'

Karin was looking well, better than Simon remembered. She had lost a strained look about her eyes and a gauntness. She even seemed to walk in with more vitality and confidence.

'I knew you'd want to hear all about it.' She sat down at the table, at ease in this house as people always were when his father was not around. Even he felt the lightness in the atmosphere.

'I should say so. Karin has been up to Seaton Vaux.'

'I hear money is no object.'

'Certainly isn't. The estate village is looking brighter already – the roofs are being repaired, everything's being painted, fencing is getting mended for the first time in half a century. And the house and gardens are going to be amazing.'

'And you got the job?' Meriel brought the teapot to the table.

'It's a bit more complicated than that. I think I did . . . but it's a huge project, beyond me on my own. I did try to explain that I wasn't a Chelsea Gold Medal winner with twenty years of experience.'

'And how was the beautiful young Mrs Philips?'

'Beautiful. Bubbling. She's like a child – she *is* a child. It's a strange set-up. He's fifty-six, she's twenty-two. He wasn't there, she was flying back to London later in the helicopter. It's another world.'

'You mustn't do yourself down, Karin. You take that contract. You can always employ other people. But you're good enough and you know it.'

'Hm. It is exciting.'

'I don't suppose you'd have any use for a young man who trained in horticulture – market gardening – and who needs a job?'

'Just who is this, Simon?' Meriel interrupted, suspiciously.

'Someone I've had to do with lately. He's young and fit. All right . . . he's an ex-con.'

'Simon, really.'

But Karin waved her away. 'Yes,' she said to Simon, 'I would. Tell me a bit more.'

Later, as he was leaving, the station called.

'Message, guv . . . DCS Jim Chapman from the North Yorkshire force is on his way down to start on the Angus case review. He'll meet you first thing tomorrow.'

'Good.'

If anyone thought DCI Serrailler felt in any way put out by the appearance of someone senior from an outside force coming in to conduct this review, they could not have been more wrong, he thought, as he drove back to Lafferton. He needed a new pair of eyes on the case, a new view of things. They had trawled over the ground and they were stale and exhausted, all of them. If someone else could give them a fillip and spot something, anything, they might have overlooked, all the better. It was going to be a shot in the arm, not an insult.

Fifty-three

The meeting was scheduled for nine o'clock. At eight twenty, the telephone rang as Serrailler was walking into his office.

'I've got Mrs Angus for you.'

He hesitated. He had neither seen nor spoken to Marilyn since the television interview but he had calmed down enough to feel able to talk to her. Nevertheless, he took a deep breath. He needed to hold fast to the understanding that what she had done had been without malice, simply in the extremes of grief and distress.

'I'll speak to her.'

Marilyn dispensed with any small talk and said without preamble, 'I just wanted you to know what I plan. I have got some people together . . . I've asked them to begin a search for David.'

'But . . .'

'I know what you are going to say but I don't feel enough has been done.'

'I can assure you that is absolutely not the case and we're not speaking in the past tense – everything *is* being done and will continue to be done.'

'Yet you are no nearer to finding him. I don't think the searches can have been thorough enough. I'm not satisfied and I won't be satisfied until I know they're being done again . . . that's what I wanted to tell you. I will organise teams and –'

'You do understand that members of the public have no rights of access, no authority to go into or on to private property?'

'Is there anything to prevent them asking for permission to search and then going ahead once we have it? I don't think there is.'

'I have to caution you –'

'I'm sure you do. But I'm going to carry on nevertheless. I simply can't stand this . . . this nothingness . . . I feel impotent and I feel angry.'

'And I do sincerely understand those feelings, believe me.'

'Then let me get on with this. I've informed you out of courtesy. That's all.'

'Can we at least talk about this before –'

'No. We'll go on until we drop . . . or until we find David. I have to find him. There's nothing else in my life of any importance at all, nothing else I have to do.'

Nathan put his head round the door. 'Guv, you seen the papers?'

Simon groaned. 'Bring them in.'

MISSING BOY'S MOTHER FORCED TO ORGANISE OWN SEARCH. 'POLICE WERE CURSORY,' SAYS MRS

ANGUS. 'I'LL FIND MY BOY MYSELF,' VOWS ANGRY MOTHER.

Serrailler was in the middle of reading through the vitriol when the desk called up to tell him DCS Chapman had arrived. He dropped the papers on to the chair and went down. Jim Chapman was one of his force's most senior officers, five years off retirement and with a reputation for thoroughness and dogged determination. He had been the SIO in two high-profile and highly successful murder hunts in Yorkshire and had the Queen's Police Medal for Bravery. When Serrailler told him he was privileged to be working with him, he meant it. Chapman was a big man with close-cropped grey hair and heavy-lidded eyes, a man with a broad Yorkshire accent and a surprisingly gentle manner.

The moment the door closed on the two of them in Serrailler's office, he said, 'I want you to know I'm for you not against you. I'm here to help not to undermine. I'm an addition not a replacement.'

'Thanks, that's appreciated.'

'And' – Chapman pointed to the papers – 'I've read them.'

'I've called a press conference for ten o'clock.'

'You'd no alternative. It's always a problem. The mother's distraught, they always believe we're not doing enough and of course we're not, no human being on earth is doing enough for her unless they find the boy. The father took his own life?'

'Yes. I think it tipped her over the edge – and do you wonder? How do you want to begin, sir?'

'I'm Jim. I'm always Jim. As I said, I'm on side. I'd like to talk to the team briefly, then get this press conference out of the way. I'll sit in but I'll not speak. This is your call. After those buggers have gone we'll get down to it. I've read most of t'paperwork on the way down and last night. Fill me in on the rest.'

Simon did, going through the team one by one, giving their background, personality, particular strengths. The DCS listened, said nothing, made no notes.

'No weak links?'

'No. We've as good a team as you could find . . . They're demoralised just now but they're still bloody-minded about it.'

'No one gone sick?'

'No.'

'Signs of strain?'

'No more than you'd expect.'

'Aye, it takes its toll, this sort of inquiry. They'd rather face bullets. We all would.'

'Do you want to talk to Mrs Angus?'

'Mebbe. Not for now. Where's your canteen?'

'I'll get something brought in for you, we've –'

But the DCS was on his feet. 'I don't want special treatment,' he said, walking out. 'Downstairs or up?'

'Down.' Serrailler followed him quickly along the corridor.

*

The press conference was an unpleasant business. Marilyn Angus's television interview had swung them all. Even the local reporters, who were always helpful, asked aggressive questions, vying with the big boys from television and the national press to be confrontational. They demanded action, they demanded answers, they pressed on detail. Serrailler was a match for them every time. He had always enjoyed a bit of combat, and he maintained a cool, sympathetic but not self-defensive stand. There was a lot of grumbling and muttering from the assembly, but they left meekly enough.

'Good morning. I'm Jim Chapman. Right, you've taken a battering this morning and over the TV interview last night. I want you to know we're together on this. I am not here to trip you up, pull you to pieces or give you a hard time. I'm here to look at the David Angus case from scratch. I'm not doubting you've worked extremely hard – no one's been negligent, everyone's given this 110 per cent.

'I'll be looking at everything, going everywhere, studying the paperwork, the forensics, the background, the data – and I want to talk to each of you. But there's nothing private or secret here, I'm not going behind your SIO's back.

'Right. I want to start from square one, inch by inch and minute by minute. I want you to take me through what you know. I want to hear your thoughts and your suspicions – the lot. Don't think that anything you say is going to be sneered at or dismissed. Nothing gets dismissed.

'This morning I want to get an idea of how each one of you in this investigating team sees the case. Tell me your ideas, your view of the scenario. Nathan, isn't it? Right, lad, you.'

The room went silent. Nathan rubbed his hand through his hair and looked down at the table for a minute. Then he said, 'Well, first off, we're looking for a body. The kid's dead. Gotta be.'

He waited but Chapman said nothing.

'I still wonder about the family, to be honest with you. What did the father kill himself for? Was it only that he couldn't face going on without the boy any longer? I know his alibi for the time the boy vanished is cast iron like, but parents are often the killers and I just wonder if there isn't something in the family situation we've missed. Dunno what though.'

'That it?'

'Yeah, well, for now . . . you wanted a view.'

'Fine. Good. Anyone else share Nathan's take on this?'

DC Clare Liscom said quickly, 'Yes, I do. I don't know about the father but the mother . . . she's behaved very oddly, even allowing for what she's been through. She's been hostile to us, she's been obstructive . . . She has another child, the daughter Lucy, but it's as though that kid hardly exists. I wonder if we should pull the whole family apart again. Look closer to home not further away.'

Kate Marshall shook her head. 'Sorry, Clare but no, I –'

'You're the FLO?'

'Was. Sorry, sir, yes. DC Marshall. No one in that family hurt David. Marilyn has been off her head with grief and dread and suspense and guilt, and then her husband tries to commit suicide, fails, tries again and succeeds. I think she is literally out of her right mind at the moment and I'm worried about her, but I don't think we'll find anything in the house.'

One by one, the others agreed or did not, and then brought up their own suggestions. Simon sat in silence, feeling huge pride in his team, in their dedication and skill, their commitment and determination. They were as focused a group as he thought could have been assembled in any force in the country.

It was a surprise when Geoff Prince spoke. He was generally silent.

'What about these villains, sir? Getting kids to nick cars for them, then trying to kill the DCI, and that sap who did some of their dirty work. Maybe they ran over the kid. Maybe he saw something . . .'

Serrailler shook his head. 'Sorry, it's not their style.'

Chapman turned to him. 'Simon?'

'I don't think it is anything to do with anyone in the family, alive or dead. I have a hunch he won't be found within a hundred miles of Lafferton. I think he was away from here within minutes of being abducted. It is the very absence of anything at all which makes me think this . . .'

'Right. Let's tick them off,' Chapman said. He went to the white board on the far wall.

1. Alive or dead. In all probability – DEAD.
2. Still in his own home. 'So, the story of his waiting at the gate is a fabrication.'

'Sorry sir, but no, we've a witness – man cycling to work down Sorrel Drive reported seeing David at what must have been a couple of minutes after his mother left him.'

'Good. Thanks.' He wiped out the second point briskly. It had been a test, Serrailler thought, neatly done.

3. Taken on foot by someone he knew.
4. Taken in a car by someone he knew.
5. Taken on foot by a stranger.
6. Taken in a car by a stranger.
7. Taken somewhere close at hand and killed.
8. Taken out of Lafferton to somewhere else and then killed.

'And that's about it. Not many alternatives, are there? Nice and straightforward. What's the worst-case scenario?'

Half a dozen people spoke at once then fell silent.

'Worst-case scenario is the random paedophile killer, passing through the place, spotting the boy standing at his gate, completely by chance, and seizing his opportunity, and driving him to God knows where. You said it. Nightmare scenario. I think we're in the middle of it.'

Fifty-four

There was warmth in the sun. Cat stood in the supermarket car park with Felix asleep in the baby-carrier of the trolley and turned her face to it. Around the perimeter, the cherry-blossom trees were breaking into the sugary-pink flower people like her mother and Karin sneered at but which Cat loved. The previous week she and Hannah had gone into Bevham alone, officially to buy school shoes but in fact to have what Hannah called 'a pink afternoon'. Her new brother had ceased to be a novelty and was not yet interesting in his own right. Cat recognised the first signs of pique. Felix had been left with Meriel while she and Hannah shopped. They had come back with carriers full of pink . . . clothes, toys, sweets, and three different shades of pink nail varnish. Hannah had been ecstatic.

'I love this,' Cat thought now, still lingering in the spring sunshine before starting to load her groceries. 'I love having time with the children, being alone in the house with Felix, the cat and things to cook, having an afternoon nap after reading, seeing Ma in the middle of the day with time to spare. I love sitting on the sofa feeding the baby and reading the paper or watching an old film on television. I love being free to have a pink afternoon with Hannah. I even love browsing round the supermarket instead of racing in, grabbing essentials and racing off again.'

The downside was the guilt. The locum was still ill, though the agency was now taking five nights, so that Chris only had Monday and Friday on call.

The baby stirred inside his blue padded suit. The soft white lining framed his small face. Cat looked at his eyelashes, and the pearl pinkness of his nails, his barely visible fringe of hair. Love spouted up and overflowed into tears. She had never cried so often, so readily, or so happily, even after the births of her other two children.

She unstrapped Felix and restrapped him into the car. He did not wake. As she clicked the buckle across his tummy, the face of David Angus came to her, as she had just seen it on the familiar poster in the supermarket. She dared not let herself think further about him, but she could not get his face out of her mind.

There was a strange vehicle in the farmhouse drive, an ice-blue Toyota Celica. Cat backed her own car up to the door that led to the kitchen and got out.

'Hello?'

Cat knew at once who the woman was, though she had never seen Diana Mason before. She looked amazing, in a cream bouclé suit with a skirt short enough to show off her very good legs but not too short for someone in her late forties. Clever, Cat thought. Felix let out a wail.

'Excuse me a moment.'

The woman watched as Cat leaned into the car, unstrapped the baby and hauled him out. He had been sick down the front of his suit. Cat realised that her jeans had a split in the side seam. She felt scruffy and angry.

'I'm sorry if this is an awful moment. I thought I'd wait a little to see if you came home.' She stretched out a hand, then smiled. 'Oh, not easy with your arms full. Anyway, how do you do. I'm Diana Mason. Simon's friend.'

There was nothing to do but invite her in.

'I've got to feed this one pretty quickly if you don't mind.' Cat could feel the milk leaking through her T-shirt as she rushed about getting the tea things, Felix on her hip wriggling and pushing his head at her chest.

Diana Mason stood, tall, cool and immaculate beside the window, watching. Bloody hell, Cat thought, struggling with the mugs.

'No saucers,' she said, 'too complicated.' Felix kicked her as she bent to get milk from the fridge. 'Sorry but I must . . .' She settled on the sofa and hitched up her shirt.

'May I sit here?'

'Anywhere.'

Cat took a deep breath as the baby latched on hard to her nipple and began to suck with vigour, his fingers curling in ecstasy. Then she looked across the room at Diana Mason. She just missed being beautiful but she was extremely attractive, with good skin and well-cut hair; she was also elegant, poised and sexy. Cat could not imagine how Simon had managed to keep her as an occasional lover for three years, but there was something about the woman's cool reserve which matched his own. They might have made a good team.

'So, you're Simon's mystery lady?'

Cat deserved an award for phrasing it so tactlessly; all the same she had not expected Diana's reaction. She simply began to cry, silently, desperately, copiously. Her tears ran down her face on to her hands and she made no attempt to stop them.

'Oh God, that was a stupid thing to say,' Cat said weakly.

It took a while. The kettle began to whistle. Cat got up, as the baby clung to her like a limpet to a heaving rock.

'No, I'm so sorry . . . you mustn't, it's scalding water.'

Diana came across and took the kettle off the stove, still pouring tears. Cat went back to the sofa. It seemed, for the moment, better to stay put and keep quiet.

The tea was made and poured, and a biscuit tin opened. A mug was put down on the small table beside her, and three biscuits on a plate. In the end, it felt quite companionable.

'Better tell me,' Cat said at last.

'May I ask what you know about me?'

'Not much. That Simon saw you in London sometimes . . . that you're a widow. You run a business but I don't think he ever said what . . . Si is good at keeping things to himself.'

'I own a chain of bistros. Except I've just accepted an offer for them. I've had enough.'

'Good offer?'

'Good offer.' She shrugged.

'So now what?'

'I've heard about you . . . once or twice anyway. Simon doesn't talk about himself or his work really but he did sometimes tell me about you . . . your family . . . this house. It means a lot to him, doesn't it?'

'I think it does.'

'I came to see you because there's no one else I can ask. I have to know what I did wrong and how to set it right. I want him . . . I want to be with him. It's eating me up. I didn't think I felt like this. I thought it was a pleasant arrangement. I was very, very fond of him . . . but . . .'

'Then he told you it was over and it changed everything.'

'I can't live without him. It's so simple. I need to see him . . . to be with him. I went to his flat and he was angry. I ring him but he doesn't take the calls. I don't know what to do or where to turn.'

Cat set Felix on her other breast, and then reached carefully for her tea. She needed to think.

She ought to tell the truth and she couldn't. Hurting someone who was clearly so vulnerable and would be tuned in to the slightest nuance in someone's voice was beyond her. On the other hand, she was not about to lie or to give Diana Mason any encouragement.

'He's your brother. You probably know him better than anyone.'

'That isn't saying a lot.'

'At least there is one thing you can tell me, please, you're bound to know.'

This is going to be the easy bit. Cat put her tea down.

'So far as I know there isn't anyone else,' she said. 'That's what you needed to know.'

'Oh God. I've got no shame left, absolutely none. I don't care what you think about me. I'm past that. You really think that? There is no one.'

Cat thought of Freya. Freya's face was there, small, sweet, pert, smiling at her from a distance.

'No,' she said.

'Then it's something I've done wrong and I need to know what. I just want to put it right.'

'It won't be you. It's Si. He's a lone bird really. You can't push him, you can't trick him and you certainly can't manipulate him. God knows, enough women have tried. He's got a good carapace.'

'I want to find the chink, the way through.'

'I honestly don't think anyone ever will. He's very, very good at shutting himself off. You must have realised that much.'

440

'I suppose it never worried me . . . before he cut me off. I just assumed he would always be there, that things were fine between us.'

'Right.'

'Cat, please can you tell me anything that would help? Anything . . .' Her eyes were still full of tears. She moved the half-empty mug round and round on a little circle on the kitchen table.

It felt like advising a lovelorn teenager. So, how exactly would she do that?

Easy.

'I think you should back off a bit. The harder you push the more firmly the door will stay locked. Cut yourself off too . . . let him understand how it feels.'

'And will he care when he does?'

'Not sure. I just know the other way is pretty doomed.'

'Oh God. I can't bear this.'

Cat wanted to slap her.

'Go on holiday. Go round the world on the money.'

'And who knows, I might meet Mr Right and forget all about him.'

'No, but you might have a good time and see a lot of interesting things and it will probably be less painful when you're on the other side of the world.'

'Maybe.'

'Unless you're determined that it won't be of course.'

'Ouch.'

'I'm sorry – brisk GP speaking.'

'You don't look like him . . . no one would think you were two of triplets.'

'I know. Nor does Ivo. He and I are quite alike but Si's out there on his own. In most senses.'

Diana laughed.

I do quite like her, Cat thought. She is not like me, she is everything I struggle to be and can never achieve – smart, cool, well presented – but I could get on with her if . . . if it were not for Si. The 'if' was what made it impossible. Cat couldn't take any woman's side against Simon and especially not this one. A meeting every so often in London was about right. No more.

'Whatever I say isn't going to make any difference, is it?'

'Probably not. I just needed to talk about him. Has he always been like this . . . closed-off?'

'He's just the way he is. He seems fine to me but then I'm his sister. Look, I don't in the least mind your having come and I do understand and I feel for you.'

Diana stood. 'But you won't talk about your brother. Fair enough.'

'I'm sorry.'

'I wanted to feel nearer to him by coming here. Does he?'

'What, come here? Yes. He just turns up. But just now they're in the thick of this missing schoolboy case. He hasn't much time for anything else.'

'Do you have a photo of him?'

'Don't you?'

'No.'

'Keep it that way. The fewer reminders the better.'

There was a small silence. God, Cat thought, I sound as if I'm dismissing a neurotic patient.

As they went to the front door, Chris's car pulled up and Sam and Hannah spilled out of the back doors then froze.

'Hello. I'm Diana.'

They scurried like mice into the house, giggling.

She went up to Chris and held out her hand. 'I'm Diana Mason. But I'm just off. You're Chris?'

'I am. But don't go on –'

'I'm not going on your account, I'm going on my own. Thank you, Cat. Thank you more than I can say.' She swept herself up and into the car and the car down the drive and away, without looking back.

Cat went up to Chris and put her arms round him. 'Hey, this is nice. I thought it was the Percys' lift today?'

'Was but a clinic was cancelled – both midwives were off with a stomach bug. So I scooped up the Percy brats and our brats and . . . who the hell was that?'

He walked into the house with his arm round Cat's shoulders.

'Si's London lady.'

'Smart. Old.'

'Desperate.'

'Tears?'

Chris felt the teapot and went to empty it and make fresh.

443

'Yes. No shame at all. She's crazy about him and, of course, because she now can't have him, it's all got a whole lot worse.'

'Easy to smile.'

'One day I'm going to throttle my brother. I'm fed up with him attracting and repelling perfectly nice women.'

'One day he'll get his come-uppance. One day . . .'

'You home for good?'

'Hope so. Dick is taking an evening surgery for me now and then and it's the agency on call.'

He went to look down at his sleeping son. From the playroom came the high-pitched sounds of an American cartoon which Sam and Hannah were forbidden to watch. She hesitated on her way to switch it off. 'Love you,' she said.

Chris smiled.

It is this, she thought, looking round the kitchen. This is what she wants with Simon. It's what a great many people want.

'You two. How many more times do I have to tell you . . .'

Chris Deerbon poured himself a mug of tea, took it over to the sofa, picked up the paper and immediately fell asleep. Mephisto jumped from the window ledge and on to Chris's stomach.

Fifty-five

Moonlight came through the long thin window and fell on to the stairs. In the hall, it shone in lozenge shapes on to the floor.

She slipped down through the house like a frail little ghost, making no sound at all.

Marilyn Angus was asleep. She went to bed before nine o'clock and slept, sometimes until after nine the next morning. Lucy got herself up and dressed and out of the house. She walked to the school bus on the corner. There were always friends. Friends looked out for her now.

She did not switch on the light until she had closed the kitchen door. The blue-white tubes shimmered alive.

She went to the fridge and took out a carton of milk.

The fruit bowl was empty apart from two walnuts and a small shrivelled, darkened apple. Before, the fruit bowl was always full of oranges, pears, plums, a pineapple, kiwis, bananas. Before.

She reached for a new packet of biscuits, slit it open and sat at the table. The fridge hummed.

What happened next surprised her. There was no difference tonight from any other night. She often came downstairs. Nothing had changed. She felt the same. Everything looked the same. But suddenly, her head was full of it, clear, whole and complete. She did not have to think it through or work her way towards it. It was there, worked out for her. Planned.

She got up, opened the door that led to the utility room and from there to the outside door. She unbolted it. It slid back smoothly and without any sound. The key turned easily. She went outside.

It was not cold. The moon was very bright. From next door, across the drive, she could hear the faint sounds of music. Somewhere across the gardens, a dog barked.

She stood looking down the drive to the gate.

There. The path. The hedge. The gateposts.

Beyond that, the pavement and the road.

There.

He had been there and then he was not there.

She tried again to imagine him. There. Not there.

She did so almost every night. The only thing different was what had happened a few minutes ago inside her head.

A car went fast down the road. The headlights flashed over the gateposts.

The dog barked again.

She slipped back into the house and her head was full and everything was suddenly clear to her. The moonlight was a pool she floated through on her way upstairs.

Fifty-six

Simon Serrailler leaned back in his chair, almost tipping it over. It was nearly eight o'clock.

'Enough. Come and have something to eat?'

He and Jim Chapman had worked solidly together all afternoon, brainstorming, picking everything apart between them. Jim had moulded himself in from the start, an outside reviewer and yet also at one with them and a part of the team. The DCS had a knack of being impartial, pointing out this or that, drawing attention to something that might have been done differently, and yet reassuring Serrailler and the rest that he was one of them.

He said, 'Let's get a pint and a decent meal. Where do you suggest?'

Now was as good a time as any, Simon thought. He had last been to his favourite Italian restaurant with Freya, it was there that he had looked at her and wondered if he had found not just a good new colleague but . . .

'Italian?'

'So long as they do a decent spaghetti.'

'Can Pavarotti sing? Come on.'

He would not want to take any other woman there but he had got on so well with the straightforward Yorkshire DCS that he felt relaxed enough to go there with him and banish the unhappy memories – the demons, as he thought.

Chapman's car was in the forecourt next to Simon's own. 'A bottle of wine?'

'With a couple of pints first, aye.'

'Then let's walk. I live not far from the restaurant, your hotel is just as near. If you don't mind walking in tomorrow, we can both enjoy a drink tonight.'

'Suits me. I've nothing to carry, I checked my bag in this morning.'

They set off through the mild spring night. The streets were quiet until they turned into the market square, where people were about, on their way to pubs and pizza houses, though midweek there were not too many of them.

A gang of youths were hanging about, frog-jumping over a couple of bollards.

'Get much trouble?' Chapman said.

'The usual – too much booze on Friday and Saturday nights. Otherwise, we're lucky.'

'You had that very nasty murder sequence.'

'Yes . . . and we lost an officer, as you probably know.'

'Always difficult. And now this.'

'More than our share, I'd say. Here we are.'

The proprietor came forward to shake Simon's hand.

'We miss you, Mr Serrailler . . . long time.'

'This is a colleague of mine, DCS Chapman. He comes from the north of England where they eat double what we do down here.'

There was one thing Simon made sure of – they went to a table on the opposite side of the room from the one he had shared with Freya. He did not feel uncomfortable or upset to be here again, he felt at home. But all the same, he steered Chapman away from the window tables.

Two pints of bitter and a menu were set down in front of them and Chapman drank half of his in a single long, slow, luxuriant swallow before speaking.

'Good,' he said. 'Now you tell me, is it shop or not?'

'Let's do ten minutes' shop and then put it away for tonight.'

'Right.' The DCS waited until Simon had drunk from his own pint, then he said, 'I tell you, Simon, we'll go into everything again, turn it all over, but I reckon even when we have we'll be looking at the same thing we're looking at now.'

'Which is?'

'The random operator. He's been driving through . . . comes from somewhere miles away. Either he's a long-distance driver employed by a firm, or self-employed, taking short jobs to get himself the length and breadth of the country. If it hadn't been young Angus, it would have been some other kid, five or a hundred miles off. He was away in ten minutes.'

Simon moved his beer glass round and round with his finger. 'Bugger.'

'Aye.'

Simon's mobile phone rang from his jacket pocket. One or two other diners looked round immediately. He went outside.

'Serrailler.'

'Guv, where are you?'

'Having a meal with DCS Chapman.'

'Sorry, but you're not going to get it finished.'

'What?'

'The Angus girl . . . Lucy. She's gone missing, guv.'

'Jesus. OK, I'm on my way.'

Simon went back inside and briefed the DCS. Chapman got up.

'No need,' Simon said, 'you eat for God's sake, this isn't your shout.'

'All t'same.'

'Dammit, we haven't brought a car.'

'Six or seven minutes – not going to make too much difference, is it? They're on to it. You have to pace yourself.'

They set off to walk briskly back through the town.

Fifty-seven

'Gerrup.'

Andy woke out of a dream of crushed limbs to find he had been sleeping with his leg folded under him. His brother-in-law stood at the bottom of his bed, unshaven, in vest and jeans. A light like sour milk came through the drawn curtain.

'What's up?'

'You are. Gerrup.'

'OK, OK, keep your hair on, what time is it anyway?'

'Time you were going. Michelle's in the kitchen.'

'Going where?'

'Any bloody where,' Pete said, banging out of the room.

Andy pulled himself out of the camp bed and went to the bathroom. His nephew had already gone, the Harley-Davidson duvet spilling out of his bed like entrails.

When he made it to the kitchen they were both there, Pete at the table with a huge plate of fry-up in front of him, Michelle with her back against the sink, smoking.

'OK, you get a cup of tea and a slice of bread and that's it. I ent doing no fry-up for you. Then you get packed and out. I've had it up to here. You think I want my kids growin' up with a jailbird?'

'What's brought this on, I've been out over a month?'

'Yes, and you'll be back before we know it. I know what happened, I know you was banged up for the night and bailed. So that's fuckin' that. I can't cope, not with this baby as well.'

'What baby?'

'This baby I'm havin'.'

'I didn't know you were havin' a baby.'

'Well, you do now. Here.' She handed him a slice of white toast on the end of a knife. 'Tea's in the pot. I want you gone in half an hour.'

'I'm supposed to be your brother.'

'You should have thought of that.'

'I've paid my way.'

'Yeah, with dirty money. No thanks.'

'Where am I supposed to go?'

'You should have thought of that an' all.'

'Look . . .'

'No. You look, And. I want me house back and Matt wants his room back and I ent arguing with you.'

She stood, pasty face with the look under her eyes that said she was pregnant. She had spots on her chin and her roots were growing out, dark brown in an earthy furrow across the corn blonde.

He drank his tea. Ate his toast. Pete piled egg yolk, sausages and beans on to his fork and stuffed it sideways into his mouth. A lump of yolk dropped on to his vest.

'Gerroff,' Michelle said and threw a cloth in his direction.

Andy looked round. Quite suddenly, he'd had enough. He couldn't have stayed another night. He got up. 'Right,' he said.

He'd little to pack and he left some bits behind. He got it all into the holdall easily enough. Twenty minutes later he was walking out of the door without saying another word to either of them. It was sunny. There were daffodils out round the edges of the blocks of flats and in the front gardens. It was mild. The air had a smell of spring in it.

'It's good,' he said to himself. 'Good.'

He wondered how the kitchen garden was coming along at the prison.

It felt like coming out all over again, just at first. It was partly the spring, partly that he would never have to crumple up his limbs in the camp bed in Matt's fetid bedroom again or watch his brother-in-law eating egg. But there was more, a strange feeling that he was renewed, emerging from a tunnel which he had thought was at an end months ago but which had had an extra, sideways section.

He walked to the edge of the town whistling and then he turned on to the road that ran round the Hill. There were some people walking dogs, and a pair of mothers with toddlers, straining up the

453

grassy banks to the top, laughing into the mild wind.

Andy climbed slowly, and when he reached the Wern Stones, he sat down, and leaned against one. He still felt crock from the impact of that van. The sun brushed his face. He looked down over Lafferton. King. That was how they played it when they were kids. King of the Wern Stones.

He'd heard the stories about last year's murders that had happened on the Hill but he couldn't connect with any of that; he had been inside and this had been another world.

He stayed there for half an hour, until the sun moved behind some clouds and his back hurt, pressed against the ancient stone. The mothers and toddlers had gone.

Andy got up. He should go. But go where? He supposed he would have to walk into town and try and see his probation officer. Didn't she have to get him somewhere to sleep? He thought about Lee Carter. He'd a house full of places to sleep.

He went to Dino's instead. The café was full of morning shoppers and the espresso machine was working overtime. Andy found a table near the counter. From behind it, Alfredo waved, tea towel over his arm, face perspiring. Seconds later, he pushed a cup of tea and two slices of toast across and shouted Andy's name.

People piled in, and after a while the door just opened for them to see there were no seats, and

454

closed on them again. It was warm and it was noisy. When someone left a newspaper, Andy reached across and grabbed it. He opened it on the soccer page and sipped his tea to make it last.

He was back for a sandwich at half past one, after mooching round the streets, failing to see his probation officer and sitting on a bench for half an hour. This is what it'll be, he thought, benches, doorways. I'm a dosser. It's what happens.

He went back to Dino's at ten past four. The place was quiet at last, just a couple of schoolkids squabbling over nothing and one woman eating her slow way through a toasted scone.

'OK, Andy, what's up?'

'How do you mean?'

'You been in here three, four times, hanging about – like we used to hang about.' Fredo pointed to the boys, who picked up their bags, and left, shoving each other on to the pavement. 'Your Michelle had enough of you?'

'Yeah, right.'

'Well?'

'I said yes, OK?'

'Right. You wan' tea, coffee, milk shake, Coke . . .'

'Tell you what . . . what was it we had? Coke float. That'll remind me.'

'You want reminding? . . . You really want a Coke float?'

'Tea then.'

'You don't wanna Coke float, but maybe you want a job?'

455

Andy took the tea and stood at the counter with it. Alfredo went on wiping down the glass shelves of the pastry stand.

'You seen me here today? Gone mental. And it's just me.'

'Why? Thought you had a million family.'

'Not so much now and Lina's had to go home, her sister's in hospital, she had bad baby trouble.'

'So there's a job?'

'There's a job.'

'What doing?'

'Everything . . . anything . . . behind here, in the back.'

'How long for?'

'No idea. A week, a month, ten years.'

'Only trouble is, I'd have to be clean, look respectable.'

'You're all right, Andy.'

'Not after a couple nights on a bench I won't be.'

Fredo stopped wiping the shelves. 'She really has thrown you out.'

'Not that I care. Blood ent always thicker than water.'

'Sure it is.' He turned to the sink and put the cloth under the hot tap.

The woman finished her scone and went out.

'There's a couple of rooms upstairs. Full of junk, nobody's lived up there for years . . . no furniture, kitchen's in a state. Nothing's turned on.'

'You mean it'd go with the job.'

Alfredo looked at him steadily. 'Not exactly. You

could have full pay and sleep on the bench or half pay and have the rooms. I'd get it sorted quick enough, there's always furniture somewhere.'

'There is?'

'No bath. Sink.'

'That's OK. You're forgetting where I've been, Fredo.'

'And no Carter. No trouble.'

'No.'

There was another pause. Alfredo was silent, still looking at him speculatively. Then, he leaned across the counter and put out his hand. Andy took it.

'Tonight, you better come home with me.'

'Thanks, Fredo,' Andy said. It seemed to be enough.

Fifty-eight

Once, they had let her take the dog for a walk, just down the avenue and back. A couple of times she had gone into the garden and played with it, throwing a ball. When she had got back home she had asked for a dog. 'One like that. It's a Labrador. I love it.'

'We're busy people, we both work, it wouldn't be fair to keep a dog, especially not a dog like that and you'd soon lose interest in taking it for walks.'

'Try a hamster,' her father had said. 'Maybe a cat one day? I'll think about it.'

'Cats make me wheeze,' David had said.

So there had been no dog, no cat and the hamster had been forgotten.

She had called in a few times and asked to see the dog and they had let her. Its name was Archie and it slept not in the house but in a big workshop at the bottom of the garden. The woman, whose name was Mrs Price, had taken her down there when she went to fetch Archie for his walk. She'd liked the workshop. It had shelves, woodwork tools, a bench and stool, and a ladder up into a roof space where there was a window, and a couch covered in an old quilt. It belonged to the Prices' son, who used it when he came home, which he rarely did now. He was in the air force serving overseas, flying Tornado jets, his mother had said. 'I can't think about it.'

The walls of the workshop had posters of planes, and others of *The Simpsons*. In the roof space there was a radio and a pile of aircraft magazines. It was a boy's den. But she liked it because of Archie and because the idea of having a whole place to yourself, with a roof space, delighted her. She thought she might mention it when she got home, but in the end did not. She thought of asking for one like it, for Christmas, but that was how it stayed – a thought, and she got rid of it fast.

All that had been Before. She had not been to the Prices' house since. She had not been anywhere. But then, standing at the door in the dark, looking towards the end of the drive and the gateposts, she had tried to think of something good, and had.

After that, everything was easy.

Fifty-nine

'What's happening, Chris . . . what is this? Why has the world gone mad . . . why is this going on?'

Cat had heard the news at ten o'clock. Chris was on call, she was alone with her three sleeping children and suddenly, she had been overcome by both panic and despair. Lucy Angus was missing. Cat sat nursing a mug of coffee, wishing that Mephisto were beside her, another warm living body, but Mephisto was out, prowling the night fields looking for smaller creatures to slaughter.

She thought of the cloud 'no bigger than a man's hand' but which was growing and darkening by the day. They were under it and the sunlight could not break through or any warmth and brightness reassure them.

Chris was on call, at an emergency birth ten miles away. A woman had insisted on having her first child at home, in a water bath, with only a private midwife attending her, but the labour had started early and urgently, the midwife was on holiday, and Chris had managed to tell Cat enough about what was happening for her to worry about that too. The baby was a breech and the labour fast. He was on his own until the paramedics arrived with a hospital midwife. What they all needed, and soon, was a holiday, Cat thought, a week or ten days abroad together, far away from Lafferton and the evil that seemed to be stalking it, away from the sadness of Martha's death and the worries about the practice and the sudden encounter with Diana Mason. She and Chris needed one another and their children, sunshine and some warm water, good food and drink and laughter, and nothing and no one else.

The phone rang again. She had it on the sofa beside her.

'How are things?'

'Paramedics are here. I've come outside for a breath. Bloody stupid woman. There, I've said it, I feel better.'

'Is she all right?'

'Just. The baby needs to be got to special care urgently . . . Mother haemorrhaged . . . God.'

'Well done.'

'Why do we do this, Cat?'

'You know why. Come home.'

'Just got to see them into the ambulance. Be twenty minutes. Love you.'

It rarely happened like that now. Mothers gave birth in hospital. Occasionally a baby arrived in a hurry before the woman made it to Bevham General, but GPs were no longer the on-call, hands-on obstetricians they used to be. By the time Cat and Chris had trained, those days had gone. It made it more frightening, and a greater risk on the rare occasions those skills were called upon. But Chris had a cool head and he had done two years in obs and gynae.

She went into the den and turned on the television. Politicians jawing. Men propelling home-made robots around a track by remote control. A pair of eagles fighting in mid-air. A man stabbing another in the stomach.

She was flicking through the channels in search of something soothing when Chris came in.

'You look shot to pieces.'

'Feel it. I thought I was going to lose them both. The ambulance met a road accident, boy knocked off his bike and killed . . . they had to stop and call out another . . .'

He slumped down beside her and leaned his head against her arm.

'It was one of those New Age nutters from Starly . . . babies should be born under bushes, or under water, no painkillers, no doctors, everything natural. God knows who this private midwife is – I've never heard of her. Glad she wasn't there. I had enough to cope with . . . didn't need white witches burning leaves. The girl hadn't had any antenatal, no idea the baby was a breech . . . it's all come as a very nasty shock.'

'They going to be all right?'

'Yes. I stopped the bleeding, got the baby out and breathing . . . the cord was wrapped round his neck of course.'

462

'Of course. Poor you.'

'Poor her . . . she was terrified.'

The television news beamed up. They sat together, watching through the wars and politicians.

Then the familiar picture of David Angus flashed on to the screen. After a couple of seconds, another, of Lucy, appeared beside it.

'I feel sick,' Cat said.

Sorrel Drive was cordoned off and police vehicles were parked on both sides. They had brought in floodlights.

It was after eleven o'clock. Simon had been into the house but Marilyn had not been able to speak to him coherently. The DC with him had pieced together something from her few hysterical sentences. Lucy had been to school as usual, come home as usual, gone up to her bedroom to do her homework and, as also seemed quite usual, not come out of it again. But when her mother had gone up to say goodnight to her, she had not been there, nor anywhere else in the house. The side door leading to the utility room had been found unbolted.

Within ten minutes of her call to the station, the avenue had been full of police.

'But how long?' Simon said, standing under a street lamp near to the house. 'We need to know exactly. She came home at twenty minutes to five. Her mother found her gone at ten to nine. What

463

happened between? We don't know. Has she been missing for twenty minutes or four hours? It's light until after seven now . . . someone would have seen her.'

DCS Chapman had been walking slowly up one side of Sorrel Drive and down the other, looking carefully around him. Now he came up to Simon again.

'Anything strike you?'

'This is different.'

'From the boy? I think so too.'

'She's gone off. Of her own accord.'

'Yes, no one has been into the house, gone upstairs, found her, dragged her down.'

'We'll comb the area but I want to check out the homes of all her friends. Though if she'd been with them openly they'd have rung in by now.'

'School?'

'The caretaker reports everything as usual.'

'What's your plan?'

Simon looked round. It was like the film set for a police drama. Nathan Coates came scooting towards them on his bike.

'Guv. We was out. I came when I heard. Anything?'

'Not yet.'

'We could put out a call, asking everyone to search their own premises.'

'They never do though. We still have to go over it. Might as well leave it all to uniform.'

'You got the river boys out?'

'Too soon.'

'OK, where do you want me, guv?'

Simon looked at him. He had pulled off his cycle helmet and his red hair stuck up like the bristles on a broom. He looked hopelessly young, and eager as a Boy Scout.

'I want a list of all Lucy's friends . . . from her school and any others. You won't get it out of the mother. Find the class teacher, try and get it from her . . . The chances are she's gone to someone and it's likely to be a friend.'

'Guv.'

Jim Chapman smiled, watching Nathan replace his helmet and cycle off fast.

'He reminds me of the advertisements you used to see in shop windows . . . "Smart Lad Wanted" . . .'

'He's the best.'

A couple of uniformed officers went past on their way from one house to the next. 'Drives half a bloody mile long,' one said. 'Who needs them?'

'Look, Jim, why don't you get off to your hotel? One of the cars can drop you down there. You've done your share of hanging about the streets at night.'

'You could be right. Besides, it's the boy's case I'm here to look into.'

They walked up the road to where a patrol car was blocking off an entrance.

'Can you drop DCS Chapman back to his hotel? The Stratfield Inn. Someone can cover for you here for ten minutes.'

'Goodnight, Simon. I'll be in the station first thing. By then I'm betting you'll have found her safe and well.'

'I hope to God you're right.'

Simon closed the door of the car and headed back towards the Angus house. It had been crawling with forensics in white suits but they were emptying out as he reached the gateway.

'Anything?'

Simon had worked with Phil Gadsby on a number of cases and rated him as the force's best. If there was anything for forensics to find, Phil found it.

'She was in her room. She was wearing jeans and a sweatshirt. She took her mac. I think she went through the kitchen into the pantry. She took some food. She's gone off on her own. There are no traces of a struggle, no blood, no one else's fingerprints. The house is clean as a whistle.'

'Thought it would be. Can you get anything from the garden?'

'We'll be back in the morning, go into all the gardens on the neighbouring houses. For now, that's it.'

Simon went towards the front door of the house. The lights were on in every room, the rest of the forensic team leaving. He waited until they had gone and the vans had driven away. It went quiet then, though uniform were still going from house to house. He thought how different it would be if this was happening on the Dulcie estate – everyone would be out on the street, or at doors and windows, kids would be following the officers, women shouting at them; someone would probably even bring out mugs of tea. Here, curtains and blinds stayed drawn. One or two had glanced out when the cars had arrived, but they stayed firmly, privately within. Nothing might have been happening at all. Now, lights were going off. No one stood at their doorway looking out and it would not have crossed any of their minds to produce trays of tea.

But at the door of the Angus house, he hesitated. If Marilyn Angus was reported as 'incoherent', seeing him, the one person perhaps more than any other she associated so closely with David's continuing disappearance, might well not help her. He had no news, nothing to offer. Others had asked enough questions for tonight.

He turned away again.

It was a soft, mild night and the gardens smelled of fresh grass and turned earth. Of spring. He tried to picture the two children, one certainly dead, one still possibly alive. How did a woman cope with the weeks-long disappearance of her son, the suicide of her husband, and now the fact that her second child was missing? This was one of the times when he found police work agonising.

Sixty

When she had reached the door of the workshop she had worried that Archie would start to bark so she spoke his name softly as she went down the dark garden. He was waiting, standing up and wagging his tail, and he bumped himself against her when she went inside. She put her bag down on the bench and sat on the floor beside him and the Labrador came and lay beside her and licked her hands. He smelled doggy and his body was heavy and very warm.

It was only when she felt safe, settled in beside him, that she let herself think. Her mother would go upstairs and might open her door and say goodnight, or might just call from the landing. Before, she had always come in. They had talked. It had been a good time of the day. Before.

No one had talked properly since. There had been terrible whispered conversations from which she had been excluded, and brief words if she had asked questions; not talking. Since her father had died it had been worse.

The dog leaned forward and snuffled her face with his wet nose.

Before, she had known David was the most important, more loved, of more interest to them, but she had not minded. It had been true. He was interesting and lovable. But once he had gone she ought to have moved up into the space he had left and instead she had been pushed down and down until, in the end, she had become invisible.

She had loved the house. Now she hated it. There was a thick grey silence everywhere, as though no air or daylight had come into it from that day. But her own room was the same and so she stayed there.

She reached for her bag and took out the biscuits, though she was not hungry. But she had brought them and so they were to be eaten, and anyway, it was something to do. She could see a little now that her eyes were used to the dark.

She hadn't worked out exactly how long she would stay in the workshop. They might find her. They might never find her. She could come out when she chose.

After a while, the dog lay down and she lay down with him, pulling the blankets from his bed over them both. She talked to Archie then. The dog gave great sighs from time to time and she went on talking until everything she had thought and felt was out there, in the quiet dark spaces of the workshop among the tools and the pictures of fighter planes.

She slept for a short time.

The lights wakened her first, and then the sound of the cars. Archie stood up ready to bark but she quietened him.

She supposed eventually people would find the workshop.

There had been no lights on in the Prices' house when she had crept down the garden and their car had not been in the drive.

But no one came. Lucy opened the workshop door and listened. She heard more cars, and voices out in the street. Saw the lights go up, like the floodlights at the sports ground. She felt a flutter of excitement in her stomach.

Archie lay down. After a while, so did she, and then slept again, her arms round the dog's neck.

Sixty-one

'*Simon, darling, please, please return this call . . . please just pick up the phone to me once.*'

'*Si, give me a ring.*'

It was almost midnight and his sister's message had been timed ten minutes earlier. He took a chance.

'Cat Deerbon.'

'Hope you weren't asleep.'

'No, the young man is having a social time. I'm downstairs. Any news?'

'Lucy? No, but I'm confident we'll find her.'

'You haven't found David.'

'Different. We're fairly sure she's taken herself off somewhere. It's a gesture, probably. Are you all OK? It sounded a bit urgent.'

'Yes and no. Look, it's a bit late. Come to supper tomorrow?'

'Depends on all this. Talk now or I'll lie awake.'

'OK, here goes, but don't shoot the messenger.'

'I promise.'

'I had a visitor this afternoon . . . Diana Mason came.'

'She came to the farmhouse? Just turned up? Bloody hell.'

'Calm, Si. Deep breaths.'

'How dare she? She doesn't even know you. How did she find you? She'd absolutely no right to come there, trying to get at you, discussing me –'

'Simon –'

'I'm sick to death of her, she's turning into a stalker. What do I have to say or do to make it plain to her? How can I get through?'

There was silence from Cat as he ranted. In the end, he sat down and drew a deep breath.

'Right. Sorry.'

'No, it's fine, you go ahead, get it off your chest. Whatever "it" is.'

'Mind your own bloody business.'

'I didn't hear that.'

'God, I'm sorry. I'm bushed and this has wound me up.'

'Well, yes.'

'Forget her. Not a problem.'

'It is for her.'

'I can't help there.'

'No?'

'No,' he said.

'Listen, I didn't swap girly confidences, I didn't give her any information and certainly no encouragement. But I did feel sorry for her. I think she's had a raw deal. Try and behave a bit less selfishly and give a little, Simon. This keeps happening and you've got to sort it, don't you think? See someone, talk to someone. You'll end up miserable and so will a lot of other people. If Freya hadn't –'

'Shut up. Leave Freya out of this conversation.'

'Why?'

'Because that was different . . . and none of this has anything to do with you.'

'Freya wasn't different, Freya *is* different, Simon, and that's because she's dead, and so she's safe – a safe woman. You can kid yourself it was all going to be fine because you never had to face real life with her. Easy to love a ghost.'

'I'm not listening to any more of this. What the hell is it all about anyway?'

'It's about my having had a very unhappy woman in my house all afternoon. You don't have to go on seeing her, but you do have to give her some sort of explanation. You can't just wordlessly drop people.'

'I'm going to put the phone down. You and I are about to quarrel seriously.'

'We already have. I've got to get through to you because no one else ever has.'

'Or?'

'Or nothing. Felix has gone to sleep and I'm going to bed. But just think about it, Si. It matters.'

The phone clicked off.

There were a few seconds, during which he had indeed started to think, before his mobile interrupted.

'Serrailler.'

'We've found her. And she's fine.'

After he had been given the details and had told Nathan to go home, Simon poured himself a whisky. He wanted to blot it out, blot out what had been said, blot out the memories of Freya and the intrusions of Diana Mason, everything. Only the news that Lucy Angus was safe gave him a measure of comfort.

Sixty-two

'Can I have a dog?'

Lucy sat drinking a mug of tea. She looked composed.

She ran away, Marilyn thought. She wanted not to be here. She wanted to be in a dark garden shed belonging to someone else, with their dog, rather than be in this house with me. She had looked at her coming up the drive between the two constables, a huge blanket wrapped round her shoulders, and seen someone she barely knew.

'Don't be angry, please don't be angry.' Lucy had started to shiver.

'Of course I'm not angry. You're here, you're alive . . . I couldn't . . .'

Lucy had walked past her mother into the kitchen.

It was ten past one. Neither of them wanted to sleep.

'A dog?'

'You never let us.'

'It's difficult . . . it wouldn't be fair.'

'Why?'

'On a dog left by itself all day. We're . . . I'm out.'

'Nothing's the same.'

'No.'

'So we could have a dog.'

'David's allergic to animal hair.'

Lucy looked her in the eyes. There was a moment of appalling silence.

'David's not here,' Lucy said at last.

The air in the kitchen seemed to contain something which made breathing difficult.

'Dad's not here. Everything in the house was dead.'

'I wasn't dead.'

'You seemed dead.'

'Oh God.'

'It was good being with the Prices' dog.'

'You shouldn't have broken in.'

'I didn't break in, the workshop's open. Why don't you answer me? You never do. I think I'm not here. Can we have a dog?'

'Lucy, let me . . . please . . . I'm tired. I don't like making sudden decisions.'

'If you mean no, say it, don't just not answer.'

'I don't mean no. I don't know what I mean. I couldn't take any more of this . . . everything. Didn't you think of that? Didn't you think about me at all?'

'Yes,' Lucy said. She got up, took her mug to the sink, rinsed it and put it in the rack. 'I thought about you. Goodnight.'

'Lucy, don't just walk out like that, we haven't talked properly, you haven't explained.'

'Yes I have. You just didn't hear me. Like about the dog.'

She went out, moving in the way she did now, her feet seeming to glide just above the floor, making no sound or stir of the air. She went upstairs. The house still felt dead but something had changed. She had made a difference just by going away. She had made a mark.

She hesitated on the landing, then went on up the final flight to the top. She pushed open the door of his room. It smelled of him, a boy smell that had not yet gone. But it will go, Lucy thought. Everything will fade soon. I won't remember him, his smell will not be here, his things just sit on the shelves and they are dead things.

She went round quietly, touching them. His books. His models. His computer. His Harry Potter lamp. His *Lord of the Rings* figures. His shoes. She wondered if it was going to be left like this for ever, like a castle full of sleeping people in a fairy tale.

She had known inside herself almost from the beginning that her brother was dead and she had just accepted it. All the time her parents had gone on about never giving up hope, she had looked at them and seen strangers who would not listen. David was dead. How could he not be?

It saddened her because he had always been there in his own odd little world, but a part of their world too, a part of hers. She hated to think about how he had died. She made her thoughts swerve away from it every time they threatened to invade her head. She went to sit on the window ledge and look down over the dark garden. She wondered if they would ever find his body or catch whoever had taken him. She had no feelings of certainty about that. Just about his being dead.

In the end, her legs got cramp and she slipped down from the ledge and glided out of her brother's room.

The house was silent again. Dead. She didn't know whether her mother had gone to bed or not. She was used to not knowing. Leaving home had made no difference to anything. In her own room, she lay and thought of dogs. Archie. Another dog. A dog of her own. Her dog would change things.

She lay down, closed her eyes and began to conjure up the perfect dog.

Along the hall, Marilyn lay in the same way, made the same shape in the bed. But they were not alike. She had never wanted them to be alike. She had never really wanted a girl. When she was pregnant with Lucy she had believed she was carrying a boy, longed for a boy and been shocked when it was not. She remembered looking her daughter in the eye, soon after she was born, and seeing someone with bold challenging eyes and a face too like her own, an attitude. Inevitably – though it had taken several days – she had loved Lucy. Who did not love their first-born? After a time, she had enjoyed having a girl.

With her second pregnancy she had not dared to expect or to hope for anything, just planned for a second daughter. David had been a joyous, miraculous surprise. Beside him, everything and everyone else in her world had receded, become shadowy and colourless. Having David, she felt she had been resurrected as a new person, invincible, all-loved. The hardest thing to bear, apart from the loss of him, was her own guilt. She had loved him too much, favoured him over all, and so he had been taken away from her. She had struggled to love Lucy since David's birth and, in a way, of course she had loved her – but it had never again been real, felt, all-absorbing love. If her daughter had been taken and never returned, the pain would have been great but bearable, just as the pain of losing Alan was bearable. In any case, she was angry with Alan, hurt at being abandoned and let down by him and amazed at his weakness.

Can I have a dog?

Lucy had looked at her with the same bright, steady, challenging eyes.

For now, they were left together. For now, there was no one else. David would surely come back, surely be found, no matter how long it took. She could not allow the thought that he would not to touch her. If it did, she knew she would crumple and disintegrate. She clung to the future, in which he was, as to a thin, steely thread, all that there was to keep her from drowning.

Can I have a dog?

She heard the cool little voice, composed and reasonable. Stubborn.

Lucy was opaque. She had never got through to her, never known her, never understood her. She did not now.

'David . . .' she said, and turned to curl up, her arms around her fantasy of his small body, as she did every time she lay down. Sometimes, she went up to bed simply in order to do this.

'Doodlebug.'

She did not know whether or not they could have a dog.

Sixty-three

'Have you been crying half the afternoon?'

Chris Deerbon picked up his pile of mail and flipped through it.

'Yes.'

'Hormones.'

'No, my brother.'

'Hormones.'

'Oh shut up, you pig, I know, I know. But I didn't give birth yesterday, they don't make me burst into tears about nothing. I can't bear falling out with anyone I love, I can't bear upsetting Si, and saying horrible things and hearing him sound so nasty.'

Chris threw a lot of torn envelopes and junk mail into the bin and came over to sit beside her.

'I know. All the same it had to be said. He does behave badly to women, he has hurt this one with no good reason. You don't like to see that side of him – why would you? Nor do I. He matters to us.'

'I wish I could get to the bottom of him, you know. But I never, never have.'

'Someone will, one day, and it'll give him the shock of his life.'

'I pity her.'

'He'll be feeling better for having one case quickly closed.'

'Have you heard anything today?'

'No, only what's been on the news. I think the child was making a point – "Look at me, I'm still here."'

'Poor kid. She's the one everyone should be looking out for, you know.'

'Now, there's something I want to talk about . . . important.'

'What's happened?'

'Something good. At least I think so. I've had a job offer.'

'What do you mean? You're not looking for a job.'

'I didn't think I was. But . . . I've been approached by a drug company. They're opening up a big project with their new asthma drug. It's trialled fantastically well, it's potentially the biggest thing since salbutamol – it really could cut serious asthma attacks in children by a third . . . even cut deaths. They want me to head up the team. They need a medic with a special interest in asthma.'

'You don't have a special interest in asthma.' Cat looked at him a long minute, until he had to glance away. 'I should think you bloody well can't meet me in the eye. What the hell are you thinking of? Drug company? Is this Chris Deerbon sitting here? You despise doctors who go and push company drugs, you always have. *Sold out*. How often have I heard you say that? *Glorified reps. Putting a respectable face on it* . . . Jeez, Chris, where are you coming from?'

'I am coming,' he said quietly, 'from a state of utter exhaustion. A state of being unable to cope much longer with not having a partner, not being able to get a locum, paying out a small fortune for agency cover. A state of being buried in bloody government paperwork about targets and quotas and anything but attention to sick people. I don't know where to turn. That's where I'm coming from.'

'You mean it, don't you?'

'Never more. God, Cat, I don't want to leave general practice. I love it. I love hands-on medicine, always have. But just now, I'm feeling burnt out.'

'The answer isn't for you to go and work for a drug company.'

'Tell me what the answer is then.'

'For me to come back to work of course. I'll get Sally to have Felix, and I'll come back every morning to do surgeries, and aim to be in harness full time sooner than I'd planned. QED.' She got up. 'I'm going to make some soup and toast.'

'Sounds good. But you can't come back, the whole point of this year was for you to –'

'I know what it was, but that was before you were so drained with exhaustion you started talking about drug companies. I'm wasted here, lovely as it is to sit on the sofa cuddling Felix and reading Maeve Binchy. Give me another week and I'll start back.'

'I daren't argue with you when you've got that look. If I agree . . .'

'You got no choice, buster.'

'If . . . will you ring Si?'

'No.'

'Oh grow up, Cat . . . or rather, show him who is grown up. I won't have my family riven by faction. There are enough wars in the world. By the way, have you spoken to your parents lately?'

'Mum rang today as a matter of fact. Why?'

'How was she?'

'Odd. But she always sounds odd these days. I can't get through to what it is . . . she has that bright, charming barrier well up. There's something and I'm damned if I can tell what.'

Cat shoved bread into the toaster. At times like this she had always found it better not to think. Not to think about David Angus and the possibility that he had died a horrible death, not to think about her mother and father and whether anything had happened between them, not to think about going back to work far sooner than she had planned. Not to think – just get on with it.

'We endure by enduring' she had read somewhere. It had struck her as one of the greatest truths she had ever read.

The soup began to bubble.

Sixty-four

'Simon, this is the second message I have left. I dislike speaking to machines. Would you be good enough to telephone me?'

Meriel quietly set the armful of narcissi she had just picked down on the waiting newspaper. The garden was rich with yellow and gold and the pink and white and scarlet of tulips. She stared out at it and the colour drained away before her eyes like blood draining from a corpse. The world was two dimensional, grey.

'Damned machines.'

She dared not speak. She would not say anything.

She said, 'Why were you telephoning Simon?'

Richard turned. 'I have something to ask him.'

'If . . .' Her throat contracted. 'To ask?'

To her surprise, he came and laid his hands on her shoulders.

He said, 'In this, my dear, you have to trust me. You have already trusted me. You have to do so for the rest of our lives. Do you think I would possibly betray that?'

Meriel Serrailler had rarely cried in her life but tears came now, though only to her eyes, where they rested, blurring the yellow of the flowers on the kitchen table.

'Whatever I may have said when you first told me about Martha, I have accepted it and I accept that what you did you did for her and for the best. I do not agree but I have never doubted your goodness of heart and motive. You must believe that. And who is to say that you are wrong? Not me. Who? No one. The very last person I would betray this to would be our own son.'

She wanted to reach out to him, but he had let her go and walked out of the room in a single movement. She took out a handkerchief and wiped her eyes slowly. She was shaken by the depth of his kindness. Beneath the usual formality his voice had had a softness and a tenderness which she had rarely known.

She sat at the table and began to trim the flowers. Gradually, looking around and through the window, she saw that the colour had come back to the garden, and was richer, brighter, more intense, the flowers shimmering with a transforming brilliance. A sense of relief and lightness of heart flooded through her. She had been forgiven.

Sixty-five

Spring slipped into early summer and warm, sunlit days. On Hylam Peak, the walkers were out in force again. Hares boxed and the lambs bounced and leapt on the fresh turf. In Gardale Ravine someone left lilac beside the grave where the child had been buried, though her body no longer lay there. On the Hill, children played about the Wern Stones and the stain left by the events of the previous year dissolved in the sun. The gardens of Lafferton were golden with forsythia.

Marilyn Angus had lost interest in conducting a search of her own. The angry and the nutters who had rallied to her public appeals had gone home.

DCS Jim Chapman returned to Yorkshire. His review of the David Angus case had been thorough and he had no criticisms of the way things had been handled; he made one or two suggestions, which were followed up and led nowhere. The face of David Angus still looked out from posters and hoardings, from shop windows and noticeboards but fading now, and sometimes torn at the corners. No one forgot but it was no longer at the front of everyone's mind.

The team battled on. The case was picked up by forces round the country and set aside again. HOLMES was accessed and data extracted and input.

There was no news, no trace, no sign. The boy might never have existed.

The calls to Lafferton police about the case slowed to a trickle and that trickle was made up of the mad and the sad and the malicious.

March went out, and an early Easter with it.

On 4th April, Cat returned home from taking morning surgery to hear the phone ringing.

'Hi, Ma.'

'Don't call me, Ma. Darling, have you fixed a date for Felix's christening? If not, could you make it May the 12th?'

'No, and I'm not sure. Why?'

'Because we've arranged to have Martha's stone in the cloisters dedicated on that day and I thought the christening might come straight after.'

'I'll talk to Chris, but I can't see why not. Only, wouldn't you prefer something quiet and more special – private – for Martha?'

'No. It would suit very well. How are you?'

'Fine. I rather like being a doctor again. Easy to say that when I've no nights, no house calls.'

'How does Felix like his minder?'

'They're in love.'

'I keep trying to ring Simon but I never get through to him.'

'Oh.'

'Is he away?'

'Not that I'm aware of.'

'Why do you say it like that?'

'Ma, I have to go.'

'Let me know about the 12th, darling. I'll do the tea.'

Meriel Serrailler clicked the phone off, as abruptly as usual.

'Bloody hell.'

But she would not think about it. Cat had not spoken to her brother for weeks. She knew nothing. She hated it.

She picked up the car keys and went out to fetch Felix from Sally Warrender.

Andy Gunton opened the window of the flat above the café and leaned out. It was evening and even in the middle of the town the air smelled of fresh greenery and turned earth. He was comfortable. Alfredo's wife had made some curtains, Alfredo and his brother had brought a wardrobe here, a table and a chair and an ancient television there.

He was happy enough. He didn't mind washing up and wiping tables and cleaning out the kitchen and mopping the floor at the end of the day. He wouldn't be doing it for ever. He had not been near Michelle. Once she had come into the café with a friend and he had hidden in the back the whole twenty minutes she was there. He had not seen Lee Carter. His case was still before the CPS. He didn't think about it.

He leaned out a bit further and caught sight of the tops of trees on the Hill.

This wasn't for ever. This was a stop on the way. He'd make it way further than this. Wouldn't he?

Simon Serrailler left the station and headed for the pub across the road. He rarely went there. The evening was softening, the sky was like enamel.

Nathan Coates was at the bar.

'Guv . . . what can I get you?'

'Thanks. I'll have half a Genesis.'

'Yeah, been quiet. Too quiet. I 'ate it.'

They found a table.

'Em's coming in. We're going to the pictures.'

'What's on?'

'Dunno. We just drive out to the multi . . . look up and see what we fancy . . . have a Chinese after. Our treat every week. It's like a date, you know, 'ave to keep the romance going. I buy her chocs and all that.'

'I'm in tears.'

He looked at Nathan and thought he knew precisely what made him tick. He loved his job but he probably had no further ambitions, knowing how lucky he was to have made it this far, out of the Dulcie estate and his petty-criminal family. He loved his wife. They were saving to move out of their small flat into a cottage in a village outside Lafferton. Then they'd have babies. QED.

'How do you see things, Nathan? In ten, fifteen years?'

'Well, DI next, probably here or maybe move to Bevham, then I'd like to go into one of the specialist units, get some experience . . . maybe paedophile unit, then an MIT somewhere. Thing is, Em can work anywhere there's a big hospital, they're all crying out for midwives, and anyway, she'll have a couple of our own and take a break . . . but she wouldn't give up, she loves it. We'd maybe go north. I had a couple of talks with Jim Chapman. He reckoned there'd be the right openings for me up there.'

Simon drained his beer. So what do I know? How much have I ever known about the people I work with, even as closely as I work with Nathan? How much do I ask them? He felt chastened.

'Let me get you another.'

'Naw, thanks, guv, here's Em, and I only have a half. Might have a pint later though.'

Nice, plump, fresh-faced Emma Coates came over. Emma, who had been there when Nathan had broken the door down and found Freya dying and her murderer getting away over the dark back gardens. They had come through it all. They deserved their ambitions.

'Hello, Chief Inspector, are you coming with us?'

Simon stood up. 'Heavens, no. Just keeping Nathan out of mischief till you appeared.'

'Thanks.'

'You'd be welcome, guv, honest, we'd like it.'

'No you wouldn't. Besides, I promised I'd call in on my mother.'

'Ah, well, better not skip that then.'

'Indeed.'

He walked across the road to his car. Blackbirds were singing madly from every garden. It was still not dark.

He sat for a moment. He should go out to the farmhouse. That was the one thing he wanted to do – just turn up there as he had always done, eat whatever was for supper, stay in the spare room after sharing a bottle or two of wine, romp with the children before they were asleep.

Either that or he should do as he had told Nathan and call in on his parents. He had barely spoken to them for a couple of weeks.

He started the engine and headed to the crossroads. Left out of town towards the Deerbons' village. Right, towards the one in which his parents lived. Straight on through Lafferton towards the cathedral and his own flat.

He accelerated and drove straight on.

In London, the trees in the parks were vivid green and ducklings like bumble bees skimmed over the lakes. In St James's Park the paths were full of strollers and lovers lay about the grass. Diana Mason sat on a bench and tried not to see them.

The previous week, the sale of her restaurant chain had gone through. She was free and she was wealthy. She had no idea what to do. She had shopped for clothes she did not want, gone into travel agents and picked up brochures for holidays she would not take. She thought endlessly of Simon. Her messages were not returned, he did not reply to her faxes or emails. She had written letters, gone to his flat, driven to Lafferton to see his sister and none of it had worked, nothing helped her to reach him. She had no idea what she might do next and could not think of doing nothing, of leaving it and trying to wean herself from him by going away, as his sister had suggested. It would not work. The further she went the more she would think about him. There was no one else, nothing else. In her turn, she did not answer messages left by friends, or respond to invitations.

She did not understand why he had turned against her so abruptly or behaved so coldly. She needed to ask someone but the only person who might have helped her had politely, pleasantly, firmly refused.

But perhaps, then, she might go and see his mother, who maybe would understand more, sympathise, confide, explain. Take her side. Speak for her.

She got up quickly. The idea gave her a burst of fresh hope and energy. It was the only thing left. It was everything.

She walked back to her flat, planning her route, her clothes. Her words.

Sixty-six

It could have been high summer on 12th May, save for the still-fresh smell of spring on the air.

The old cloisters of St Michael's Cathedral surrounded a small grass quadrangle. This was not a burial ground, but memorial stones to members of the congregation were laid here level with the ground and formed a cross. That to Martha Serrailler was one of the last, at the south corner.

They stood in the patch of sun. Richard and Meriel. Cat and Chris with their children. Martha's godfather, an old medical colleague of Richard's, leaning on two sticks. Shirley and Rosa from Ivy Lodge. And, just as they were about to begin, Simon, who stood next to his mother, and did not meet Cat's eye.

The dedication was short and simple. Plain words. A short Bible passage. The first prayer. Cat looked down at the slab. '*Martha Felicity Serrailler. 1977–2003. Blessed are the pure in heart.*'

There were three simple posies of white flowers beside it, one of them from Ivo in Australia. He is never here for anything, Cat thought – marriage, births, deaths. Celebrations or wakes. He might as well not be a part of the family at all. Why? What had made him go to the other side of the world and stay there for seven years without a single return visit home? She wondered if he so much as remembered their faces. Certainly, he would have next to no memories of Martha.

Cat herself felt little now for the fair-haired, speechless girl who had been her sister. Martha's life had been sealed away and, ultimately, it had been a mystery. Perhaps Simon had been right and her death was a mystery too. Who knew?

She wanted to look at him and could not. He kept his eyes down. He wore a pale grey suit in which he should have looked older but which actually made him seem like a tall schoolboy. She looked down at Felix in his carrying crib, oblivious to the voices and the birdsong and the sun on his face, as well as to the fact that he was dressed in cream silk and lace, the Serrailler family christening gown.

A sudden pain shot through her heart, for David Angus, for Martha. For Simon. After the christening, back at her parents' house, she would take him aside, out into the garden away from everyone else. This stupid feud had to be brought to an end.

'Let us pray for Martha. Let us hold the mystery of her life before God and trust her to His care. Lord, grant her the understanding of Your presence, the knowledge of Your love and the grace of Your protection and help her to grow in new life with You.'

'Bring us, O Lord, at your last awakening,
    into the house and gate of heaven.
To enter into that gate and dwell in that house
Where there shall be no darkness nor dazzling
    but one equal light;
No noise nor silence, but one equal music;
No fears nor hopes, but one equal possession;
No ends nor beginnings, but one equal eternity;
In the habitations of thy glory and dominion,
World without end.'

Sam's small voice piped out into the sunlit quiet before the others. 'Amen.' His sister trod on his toe.

Cat looked up. Simon had her eye and could not look away now. Slowly, he smiled.

They went into the Lady Chapel by the cloister door. People were already there, godparents and friends.

Felix woke as he was lifted from his basket, and lay in Karin McCafferty's arms, his eyes widened in wonder at the flickering candles and the glint of gold and blue on the chapel roof, the shine of the silver christening jug.

He gave a tiny gasp when the water touched him but then was still again, gazing round.

Hannah dropped her candle. Sam grinned in triumph.

They went out into the sunshine of the May afternoon and gathered round Felix in admiration. Cameras clicked.

'Hi,' Simon said from behind Cat.

She put out her hand and he held it. 'Hi.'

There was no need, after that, to take him away into the garden and say anything at all.

David

Cave. Cellar. No matter what name it was given. A dark, cold, damp, deep hole underground. No matter where. Just far from home, Lafferton, the gate of the house and the last moments of safety.

The small body was curled up and bent to one side, one arm forward, one back.

As the weeks and months went on, the same thing happened to it as to all bodies so that soon it was not a body, merely bones.

If they were ever found, the bones of the boy, they would be moved and examined and then they too would be buried in sacred ground with a stone above.

If they were found.

Sixty-seven

He had a week's leave. It was late June. People spoke of it for years afterwards, the long, long spring, the hot, hot summer.

Simon had packed his drawing things into the canvas bag, the few clothes he ever took abroad with him, half a dozen paperbacks. He was leaving at five the next morning to catch an early flight. He would be in Venice by early afternoon, meeting Ernesto and his boat at the terminal.

He was switching off the refrigerator and propping the door open when the telephone rang. He was off duty now. It had to be family.

'Guv? I know you're on leave only . . .'

'Go on, Nathan.'

'Thought you might like a bit of good news.'

'Always do with it.'

'Report came in via Interpol . . . they traced connections in five countries so far . . . them stolen cars . . . looks as if we got Lee Carter sewn up. Right little racket. He got the cars nicked and changed the plates and that. Set up false documents and bunged them off abroad in ones and twos.'

'Where to?'

'Russia mainly. Few other places I've never even heard of, to be honest with you.'

'Criminal underworld in Russia?'

'Yeah, and they like flash cars. CPS won't throw this one out. One thing though . . . we let that Andy Gunton get off with TADA.'

'Taking and driving away is all he was doing.'

'You don't reckon he was in on the rest of it, then?'

'Do you?'

There was a pause. Serrailler had no doubts that Andy Gunton had been small fry. But he wanted Nathan to make up his own mind. 'Naw,' the sergeant said in the end. 'He needed some cash, he got stupid.'

'Agreed. I feel sorry for Andy Gunton. Don't quite know why.'

Nathan laughed. 'You meet his sister Michelle, you'll feel a lot sorrier. I tell you what though, guv. You put the fear of God into the both of them, him and Carter, when they thought you was looking them over, regarding the missing kid.'

'Oh I know. Carter's low life, Gunton's been stupid, but they're not child abductors. Never crossed my mind. Besides, forensics went over those aircraft hangars on their hands and knees.'

'Where is that kid, guv?' Nathan sounded close to tears. 'Where've they got him?'

Serrailler sighed. What was there to say? What answer did he have?

'I get sick thinking about it,' Nathan said.

'We'll have them, Nathan.'

'Yes?'

'Yes. And if not us, someone else, some force somewhere.'

'You believe that?'

'I wouldn't be in this job if I didn't.'

'Right.'

Simon put the phone down, Nathan's last word in his ears. *Right.* But it wasn't right. He knew it, the DS knew it. It was as wrong as it could be. Not everything worked out. Not every killer was caught. Not every missing child was found, alive or dead. Sometimes there was no resolution. Sometimes, you had to live with that, and it was the hardest thing of all. He sat in his chair and looked out at the sky beyond the window. He felt drained, but it had more to do with frustration than overwork. You lived for that closure, he thought – case solved, a charge, a conviction. File shut. When it was so long in coming, or never came, the sense of exhaustion was compounded by a flat, morale-sapping sense of failure. He had it now. The whole team had it. They knew David Angus was dead, all their sense and experience told them so. Knew it, but did not know it. They knew nothing and it drove them crazy.

He closed his eyes. Crazy. A lot of things had happened to make him crazy. Martha's death. David Angus. Things in his family which troubled him, but which he could not properly define.

And Diana.

Diana made him not crazy, but furious, with a desperate need to defend himself, his space, his privacy, his entire life and being. He hated the feeling that she was watching him, prying into corners of his life he had always kept away from anyone. Above all, he hated the messiness of her feelings, poured out over him. What he had thought was an easy, casual friendship had been turned inside out. He stood up and walked to the window, back to the chair, back to the window again, irritable and angry, with Diana, with himself.

The phone rang again, saving him.

'Guv . . .'

'Now what?'

'A call just come in from West Mercia force. Seven-year-old boy gone missing. Left his house for the village school about quarter of a mile away. Called in at the shop for sweets and wasn't seen again after. They've done all the local stuff. Nothing. It's been twelve hours. They just rung us.'

'Who's in charge?'

'DS Phipps. Asked for you. I said you was on your holidays.'

Simon stared out of the window at the darkening sky.

It was the worst news, and he had been dreading it. Somewhere, another child. Another disappearance. More agony. He had no need for it to be his again. He was on holiday. He could leave it to them.

I've had enough, he thought. He could not tell whether he simply needed his break or whether the sense of staleness and dissatisfaction went deeper. Had he, indeed, had enough?

David Angus's face was outside his window, set against the sky, filling his mind.

Whoever is doing this will go on, Simon thought. There'll be another. And another. Because people like this, the child molesters, the child abductors, the child killers, they don't stop. Ever. Not until we stop them.

He realised that nothing else mattered now. Not his own feelings, not Diana. Even his worries about his own family. Nothing mattered but this. There was no time for anything else.

He lifted the phone, called the station and got the number for the West Mercia force.

After he had talked to DS Phipps, he would ring Ernesto.

Venice, too, would have to wait.

Now read the first chapter of the
next Simon Serrailler case

THE RISK
OF DARKNESS

Also published by Vintage

One

There was no fly and there should have been a fly. It was that sort of room. Grey linoleum. Putty walls. Chairs and tables with tubular metal legs. But in these places there was always a fly too, zizzing slowly up and down a window pane. Up and down. Up and down. Up.

The wall at the far end was covered in whiteboards and pinboards. Names. Dates. Places. Then came:

Witnesses (which was blank).

Suspects. (Blank.)

Forensics. (Blank.)

In each case.

There were five people in the conference room of the North Riding Police HQ, and they had been staring at the boards for over an hour. DCI Simon Serrailler felt as if he had spent half his life staring at one of the photographs. The bright fresh face. The protruding ears. The school tie. The newly cut hair. The expression. Interested. Alert.

David Angus. It was eight months since he had vanished from outside the gate of his own house at ten past eight one morning.

David Angus.

Simon wished there was a fly to mesmerise him, instead of the small boy's face.

The call from DS Jim Chapman had come a couple of days earlier, in the middle of a glorious Sunday afternoon.

Simon had been sitting on the bench, padded up and waiting to bat for Lafferton Police against Bevham Hospital 2nd Eleven. The score was 228 for 5, the medics' bowling was flaccid, and Simon thought his team might declare before he himself got in. He wasn't sure whether he would mind or not. He enjoyed playing though he was only an average cricketer. But on such an afternoon, on such a fine ground, he was happy whether he went in to bat or not.

The swifts soared and screamed high above the pavilion and swallows skimmed the boundary. He had been low-spirited and restless during the past few months, for no particular reason and then again, for a host of them but his mood lightened now with the pleasure of the game and the prospect of a good pavilion tea. He was having supper with his sister and her family later. He remembered what his nephew Sam had said suddenly the previous week, when he and Simon had been swimming together; he had stopped mid-length, leaping up out of the water with: 'Today is a GOOD day!'

Simon smiled to himself. It didn't take much.

'Howzzzzzaaaattt?'

But the cry faded away. The batsman was safe and going for his hundred.

'Uncle Simon, hey!'

'Hi, Sam.'

His nephew came running up to the bench. He was holding the mobile, which Simon had given him to look after if he went in to bat.

'Call for you. It's DCS Chapman from the North Riding CID.' Sam's face was shadowed with anxiety. 'Only, I thought I should ask who it was . . .'

'No, that's quite right. Good work, Sam.'

Simon got up and walked round the corner of the pavilion.

'Serrailler.'

'Jim Chapman. New recruit, was it?'

'Nephew. I'm padded up, next in to bat.'

'Good man. Sorry to break into your Sunday afternoon. Any chance of you coming up here in the next couple of days?'

'The missing child?'

'Been three weeks and not a thing.'

'I could drive up tomorrow early evening and give you Tuesday and Wednesday, if you need me that long – once I've cleared it.'

'I just did that. Your Chief thinks a lot of you.'

There was a mighty cheer from the spectators and applause broke.

'We're a man out, Jim. Got to go.'

*

Sam was waiting, keen as mustard, holding out his hand for the mobile.

'What do I do if it rings when you're batting?'

'Take the name and number and say I'll call back.'

'Right, guv.'

Simon bent over and tightened the buckle on his pad to hide a smile.

But as he walked out to bat, a thin fog of misery clouded around his head, blocking out the brightness of the day, souring his pleasure. The child abduction case was always there, a stain on the recesses of the mind. It was not only the fact that it was still a blank, unsolved and unresolved, but that the boy's abductor was free to strike again. No one liked an open case, let alone one so distressing. The phone call from Jim Chapman had pulled Simon back to the Angus case, to the force, to work . . . and from there, to how he had started to feel about his job in the past few months. And why.

Facing the tricky spin-bowling of a cardiac registrar gave him something else to concentrate on for the moment. Simon hooked the first ball and ran.

The pony neighing from the paddock woke Cat Deerbon from a sleep of less than two hours. She lay, cramped and uncomfortable, wondering where she was. She had been called out to an elderly patient who had fallen downstairs and fractured his femur and on her return home had let the door bang and had woken her youngest child. Felix had been hungry, thirsty and cross, and in the end Cat had fallen asleep next to his cot.

Now, she sat up stiffly but his warm little body did not stir. The sun was coming through a slit in the curtains on to his face.

It was only ten past six.

The grey pony was standing by the fence grazing, but whinnied again, seeing Cat coming towards it, carrot in hand.

How could I leave all this? she thought, feeling its nuzzling mouth. How could either of us bear to leave this farmhouse, these fields, this village?

The air smelled sweet and a mist lay in the hollow. A woodpecker yaffled, swooping towards one of the oak trees on the far side of the fence.

Chris, her husband, was restless again, unhappy in general practice, furious at the burden of administration which took him from his patients, irritated by the mountain of new targets, checks and balances. He had spoken several times in the past month of going to Australia for five years – which might as well be for ever, Cat thought, knowing he had only put a time limit on it as a sop to her. She had been there once to see her triplet brother, Ivo, and hated it – the only person, Chris said, who ever had.

She wiped her hand, slimy from the pony's mouth, on her dressing gown. The animal, satisfied, trotted quietly away across the paddock.

They were so close to Lafferton and the practice, close to her parents and Simon, to the cathedral which meant so much to her. They were also in the heart of the country, with a working farm across the lane where the children saw lambs and calves and helped feed chickens; they loved their schools, they had friends nearby.

No, she thought, feeling the sun growing warm on her back. No.

From the house Felix roared. But Sam would go to him, Sam, his brother and worshipper, rather than Hannah, who preferred her pony and had become jealous of the baby as he had grown through his first year.

Cat wandered round the edge of the paddock, knowing that she would feel tired later in the day but not resenting her broken night – seeing patients at their most vulnerable, especially when they were elderly and frightened, had always been one of the best parts of working in general practice for her, and she had no intention of handing over night work to some agency when the new contract came into force. Chris disagreed. They had locked horns about it too often and now simply avoided the subject.

One of the old apple trees had a swathe of the white rose Wedding Day running through its gnarled branches and the scent drifted to her as she passed.

No, she thought again.

There had been too many bad days during the past couple of years, too much fear and tension; but now, apart from her usual anxiety about her brother, nothing was wrong – nothing except Chris's discontentment and irritability, nothing but his desire to change things, move them away, spoil . . . Her bare feet were wet with dew.

'Mummmeeeee. Tellyphoooooonnne . . .'

Hannah was leaning too far out of an upstairs window.

Cat ran.

It was a morning people remembered, for the silver-blue clear sky and the early-morning sunshine and the fact that everything was fresh. They relaxed and felt suddenly untroubled and strangers spoke to one another, passing in the street.

Natalie Coombs would remember it too.

'I can hear Ed's car.'

'No you can't, it's Mr Hardisty's, and get down-stairs, we'll be late.'

'I want to wave to Ed.'

'You can wave to Ed from here.'

'No, I –'

'Get DOWNSTAIRS.'

Kyra's hair was all over her face, tangled after sleep. She was barefoot.

'Shit, Kyra, can't you do anything for your bloody self? . . . Where's your hairbrush, where's your shoes?'

But Kyra had gone to the front room to peer out of the window, waiting.

Natalie poured Chocolate Frosties into a blue bowl. She had eleven minutes – get Kyra ready, finish off her own face, find her stuff, make sure the bloody guinea pig had food and water, go. What had she been thinking. *I want to keep this baby?*

'There's Ed, there's Ed . . .'

She knew better than to interrupt Kyra. It was a morning thing.

'Bye, Ed . . . Ed . . .' Kyra was banging on the window.

Ed had turned from locking the front door. Kyra waved. Ed waved.

'Bye, Kyra . . .'

'Can I come and see you tonight, Ed?'

But the car had started. Kyra was shouting to herself.

'Stop being a pest.'

'Ed doesn't mind.'

'You heard. Eat your cereal.'

But Kyra was still waving, waving and waving as Ed's car turned the corner and out of sight. What the hell was it about bloody Ed? Natalie wondered. Still, it might give her a half-hour to herself tonight, if Kyra could wangle her way next door, to help with the plant-watering or eat a Mars bar in front of Ed's telly.

'Don't slosh the milk out like that, Kyra, now look . . .'

Kyra sighed.

For a six-year-old, Natalie thought, she had a diva's line in sighs.

The sun shone. People called out to one another, getting into their cars.

'Look, look,' Kyra said, dragging on Natalie's

arm. 'Look in Ed's window, the rainbow thing is going round, look, it's all pretty colours moving.'

Natalie slammed the car door, opened it again, slammed it for the second time, which was what she always had to do, otherwise it didn't stay closed.

'Can we have one of them rainbow-making things in our window? They're like fairyland.'

'Shit.' Natalie screeched to a halt at the junction. 'Watch where you're going, dickhead.'

Kyra sighed and thought about Ed, who never shouted and never swore. She thought she would go round tonight and ask if they could make pancakes.

It was the sun, brilliant on the white wall, that woke Max Jameson, a sheet of light through the glass. He had bought the loft because of the light – even on a dull day the space was full of it. When he had first brought Lizzie here she had gazed around her in delight.

'The Old Ribbon Factory,' she had said. 'Why?'

'Because they made ribbons. Lafferton ribbons were famous.'

Lizzie had walked a few steps before doing a little dance in the middle of the room.

That was the loft – one room plus an open-tread staircase to the bedroom and bathroom. One vast room.

'It's like a ship,' she had said.

Max closed his eyes, seeing her there, head back, dark hair hanging down.

There was a wall of glass. No blind, no curtain. At night the lamps glowed in the narrow street below. There was nothing beyond the Old Ribbon Factory except the towpath and then the canal. The second time, he had brought Lizzie here at night. She had gone straight to the window.

'It's Victorian England.'

'Phoney.'

'No. No, it really is. It feels right.'

On the wall at the far end of the room was her picture. He had taken the shot of Lizzie, alone beside the lake in her wedding dress, her head back in that same way, hair down but this time threaded with white flowers. She was looking up and she was laughing. The picture was blown up twelve feet high and ten feet wide on the white wall. When Lizzie had first seen it, she had been neither startled nor embarrassed, only thoughtful.

'It's the best memory,' she had said at last.

Max opened his eyes again and the sunlight burned into them. He heard her.

'Lizzie?' He flung the clothes off the bed in panic at her absence. 'Lizzie . . . ?'

She was halfway down the staircase, vomiting.

He tried to help her, to lead her back to safety, but her unsteadiness made it difficult, and he was afraid they would both fall. Then she stared into his face, her eyes wide and terrified, and screamed at him.

'Lizzie, it's OK, I'm here, it's me. I won't hurt you, I won't hurt you. Lizzie . . .'

Somehow he struggled with her to the bed and got her to lie down. She curled away from him making small angry sounds inside her throat like a cat growling. Max ran to the bathroom and sluiced cold water over his head and neck, scrubbed his teeth, keeping the door open. He could see the bed through the medicine cabinet mirror. She had not stirred again. He pulled on jeans and a shirt, ran down into the brilliant room and switched on the kettle. He was breathing hard, tense with panic, his hands sweating. Like a bitter taste, the fear was in his mouth and throat all the time now.

The crash came. He swung round in time to see Lizzie sliding in terrible slow motion from the top of the stairs to the foot, lying with one leg under her body, arms outstretched, roaring in pain and fright like a furious child.

The kettle gushed out steam and the sunlight caught the glass door of the wall cupboard like fire.

Max felt tears running down his face. The kettle was too full and splashed as he poured it, the water scalding his hand.

At the foot of the stairs, Lizzie lay still and the sound that came from her was the bellow of some animal, not any noise that she would make, not Lizzie, not his wife.

Cat Deerbon heard it, holding the telephone.

'Max, you'll have to speak more slowly . . . what's happened?'

But all she could make out, apart from the noise

516

in the background, were a few incoherent, drowned words.

'Max, hold on . . . I'm coming now. Hold on . . .'

Felix was crawling along the landing towards the stairgate, smelling of dirty nappy. Cat scooped him up and into the bathroom, where Chris was shaving.

'That was Max Jameson,' she said. 'Lizzie . . . I've got to go. Make Hannah help you.'

She ran, zipping up her skirt as she went, avoiding his look.

Outside, the air smelled of hay and the grey pony was cantering round the paddock, tail swishing with pleasure. Cat was out of the drive and fast down the lane, planning what had to be done, how she could make Max Jameson understand, finally, that he could not keep Lizzie at home to die.

THE SIMON SERRAILLER CASES

HAVE YOU READ THEM ALL?

BOOK 1: THE VARIOUS HAUNTS OF MEN

A woman vanishes in the fog up on 'the Hill', then a young
girl and an old man both disappear in quick succession.
A coincidence, or is there a killer in Lafferton?

BOOK 2: THE PURE IN HEART

A little boy is snatched at the gate of his home. A young
woman hovers between life and death. An ex-con struggles
to go straight. What links these three lives?

BOOK 3: THE RISK OF DARKNESS

Children have been vanishing. There are no leads, just a
kidnapper at large. Then another child is snatched – this
time in Yorkshire. Has the abductor struck again?

BOOK 4: THE VOWS OF SILENCE

A gunman is terrorising young women. What links the attacks?
Is the marksman with a rifle the same person as the killer with
a handgun or do the police have two snipers on their hands?

BOOK 5: THE SHADOWS IN THE STREET

Two local prostitutes have been found strangled,
then another girl vanishes. Are these killings by an
angry punter or is a serial killer at large?

BOOK 6: THE BETRAYAL OF TRUST

Heavy rain falls on Lafferton, flooding the town. But
as the water slowly drains away, a shallow grave and a
skeleton are revealed. But whose is it?

BOOK 7: A QUESTION OF IDENTITY

One snowy night an old lady is murdered. The police
track down a name – Alan Keyes. But how do you
catch a killer who doesn't exist?

BOOK 8: THE SOUL OF DISCRETION

Serrailler faces his most dangerous challenge yet. In an undercover
op, he must inhabit the mind of the worst kind of criminal.
But can he do so without losing everything?